Elementary

All-New Tales of the Elemental Masters

Edited by
Mercedes Lackey

DAW BOOKS, INC.

DONALD A. WOLLHEIM, FOUNDER

375 Hudson Street, New York, NY 10014

ELIZABETH R. WOLLHEIM
SHEILA E. GILBERT
PUBLISHERS

www.dawbooks.com

First Printing, December 2013
1 2 3 4 5 6 7 8 9

DAW TRADEMARK REGISTERED
U.S. PAT. AND TM. OFF. AND FOREIGN COUNTRIES
—MARCA REGISTRADA
HECHO EN U.S.A.

PRINTED IN THE U.S.A

Contents

Fire-Water
Samuel C. Conway

As he did every day, Octli poked his nose first from his burrow to sniff for the scent of blood. He found none, so next came his eyes, scanning the landscape for telltale shadows. Next came his long, long ears, and only when they detected no lurking hunters did the rest of him follow.

He sat motionless for some time, smelling, watching, listening, until at last he felt safe enough to forage for his breakfast. With so many eager fangs waiting out there to sink into his pelt, Octli could ill afford to be careless.

Still, as careful as one might be, the world has a way of doing what it will. Octli had just enjoyed some tender clover and was about to start digging up a wild yam when the sun winked at him. Instinctively he froze, becoming one with the landscape. The sun winked again, a shadow, a circling hunter.

Octli bolted for his burrow but was too slow. Something crashed down upon his back and drove him to the ground. Its weight held him down, his middle squeezed tightly. A cloak of feathers fell over him and blotted out the sun. A savagely hooked beak descended to Octli's ear. He closed his eyes tightly.

"Peace," the beak's owner said. "I will not eat you."

Octli's eyes flew open. "You won't? Is this a trick?"

"No trick." The bird lifted his foot from Octli's back and allowed the rabbit to stand. "I am not here for food."

"What, then?" Octli said nervously, backing away from the bird's fiery gaze.

"I have come to ask for your help."

Octli had expected to hear any one of a number of things, but that had certainly not been among them. "Me?" he sputtered. "How could I do that?"

"I do not know." The bird sighed. He ruffled his feathers and shook them all out, first his body, then his head, and finally his tail. "But I hoped that you would."

"Well . . . I . . . I suppose that I must. You did spare my life."

"Your life was never in danger from me."

Now that his terror had subsided, even if only a little, Octli looked more closely at the bird and realized that was true. The long, lanky and naked legs meant this bird was not the sort to eat a rabbit, although if hungry enough, anyone with a beak like that would hardly be fussy. No, this bird was the sort who preferred fish for his supper. "I am grateful for that," Octli said, still eyeing the long, long, long talons upon which the bird rested. "You will forgive me, though, if I continue to shake for a while."

"If you must." The bird settled his feathers once more. "Will you help me?"

"I ought to," Octli said warily, "but I still do not know why you are here."

The bird glanced over one of his shoulders, then over the other. "I am here because of my Master."

"He sent you to me?"

"No." The bird stared at the ground. "I am here *because* of him. If he knew, he would be very, very angry."

Octli peered at the bird, who, standing with his head bowed and his wings drooping, looked far less horrifying and far more miserable than he had before. Octli began to pity him. "I . . . would like to help you, yes . . ."

The bird raised his head hopefully.

". . . but first you must tell me what troubles you."

"It is my Master." Again the bird glanced furtively about. "We are of the Water, you see, and my Master has declared war on one who is of the Fire. They are in constant battle, and the land suffers for it. Water floods where it should not, Fire rages where it must not, and nothing comes of it but misery for all. Their hatred for each other has made them blind to the suffering they are causing."

"Why, though?" Octli asked. "Why do they hate each other so?"

The bird shrugged his wings. "They are Men. Who can guess why they hate each other? I imagine that they themselves do not even know why."

"I see. But what can I do?"

"You are of the Earth," the bird said eagerly. "I thought perhaps if another Elemental were to intervene, we could put a stop to the fighting."

"What about your brothers of the Air?" Octli asked.

The bird clicked his beak and shook his feathers out again. "Them!" he snorted. "There is no talking sense to them. I have always found them so . . . so . . ."

"Flighty?" Octli offered, but when the bird drew himself up and glowered, he hurriedly added, "Yes, I can see that you need help. I do not have any such power myself . . ."

The bird hung his head.

". . . but I know of one who does. An Earth Master."

The bird perked up. "Do you think he will help me?"

"She," Octli corrected. "That I do not know. There is only one way to find out."

It took a long time to travel to where the Earth Master lived. Octli's legs were built for speed, but he needed to rest frequently. He refused all of the impatient bird's offers to carry him—those talons were just a bit too long and a bit too sharp and a bit too frightening for such a trip. The sun had sunk very low, then, before Octli arrived, panting, at a little stone house sitting all by itself at the base of a mountain.

"Mother!" he called. "Earth Mother!"

She emerged slowly, one carefully placed foot at a time, but Octli knew that it was not because of her age; she simply never had any reason to hurry. Mother smiled down at the rabbit and brushed a long white wisp from her eyes. "Well, hello, little one," she said in a voice that was both as soft as sand and as powerful at the mountain that loomed above them. "Have you come to share my supper?"

"Well, I . . . no . . . but . . ." Octli fidgeted, his nose catching the scent of something very rare inside the house. "But if you had more than enough for yourself, I would not refuse your kindness."

With a chuckle the old lady turned and disappeared into the shadowy interior of her house, returning a moment later with the tender and delightful fruit called *tomatl*. "Now tell me," she whispered as she set it down before Octli's nose. "What is it that bird wants of me?"

Octli froze in midbite and almost spat out his treat. "I . . . he . . . you . . ." he said in astonishment.

She laughed. "His shadow crossed over you twice, but you never even blinked. I know that even a *tomatl* could not entrance you so much as to make you blind, so you and he must be friends."

"Well . . . sort of . . ." Octli said sheepishly.

The old lady smiled and stroked Octli's ears. "Eat your supper. Let me speak to your friend." With that she stood and pointed up at the circling silhouette, then pointed to the ground before her feet.

The bird tucked his wings and plunged, rocketing toward the sand and only stretching his wings at the very last moment before he thumped down and sprawled out submissively, his beak on the ground. "Please, Earth Mother," he squawked, "do not punish me. I came to plead for your help. Terrible things are happening: the Fire splits the rocks, the Water drowns the fields! Rivers boil and rage!"

"Would you like a *tomatl*?"

"I . . . what?"

"A *tomatl*. Would you like one?"

"Er . . . I . . . no, thank you." The bird gave Octli a dumbfounded look, which Octli could only answer with a shrug.

"No, I did not think so. Please forgive me that I have nothing else to offer you. Welcome to my home, Son of the Air."

Bewildered, the bird rose to his feet and shook the dust from his wings. He gave Octli another uncertain glance, then said, "It is, um, Water, actually, Lady. I am of the Water."

"Oh! Please forgive me," Mother said, throwing up her hands. "I did not recognize you, all flapping about in the dirt as you were."

The bird cleared his throat and looked down, but said nothing.

"Now," Mother said as she hunkered down on her heels. "Tell me, what is the matter?"

Never taking his eyes from the ground, the bird recounted the tale of the dreadful fight between his Master, who really was just a mage but who insisted on the loftier title, and the Fire Mage, who also liked to be addressed as "Master," and how the fight was scarring the land and harming everyone nearby, be it Man, Beast, or Elemental. Mother listened to it all while chewing thoughtfully on a bit of dried *tomatl*. When the bird had finished, she pondered the story for a while before she said, "I can see that you have quite a problem."

"Yes, my Lady."

"So answer me one question. Why is it that I should help you?"

The bird opened and closed his beak, but no words came out.

"Answer me. Why should I help you?"

One yellow eye opened and glanced pleadingly at Octli. "I . . . please . . ." he began.

"Answer me. Why should I help you?"

The bird sagged, defeated. "I do not know, my Lady."

"I see. Then I will tell you the answer."

"My Lady?"

Mother reached down and hooked her finger beneath the bird's beak, gently lifting the reluctant gaze to hers. She smiled. "Because you asked me to."

They set off at first light, but even so, the sun was nearing its peak before they reached the battleground. Mother never hastened her thoughtful and deliberate pace and stopped quite often to sniff at flowers or to comment on the beauty of the clouds, while the bird who rode on her shoulder did not dare to make any impatient noises. His gaze darted about with increasing agitation, however, as the signs of war became more obvious. Here a field buried in mud, there a shed burned to ashes. Each time Mother stopped, leaning on her stick, and surveyed the scene grimly. "This," she muttered, "will not do at all."

The bird pointed the way to a hilltop overlooking a village that had clearly seen happier times. Some of the fields were swamped in water as deep as a man's ankles, while others had been blackened to dust. People struggled to coax what crops they could out of the few little patches of green earth that remained. As Mother frowned, a column of white steam gushed skyward in the distance.

"They are at it again," the bird said mournfully.

"So I see." Mother glanced down toward Octli, who had been following at her heels. "Little one, would you do me a kindness?"

"Of course, Earth Mother," Octli said eagerly.

"I need to get their attention, those two," she said, nodding toward the geysering steam. "Could you give me a thump?"

Octli blinked and peered down at his long hind foot. "A thump, Earth Mother?"

"Yes. You know, something to make them take notice."

Octli was skeptical, but he did not question the old lady's wisdom. Planting his forepaws firmly on the ground, he stamped his hind leg as hard as he could. To his astonishment, the entire hillside rocked as a wave rushed through the soil and down through the village, leaving the people staggering about in alarm.

"A few more, please."

Octli obeyed, watching with amazement as the little taps of his foot rocked the world to its heart and turned the village into a disturbed anthill. He was even more amazed when he saw the soil itself shift and roll, rise and dimple, shaping itself into the very semblance of a face—his face, ears, whiskers, and all.

"There," Mother said brightly. "I think they ought to notice that."

Octli shivered. All of the villagers were gaping and pointing at his image on the hillside, and Octli's instincts began to whisper urgently in his ear. "Should I hide, Earth Mother?" he said shakily.

"Hide?" She laughed. "Don't be silly, little one. You would miss all of the fun."

It did not take long before two glowering figures appeared, stalking in the same direction but quite far apart, each refusing to acknowledge even the breath of the other. The fat one boiled with rage while smoke rose from the skinny one's ears.

"What is this?" the fat one shouted, jabbing his finger at Mother. "What do you think you're doing here, you old goat?"

Mother smiled and began drawing some little pictures in the dirt with the end of her stick. "I only came to watch," she said sweetly.

"Be on your way!" the skinny one growled. "Your trick has interrupted a very important duel. I was just about to defeat this tub of fat—"

"Shut up, Stick Man!" the fat one barked back. He raised his hand, and water bubbled from the ground at his feet, only to be rendered to steam by a blast of flame from the skinny man's fingers.

"Now, now, boys," Mother said. "Pay no attention to me. Just go about what you were doing."

The Water Mage clenched his fists and squinted, but his piggy eyes flew open wide when he realized who was perched on the old lady's shoulder. "You!" he bellowed. "Where have you been? What is all this?"

The bird cowered, but the old lady said, "This one? He came to tell me that his Master was the most powerful man in all the world. I simply had to come and see for myself."

The Water Mage was taken aback, and drew himself up. "Well, then," he grunted.

"And this one," Mother continued, nodding down to Octli, "he told me that there was a Fire Mage here who was of such might that he was one with the gods."

"What?" the skinny man said, his mouth falling open. "I mean, yes, naturally. Er, who is he again?"

"Insolent little pest!" the Water Mage roared toward Octli. "You will drown!"

"No!" the Fire Mage shouted. "Leave the little one alone! I like him."

Mother held up her hands. "Now, boys, settle down, both of you. I can see that there is only one way to prove who here is the greater Master."

"How?" they both asked at once, then squinted ruefully.

Mother stood up and adjusted her shawl. "A duel!" she said.

"But that's what we—"

"To the death!" She raised her stick high. "The greater power will destroy the weaker!"

Octli gasped. "Earth Mother?" he whispered uncertainly, but the old lady did not look down.

The two mages also gasped, but after glancing at each other, their furious expressions returned. "Yes! Agreed!" the Water Mage said.

"To the death!" the Fire Mage added.

"Good." Mother swung her stick up over her head, then brought it down to the earth with a *crack*! Right away the soil erupted, spitting forth a dense field of stubby green leaves all bristling with angry spikes. "Neither will touch the other, as these branches will ensure."

"Ouch!" the Fire Mage yelped, having put it to the test. He thrust his finger into his mouth and grumbled while the Water Mage barked with laughter.

"Let us begin," Mother said, settling down on her heels. She scooped up a very startled Octli and settled him into her lap, and her gentle hand on his ears kept him from darting to safety. "May the greater power forever destroy the other!"

The Fire Mage struck first, a surge of molten rock rising from the soil and rolling toward his opponent. The Water Mage countered with a wave of his own that met the glowing tide head-on and exploded into a hissing, sizzling chaos that boiled among the spiky leaves, making them quake and twitch as though in agony.

Octli looked up toward the bird. "This is your fault," he whispered. "They are going to kill each other!"

"Me?" the bird hissed. "I wanted to stop it. You are the one who started this!"

Both of them, though, fell silent when they realized that Mother was looking at them. "You do not trust me?" she whispered, sounding hurt.

Octli winced. "I am sorry, Earth Mother."

"Forgive me, Lady," the bird said.

Mother nodded. "Just watch," she said, "and relax. We are going to be here for some time, I think."

Indeed they were. Then sun made its patient way across the sky, shortening the shadows and lengthening them again, while the two men, roaring like bulls, hurled their energies at each other over and over again. Each time the two forces met, they fell, hissing, onto the spiky branches below, soaking into the leaves and turning them gradually from green to blue.

At long last, the Water Mage choked and fell to his knees, his chin sinking to his chest. His tunic was soaked with the sweat that fell like rain from his forehead.

"I win!" the Fire Mage panted, but when he thrust forth his arm for the killing blow, only a little candle flame trickled from his fingertips, and then he, too, fell to his knees and gasped for breath.

Only then did Mother stand, stretching her arms behind her. "My, what a ferocious battle," she yawned. "Are you boys all finished now?"

Both of them clearly wanted to answer, but neither had enough wind for words. Mother stepped to the edge of the spiky branches and tilted her head. "Well, now, we still need to find out which of the powers was greater. But I do not see them. Where do you suppose they went?"

The men, still winded, climbed to their feet. The Fire Mage pointed accusingly at the leaves before him. "You tricked us. You stole our powers!"

"Stole? Me? Why, I did no such thing. I am merely keeping them safe for you."

"Where?" the men demanded.

Mother pointed to the quivering blue leaves. "In there, of course. I must say, too, that they are getting along together far better than you two."

Snarling at each other, each man seized a leaf and, yelping at the prickly spikes, broke them open. Neither was quite certain what to expect, but certainly neither expected to find something that looked very much like milk. The Water Mage would have bellowed in anger if he could have stopped panting, and the Fire Mage looked as though he were about to cry. "You destroyed them," he whimpered.

"Nonsense!" Mother laughed. "I simply mingled them."

"Mingled? You crazy old witch! Fire is the enemy of Water!"

"So you keep saying." Mother pointed to the liquid that was dripping from the skinny man's fingers. "You are letting it get away. If you want your power back, you are going to have to take it inside of you quickly."

The Water Mage just stared dumbly at her for a moment, and then with a flicker of understanding, he held the leaf over his mouth and gulped its contents down. Right away his eyes bulged from his head, and he began to gag. "Oh! Ow! It burns like fire!"

"What are you talking about, you idiot?" the fat man wheezed, and he, too, took a drink. Immediately he fell onto his bottom. "It does burn like fire, but it's wet like water!"

"I told you. I mingled them," Mother said as she drew some more pictures in the sand with her stick. "And you had better hurry and take them back into you before the land swallows them first and you lose them forever."

Both men gasped and, ignoring the painful spikes, began frantically snatching up leaves. Eagerly they broke the leaves open and guzzled down what they found within. They swallowed, coughed, swallowed, gagged, swallowed, wheezed, and swallowed. Soon both began to sway on their feet. Their faces were bright red, and they sweated heavily. The fat man rubbed at his eyes, blinking them blearily, and turned to speak to his rival, but all that came out was a thunderous belch that echoed clear down to the village below. The two men gawked at each other, then burst out laughing.

Mother smiled and lifted Octli from her lap, then used her stick to help herself to her feet. "I think that they have learned their lesson," she said.

The bird, who had been watching this strange scene in puzzled silence, hopped to the ground in front of Mother. He looked worriedly over his shoulder to where the two mages were hugging and professing their mutual admiration and affection in words that were not at all clear to anyone else. "How long will this magic last, my Lady?" he asked.

"Not long. They may not feel very friendly when they first wake up, but as long as you remind them of how much more powerful their energies were when combined with a tiny bit of the Earth, I think that we can make their friendship last a long time. I will leave you with that task."

The bird dipped his head low and spread his wings in a regal bow. "Thank you, my Lady. I will make sure that they do not forget." With that he leaped into the air and rejoined his Master, who was now leaning heavily on the Fire Mage as the two wobbled their way noisily back down to the village.

Mother turned to go, but paused when she saw Octli sniffing curiously at one of the leaves. He started guiltily and backed away, but she smiled and said, "You may try some if you would like."

"It is kind of you to offer, Mother," he said, and nibbled carefully, and with the leaf came the water and the fire at the same time. "Oh!" he croaked, hopping backward and shaking his head. "This is . . . very different." After a moment his head began to feel strange. He looked down the hill to where the two mages were stumbling along, singing merrily and clapping each other on the back. He took another bite, and then another, and by the third, he was beginning to understand why the men were behaving so. "I think I like this. May I share the magic with some of my brothers?"

"Of course, little one. Invite them all. There is plenty for everyone."

"Oh, I don't know about that, Mother," Octli said, his voice becoming less steady. "I have quite a lot of brothers."

Author's note: To the Aztecs, the Centzon Totochtin *were a group of four hundred rabbit-deities who would gather together to enjoy the intoxicating beverage originally known as* octli, *and later called* pulque, *which was the great-uncle of what we now know as tequila. While originally prepared by the mingling of Fire and Water magics, the arrival of the Spanish brought about new methods of preparing* pulque *through a tedious fermentation process that made the drink available to all humankind. Most* pulque *today is created by this method, but those of us "in the know" still prefer the original recipe.*

Fire Song

Diana L. Paxson

"To you, Hestia, the first and the last . . ."

Kyria smiled as her mother tipped her wine cup over the hearth. It always amused her that Eudocia, otherwise so unworldly, should be so dedicated to the rituals of household piety. "When I see you do that, I know I am home."

Flames leaped, and the coals sizzled as the drops hit them. For a moment Kyria glimpsed the bright shapes of salamanders dancing there. She did not see them well—her Element was Water—but after she had learned to see the nymphs, she found that she could tell when the spirits of other Elements were near. Did the salamanders appreciate the drink? Did the goddess mind sharing the offering?

The firelight struck sparks from the curls of the child, dark like her own, who slept in her arms. Empedocles was not a fretful child, but he was never still except when he was sleeping. Bright eyes—gray like his father's—darted ceaselessly about, taking everything in. When he closed them, both of them could rest.

Firelight flickered on the whitewashed walls, illuminating the hangings that Eudocia had woven when the family first came to Kumae and the ancestor figures in their niche by the door. Their quarters were small, but a Pythagorean philosopher needed little. Most of Archilaus' time was spent in the long room and courtyard that the tyrant Aristodemus had given him for his school.

"Do they not honor the goddess at Akragas?" her mother asked.

"Oh, of course," Kyria replied. In some lands there might be barbarians who did not offer to the lady of the hearth, but no one who spoke Greek would dare deny Hestia her due. "But my husband's mother is hearth-priestess there."

Shifting the limp weight of the child, she winced at the prickle of returning circulation in her arm. Empedocles was only three, but he was growing fast.

"Would you like me to take him?"

"I'm all right. Sit down, Mother—you've been on your feet all day!"

This was the first visit Kyria had made to Cumae since her marriage. She had wanted to show her son to his grandparents, but she was beginning to wonder if this had been a good time to come. Her mother had looked anxious ever since they arrived.

But maybe she had reason to worry. There had only been a few ships in the harbor. In the marketplace, people spoke in low voices and hurried off as soon as their business was done. Work on the moat that the tyrant had set the people to dig around the town had been abandoned. According to their cook, it was because one of the women carrying earth had said that she only veiled her face when Aristodemus passed by. After all, she said, Aristodemus was the only real man there.

That was enough to shame the men into striking, but a rebellion needed a leader. The tyrant had survived challenges in the past. *Surely,* thought Kyria, *he will weather this one.* But suddenly it was not only because she missed her husband that Kyria wished Meto had come with her.

For a moment her mother stood still, rubbing her hands. Then she was in motion once more, stacking the wine cups, straightening a cloth.

"Something *is* wrong! You jump every time you hear a sound. Why has Father gone out with the older students when he meant to celebrate with us here at home?"

Eudocia looked at her daughter for a moment, then picked up one of the plates and began to scrape the remains of the barley and greens into a bowl.

"There have been . . . rumors . . . that the sons of the nobles the tyrant drove out are plotting against him. Aristodemus has been very generous, supporting the school all these years. When he asks for counsel, of course Archilaus must come."

"But will the tyrant listen?" Kyria asked. "I always thought he viewed Father as an ornament, as if supporting a philosopher would persuade people that he was a gentleman. That's not the reputation he has elsewhere, you know. In Sikelia they say he's no more than a thug who used his success as a soldier to raise the mob against the nobles and has employed foreign mercenaries to keep himself in power."

Kyria flinched as her mother, glancing around in fear, clapped a hand over her mouth. But they had dismissed the cook when it became clear that Archilaus was not going to be home for dinner. The only other person in the house was Lysander, the philosopher's youngest pupil, and he had been sent to bed some time ago.

"Foolish girl, you never did know when to keep silent!" Eudocia let go when it was clear that they were alone. "And now the gods have punished you with a son who cannot speak at all!"

Empedocles jerked awake as Kyria clutched him. Shock kept *her* speechless as her mother went on.

"Do you think I haven't noticed that he never cries? I thought at first it was because you do everything for him before he can ask. At that age, you babbled like a brook. I told your father; but he only laughed and said the boy is a born philosopher, but I know!"

"Everyone says that boys speak later than girls. Every child is different. There is nothing wrong with my son!" Kyria cried. Surely she did not delude herself when she recognized intelligence in that flickering gaze. What need did Empedocles have for words? Everyone loved him. Kyria was not the only one who always knew when he was hungry or wet—his nursemaids felt the same.

She didn't even try to fight her tide of anger. "I thought you would be pleased to see him, but you are a foolish old woman. As soon as I can find a ship to carry us, we'll be gone!"

Empedocles squirmed in her arms, and she set him carefully in the chair. "Stay there. Mama has things to do!" For a moment he glared back, but then some falling coal sent a spurt of flame from the hearth, and he laughed.

She began to gather the child's gear into a basket, once more amazed at how much was needed for the comfort of one so small. Her own gowns rolled swiftly into a bundle. She was tightening the last knot when the curtain to the back room stirred, and Lysander, still rubbing his eyes, walked into the room.

"Someone is shouting outside," he said. At eight, his features were still child-soft, but there was a good brain beneath that tousled brown hair.

Kyria opened the front door. The wind that swirled down from the acropolis carried faint cries. There was a hint of smoke as well.

"Lysander, get your cloak. Mother, perhaps you had better make up a bundle for yourself and one for Father, too. Pythagoras himself fled when there was a revolution in Crotona. Do you think Archilaus will be any safer if Aristodemus falls?"

"I have a bundle . . ." Eudocia said in a defeated voice. "Archilaus forbade me to pack, but I have been ready for the past two days."

Kyria took a deep breath. Any possible response to *that* went so far beyond what she could properly say to her mother that she had no words. And anyway, there was no time. The shouting was louder now. She had heard shouts like that from the arena when they were holding the Games. Empedocles slid down from the chair and took a step toward the door.

As Kyria plopped him back down on the seat, she heard the sound of running feet on stone. One of the philosopher's students burst around the corner, his red hair blazing in the light from the open door. White wisps of hair standing on end and tunic awry, Archilaus followed, supported by Polycritos and Nicolaus, the oldest of his students.

"Aristodemus is dead!" The boy skidded to a stop. "And my father—" He gulped, new tears cutting a pathway through the dirt on his cheeks.

Kyria remembered that he was called Picus, son of a Roman who came to Kumae with the exiled King Tarquin, and stayed on as one of the tyrant's guards. Kyria reached out, but he stood rigid, at fourteen too old to accept comfort, but not old enough to deny his need.

"Thymoteles has seized the citadel." Archilaus was shaking, but his voice was calm. "You women and the boys must go. They will want Picus because of his father, Polycritos because he is my student, and Lysander and Nicolaus, whose fathers are foreign merchants, to hold for ransom. But I can keep them talking while you pack and get away."

"No, master!" Polycritos said hoarsely. "You must get away. I've heard my father and his friends talking over their wine. It was always what they were going to do someday, but now that day's here. They hate you—hate everyone the tyrant favored. I must be the one to stay."

"But he'll punish you—" Archilaus began.

"Tie me up!" said the boy. "Decide where you'll go, and I'll tell him you went the other way."

"It's a good plan," Kyria agreed, slinging her bundles over one shoulder and sliding one arm through the handle of her basket.

"Please, master." Polycritos was weeping now. "My father has shamed our house. At least let me do this for you!"

Kyria settled Empedocles on one hip. "Nicolaus and Picus, there's rope in the kitchen. Get it, and pack a basket with all the food you can find. We'll make for the harbor. Do as Polycritos says and come after us." She turned to her parents. "*Please* follow me!"

Had he been present, her husband could have summoned spirits of the Air to add a compulsion to his words, but the emotion behind Kyria's appeal was enough to sweep her mother through the door. Eudocia seized her husband's hand. Still protesting, he let himself be pulled down the narrow lane. The ruddy glow above the acropolis gave enough light to show their way.

"The mercenaries stopped to loot," breathed her father as he stumbled along. "I tried to save some of the scrolls, but the soldiers were between me and the library . . ."

And were the books more important than your family? Kyria bit back the question, knowing that her father would probably reply that, unlike the scrolls, his family could run away. And hadn't she just proved him right, after all?

"May the gods keep them too busy playing with the tyrant's possessions to look for his friends!" she replied.

As they neared the corner, she heard footsteps and stiffened, but it was only Nicolaus and Picus, bundles thumping against their backs as they ran. Ahead, a door opened, and lamplight spilled out across the stony lane. The house Aristodemus had given his philosopher was at the very edge of the heights that looked west toward the long, straight stretch of beach and the Tyrrhenian Sea. The tyrant's favorites were abandoning their mansions now. Kyria glimpsed bright cloth and a glint of gold as people pushed through the doorway. One of them was weeping; another mumbled angrily.

"It's Telarchos!" her father cried, and looked surprised when Kyria held him back. "He's a warrior! He'll protect us!"

"Not against such odds," she hissed in reply. "He'll try to fight, and anyone with him will be killed. Let them go." She nodded as Telarchos' household started off in the direction of the Processional Way. "Everyone who takes that route will distract the rebels from looking for us here."

Kyria held them back until the other fugitives had rounded the corner and even the sound of weeping had faded away.

"Lady of the Citadel, guide us," she whispered as an owl swept overhead on silent wings.

The houses of Kumae's citizens sprawled down the hillside between the acropolis and the bay in a warren of passageways. Memory led her down the narrow street beside Telarchos' mansion. Their cook's daughter and she had gone that way once when they were children, eager to spy on the Dionysian festival. They made their way through an alley, then endured a tense moment waiting for another babbling group to pass before they returned to the road.

"Hsst!" Nicolaus, who was in the lead, turned suddenly into a narrow passage between a shed and a donkey pen, waving at the others to follow. Behind them, the regular tramp of hobnailed sandals rang against stone. Kyria pressed herself against the wall, willing the shadows to enfold them. She could hear her mother's harsh breathing, her father's whispered affirmations of divine harmony. Even Empedocles held still. If he was indeed mute, she could only be grateful for it now.

"Etruscans!" Nicolaus shaped the word as the shadows of cone-shaped helmets jerked along the wall. "Thymoteles hired them."

"Barbarians!" muttered Archilaus. "Students and teachers are noncombatants—sacred to the gods!"

"Not always." Nicolaus stifled a grin. "Picus grabbed a bronze vase and brained the man who stabbed his father. That's another reason they might be after us." They all held their breaths as the patrol marched by.

"They've cut us off from the harbor," Kyria observed when the soldiers had passed. "We'll have to get to one of the northern gates and work our way around past the lake."

"But that is a dreadful place! Birds that fly over it fall dead from the sky," Eudocia exclaimed. "No one in their senses goes near."

"Then they won't be looking for us there," Kyria said stoutly. Meto and she had ventured there once, and her nose wrinkled even at the memory, but there was a path though the trees that lined the rim. "If we skirt the lake and head for the fishing village by Baios' tomb, we can hire a boat." The coins that would have paid for her passage on a merchant vessel should be more than enough to bribe a fisherman to carry them across the bay. It was not a perfect plan, but no one had come with anything better. Shifting Empedocles to rest against her shoulder, she stepped back onto the road.

By the time they slipped through the small gate that the refuse collectors used, flames were devouring the acropolis. They were far from the only party leaving the city, but no one else took the road to the lake that reflected the bloody sky. Lake Avernus was a gloomy place even at noon, black beneath the shadow of the trees that lined its shores and an oily gray in the sun. It was the only water Kyria had ever encountered that made her want to flee. She had never seen a bird drop from the sky above it, but few swam there. The peasants said that Odysseus had come here once, seeking the ghost of his father, and later Aeneas stopped by on his way to Latium. At midnight, it was a place of terror where gibbering spirits rode the wind to the gate of Hades, which must surely be somewhere nearby.

The citadel was still burning when the fugitives huddled to rest beneath a stand of pines. The fallen needles had a dry, musty smell.

"I hope it all burns!" muttered Picus. "My father will have a noble pyre!" Through the tangle of branches they could see the stark silhouette of the acropolis against a sky of flame. The glow illuminated the faces of her companions. Except for Empedocles, who bounced in her arms, pointing, they were all marked by fatigue and fear.

"How did the rebels get past the tyrant's guards?" she asked.

"Xenocrite let them in!" spat Nicolaus.

"She is the daughter of one of the exiled nobles," explained Eudocia, "but she always seemed happy with the luxuries Aristodemus gave her."

"She said that she would rather carry earth like the other women, if it was for her father, than lie in a usurper's soft bed," answered Archilaus. "Thymoteles cut Aristodemus' throat before he could answer her."

"Hermes, God of Travelers, help us!" whispered Eudocia. "I hoped we would be safe here for the rest of our lives."

Kyria patted her mother's hand, understanding how hard this flight must be for a woman who rarely left her home.

"Pythagoras taught that impermanence is the nature of all things physical," said her father sternly. "In other lands, men look at the earth and think it eternal, but here, where water burns and the land itself rises and falls like the sea, we cannot deny that his words were true. Even our bodies are only temporary habitations. The soul moves from one to another until it is perfected."

But bodies are precious, too, thought Kyria, acutely conscious of the warm weight of the child in her arms. *I do not care who Empedocles was before, or who he will be. I know only that the body he wears now came from my own, and I will give my last drop of blood to preserve it.* If her child never spoke a word, the bright spirit that burned within him could still bring light to the world.

"Is the fishers' village far?" whispered Lysander in the silence that followed.

"We could reach it by dawn," said Nicolaus, "but some of the nobles that Aristodemus banished live there."

"The rebels will still be in the city," said Kyria. "If the villagers will not help us, we can buy food and continue on."

"Fisherfolk live all along the bay," her father said calmly. "We will find another village."

"But not until we have light," said Kyria. "We should eat something now, and get whatever rest we can."

Dawn brought a smoke-dimmed sky and a muggy heat, as if summer were already here. From the knob of ocher stone where the citadel still smoldered, a land scored by canyons and craters stretched westward. Men called them the fields of fire, though except for the places where sulfurous vapors burst from the earth, there was rich soil.

The track they followed wound south, crossing a hillside where a few goats grazed and buttercups glowed in the ripening grass. Farther off, tall cypresses stood like green columns for a roofless temple, framing a glimpse of sparkling blue bay. It would have been a lovely day for a walk if not for the smoke in the air, but as the sun rose, the wind shifted, bringing the scent of the sea.

Empedocles wriggled until Kyria set him down. She untied the cord that bound her peplos below her breasts to make a leash for him. Though her mother frowned, he had run off too many times to go free. His tongue might lag, but there was nothing wrong with his legs.

The day grew warmer. Kyria settled into a mindless progress, retaining just enough focus to keep hold of Empedocles' leash, when Lysander pulled on her sleeve.

"I hear hoofbeats!"

Nico knelt and laid his ear to the earth. "Horses! More than one. They must have gotten them from the citadel."

Kyria cast a quick look around. The pines edging the road could give no cover. They were widely spaced, their branches bushing out like a sunshade well over the height of a man. Where the slope fell away beyond them, brush covered the hill.

"Down there!" she cried, grabbing the child. Stiff twigs tore at skin and gown as they slid down the bank, but when the first of the horsemen rounded the bend, all of the fugitives were out of sight, nursing their scratches as they crouched among the leathery leaves.

The horsemen laughed and passed a wineskin back and forth. They wore odd bits of looted finery, and ambling behind them was a laden mule.

"We're too late," wailed Eudocia when they had gone.

"No," said her husband. "We are saved. If we had made it to the village, we would be there now, waiting as the fisherman got his boat ready for sea."

"If we had found someone willing to take us at all," added Picus grimly.

"The gods are watching over us!" exclaimed Lysander. "We would have fallen right into their hands."

"But if we cannot go to the village, what will we do?" Eudocia's voice wavered, but she was not weeping. Indeed, she was holding up better than Kyria had expected.

"Go back to the fork," Archilaus replied. "That road follows the shore."

Kyria shaded her eyes with her hand. Before them lay a rolling countryside of dull green brush and pasture where the grass was ripening to gold. Some five leagues to the east, the double peaks of Vesouvios floated on the horizon. She had to believe that somewhere along the curving coastline they would find a ship. Empedocles was already scrambling back up the slope. With a sigh, she followed him.

The fugitives kept moving throughout that day. For a time the road edged the coast, but they found no one with a boat big enough to carry all of them. Now the track led inland. The boys ranged ahead to watch for other travelers, and the more identifiable members of the party were usually able to hide before they were seen. From time to time they saw shepherds on the hillside, but by the time any news got to the rebels, surely the fugitives would be gone.

As the sun sank westward, their footsteps slowed. Empedocles' enthusiasm for running had failed long ago. Kyria's nostrils flared at a whiff of sulfur on the wind. "You're tired, little man." She jiggled him in her arms, wondering how much farther she could carry him.

"What cannot be changed must be endured," said her father, but he, too, sounded weary.

The country here was ridged and broken, good only for

goats. She hoped they would find a source of good water soon. The last spring had had an odd mineral taste, and the nymph was a sickly creature who snarled at her.

"How much will Thymoteles care that you escaped?" she asked softly.

Archilaus' brow furrowed. "Logically, their first concern should be to secure the city." The tall cypresses laid bars of shadow across his face as they passed.

"But most men are not logical, I have heard you say—"

He sighed. "Some of them desire to obliterate everything Aristodemus achieved."

"And you fear they will identify the tyrant's philosopher with the tyrant?"

"Perhaps, though the gods know Aristodemus was not willing to learn very much from me. But Thymoteles has a more practical reason to want me out of the way. I told him that if he murdered Aristodemus instead of giving him a trial, his name would be despised in every city where Greek is spoken."

"And he knows that you will bear witness against him if you live," Kyria said.

She had no illusions regarding their fate if they were captured. Her parents would be killed. She herself would fetch a good price in a slave market somewhere far away. And her son—would she see his bright spirit extinguished by fetters, or watch him die as Andromache had watched when her child was thrown from the walls of Troy?

Her arms tightened protectively around Empodecles, who stirred. His eyes grew bright as he looked around him. Ahead, the road crossed a ridge of land that swelled upward, where the rim of a caldera showed above the trees. When they came to the crest, they paused.

"Master, is that the place you spoke of, where Hephaestus has his forge?" asked Lysander.

"Or Hestia her cauldron." Archilaus smiled. "Vesouvios is another." He nodded toward the distant mountain.

"And Aitne in Sikelia, where I live now," added Kyria. For some time she had been feeling a deep throbbing beneath the ground. When she extended her awareness downward, she sensed water, but it was strangely blended with earth and fire.

This is a country for Titans or gods, not men, she thought with a sudden unease. *I want to go back to the sea.*

"What's that?" Picus was looking back the way they had come. A moving haze of dust veiled the road.

"Lysander, you have the best eyes." Nico lifted him. "What do you see?"

"Mounted soldiers," the boy squeaked, "coming fast!"

"Get off the road!" To the left, there was a gap in the brush. Kyria started downward, her sandals slipping in the loose pale soil, and the others followed.

It was no more than a goat track, winding down through a tangle of scrub oak mixed with myrtle and buckthorn. The aroma of sun-warmed sage scented the air. When the path began to climb again, she paused to peer back through the branches. The horsemen still pounded along the dusty road. Sunlight glinted from their pointed helms.

Etruscans . . . They would not give up easily. Despite the heat of the sun, she shivered.

Above them, a few pines stood stark against the sky. They climbed toward them until suddenly the path fell sharply away, and they found themselves on the rim of the caldera. Most of the crater floor was a wasteland of bubbling mud and tumbled stone where only plumes of vapor grew, but on the western side, there was a green grove. The smell of sulfur drifted up on the wind.

"Hestia help us!" moaned her mother. "This place belongs to the gods. We cannot go there!"

"I'd rather trust to the mercy of the gods than men," Kyria replied.

The place might be holy, but *someone* came here, for when they reached the base of the slope, they found that the path joined a road whose ruts were overgrown with grass. At the edge of the woods stood an altar of honey-colored stone that looked as if it had been there since the gods imprisoned the Titans underground. Archilaus bent to trace the weathered inscription.

"To Hestia and Hephaestus . . ." He straightened. "Holy ones, if ever we escape this peril, I promise you an offering."

Now that they were on level ground, Kyria could set Empedocles down. As he trotted alongside, her spirit as well as her back muscles began to ease. Green grasses waved beneath oak and olive and the glossy-leafed unedo, whose pebbled fruits were just beginning to swell. She glimpsed the cliffs that rimmed the crater above the trees.

The boys came dashing back from their explorations to show her a rivulet that formed a small pool. Kyria scooped up cool water, feeling senses that had been deadened by fatigue revive.

"Nymphs of this forest pool," she whispered, "I thank you!"

Sunlight struck the water as a breeze stirred the branches, and shifting focus showed her a shimmer of opalescent forms and flickering wings. Empedocles sat down suddenly, eyes wide. Then he pointed and laughed. He could see them! She had suspected it, but this was the first time the child had been in a place where the sprites could so easily appear.

One of the nymphs darted toward the boy, evaded his grab, and hovered in front of Kyria. "Rest, Despoina. Drink! You are safe for now, but this is not a good place for humankind."

Kyria nodded. Below her she sensed not solid earth, but contorted caverns where Earth and Water and Fire all strove for mastery. Tartarus was close to the surface here, and clearly the Elements were still at war. She tried not to think about what might happen if those titanic powers, so much greater than the sprites she knew, should ever break free.

But for now, there was peace in the grove. Her parents had settled with their backs against an oak tree. Empedocles lay curled on the grass. Even the boys were sitting, playing some game with pebbles and a board scratched into the soil. *Surely,* thought Kyria, *we can stay here for a little while . . .* Her eyelids closed.

When she opened them again, the setting sun was sending shafts of fiery light between the trees. But what had wakened her was a spray of droplets cast by a frenzied cloud of nymphs calling her name. As she sat up, she heard shouts and the neighs of horses

Kyria lurched to her feet, heart pounding. The boys ran toward her, eyes wide, but her mother clung to her husband's arm, weeping.

"Our pursuers have found us. You must go," Archilaus said quietly. "A wise man knows when it is time to make an end, and your mother and I cannot run anymore."

The day's effort had worn away their flesh and left dark smudges around their eyes, but Kyria could not, *would* not, accept defeat now.

"You survived a shipwreck, and you will survive this!" she cried. "If this is Hestia's cauldron, then let her protect us. Picus, Nicolaus, help them!" She pointed toward the wasteland beyond the trees.

Somehow, she got her parents moving. As they stumbled past the last of the trees, she heard a shout and saw the Etruscans urging their mounts down the slope.

The shadow of the western rim lengthened swiftly across the crater floor as the sun dipped behind it. Their feet kicked up beige dust as they raced toward the tumbled rocks on the other side. The slope there was steep, but perhaps they could climb it, perhaps they could throw rocks. She only knew that she was *not* going to simply sit down and wait to die.

Their pursuers had reached the flat ground. By now most of the crater floor was in shadow, but they urged their horses toward their prey. The first three riders were well into the mud pool before they realized they were not on solid ground. Horses plunged wildly as the viscous mud caught at their hooves, then fell, screaming as the searing mud sucked them down. Only one of the soldiers managed to struggle back to his companions, and Kyria did not think he would be fighting for a while.

The boys had pushed her parents behind a formation of curdled stone. The slope around it looked half melted, stained in patches of bright yellow, ocher, and gray. Empedocles and she tumbled into place behind another. The forces that had been merely disturbing when she sensed them from the grove now beat against her awareness. The stone beneath her was warm, and a reek of rotting eggs filled the air. She stifled a shriek as vapor hissed from some nearby hole, and another at Empedocles' chortle of delight. She fought back an impulse to slap him. If his life was going to be cut short, he might as well end it laughing.

As the sun set, the crater became a cauldron of shadow.

She could hear voices from the other end, but could not see their foes. Even on foot, the Etruscans would hesitate to cross the crater floor in darkness. The fugitives would be equally invisible. But they must do something, or they would gain no more than an uncomfortable night and capture in the morning.

The cliff behind her was faintly visible in the afterglow. The boys and she might be able to climb it, but her parents had barely been able to get this far. Her father had the comfort of his philosophy. It was her mother for whom Kyria wept, only now recognizing how much courage she had shown.

At the other end of the caldera, light sparked, faltered, then settled into a steady flame. In moments another torch was glowing, and then a third, and they began to move. There was a hollow rumble from beneath the earth as someone dislodged a stone. For a moment the torches paused, then came inexorably on.

Kyria blinked back tears. It had all been for nothing, their escape, their journey, and this last desperate dash. She had scorned her mother as useless, but she herself had done no better.

As their enemies drew closer, the torches began to swing about, poking into each hole and behind each rock formation, lest they miss the one where their prey lay hidden.

"Meto, forgive me for not coming back to you. And you, my little one," she whispered into Empedocles' hair. "I should never have brought you here . . ."

His eyes glinted as he turned to her, then he pointed at the torches and laughed. Kyria stifled a gasp. Being of Water, she had always found the salamanders hard to see. But she was seeing them now, dancing in the flames.

The nearest soldier thrust his torch at a tumble of rock and recoiled as the earth emitted a burst of reddish steam. The next man swung and swore as glowing steam billowed around him, and then the third. The salamanders were dancing, and now she saw nymphs with them, manifesting somehow from the earth's vapors at the touch of the flame.

"Fire an' Water," Empedocles said clearly. "Burn! Make bad men go 'way!"

Steam roared from every vent on the floor of the caldera as if Medea's dragons were imprisoned below. The earth groaned, and rocks came clattering down the cliff. The sprites danced in the glowing clouds, tugging at the men's clothing, nipping at faces and hands. The Etruscans cast away their torches and fled, but the clouds continued to grow. Screams of terror turned to cries of agony as the Elementals drove them into the sucking mud and boiling pools. It seemed a very long time before the last pleading voice fell still.

The vapors subsided, but the salamanders returned, flickering around Empedocles in a garland of living flame. He tugged at his mother's hand, and she let him lead her out from behind the rocks.

"Come!" Kyria's voice wavered only a little as she called. "It's safe now."

One by one the others emerged from their hiding places and joined her. Guided by Empedocles, they made their careful way back toward the grove. When Eudocia stumbled, Kyria took her arm.

"My son can talk . . ." she said after a while.

"Yes," said her mother, "but what is he going to say? Oh, my dear, you *are* going to have an interesting time with that child . . ."

Author's Note: The story of the two women who helped bring down the tyrant Aristodemus can be found in Plutarch's essay "The Bravery of Women." Cumae is one of the few places in the region built on solid ground. The use of fire to cause condensation in the vapors from the fumaroles of Il Volcano Solfatara has been a tourist attraction since ancient times. The Campi Phlegrei ("Fields of Fire") is actually an eight-mile-wide super-volcano between Cumae and Naples whose topography changes constantly. It is showing signs of activity today.

Sails of the Armada
Kristin Schwengel

July 29, 1588

"Exsurge, Domine, et Vindica Causam Tuam." His eyes on
the open seas, Rodrigo snorted under his breath, then repeated in his native Galician the phrase the *capelán* had used
in the morning's prayer service. *"Arise, O Lord, and vindi-
cate thy cause.* A grand and glorious motto for this misbegot-
ten 'Enterprise,' is it not? To make a grasp for power into a
holy crusade?"

Tareixa's only answer to his frustrated thoughts was to
flick the water with her silver-black tail, splashing the salt
spray against the side of the *galleas*. Rodrigo grinned for a
moment, watching her sinuous form through the deck rails as
she rolled and turned in the waves, enjoying the beauty of a
clear sky after the recent days of storms. Her mood seemed
playful, as though she was urging him to join her in the water.

It was how they had met, when he was a young boy swimming in the *ría*, the deep ocean inlet near his home. She had
come upon him and had swum with him, her giant body
dwarfing his. As the years passed, she spent more and more
time with him in the *rías*, away from the rest of her kind in the
deeper ocean waters. When she was near, he was always aware
of her presence in the back of his mind, and he had learned to
interpret her moods, to communicate with her after a fashion.
True language was beyond her, but she could understand the
feeling or intent of his words or thoughts, and sometimes he
could create pictures in his own mind that she could share.

Sensing eyes upon him, Rodrigo pulled his attention from the sea, sorting through the pile of rigging draped over his knees and setting aside coils in need of minor repairs. A separate heap awaited those that were so worn, they could only be shredded back to hempen fibers, to be used for cleaning the ship and her *canone*, or mixed with pitch to fill the inevitable cracks in her hull. Glancing up under his lashes as he worked, he saw Don Ruarte, the *capelán* assigned to the *San Lorenzo*, standing near the rails at the side of the forecastle, above the deck where he sat.

To most, Don Ruarte looked like any other priest, with only the gold chain given him by the King to indicate that he was one of the most senior priests of the fleet. But when Rodrigo observed the Don, he also saw *sílfide*, spirits of Air, which the Don held bound to him. Don Ruarte, like several clerics Rodrigo had noticed on the decks of the other ships, was a *mago dos ventos*, a mage of the winds. Rodrigo had also seen at least one *mago da auga*, one who could command the spirits of Water, the *náiade* and *nereidas,* as Don Ruarte commanded those of Air. Though the black-clad Don now looked forward over the bowsprit, his fingers raised as he sifted through the winds that pushed the Armada onward at its ponderous pace, Rodrigo was sure that, moments before, those piercing ice-blue eyes had been turned his way.

The Don had taken to watching Rodrigo once the fleet had begun its slow progress northward from the mouth of the Tagus, just beyond Lisbon. Rodrigo had been pressed into service that March, seized from Lisbon's streets while taking a day away from his family's trading ship. When he had been forced to join the Spanish forces, he'd feared becoming a *buenaboya*, a "volunteer" chained to the ranks of oars in the dank, poisonous hold, but the Neopolitan crewmasters had recognized the usefulness of another experienced sailor, even if he was a Galician.

Rodrigo had become a boy-of-all-work on the flagship, assigned to odd tasks, acting in relief of both ship's boys and apprentice mariners, but officially neither one nor the other. He obeyed every command with alacrity, knowing that one more would always be welcome among the *buenaboyas*, especially as illness took its toll during the Armada's slow progress. Yet despite his determination to efface himself among more than a hundred other sailors, to be a nameless pair of hard-laboring hands aboard a ship full of crew and soldiers, Don Ruarte had taken notice of him, had picked him out as different from the rest. As Rodrigo's eyes could see the *sílfide* accompanying the Don, could the *capelán* have seen something unusual about him?

Daring another glance between the rails, he could just make out Tareixa's spined body breaking in a glossy curve between the waves. Had the *mago dos ventos* seen her as well? Her snakelike form was nearly half as long as the ship itself, although her sinuous coils and serpentine movement made it difficult for even his practiced eye to spot her, especially if she stayed just below the surface, where her shimmering skin matched the colors of the sea. Rodrigo frowned and bit his salt-cracked lip. After all the years he had known her, after she had even followed him from Galicia to Lisbon and out to sea again, should he try to warn her to keep away?

He looked back up at Don Ruarte. He had never heard anyone among the Spanish speak of a *mago*, openly or secretly. Nor did folk in his home village, but he had still grown up with an awareness that, at one time, the *magos* had openly communicated with and commanded the spirits of Air, Fire, Earth, and Water, and that the Inquisitors had sought out and destroyed all of the *magos* whom they could find, claiming them heretics. Yet here was the Don, holding the winds in his fingertips as the Spanish sought to hold all of Europe and, it seemed, the whole of the globe.

If one could not see the *sílfide*, one might think that the Don simply held his hands up in supplicating prayer to Our Lord. Perhaps that was all any of the Spanish soldiers and sailors saw, or they were as silent as he if they saw more. But surely the King, or at least the *Capitán-General*, the Duke of Medina Sidonia, knew that what was supposed to be a forbidden heresy was being practiced aboard the ships. It could not be by chance that the flagship of each squadron carried a priest who was also a *mago*. And if they had been placed by design, surely these were the most powerful *magos* in Spain, each assigned to bend the winds or waves to do his bidding, which was the bidding of the King. This Armada was commanded to bring soldiers to join with the land armies of the Duke of Parma in Flanders, to invade England and add it to Spain's other conquests. Rodrigo's jaw tightened in bitter resentment at that thought before turning back to the piles of rigging, his callused hands working along another length of rope. More than a hundred years of Spanish rule had not been enough for his people to forget their heritage, nor their sympathy for others who struggled against Spain.

The winds shifted slightly, and at a command from the *contramaestre*, the officer of the deck, he left his coils of rope and sprang to his position along the port lines of the *palo de mesano*, the third mast from the fore of the ship, hauling on the lines with the other men, bringing the lateen sail around to catch the dancing breeze. The triangular sail snapped once, twice, then filled as the decksmen raced to secure the ropes, the mast swaying with the pull as the flaxen sail curved outward, filled by the new wind. The timbers shuddered as the ship slowly came around, gaining every bit of speed possible from the air current that Don Ruarte had caught between his thin fingers and sent with them. The ship's carpenters and divers had managed to repair the fragile rudder damaged by waves during the last storm, but the *San Lorenzo* would still be hard-pressed to catch up to the rest of the Armada before the coast of England was sighted.

The trill of a pipe played by one of the ship's boys marked a change in the watch, and Rodrigo hastened back to the pile of rigging, tidying the coils for Alonzo, the apprentice who came to take over the task. Free of duties for the next eight hours, he made his way across to the starboard side of the deck. Leaning against the rail in a cramped corner, he could just make out distant sails with the Burgundian cross of King Philip to the north. Rodrigo glanced up once more at the *San Lorenzo's* full sails. With fortune, they would rejoin the fleet by late morning.

His eye was caught by the movement of a small *patache*, a scout and messenger ship, coming from the north, tacking back across the wind to approach the *San Lorenzo*. The helmsman gave orders to bring in the sails so that the *San Lorenzo* held her position, rocking in a trough between the waves while the faster ship came to her. When the *patache* was near, but not so close as to risk fouling either ship's rigging, she drew in her sail and let down a small oared boat, which drew to the side of the much larger *galleas*.

"Dispatches for Don Hugo de Moncada from the Duke de Medina Sidonia!"

At the shout from below, the *alférez de mar*, third in command to the ship's *capitán*, nodded, and the decksmen lowered the boarding ladder. Securing the small boat to bob in the waves beside the *San Lorenzo*, the messenger and his oarsmen scrambled up the rope ladder to the broad deck. The *alférez* whisked the messenger to the *camarote*, the highest tier of the sterncastle, to meet with Don Moncada in one of the private cabins, while the oarsmen were offered water from the best casks left in the hold.

Still keeping to his idle pose, partly hidden by the bundles of hammocks and sleeping partitions stowed along the rail, Rodrigo strained to hear them.

"What news of the fleet?" one of the decksmen murmured.

"A scouting ship sighted the coast," replied one of the oarsmen, "but the Duke has ordered delay for repairs and redistribution of shot rather than striking the heretics in their port, as *El Draque* attacked Cadiz."

Rodrigo concealed a wry smile. That sailor, at least, believed in the proclaimed intent of the Armada to restore the practice of the true Catholic faith to England. And of course, to avenge the bold attack of the previous year, when the Englishman Drake had managed the destruction of some of the first ships of the Armada gathered in the port of Cadiz.

"Surely they are not still in port!" protested another of the sailors. "They must have been out to sea long before this."

"The scout ship took up a fisherman, and he said that their ships were still in the harbor, there being no wind to bring them out against the tide."

"But are not their ships able to make use of the faintest of winds?"

The oarsman snorted. "They still need some breeze to fill their sails, however fast their ships may be once they have it." He gestured to the lower decks of the *San Lorenzo*. "They have not your oars to carry them forward despite a calm."

Those oars were what set the *galleas* apart—with the sails of a galleon and the oars of a galley, the *San Lorenzo* and her three sister ships could use either to close with the enemy's ships.

"Does the Duke then expect a sea battle soon? Are we not to go straight up the Channel to Flanders?" asked another decksman.

"Perhaps. If it comes to that, I only hope those prancing soldiers with their fancy clothing and private servants prove their worth when we grapple the heretics," the oarsman snarled. The decksmen responded in a chorus of embittered agreement, as all of them had suffered the injustice of the preferential treatment given to the soldiers and their officers. Rodrigo let his attention drift away from the complaints of the underfed and underpaid. He wondered, not for the first time, if the English were such heretics as the *capelán* had claimed them to be. Was not Don Ruarte himself engaged in what was said to be heresy? Or was it only heresy to be an opponent of the Spanish crown?

July 31, 1588

When morning arrived, the sails of the English were clearly seen to the west, following the Armada's progress into the Channel. The ship's boy piped "All Hands," and Rodrigo and the men of his deck watch stayed at their positions, joined by both the men of the next watch and those of the previous, whose bleary eyes revealed their shortened rest. All traces of night hammocks and personal belongings of the sailors and soldiers who slept above-decks were quickly secured below, clearing the decks for whatever battles might come.

The *galleasses* had been assigned to the center of the *lunula*, the crescent formation the Armada had taken, where their heavy *canone* could protect the slower, more lightly armed cargo ships. From the *San Lorenzo*'s deck, Rodrigo could clearly see the long stretch of the horns of the *lunula* to the north and south.

He could also see the English fleet ranked to the west. In the night, they must have tacked dangerously close to shore in order to come around behind the Spanish fleet, so that the wind now favored them. One of the smaller English ships advanced toward the center of the crescent, fired a single shot, then brought her sail around and retreated to rejoin the ranks of the English fleet. From the Spanish soldiers on the gundecks below came angry shouts responding to the challenge of that defiant shot, even though the English were far beyond hailing distance. Rodrigo's stomach turned and tightened as he stood with his deckmates, their hands ready to pull the lines of the sails, ears straining to hear above the sound of wind and wave, waiting, all eyes on the ships slowly approaching the southern vanguard.

Making every use of the winds behind them, the line of English ships passed behind the trailing curve of the *lunula*, each ship firing in turn as she passed first the southern vanguard, then the northern rearguard. Even from the distance, the roar of the *canone* rang across the seas to thunder in Rodrigo's bones. At the first volley, he felt a surge of startled terror from Tareixa, his own dread and anxiety echoed back to him, and then her presence disappeared from his mind. He hoped that she had only fled, vanishing to safety into the deeper waters, and that she had been close enough to the *San Lorenzo* that she would not have been injured by any shot falling to the sea.

"Cowards!" shouted one of the soldiers on the gundeck. The cry was taken up by many more voices as it was clear that the English would not come near the main formation. Instead, they tacked to the wind and came around to repeat their slow pass in reverse, continuing to focus their fire upon the rearmost ships of the *lunula*. Rodrigo could see some of the ships of the rearguard scattering from their stations and hiding among the main force, but even the few ships that stayed in position and faced the near-constant firing did not seem to be much damaged, sending off their own, equally ineffective volleys in return.

His stomach considerably calmer with the realization that the *San Lorenzo* was not likely to be engaged, he watched the distant encounter unfold. He was even able to spot some of the splashes where shot struck the sea. Suddenly curious, he glanced up to the forecastle, where Don Ruarte stood in his usual place, hands idle at his sides, brow furrowed in frustration. His *sílfide* hovered around him, but neither the Don nor the Air spirits seemed to be acting in any way to change the winds. Rodrigo wondered for a moment what orders the Don had been given in the event of battle. Was he only to act if the *San Lorenzo* herself was engaged? He had no chance to wonder further, for after only a few passes of their line behind the *lunula*, the English broke off their attack and regathered their fleet as the winds carried the Spanish ships farther up the Channel. As the *contramaestre* ordered the men of the previous watches back to their rest, Rodrigo saw only one Spanish ship falling behind, her foremast broken and sails a useless tangle, while the rest of the Armada sailed on unhindered.

August 2, 1588

Anticipation hummed in the air aboard the *San Lorenzo*. The dawn had at last brought with it a wind favorable to the Armada, and the ship's boy once again piped "All Hands" to gather the men. The *Nuestra Señora del Rosario* had indeed been taken by the English after her mast had broken two days ago, but the rest of the Spanish ships had continued on, regrouping into a compact protective formation. After that first brief encounter, the English had made no further move against them, and now, for the first time, wind filled the Spanish sails. A group of the English ships tried to slip close to shore past the Spaniards to flank their landward side, but the *Capitán-General* led his own squadron to block them, forcing the English ships to move farther seaward past the rearguard and open themselves to fire.

In the tighter formation, the roar of the nearby ships' *canone* echoed louder, ringing in Rodrigo's ears. Aboard the *San Lorenzo*, the sailors were unable to hear any spoken commands during the volleys and acted by watching the helmsman, reading his gestures and hauling lines as he directed. The acrid smoke from both English and Spanish guns drifted over the seas to sting the eyes and the throat, even obscuring parts of the *galleas* from Rodrigo's view for moments. Although the gunners of the Spanish ships fired their ready-loaded volley and immediately moved to the upper deck, preparing to grapple and board, the English soldiers stayed to their gundecks and fired repeated volleys. Even so, the English ships still stayed so far away that little damage was done to their targets.

At a command from Don Moncada, the helmsman made for a spot nearer the shore, where the largest of the English ships—the *Triumph*, Rodrigo heard one of the men shout— and five others were stalled by falling winds, separated from the rest of the English fleet and trapped between the Armada and the jutting spur of land.

Looking up, Rodrigo saw Don Ruarte standing as far to the fore as he could, and this time his hands were outstretched before him. The *sílfide* swirled around him, and to Rodrigo it was clear that they were controlling the winds that kept the *Triumph* and her sister ships motionless near the spit of land while the *San Lorenzo* and the other *galleasses* closed the distance.

As the smoke briefly cleared and he could see the English sailors frantically laboring to shift their sails and free their ships from the strange calm, something about their struggle captured Rodrigo's sympathy. Their fierce independence tugged at his Galician spirit, and a flood of hot anger filled him. A rush of confused concern from Tareixa filled his mind, startling him with the sudden return of her presence in his thoughts. He thought she had fled to the deep seas, even home to Galicia, after the first firing of the *canone* two days ago, and for an astonished moment his hand fell slack on the line. The desperation of the English sailors and his own anger at the Spanish who controlled him and his country, and now sought to control yet another, made him burn with the desire to aid those struggling ships. He could do nothing himself, but now that she had returned, could she? Was Tareixa strong enough, would she understand, if he asked her to interfere?

Still hauling on the line, obeying his orders, he spoke in his mind to Tareixa, as clearly and simply as he could, *"Hold our ships."*

Her response was a surprisingly complete picture of herself and others of her kind, whom she must have found when she fled the noise of the battles, creating roiling eddies and cross-tides in the seas around their ships. Rodrigo was delighted when their efforts were successful, strengthening the shifting tide-race to hold back the *San Lorenzo* and the other *galleasses*, despite the labors of the oarsmen, sailors, and even Don Ruarte, who glowered furiously at the skies but spared not a glance for the seas. Barely beneath the apparently placid surface, Tareixa danced in turbulence until the *mago* wearied, and what winds he had held drifted away from his control.

A sudden southerly breeze immediately filled the sails of the *Triumph* and her companion ships. Rodrigo wondered if the English had *magos* of their own aboard their ships, who had taken advantage of Don Ruarte's exhaustion to seize the winds away from him.

With the change in the wind, the English pressed the advantage of their more agile ships, aiming their fire downward to the exposed rowing banks of the *galleasses*, and the screams of wounded and panicked *buenaboyas* haunted Rodrigo's ears, filling him with a strange relief that he was not among them. Despite the confusion, the helmsman immediately began bringing the *San Lorenzo* around, returning her to her place in the center of the formation, where some of the nimbler Spanish ships could hold off the English attack, for they still would not risk being grappled and boarded.

His heart thrilling at the success of her efforts, Rodrigo sent an image to Tareixa of deeper waters, hoping she would understand to sink lower and be safe from the shot that failed of its target and hissed into the frothing seas.

August 4, 1588

Each day now began with the ship's boy piping "All Hands" until it could be seen whether or not the English would move to engage them. The Spanish ships had continued sailing inexorably northward along the Channel the previous day, but overnight the *Santa Ana* and the *San Luis* had fallen behind. Despite the calm winds, the English seemed determined to take these two ships, and Rodrigo could see them lowering their boats in order to be towed into a position to attack.

The *San Lorenzo* and the other *galleasses* used their oars to retrieve the stragglers, taking the two ships in tow and drawing them back from the battle. As before, the English were determined to stay far enough distant that they could not be grappled and boarded by the far greater numbers of the Spanish soldiers, and for some time the *canone* filled the sky with thunder and smoke before a light breeze came up to clear the air and fill the sails. Fatigue numbed Rodrigo, and he no longer felt the terrors of the first battle encounter. Instead, his heart filled with a secret delight each time he saw the English evade the slower Spanish ships, each time they held off the larger force of the *grande* Armada.

Although the stern lantern of the *San Lorenzo* had been shot off in the fray, there had been no significant damage to the stern, nothing that affected either her fragile rudder or the stern hold full of gunpowder. Seeing that his ship had sustained no injury, Don Moncada commanded that she engage the *Triumph*, whose foolhardy captain had once again misjudged the wind and found himself becalmed between the *San Martin* and the *San Lorenzo*. With a flicker of his eyes to the fore, Rodrigo saw Don Ruarte, a closed fist upraised as he held the winds still to trap the English ship. The slaves and *buenaboyas* rowed the *galleas* into better position, ready to fire upon the *Triumph*. The soldiers on the deck shouted themselves hoarse with anticipation, anxious to engage with one of the elusive English ships. This was the moment they had longed for after all these months at sea, when their skills with the arquebus and the sword would finally be put to the test.

Rodrigo mourned the absence of Tareixa's kin. With the unpredictability of most of their kind, they had sought deeper waters in the past two days. Alone, Tareixa could not provide more than a slight delay to the forward progress of the *galleas*. As he scrambled to prepare the lines for the moment when the grappling hooks would be swung out, he glanced down to the seas, catching a glimpse of Tareixa's form, silver-green in the sun, snaking around and ahead of the *San Lorenzo*, creating small eddies and cross-currents to slow the ship as she shuddered between the swells, timbers creaking. Some foreboding caused him to look up, and he saw Don Ruarte in the forecastle, his sharp gaze fixed on the same place where Rodrigo's eyes had just been. Before the Don could turn again, Rodrigo bent to his task, once more bidding

Tareixa seek the safer depths and move farther from the *San Lorenzo*.

The glance to the sea had been only a moment of distraction for Don Ruarte, but it was enough. His grip on the winds had eased just enough that the breeze slipped free, filling the *Triumph's* sails, once again sending her coursing away. Although the *San Juan de Portugal* and another *zabra* gave chase, they seemed to make no progress against her. In his head, Rodrigo caught an echo of Tareixa's glee—these smaller ships were proving easier to delay than the great *galleas*. Although he had only once asked her to hold back any of the Spanish ships, she had begun to do so of her own will, delighting in her successes. As before, with the change of the wind, the Spanish ships continued on to the east, and once more the English drew back from the attack and allowed them to proceed.

August 8, 1588

"Hell-burners! Slip anchor!" Don Moncada's shouted order drew the men from the rails, where they had watched in frozen fear as dark shapes had emerged from the night, glowing as the sparks set by the departing crews had taken hold, turning the unmanned ships into drifting weapons.

The enthrallment of the floating fires broken, the men of the *San Lorenzo* leaped into action. Drilled with the rest of the sailors, Rodrigo lunged to a place on the arms of the fore *cabrestante*, straining to turn the wheel to bring up the rope of one of the two anchors that held the ship in the shifting waters off Calais.

"We'll never bring it up in time!" the *contramaestre* shouted. "Cut the lines!" Several men raced for axes from the arms chests, the strongest hacking in desperation at the arm's-width ropes until one broke and the ship shifted, now held by only the aft anchor. As soon as the *galleas* was moving again, dragging her second anchor until the men cut that rope, the helmsman guided her out of the path of the oncoming fireships while the slaves and *buenaboyas* rowed for their lives. The immediate danger past, Rodrigo and the other sailors stood on the deck, watching the blazing English ships drift idly past without so much as brushing the *galleas*, or any other of the Armada's ships.

"Perhaps it is time to make him 'El Draque' in more than just name?" Rodrigo was startled by the dry, rusty voice, so clear in his head that he thought it spoken aloud, until he realized the men beside him did not respond to it. He turned to the sea, where he saw nothing but blackness. In the back of his head, however, he felt echoes of Tareixa's joy and pride of accomplishment.

Again he heard that rough rasp, the sound shaping itself into laughter as a clear picture flashed behind his eyes. Legends named them draconets, the smaller kin to the dragons. No bigger than a dog, agile and nimble, they still possessed the fire of their much larger cousins.

"As you will, but have a care," he thought to the darkness over the sea, unused to sharing his mind with one who had such clear command of language. The raspy laugh was filled with anticipation as a warm breeze whisked past his cheek, moving counter to the salty sea breeze. He turned to look in the direction of that counter-breeze, spying the stern lantern of the *San Salvador* of Oquendo. No sooner had he identified the ship when an explosion in its stern lit the night, followed by several smaller blasts as fire ripped through the gunpowder stores. The breeze carried the screams of the dying across the water, along with shouts of command as the men struggled to put out the fire and save what they could.

"She will be taken, but not, I think, by El Draque." The draconet's rusty voice filled Rodrigo's head and he nodded. Although the draconets were not known for the gift of prophecy of their larger cousins, he did not doubt the truth of what this one told him.

"Now," the rough voice said, *"I must return to my home. This salt-wet air is no friend to my kind. I was far from my usual paths when the little one found me."* Once more, a warm breeze flitted past Rodrigo's cheek, this time moving to the south at speed.

Rodrigo smiled at the description of Tareixa as a little one, for she could easily swallow the draconet whole. But her mind and spirit, and that of most of her kin, was childlike and playful. "Farewell," he whispered to the darkness.

"Farewell to whom? To the poor souls of the *San Salvador*? Why should one smile at their loss?"

Rodrigo ducked, but he was too slow to avoid the iron grip of Don Ruarte.

Leaving the *San Lorenzo* to the sea winds, the Don dragged the struggling Galician to his tiny cabin space within the *camarote*. Once inside, he placed his body in front of the door and released Rodrigo. Rodrigo's lunge for the small window was halted when the air around him vanished, leaving him gasping for long moments until the Don loosened his grip on the winds and he could drag breath into his aching lungs. He turned back to his captor, who stood watching him with folded arms and narrowed eyes.

"The Inquisitors claimed they had rooted out the last of your kind," Don Ruarte said. "So successful were they that few now even believe in the existence of the great sea serpents and the fire lizards, much less that there were those who could speak with them and command them. How is it that you, or the one that taught you, survived?"

"I do not command." Rodrigo kept his head down, avoiding the Don's direct question.

"Answer me, or suffer the consequences." The Don's voice, though quiet, was steel. "I do not need the tools and implements of the Inquisitors to wrack with pain. Who taught you? How many more serpent-speakers are there? Where are they?"

"I know of no others," Rodrigo said at last. It was nothing more than the truth, but it did not satisfy the Don. The air around him thinned, his lungs protesting as he took great sucking breaths that barely sufficed.

"Who taught you? Where are they?" the Don repeated.

"No man taught me," Rodrigo gasped out. Again the truth did not please Don Ruarte, and the tightness in Rodrigo's lungs increased as he struggled for air.

"How did you learn, then? Did the sea creatures themselves come to you and ask to be yours?" The Don eased his hold on the air, and Rodrigo took several blessed breaths.

"As a child, I played with them in the *rías* near my home. A few came that far inland."

Don Ruarte glowered at him, but finally he seemed to accept that Rodrigo told the truth. He drew himself up to his full height. "As a senior priest of the *Grande y Felicissima Armada*, I have authority to deal with heresy aboard this ship as I see fit. You have practiced that which is outlawed and banned in the territories of His Most Catholic Majesty, and you have practiced it in the interest of heretics and enemies to Spain. The sentence for this treason is death, and I will execute that sentence myself." He raised one hand, slowly closing the fingers together, and with each tightening of his hand, Rodrigo felt the thinning of the air around him.

In the last moments before blackness took him, Rodrigo sent Tareixa a picture of the open sea as a warning to flee, to seek out a place where she could be safe from his kind.

Crushed by the loss of the one she followed, Tareixa sank to the chalky floor of the seas of Calais, stunned near to immobility. Then, in a lightning instant, her emptiness transformed to blinding rage, and she lashed her tail, driving herself upward to the great ship that her friend had sailed upon. Heedless of her own safety, she bore her sinewy body straight into the vulnerable rudder, her weight and speed causing the ship to swing around to collide with first one, then another of the ships beside it, the wood of the rudder split and useless. Her vengeance begun, she fled before that sharp, dark presence on board the ship could seek her out and snare her as it had her wind-friends. But she did not flee far, staying long enough to see that this ship moved no farther before she followed the others of the fleet.

For the rest of the season, Tareixa and her kin hounded the ships that sailed around the great island. She delighted in snaring and hindering and pushing them until enough of the ships had fallen to satisfy her, whether they were stranded by tides or dashed against the rocky shores or sank in the storms of the deeper seas. Only when her fury had eased did she leave the scattered remains of the fleet, her kin returning to their deeper homes. Only then did she retrace her path back around the land. Only then did she seek out the place where she had sensed a cold, fresh inlet to the sea.

Only then did she find a lonely *ría* where she could be alone and undisturbed, and mourn.

Author's Note: The Spanish Armada of 1588 was devastated more by weather and the voyage north around Scotland to return to Spain than by any of the encounters with the English ships. The gunpowder explosion aboard the San Salvador *actually occurred a few hours after the first battle engagement on July thirty-first, although it was not a result of the battle itself and is believed to have been an act of intentional sabotage. The* San Salvador *was then boarded and taken by Sir John Hawkins. All other events in this story take place according to the known history.*

The Wild Rogue

Fiona Patton

The London Chronicle, *March 4, 1783*
"On Monday night about eleven o'clock, the body of an unknown man was found wedged under the dock at Blackfriars by members of the Bow Street Constabulary. Foul play is suspected."

"Master Christopher?"

The small cell in London's Wood Street Compter was dark and cold and smelled of urine and vomit. The young man seated against the far wall had awakened some time ago, but after ascertaining that it was not yet time for either release or breakfast, had gone back to sleep. Now, recognizing the voice as belonging to his elder brother Edward's manservant, he slowly opened his eyes.

"Hullo, William," he said with a yawn. "Is it morning already?"

The heavyset man standing outside the cell showed a flash of relief before schooling his expression to one of aggrieved respect.

"It's just past seven, Master Christopher. Will you come out of there now, sir?"

"Is the fine paid?"

"Yes, sir."

"Was it high this time?"

"It was . . . steep, yes, sir."

Christopher snorted. He wasn't surprised. The Sessions of the Peace-Inferior Court judge—and wasn't that just a mouthful to get one's head around when one was a little too influenced by drink?—had added miscellaneous breaking of the peace—which meant whatever the judge chose to make it mean—to the list of charges the night before.

"And my brother?" he asked.

"Is waiting outside, sir."

"Then we won't keep him a moment longer."

Christopher rose and, after making a show of folding his newspaper and throwing his plum-colored frock coat over his arm, ambled to the front of the cell, where a young man in a deep blue uniform immediately opened the door for him.

"Thank you, Constable. It *is* Constable, isn't it . . . ?" Christopher peered at him through the gloom, "Cedric?"

The young man couldn't help but blush. "It is, sir, yes," he answered. "Thank you for remembering. We're all to be constables now, sir."

"Thief-takers and Charlies no more, eh? Proper officers of the law?"

"Yes, sir."

Christopher rubbed at the back of his neck. "To that end, I'm afraid my memory of last night is rather spotty. Did I damage anyone?"

"Oh, no, sir, not as such. You had a fearful barney with Jakey, that is, Constable Jake Townsend, sir, but what with him being a former boxer and all . . ."

"I came out rather more worse for our encounter than he did?"

"Yes, sir."

"That explains the bruises. Give him my regards when you see him next."

"I will, sir."

"Right. Well, then, come along, William," Christopher called over his shoulder as he headed up the prison steps at a brisk pace. "We don't want to keep the Baron Clive of Plassy Lord Lieutenant of Shropshire waiting, now do we?" Nodding to the police officers in the hall, he pushed through the main doors, then stood a moment, blinking in the bright spring morning. A smart coach waited in Mitre Square, and he crossed to it in three long strides, pulling himself in without waiting for the coachman to disembark.

The man inside had been dozing and he gave a start and then a rueful smile. "All right, Kit?" he asked with a yawn.

Christopher's careless demeanor faded. "As right as I'll ever be, Teddy," he answered. "You can drop me off at my rooms in Thames Street, if you would be so kind," he added as the coach lurched forward.

Edward shifted uncomfortably. "No, I can't," he replied. "I'm under strict instructions from our sisters to bring you home." At Christopher's pained expression, he raised his hands in a helpless gesture. "These violent bouts of drunken melancholia frighten them. They frighten *me*. So you will come home, bathe, change, reassure Lottie and Lizzie that you're all right, and then have breakfast in that order. After which, I'll have Tom take you to Thames Street if you must go."

"I must. I'm meeting someone." Christopher shook his head as his words evoked a worried frown. "Your senior East India Company agent, Teddy," he explained in a tone of exaggerated patience. "Who'd you think it was, some doxy out of Southwark?"

Edward shifted again. "No, of course not. It's just . . ."

"Just . . . what?"

"Nothing. Never mind." As the coachman maneuvered them out of the city proper and onto High Holborn Street, Edward made to speak, thought the better of it, tried again, then sat rubbing the thumb and index finger of his left hand together, his expression increasingly distressed.

Finally Christopher reached over to cup a hand over his. "Stop that," he ordered. "If you set your coach alight, you'll have the devil of a time explaining it to your stable master."

Edward smiled. "I'll tell him I dropped a cheroot."

"You don't smoke cheroots."

"I'll tell him you dropped it, then."

"I don't smoke cheroots, either; I can't keep the damned things lit."

"That's because the undines don't like smoke."

"The *undines* leave me to do as I please."

Both men fell into an uncomfortable silence, but as the coach turned onto Oxford Street, Edward glanced over with a hesitant expression. "So what happened this time?" he asked.

Christopher stared out the window, watching the estates of England's minor nobility pass by before giving a brief shrug. "I called on Philippa," he answered, his casual tone of voice belied by the angry set of his jaw.

"And?"

"And I was told by her father's butler"—Christopher spat out the words—"that she would no longer see me. Apparently, she's suddenly engaged."

Edward chewed the inside of his cheek. "To whom?" he asked finally.

"Does it matter? To a man whose parents were married. To each other."

"I'm sure that has nothing to do with it, brother."

"And I'm sure that has everything to do with it, *half*-brother."

Edward gave him a reproachful look. "That distinction matters to no one except yourself," he chided.

"Myself," Christopher agreed bitterly, "the whole of London society, and Philippa Torrington, apparently."

Edward sighed. "If you'd let me, I could introduce you to any number of Henrietta's friends who would be thrilled to marry such a *talented Water Mage*, regardless of his parentage."

Christopher bared his teeth. "No, thank you," he grated. "I don't need you or your intended to matchmake for me, and I don't need to find a woman thrilled to marry me because I'm a talented Water Mage."

"Better that than trying to make a life with someone who doesn't know; we've both seen how hard that's been on Becky."

"Becky's a Fire Mage with our father's temper . . ."

"Made that much more difficult to control because she's married to a . . ."

"Pompous ass."

"Kit . . ."

"What?"

"Oh, nothing. You're right. He is a pompous ass. She never would have accepted his proposal if . . ." Edward broke off, his expression distressed once again.

"If Father'd been alive," Christopher finished for him.

"Everything went wrong after Father died," he added in a hoarse whisper. He closed his eyes as nine years fell away as if they'd been a single day.

"What do you mean, he died in the bath? He's a Water Mage!"

"His doctor says it looked like suicide, Kit."

"The devil take his doctor! What about the undines?"

"They weren't there."

"How could they not be there? Where were they?"

"I don't know! Ask them, Kit. They love you; they'll speak to you."

But they hadn't, not for nine long years, no matter how often he'd asked or begged or demanded, they couldn't or wouldn't tell him what had happened that night. Keening in distress, the little creatures had just eddied about him like tiny whirlpools, their pale, delicate features distorted with unhappiness, until he'd finally stopped asking. Now they hardly interacted at all, and Christopher spent more time staring into the bottom of a glass than into any pond or pool.

They passed through the gates of the Clive family's Bloomsbury house in Queen Square a few moments later. An ornate coach with the emblem of the Royal Astronomer was parked before the door, and Edward's brows drew down as he alighted.

"What's Uncle Neville doing here at this time of the morning? I hope nothing's happened to Grandmama."

"He's probably just stopping in on his way to another exotic locale to plot the course of yet another planet," Christopher scoffed, turning his gaze from the splashing fountain in the center of the courtyard.

"Then why are there no sylphs hovering about his coach?" Edward insisted. "The roof's usually festooned with them."

"Because they're . . . with him?"

"And they're with an Air Mage inside a Fire Mage's home because . . . ?"

"They . . . love him? But even so, we might want to hurry."

Together, the brothers took the townhouse steps two at a time.

The London Chronicle, *March 5, 1783*

"On Monday night about nine o'clock, a group of men

carrying knives boarded the East India Company ship Wood-ford, *threatened the passengers, and made off with goods totaling three hundred and five pounds, ten shillings."*

The small cell in the Wood Street Compter was dark and cold and smelled of urine and vomit. Christopher groaned as a return to consciousness brought the return of bruises he hadn't realized had set quite so deeply and a twisting, inexplicable sense of . . . grief?

Raising himself up into a sitting position, he carefully opened his eyes. The room swam dizzily in front of him as he tried to sort out this latest visit from the last. He'd exchanged blows with Constable Townsend . . . no, he corrected himself . . . that had been the night before. He'd gone to see Philippa . . . again, the night before. He . . . A memory surfaced, hovering shakily in his mind's eye, and he made a grab for it before it could vanish again. He'd had a fight with . . . Uncle Neville? No, that didn't seem right. With . . . Teddy. That seemed equally wrong, but once dredged up, the memory remained, fuzzy with drink, but distinct enough to relive angry words, first growled, then shouted . . . His sisters' faces, white with fear, his brother's face white with uncharacteristic anger . . . Storming out, finding a tavern, drinking, raging, trying to drown out the resurgent tide of grief and guilt, blows.

His hand strayed to his upper lip, finding it split and puffy. His throat felt raw, and there was an acrid odor of spellcasting about him. He frowned. Had Teddy and he used magic against each other? They never did that. True, they'd had some dandy fights as boys—like their sister Rebecca, Christopher had their father's temper—but they'd never resorted to hurling spells at each other.

He cautiously felt about himself. His clothes were more or less intact, torn and dirty, but without scorch marks or damp patches. The smell remained, however, a magic he didn't quite recognize but seemed to think he ought to, wrapped about a knot of pain and anger that seemed familiar but strangely unreachable.

A sudden chuckle snapped him out of his reverie, and he turned to see an older, heavyset man with a short, grizzled beard and lank gray hair leaning against the bars of the op-

posite cell. When the man saw he had Christopher's attention, he touched his forelock with a sardonic expression.

"As I live and breathe," he noted, "if it isn't little Kit Walcot, all growed up."

Christopher squinted at him. "Do I know you?"

The man shook his head. "Me? No. You wouldn't remember me, lad, not after all this time, but I remember you. Why,
the last time I saw you—before last night, mind, when you
tried to take on the entire custom of The Bird and Babe—it
woulda been over twenty years ago. You was waitin' on the
Madras docks for a ship to speed you off to England. Your
ayah was too small to lift you high enough to see, so I took
you up on my shoulder. You were a sad little bantling that
day. O' course, you would be, what with your mam just pas-
sin' and all, but the boats made you smile. Them, and the
little creatures swirlin' about in the water. They came right
up to the dock to comfort you, as I remember it."

The man pressed a hand against his chest. "Henry Keeling. I fought for your daddy at Plassey and a few other battles
besides that never made it into the papers back home. And I
knew your mam. She had a rare gift for lightin' up a room."
He laid a finger along the side of his nose. "A very rare gift.

"Your daddy now," he continued before Christopher could
say anything, "was the devil's own cunning man, and that's
a fact. Robert Clive was a rare flash cove who could've whistled up a monsoon and danced it all the way to London if
he'd had a mind to." Keeling raised his hands disarmingly.
"No need to look so suspicious, lad. There was only a few of
us in the know, but we that was, were all trusted to keep his
secret. And we did keep it. Some of us took it to the grave,
just as he did.

"A bad business that." Keeling shook his head. "Folk sa-
yin' he'd topped hisself. That wasn't right. He never would
of done somethin' like that. Never. Had to have been somethin' else, don't you think?"

*A twisting, inexplicable sense of grief, a knot of pain and
anger . . .*

"Now, a little bird's told me that you've inherited more
than just his looks and his appetite for fightin', yeah?" Keeling continued, again before Christopher could say anything.

"Of course, that same little bird's told me that was about all you inherited from him."

Christopher shot him a cold look. "He left me a living," he retorted stiffly.

He left me . . .

Keeling nodded. "I heard, as an agent for his *legitimate* children's shippin' interests in the East India Company—a company I might add that he, along with a loyal army at his back, mind—helped to build to the dizzying heights it now enjoys."

Christopher leaned his head against the damp stone wall and closed his eyes. "What do you want?" he demanded.

"Me? Merely to broker an introduction between yourself and my employer," Keeling replied. "One David Hart, who happens to be what you might call a purveyor of exotic antiquities, a man who can appreciate a fellow's exotic abilities and a man who can see him well breeched for them, if you catch my meanin'."

More memories began to surface, one by one: angry words first growled, then shouted. A door slamming on home and family. Nearly everything Christopher had was at Lord Edward Clive's sufferance, whether he wanted to admit to it or not. That hadn't mattered before, but now . . .

He left . . .

"Go on," he said wearily.

"There's this antiquity of a singular design, see," Keeling explained, "what went into the drink and can't be fetched up by conventional methods. It needs fetchin' up by those of a watery nature who just might be persuaded by a flash, young cunning-man if he was to ask them in just the right manner."

"You need the undines to bring it to the surface, and you want me to convince them," Christopher interrupted.

Keeling chuckled. "Straight to the point, just like your daddy."

"Where did it fall?"

"Into the Thames off Blackfriars, well beyond the low tide mark."

Christopher raised his head to stare at the man as if he'd gone mad. "You can't possibly be serious?"

"Deadly serious."

"The undines don't enter London waters. They haven't for well over a century."

"No, they don't," Keeling agreed. "Not since fair Prince Henry died from the typhoid fever he caught sportin' with them in the Thames in 1612. But it's no bootless errand, this. If the cunning man were flash and beautiful, and as beloved of the watery ones now as he was when he was a child, and if he were to start in a particular spot upriver where they've been known to frequent, and was to draw them down to Blackfriars with him swimmin' in their midst, and them wrapped in his shields with him, it could be done."

"Westminster Bridge is the closest they ever *frequent*," Christopher shot back. "And any cunning man witless enough to try and swim to Blackfriars would sicken before he'd gone a hundred yards. A school of undines couldn't keep him healthy in that filthy cesspool, no matter how beloved he might be."

Or how beloved he might have been, his mind added bitterly.

"Oh, there's ways to stay safe in any waters," Keeling replied with a sly smile. "Ancient ways."

Christopher's eyes narrowed. "You mean magical ways."

Keeling shrugged. "All it takes is a simple charm, one that even Prince Henry might have worn if he'd stopped to think of it."

"A charm won't protect the undines."

"No, but you can. I've seen you do it as a babe before you even knew you could do it. On the Madras docks you sent out a shield like a little tube and drew them right up to you through it, laughin' the whole time."

He straightened as Cedric appeared, a ring of keys in his hand. "O' course, if you're happy lickin' your half-brother's boots for sixpence a week, I can't help you. But I'd like to help you. When a man's carried a little fellow on his shoulder, he gets to thinkin' of hisself as a kind of godfather. But you ponder on it, now, Master Kit," he added as the constable released him. "And if you change your mind, have the boy here get a message to me."

Angry words first growled, then shouted. A door slamming on home and family. An unbidden memory swimming before his eyes as he stormed across Queen Square, the memory of Uncle Neville and his father standing on the Madras docks together, deep in whispered conversation while another man lifted him high onto his shoulder. A sense of urgency spurned on by the scent of magic and a knot of grief and anger . . .

You'll never make it. One mouthful, and you'll sicken, whatever Keeling thinks his charm might do, his mind jeered. *You'll sicken, and then you'll drown. The undines won't come. They won't help. Just like they didn't help Father.*

They might. Even he could hear the plaintive note, and it made him bare his teeth in anger.

They won't!

But they might. And if they did, wouldn't that be worth it? Wouldn't it?

. . . Yes.

"Wait."

The air was chill as Keeling led him through the narrow Southwark streets, and Christopher wondered, not for the first time that morning, if he'd made the right decision. He'd frequented many of the borough's dockside stews, but this area was deep within the maze of twisting alleyways and closes, and he doubted he'd be able to find his way out again if the other man decided to abandon him here.

His pace slowed, and Keeling glanced over with a sly smile. "Not nervous, are you, lad?" he asked in an innocent voice.

Christopher frowned at him. "Should I be?"

"Not at all, a big, strong fellow like you. Ah, here we are."

The street opened up to reveal a dilapidated house with peeling paint and yellowing plaster. It might have been splendid once, two or three centuries before, but now it had a deserted air that hinted of dark secrets and danger. Keeling took him around the back to where a man in a shapeless black hat pulled low over his eyes loitered by a locked garden gate. Keeling gestured impatiently, and the man passed an insolent gaze over them both before pulling a key from his pocket. As the gate opened, Keeling waved Christopher forward. With a certain amount of trepidation, he passed through.

Powerful spells tingled across his body, triggering a deluge of memories: *a door slamming on home and family, a tavern*

*full of angry men shouting, blows, Keeling pulling him from
the fray and the high-pitched shriek of police whistles* . . .

When he came back to himself, he stood in a surprisingly
well-maintained garden dotted with rose bowers and ivy-
covered alcoves. A marble fountain splashed in the center,
and Christopher averted his gaze as Keeling lead him down
a crushed-stone path to a cane gazebo at the bottom of the
garden.

The man waiting inside was the most extraordinary-
looking person Christopher had ever seen. Although of aver-
age height and dress, he had piercing gray eyes that almost
glowed with power, and eyebrows so sparse and pale, it was
as if he had none at all. Christopher gave the two men flank-
ing him no more than a single dismissive glance as Keeling
sidled up to the man respectfully.

"Kit Walcot, sir," he said. "Kit, this here is Mister Hart."

The man thrust out a hand, and Christopher accepted it
stiffly, trying not to react as a spell shot up his arm and across
his temple. He knew a moment's disorientation as another
spat of angry memories flowed over him before Hart released
his grip and turned to the man at his right as if nothing had
just transpired.

"A pint o' purl all 'round, Georgie."

One of the men peeled off, disappearing into the house,
and Hart looked Christopher up and down with an appraising
eye. "Henry here tells me you're a dab hand with the water
ways," he said bluntly.

Relying on his upper-class education to get past the sudden, fearful churning in his stomach, Christopher inclined his
head.

"He also says you're a bottle cove that falls to fighting
when he's in his attitude," Hart continued, watching him
closely. "And he's not the only one I've heard that from. Now
I need a dab hand, and I'm prepared to pay if the hand is
prepared to do as he's told, but only if he stays off the bottle
while he's doin' it. If that's going to be a problem for you,
the gate's back the way you came."

Georgie returned with a wooden tray of tankards, and
Christopher accepted his before giving Hart a pointed look.
"The bottle doesn't rule me except when it pleases me to al-

low it," he answered, taking a measured drink before handing the tankard to Keeling. "Henry tells me you need an item recovered from the Thames. I told him it couldn't be done."

Hart's eyes narrowed. "Did you now? So why are you here, then?"

Why *was* he here? Was it really just because he missed the undines so much it felt as if he'd had a hole torn through his chest? Ignoring the suddenly overloud sound of splashing from the garden's fountain, Christopher made himself shrug. "I have a few gambling debts," he said, playing the feckless gentleman card. "And because, if it can be done at all," he added, "I can do it."

"And if you can't?" Hart pressed.

If you can't? If they won't?

"If I can't, then I'll drown, and you won't have to pay me."

Hart snorted. "Fair enough." He drained his own tankard. "To business, then. The item I need fetchin' up's housed in a small, leaden box about yea big." His hands traced out a space five inches square. "Weighs no more'n a pound or two. You go in just north of Westminster Bridge, call the water folk to you, an' take 'em to Blackfriars. Two of my men'll be followin' along the bank, with Henry here to keep things honest on both sides. You have the water folk draw up the box, you pass it to my men, they pay you, and we go our separate ways."

Something in his voice caused the hair on the back of Christopher's neck to rise, but he kept his expression even. "And the payment is . . . ?" he asked.

"Forty shillings."

"Agreed. When do we set out?"

"Directly."

Keeling's particular spot upriver turned out to be a secluded pool carved from the north bank, just past Westminster Bridge. Sheltered by a stand of willow trees, their long, graceful limbs trailing in the water, the pool would be teeming with salmon fry and undines come summer, but today the gray water slapped against the rocks, empty and uninviting. Christopher stared into the depths for a long time, feeling the strange sense of magic and urgency growing with each passing moment, before abruptly pulling off his coat. It had been a long time since he'd needed to build shields against cold water. *Nine years,* his mind supplied accusingly, *since you needed to build anything at all. Are you sure you even remember how?*

Shut up.

Closing his eyes, he reached out, not for the vast currents of energy surging past him in the Thames, but for the thin rivulets of power that trickled into the pool at his feet. Trailing his thoughts in their midst like he might trail his fingers in their physical counterparts, he scooped up small handfuls of energy, flicking the sparkling droplets of green and blue power around him as he'd done when he was young, before—

He brushed the resurge of memories away with a shake of his head. As he'd done when he was young, as his father had taught—

Again he brushed the memories aside, concentrating on the shields, only on the shields. When he had enough layers swirling around him so that he felt more or less secured against the frigid river waters, he gestured to Keeling, who stepped forward.

"This here's a Fire charm," the older man said almost apologetically, "but it should burn up most diseases you may come across if your own magic don't fight it."

"Most?"

"Everythin' has its limits, so best not dawdle about, yeah?" Doing up the chain's clasp on the back, Keeling leaned in close. "You've been estranged from the little ones for far too long, lad," he whispered so quietly that Christopher could barely hear him. "You're gonna need 'em now, so don't let pain and pride get in the way. Don't force 'em, don't question 'em, just call to 'em. They'll come to you, 'cause all they've ever wanted to do was just be with you." He squeezed Christopher's shoulder. "Just like all them years ago in Madras, eh?"

He moved off quickly, joining Hart's two men farther up the bank. "Off you go, colt," he shouted, his voice slightly jeering now. "Earn your pay."

With a deep breath to still the sudden overloud pounding of his heart, Christopher stepped into the pool.

It had been nine years since he'd summoned the undines to him for any reason other than accusatory interrogation, nine years since they'd sent sprays of rainbow-colored water at him from the fountains at Eton, nine years since they'd danced for him at Queen Square, nine long years.

They won't come.

They will come. His father's voice took him by surprise, and he almost stumbled, throwing his hand out to hit the water in a spray of cold gray droplets as his shields faltered.

"How?"

The word skipped across the surface of the water, evoking no answer but the call of ravens on the bank. Shaking himself firmly, Christopher gathered the remnants of his shields about him once again and stepped deliberately out into the Thames.

The cold hit him like a knife thrust, causing him to gasp out loud as the current immediately tried to jerk him into deeper water. His outermost shield shredded under the on-slaught, the next shuddered . . .

Concentrate, boy! You were trained better than this!

His father's voice again, dark with disapproval. Struggling against the current, Christopher fought to plant his power as he planted his feet. He steadied, took a deep breath, rebuilt his shields, reached out, and called.

For a long time there was no answer save the roaring of the river, and then, slowly, he felt them, a school of silvery undines speeding up the Thames. He opened his mind and his arms to them, and as they swept him up in their embrace, nine years of hurt and recriminations melted away. He stood there for what seemed like forever, drinking in their presence. Then, drawing them into his shields with him as if it was the most natural thing in the world, he turned and plunged into the river proper.

The swim to Blackfriars was the longest he'd ever made. Despite his shields, the water was bitterly cold, the current powerful, and the waves unpredictable, threatening to over-whelm him at every stroke, his untrained talent no true match for them. The undines did what they could to send him strength, but as he drew closer to London and the waters grew increasingly dark and fetid, they fell back, one by one, until only four of the largest of them were able to stay by him, growing more and more agitated moment by moment.

Tiny hands caught at his arms and legs, trying to draw him to the safety of the bank, but he swam on, and they swam with him, keening their distress. His head began to throb, the cold leaching in through a dozen rents in his shields as his focus began to slip, then deserted him entirely.

He went under.

Christopher!

His father's voice, strong, commanding, and impossible to ignore, sounded in his ears.

Christopher! To the undines! Now!

His eyes snapped open to see the delicate creatures writhing in the murky waters beside him. With a surge of will, he threw a shield around them like a net and dragged them to the surface. Then all he could do was swim.

By the time he fetched up against the dock at Blackfriars, he was fading in and out of consciousness, his only thought to maintain the shield around the undines who clung desperately to his face and neck. But there was still Hart's box to retrieve, so scrabbling at the wooden pier made slippery by years of rot and excrement, he blinked rapidly to try to clear his mind before sending out a shaky tendril of power into deeper water. He found it just within reach. Before he could lose it again in the shifting tide, he threw a pulse of power into the tendril to strengthen it.

"On the Madras docks you sent out a shield like a little tube and drew them right up to you through it, laughin' the whole time."

"Wul, les hope laughin's . . . not . . . impor . . . ant," he slurred. Trusting to instinct to do the job properly, he formed the tendril into a tube of clean, clear water, then made his request to the undines as best he could through chattering teeth and a heavy, encroaching darkness. He had to repeat himself twice to be understood, and finally it was only the promise that he would leave the river that convinced them, but eventually the two largest turned and plunged down the tube.

"Just a little while longer now, Christopher. Can you hold on a little while longer?"

"Yes, Papa."

"Good boy."

Time flowed past on a tide of resurging memories: *the*

vague, fuzzy recollections of his first year in India, his mother lighting candles with a flick of her wrist, his father standing tall and proud in a host of red-jacketed men, danger, fire, then England, a new land, a new family, safety. His father's death looming like a storm on the horizon, heavy with loss and confusion, and he turned away, only to see Uncle Neville standing in his brother's parlor, his face a mask of grief. His lips moved, and Christopher strained to hear his words, yet the now familiar magic rose up to block him—his own magic, he suddenly realized, cast to hide a plan hatched by the children of Robert Clive. A plan to catch the man who'd ordered their father murdered for a magical artifact in a small leaden box three days ago . . .

Three days . . . ago . . .

"Kit!"

Three days . . .

"Kit, boy, answer me!"

Shaking the memory away, he stared up at Henry Keeling, crouched on the dock above him.

"Do you have it?" the older man shouted. "The box?"

He blinked, and saw it clutched in his hands just below the surface of the water. "Y . . . yes."

"Then here, take my hand and I'll pull you up!"

He looked down to see the four undines who'd made the journey with him all the way from Westminster Bridge, lying half in and half out of his ragged shield, their eyes glassy, their delicate features unresponsive. He shook his head.

"N . . . no," he rasped. "Undines . . . can't leave them . . . Must . . . take them back."

"S'all right, lad! It's raining fit to drown a man up here! They'll be fine once we get you all out of there!"

"Oh . . . all right . . . then . . ."

Strong arms pulled him from the water. His last sensations were of the undines' tiny fingers tangled in his hair and the high-pitched shriek of police whistles as the rain washed the Thames from his body.

The London Chronicle, *March 6, 1783*

On Wednesday night about nine o'clock, three men were taken into custody by the Bow Street Runners on charges of theft and murder in connection with the attack on the East India Company Ship Woodford.

His rooms in Queen Square were bright and airy and smelled of sandalwood and lavender. When he awoke, Christopher lay in bed for some time, enjoying the feel of clean sheets and the sound of birds singing outside his window, before finally opening his eyes. The man sitting by the bed and reading a book looked up with a smile.

"All right, Kit?" he asked, his voice warm with love.

Christopher smiled weakly in return. "As right as I'll ever be, Teddy," he answered, striving to allow the relief he felt to color his voice. "Did we get him?"

"We got him. Keeling arrested his men on the dock, and they gave Hart up at once. He's in Newgate as we speak. He'll hang for certain."

A memory from the night before surfaced slowly. "Keeling's a Bow Street Runner."

Edward nodded. "And one of the men whose been guarding our family unseen for the past nine years."

"And the undines?"

"Are waiting for you, safe and sound in the courtyard fountain."

"They couldn't tell me that Father never died that night."

"I know. He was too strong a Water Master. He swore them to secrecy, and they couldn't disobey him, no matter how much they wanted to." A tiny salamander scampered across Edward's shoulder, and he smiled at it gently. "We were in danger, all of us. The mages he'd battled with in India had followed him here. He had to draw them away to protect us all."

"I know. I just wish I'd known before."

"So do I."

Pushing himself up, Christopher settled against the headboard. "What about the antiquity, that thing in the leaden box that Father died for, where is it?"

"Uncle Neville took charge of it for the White Lodge."

"I hope it was worth it." Christopher couldn't help the note of bitterness that crept into his voice, but Edward just nodded.

Setting his book to one side, he stood. "Hungry?" he asked.

"A little, if I can ever get the taste of the Thames out of my mouth."

Edward grimaced. "Well, Mrs. Cooper has a roast of beef on, so if anything can drive the taste away, it will be that."

He held out his hand to help his younger brother rise, and Christopher accepted it without hesitation.

The next morning, Robert Clive's body was finally properly interred in St Margaret's Parish Churchyard at Moreton Say in Shropshire. This time there was no taint of possible suicide, no feelings of anger, or betrayal, no confusion, only simple grief. Henry Keeling stood behind the family, his dark blue uniform dotted with the rain, a comforting presence that Christopher had only just begun to realize, had always been there.

As the rest of the family made their way to various coaches, Uncle Neville drew Christopher aside.

"I'm not going to ask you to join the White Lodge like Edward and Rebecca," the older man said, "because I know you won't; there's far too much of your father in you. However, London's new police force could certainly use a magistrate with an understanding of the city's more exotic activities. I'm sure I could put a word in the right ear . . ."

Christopher shook his head. "I really don't think I'm magistrate material, Uncle Neville." He glanced over at Keeling. "But something like it, maybe. I have to talk things over with my godfather first."

Neville smiled. "Fair enough. Keep in touch, my boy. Life's too short and the world's too wide for family to be strangers, yes?"

"Yes."

The older man headed for his own coach, leaving Christopher and Keeling standing together in the rain while a dozen undines sported in the growing puddles at their feet.

Feathers and Foundations
Elizabeth A. Vaughan

Thomas Davies, late of His Majesty's Royal Army, recently sworn Yeoman Warder of the Tower of London, and reluctant Ravenmaster, stood at attention, eyes forward, sweat gathering under his collar.

Before him stood Lieutenant-General Loftus and Colonel Doyle, positioned at either side of a great wide mahogany desk. Behind the desk sat His Lordship, the Constable of the Tower, Field Marshall Arthur, Duke of Wellington.

Behind the Duke perched three of the Tower's resident ravens, their blue-black feathers pressed against the glass. Their claws skittered against the stone sill as they fought for position.

Tom kept his eyes straight ahead, trying not to watch the birds.

"A disgrace," Lieutenant-General Loftus sputtered, his thick eyebrows almost meeting in a scowl. "Their constant, frantic cawing, their struggles to fly outside these walls—"

"They can't," the Duke observed mildly, focused on the papers in front of him. "Their wings are clipped. Have been since . . . since—"

"Charles the Second, sir," Colonel Doyle supplied.

"Charles the Second," the Duke agreed as he leaned back in his chair and formed a steeple with his fingers. "Wise precaution, given that the Empire will fall if the ravens leave the Tower."

"Britain, sir," Colonel Doyle said.

"Pardon?"

"Britain, sir," Doyle repeated calmly. "The folklore implies that the Crown and Britain will—"

"They have never acted like this," Loftus snapped, glaring at Tom. "Chasing visitors, attacking them. Why, Lady Wilson claimed one of those blasted birds flapped up and stole an earring from her ear!" Loftus snorted. "Never had these problems under the prior Ravenmaster, let that be known."

"Damn visitors." The Duke scowled at Loftus. "This is a military fortress, not a seaside resort. Bad enough we have families residing within. Letting civilians in to mill about. Nothing good in that, not one thing good."

"Their croaks are frantic, and continue for hours," Loftus continued before the Duke could pontificate on his desired reforms. "Their destruction of property is known, making off with all sorts of small items, plucking at buttons, attacking shoelaces, and their scat—"

"Chalk," Colonel Doyle said.

Loftus bristled. Tom kept his eyes on the far wall.

The Duke raised one eyebrow. "I beg your pardon?"

"Chalk," Doyle said firmly. "Bird scat is called chalk due to its white appearance."

"Regardless," Loftus snapped, "the damage it does to carriages is extensive. They startle the horses, tear up the grass, attack the flowers. Even the leading in the stained-glass windows of the Chapel is not safe from their marauding. Why, the animals in the Tower menagerie have also been acting up, rousing and carrying on as if the world were ending."

Tom kept his military stance, making every effort not to watch the birds, their feathers splayed against the glass. They were pecking at the putty there, as if to spite the Lieutenant-General. They beat their wings and chortled as their beady eyes gleamed and their sharp black beaks stabbed at the cracks.

"There's another thing that doesn't belong in this venerable fortress, that collection of animals. But come now." The Duke barked a laugh. "You cannot blame the lad for these things, surely. He's been on duty for, what, less than a month, if I remember correctly."

"Two months," Colonel Doyle chimed in.

"And it's two months I've been Constable of the Tower."

The Duke snorted and waved a hand over his papers. "No easy thing, adjusting to our roles, now is it, lad?"

Tom blinked, realizing he was being addressed. "No, sir."

Wellington turned in his chair, glaring at the window behind him. The birds squawked, flapped their wings, and fell from the sill to glide down to the Tower Green.

The Duke turned back, fixing Tom with an intent look. "Get your soldiers under control, Ravenmaster. Dismissed."

Stepping outside into the early evening air, Tom took a deep breath that he regretted at once. With no breeze, the smell of the cesspool of a moat and grounds was thick and foul. Mayhap, with luck, the breeze would pick up from the Thames later.

A flash of dark movement to his left caught his eye. He ducked his head, but the raven still managed to strike his black Tudor bonnet, knocking it askew.

With a triumphant croak, the bird glided past to land on the Tower Green. It folded up its wings and strode off, its cackling echoing from the stone walls, its blue-black body an odd contrast to the deep green grass.

Tom adjusted his hat and sighed. To any other eyes, the Tower green seemed lush and healthy. But as an Elemental Master of Earth, he wasn't fooled. The lush green, the flowers planted in the beds along the buildings all hid corruption and taint.

Much like a battlefield, where the dead lay in green fields—

A raven croaked right next to him, and for a moment Tom was back in the fields of the dead, with the birds feasting—

He jerked back to this time and this place and drew another deep breath, almost grateful for the stench.

The ravens strutted around the lawn, cawing to one another, seemingly ignoring him. He wasn't fooled by that, either. They knew full well what time it was, and he knew they were taunting him, and—

He snorted. They were birds, creatures of Air, with little brains or common sense. He was assigning them thoughts and feelings and conspiracies where there were none.

He was as daft as his family back on the Isle of Wight

claimed, shaking their heads over his notion to become a Yeoman Warder. They were right, of course, but it mattered not. He loved the Tower, with its history and stories that spanned centuries of time. The only thing that could lure him to the city was the history found here.

That and the anguish the stones held. That pain had called to him, and he'd answered, but not without a cost.

He'd had to cut himself off from his Element, shield himself against the very earth beneath his feet. So far, he'd managed, but it was a close thing. How much longer could he sustain his shields without access to healthy, growing land? Eventually, he'd need to find a way to deal with that problem, but for this moment, he had a different and more difficult task.

He needed to pen the ravens for the night.

It was a tradition, of course, but also a necessity. Foxes were known to get within the walls, coming up out of the river. Other predators, owls and the like, roamed the dark. With their clipped wings, the fool birds were vulnerable, but try to tell them that.

His fellow Warders always enjoyed the entertainment, watching him try to get the ravens in their pens. This evening was no different, and it was long past the hour for his own supper before he'd even managed the first.

The birds gathered around him, just out of reach. Tom let loose a blistering oath from his soldiering days, directed at the foul harbingers of death.

A young chambermaid hurrying past with a bundle of laundry gasped and rushed off.

Tom blushed, clearing his throat in his shame.

Almost as one, the birds cawed and croaked and flapped their wings. Then the biggest one cackled, and the others started to leap into their cages. He slammed the wooden doors shut, securing them tight for the night. Their black eyes peered at him through the wooden slats.

"Air," he said, hot, tired, and disgusted.

Their mocking cries followed him all the way across the Tower Green.

He'd no watch this night, and felt thankful for that as he trudged back to his quarters. A change, a quick wash, some supper, and then bed, he decided. For he'd have to be up at the break of day to tend his charges, release them from their cages, and feed the evil things their meat.

But upon opening his door, there on his small table sat a small package, covered in rough brown paper and tied with twine. Addressed to him in his ma's handwriting, her pride clear in every letter of his name and title. Tom smiled as the stress of the day eased from his shoulders.

Homesickness and joy both swelled in his heart. There'd be letters, and biscuits if he was lucky, wrapped in that bundle.

He'd wash first. Have a bit of supper. And then he'd open his box and have a bit of home.

There were biscuits. Chocolate ones, with walnuts, mostly reduced to crumbs. That didn't stop him. He scooped up the crumbs with his fingers, munching as he propped himself up on his bed and read his letters.

Ma's first, thanking him for his letter where he'd told of his swearing-in ceremony. His family had all wanted to attend, but their strong Elemental ties made it impossible. As bound to the Isle of Wight as they were, as foul as London was, it would only have brought them illness and misery.

He could hear her joyful voice in her words, telling of all the village gossip. Of young lads leaving for the city for work in the mills and factories. Of lasses either pining or following, and the joys and sorrows thereof. She ended with the usual note. *"You have a good position now, son, and I hope and pray that you are seeking a good wife. Someone to make you happy. Someone to make you a home."*

He rolled his eyes a bit at that one. Unlikely as not that he'd find a woman who'd deal with living in the Tower, his birds, and his magic. Best leave that for another day.

His brother's letter next. *"You're still daft for being there, no matter how the stones call to you,"* and continuing on to insult his intelligence in laughing sentences. But then the letter went on to speak of the crops in a general sense and the rector's daughter's flashing eyes with a great deal more detail.

Tom lifted an eyebrow and smiled. Even if his brother

made no mention of an attraction, his ma might soon be busy planning a wedding. Good enough. Take the pressure off his own back.

With a chuckle, he turned to his da's letter, good and thick, with his no-nonsense attitude coming through the sprawling words.

Da started with the fields and the crops, talking about the planting and the condition of the soil. Then there was that far creek, and how it dammed up in a recent storm and washed out the banks, flooding the far most field. *"Little damage, son,"* Tom was relieved to read. *"But I need to rouse your brother and some lads to go in and clear the debris. Just waiting for a fair dry spell to make the work easier. And no worries on your part,"* his da continued. *"I'll be overseeing the work."*

Tom snorted. Aye, that his da would, until he waded in to show them all how it was done.

"Something else, eldest, that you should know," the letter continued, the writing a bit larger, the ink thicker, as if his da had reached the bottom of the bottle.

Tom stiffened a bit on that, his attention caught as it was meant to be.

"There's been some odd doings here, what with the live-stock. The cattle have been gathering in odd ways and bel-lowing their fool heads off. The sheep have taken to running in panicked circles. The chickens flap their wings and shriek in panic for no reason I can see. Why, even the old cock has taken to crowing at midnight. The songbirds your ma enjoys so much have fled the woods, it seems, and large masses of them have been seen flying off the isle.

"Do you remember Portsmith, a few years back? The earth tremors that hit? Your uncle on your mother's side talked of seeing such things, of tension in the air and land. And your cousin from Holme-on-Spaulding-Moor, in York-shire, back in 1822. Said he never had such a fright as the land shifting below him.

"Never seen the like myself, and I'm wondering if you noticed anything there, in your sprawling city, far from the comforts of home and land. It worries me, what such a thing could do in London.

"But all's well here," his da continued. *"This family sees to the land, and the land sees to the family. Mind that you see to your own place as well, my son."*

Tom lingered on his da's signature, running his thumb over the ink, but there was nothing more, no magical impressions or hidden words. His da would be cautious until he knew such things were safe.

Tom sighed. Portsmith, Holme-on-Spaulding-Moor. Da was talking about the earthquakes that had rumbled through years back. Tom'd been serving then, out of the country, but he'd heard how the family and other Earth Mages had banded together to ease those quakes from what they might have been. He wasn't sure exactly what they'd done, or how they'd done it, and he cursed himself for a fool for not asking further. All he knew was, it had taken them all working together to mitigate the force and consequences.

And here he was, a lone Earth Master in the City of London, and warning signs abounding.

Could that be it? The ravens, the lions roaring in the Lion's Tower, the upset in the menagerie. Were the creatures all trying to speak to the state of the land?

He looked down at the letters surrounding him without really seeing the pages. It seemed a mite too convenient that such information would arrive just at this moment. His family's powers lay with the Earth, with the occasional Air and Water allies. And the Earth was tied firmly to the present and the past, with no tendency toward foresight. But Tom knew well enough that the Elemental forces of magic had their own paths. To dismiss this as coincidence was to risk ignoring a warning.

That he would not do.

A few days later, Tom got his chance to investigate—after the Ceremony of the Keys, when the Tower was locked up secure for the night, and its residents settled in and cozy in their beds. His watch was the White Tower this night, the oldest tower, and the one with the deepest cellars . . . dungeons years past.

He waited at his post until there was nothing but the depths of the night and the sound of his own breath around

him. Then he took up his lantern and headed down the twisting stairs. He'd go down, take care of this business, and then
nip back up to his position. And if any should find him, well,
he'd say he'd heard a noise.

It was cooler there within, the stones radiating damp and
chill. His breath fogged out ever so slightly. Standing at the
base of the stairs, he held the lantern high and saw small,
cramped halls running off in each direction, crammed with
crates, barrels, and old furniture. To see it, you'd think it was
nothing more than Granny's attic that needed cleaning out.

Tom knew better. He checked his shields, holding them as
tight as he could. His was a simple plan. Get to the deepest
part, extend his focus into the foundations and farther, down
to the very depths of the earth, and see if he could sense any
tensions in the land below. Just a swift, simple probe, and
then he'd return to his duties—

He heard a clatter from behind a crate to his left and piv-
oted, his lantern swaying in his hand, causing the shadows to
dance. "Who's there?" he whispered, his heart pounding.

A glimpse, nothing more, of a rat, its tail disappearing
into shadows.

Tom barked a laugh at himself and his racing heart, then
focused on the task at hand. Lifting his lantern again, he
headed down the narrow ways, ignoring the cells to the sides,
down to the deepest part of the "cellar," trying to catch his
breath.

He found a place then, between crates and barrels, and set
the lantern down. He plucked at his uniform, adjusting it here
and there, as he willed his heart calm and his breath steady.

Normally, he'd call his Elemental allies and ask them to
aid him in this task. He was strong in his own Element. But
he'd not call any to this place. With the filth of London all
about them, the sickness in the earth below the Tower, and
the foulness of its moat waters, he hadn't the heart.

No, he'd do it himself. But not the usual way, of merging
with an area below his feet, slowly expanding into the land in
a strong wave. He'd not expose himself, either. He'd seek
down into the bedrock below them, more like a needle thrust.
He'd shape his power thin and sharp and send it down fast, like
a weighted rope. Once he'd the answers he was seeking, he'd

pull back, just as fast, just as quick. A lightning thrust in and out, swift and sure.

At least, so he hoped.

He centered himself, adopting a firm stance, his heart beating slow and sure. He barely opened his lips, concentrating on deep regular breaths.

One last breath. He lowered his shields and braced himself for the onslaught.

The pain came as a wave, rocking him. The sickness of the stone and earth around him, the corruption of all that was natural. Worse, the stones held pain, centuries of pain, that cried out like a wounded animal. He'd felt it from the Tower before, and he'd vowed to find a way to cleanse the stones. "Soon," he whispered. "Soon."

He drew another breath and concentrated on his needle of power, bright and hot and sharp. Once the image was fully formed, he lanced it down between his feet, sending it plunging past stone and brick and layers of earth, down to the very foundations of the land. His body trembled, sweat forming at his collar, but he held on to the power and the needle and sent his awareness after it, abandoning his physical senses.

Here, deep within, he reached the place where the stone was solid and impenetrable, seemingly one piece. He'd heard heathen tales that told of the world on the back of a tortoise shell, traveling through the universe. The image was an apt one. Here, at these depths, there was no foulness, no sickness. He took a moment to revel in the feeling. The earth was clean and strong and . . . stressed.

He stopped his plunge, hovering the tip of his lance just above the source.

The stone vibrated with tension and power. Raw Elemental power shimmered with the tiniest of ripples now and again.

This was more than he knew how to handle, more than any one Elemental Master could handle, and well he knew it.

Under London. Under the Tower.

He distantly sensed his body, trembling and sweating, but his focus remained on the foundations below him. The threat was real and imminent. It would take weeks, months to gather enough Masters to solve—

He didn't have to solve. All he had to do was drain. Allay. Ease.

Tom was fairly certain that somewhere above his body swallowed hard, for in truth this could mean his death.

He didn't take the time to think. He lowered his needle, not to pierce, merely to touch, to connect, to—

Lightning sparked at the point, surged out, up the needle, up the link. Up his power to arc and dance through his body until each individual hair seemed to stand straight up. The world was at once the foundations of stone, the cellar walls, the insides of his eyeballs.

It was glorious and terrifying, and he surrendered to it, feeling his life ebbing as the earth below—

Denial, defiance, and the stones of the White Tower above tore through him, taking the burden, pulling the arc away, pulling him away, until he was every brick, every rock, every pebble, every blade of grass, every feather . . .

The bedrock below grumbled, settling down, easing . . .

He heard voices then, roused in anger, with shouts and rough hands on his shoulders. The energies were torn from him. He staggered and collapsed into the hands that seized him.

Thomas Davies, late of His Majesty's Royal Army, recently sworn Yeoman Warder of the Tower of London, and reluctant Ravenmaster, sat collapsed in a chair, cold and sweating under his uniform, barely able to focus his eyes on the men before him.

Before him were arrayed Lieutenant-General Loftus and Colonel Doyle, standing at either side of a great, wide mahogany desk. And behind the desk was His Lordship, the Constable of the Tower, Field Marshall Arthur, Duke of Wellington.

Behind the Duke, at the huge window, three large ravens, their blue-black feathers pressed against the glass. Their claws skittered against the stone sill as they fought for position.

Behind Tom, his fellow Yeomen stood in judgment.

"Dereliction of duty." The Duke's anger boomed over his head. "Leaving one's post in the dead of night—and found in this condition. Was it liquor? Opium?"

Tom managed to shake his head, trying to speak. His shields were in tatters, his resources drained. He gripped the armrests of the wooden chair, trying to stop their shaking.

". . . court-martial . . ." The Duke's word seemed to come through a fog.

Tom shook his head, trying to deny it.

"Beg pardon, your Lordship." Loftus' voice cut through Tom's confusion. He heard Loftus move closer, felt a firm hand on his shoulder. Tom managed to lift his head to meet the man's gaze.

"On your honor." Loftus was staring at him intently. "You saw the lads, didn't you?" he asked.

Tom jerked his head in astonishment. "Milord?" he croaked. "I—"

The ravens started up with raucous cries, drawing everyone's attention before he could offer any further explanation.

Loftus nodded his head as if satisfied. "There's no shame in it, son."

The other Yeomen exchanged glances, and to Tom's confusion, their attitudes seemed to change in an instant.

"Lads?" the Duke demanded. "What lads?"

"The Little Princes, your Lordship." Loftus squeezed Tom's shoulder with what seemed to be sympathy, then stepped back to his position by the desk.

"Princes?" The Duke's eyebrows rose, his confusion as deep as Tom's own.

"Slain by the command of King Richard the Second," Loftus said quietly.

"Richard the Third, sir." Colonel Doyle whispered.

The room was silent, the ravens were silent, and all Tom could here was his own harsh breath.

"Ghosts?" the Duke asked, and something in his tone made Tom raise his head to look at the man. Veteran of many wars, a fierce leader of men, he now looked . . . shaken.

"Aye." Loftus' voice was resigned and chagrined and resolute, all at the same time. "And not a man here hasn't been touched by one over the years."

In the following quiet, every Yeoman nodded, their faces just as solemn. No laughter, no mocking.

The Duke drew in a breath and leaned forward in his chair. "There will be no court-martial," he said briskly. "See to it that this doesn't happen again," he barked. "Dismissed."

Willing hands helped Tom out of his chair and into the dawning day. He blinked in confusion. How long had he been caught within the stone?

"It's a rite of passage, seeing the lads. Takes it out of a man." Loftus' voice was gruff, but his grasp on Tom's arm was strong and supportive. "A good night's sleep, and you'll be right as rain."

Loftus was right, but for the wrong reasons.

Tom sat in his quarters, a pen in his hand, ink close, trying to think on his letter to his da. His table faced the window for the breeze coming off the river. His teacup sat empty in its saucer. Ink dripped from the nib of the pen to the paper below, and he watched as the blot expanded.

He'd been told to sleep, told that he was off duty until the next day. He'd felt better when he'd woke, that was sure. A dose of his ma's stomach powders helped as well. But there was something else, and he wasn't sure what it meant or how it had come about.

Whatever else had happened while he'd lingered in the foundations of the Tower, down to the very bedrock of the land, he'd anchored himself somehow—

No. Tom shook his head. In this, in all magic, there was a danger in not being honest, or at least, in refusing to look at the truth. He'd been anchored, been . . . claimed in a way he'd never felt before.

Elemental Masters of Earth were bound to the land, aye, but it was a bond that formed over time, as one worked with the soil and the stone. His mentors, his teachers, his da had all explained that to him. Like the roots of a tree, so would grow his connection, and while those roots would bind him, they'd also support and nourish. But whatever it was that had happened below, it had been fast and harsh. Like a fist around his heart. Like the clutch of a dying man on a battlefield.

Whether it was for good or ill, he did not know.

How to explain all this to his da? How to acknowledge the warning and offer reassurance without risking exposure?

How to explain to his da the risk he had taken? How to ask if his da knew of the like, of the land, of the very buildings, locking in on a soul?

How to ask if any of Da's acquaintance knew aught about ravens?

The blot ceased to expand. Tom dipped his pen again, careful to drain off the excess ink. While he had his letters, words had never been his gift. He'd no idea where to start.

A flutter of wings drew his attention to the open window. Two of the ravens settled on the sill, filling the opening, all blue-black feathers and black, gleaming eyes. The larger one croaked at the other, pecking at the smaller one's head.

The smaller one bobbed, something dangling from its beak. Spreading its wings, it glided to the desk.

"Here now." Tom set down his pen. "None of this." These creatures could do some real damage if—

The bird cackled, opened its beak, and dropped a gleaming earring into his teacup.

Hearth and Family
Dayle A. Dermatis

Klara drew the rounded loaf of bread from the oven, sliding it out on a long, flat wooden paddle. The scent of yeast and wheat spread through the mill cottage, and her mouth filled with moisture as her stomach twisted painfully. She was past hunger.

Still, the fire salamanders writhing and playing in the flames made her smile, and she thanked them before she pushed the iron door shut, letting the cottage fall into cool shadows.

Even as hungry as she was, Klara knew the bread was too hot to eat just yet. She set the loaf on a windowsill and covered it with a towel of red-and-white checked cotton, faded and often patched.

Turning to the burlap bag of flour, she saw again what she'd seen before she'd baked this single loaf: not enough to bake another loaf, not even a small one.

Oh, there were bags of grain in storage, safely locked away from prying dormice—but with her beloved Hermann dead from a fever and Otto, her dear boy, conscripted and later killed (so she'd been informed by official, dispassionate letter) in the *Märzrevolution*, that horrible revolution of 1848, the mill was as silent as the Water Elementals in the river.

Fire was her Element, not Water like Hermann's. The undines and naiads acknowledged her, but she had no power to call them, to beg their assistance. And she couldn't run the mill without them, not alone.

One last loaf of bread, which she'd make last as long as she could. One scrawny chicken, no longer laying, that would make a meager stew along with the garden vegetables. The goat could take care of itself, thank goodness. The rich, loamy earth here near the river meant she could grow a small but decent kitchen crop without special help, and she traded some of the small bounty at the local market, but it wasn't enough.

Hermann and she had been hard workers, and the mill, built by her father, had served them well for many years. Between selling flour, grinding grain for others, and her own baked delicacies, they had thrived, had had a comfortable life. She wasn't the type to give up, but right now, with the delicious scent of that final loaf of bread pinching her empty stomach and no solution in sight, she felt tired, defeated.

Old, even, although she was far from that.

She picked up the broom and began sweeping, long, steady strokes to move what little dust lay on the floor. It felt good to move, to do *something*.

She had no idea what to do next, where she could go. Into the city, she supposed, and try to find a job at a bakery, if the salamanders would have her. But the thought of a city made her shudder: the noise, the smell, the lack of air and streams and trees.

If she had any money left, she might have considered going to America. That's what Hermann had wanted to do before he died. She was the one who'd always said no, always feared the change.

Her mother had been an Earth Magician, and they tended to nest, to bond to the land that was a comfort to them. Although Klara herself was a Fire Magician, her mother's early teachings had settled deep within her. She loved the mill and attached cozy cottage, loved the plot of earth and the cool green forest and the ever-changing river and the huge oven with the salamanders who never let things burn.

But she had loved Hermann even more, and he was gone, and so was Otto, and now she would lose the mill, her land, and the last of her heart, too.

She sat in the rocking chair her grandfather had carved for

her grandmother and picked up a piece of mending. Let it rest, untouched, in her lap.

Then she heard something. Living alone, in the forest, away from the town, she'd long grown used to its sounds: the constant splashing of the river, the breeze ruffling the leaves, the soft crunch of animals through the pine needles. The snuffling of a wild boar, the drumming of a grouse.

This was different, unfamiliar.

Hushed voices?

She turned toward the window and saw the fresh loaf of bread—her last loaf of bread—was gone.

She went to the kitchen and grabbed a butcher's knife. Without truly thinking, she cracked open the oven. She didn't know if the salamanders could help her, but their presence soothed her.

Hiding the knife in the folds of her skirt, she eased open the door and crept along the side of the mill to peer around the corner.

The tension rushed out of her. They were just children!

No, she realized as she watched the scrawny twosome huddle beneath the window as they tore into the bread. They were perhaps thirteen or fourteen, nearly adults—the boy old enough, as her Otto had been, to be taken into the military. Their small stature fooled the eye.

Like Klara, they were near to starving.

Her first instinct was to drive them away, reclaim what few crumbs were left of the loaf. She hadn't enough food to feed herself, not in these hard times, much less feed two growing children.

But the boy reminded her of Otto, and they were both innocents, and Klara couldn't have lived with herself if she did anything less than help two starving children. To send them back into the forest . . . no.

She'd have to butcher the goat.

She cleared her throat.

The two leaped to their feet, eyes wide in their dirty faces. The boy took a half step forward, protecting the girl. Twins, Klara realized. Probably blond beneath the grime.

"*Ach*, if you're going to be eating my bread, we should be properly introduced," she said. "My name is Klara."

"I—I'm Georg, and this is Frieda," the boy said.

"We're sorry for taking your bread," Frieda said. "It's just . . . we haven't eaten . . ."

They hadn't eaten for longer than she had, Klara guessed, and they were still growing.

"Wash up down by the river, and then come inside," she said, nodding at the mill. "We'll see what we can do."

As they rounded the corner, she caught movement out of the side of her eye. There, in the river, the undines and naiads leaped and splashed and waved. Klara turned to stare at the children.

Were they Elemental Magicians, too? Could one of them be a Water Magician?

Klara asked Georg to fill the heavy iron pot with water from the river. Opening the small door in the front of the hulking black stove, she fed in kindling to catch the coals, then larger pieces. One of the salamanders leaped out to twine along her arm, sinuous as an otter, before diving back into the growing flames.

When Klara stood, she saw Frieda staring at her, but the girl quickly looked away when she saw the woman's gaze on her.

"Some vegetables from the garden, I think," Klara said.

Georg, who'd just come in with the pot, said, "I'll do that."

He came back faster than she expected, bearing a cabbage, some onions and carrots, and a beetroot she hadn't realized still existed. Before she could say anything else, he darted back outside.

"He's off to find mushrooms," Frieda said. "He's good at that." She picked up a knife and began deftly chopping vegetables.

Mushrooms, Klara thought. She still had a bit of butter, tied in a sack and cooled by the river. Her mouth watered.

She picked up another knife and asked Frieda how the two had come to be in the forest.

Their story came as no surprise; it was one she'd heard in town, at the market, over and over again. Germany in the 1840s was a place growing harsher and harder. The potato blight meant famine was a constant threat—if it wasn't here already—and it was little better in the cities, with food prices soaring. Frieda's and Georg's parents had been unable to see how they could feed a family of four and quietly argued whether they should stop hiding Georg from conscription.

Frieda and Georg had overheard the debate and chosen to leave rather than risk what they saw as worse.

"Normally Georg is good at finding his way through the forest," Frieda added. "But this time, we got lost. We were trying to get to the town, but he couldn't see the way."

Klara knelt to open the stove again and add more wood, and when a salamander paused in its joyous leaping, she whispered, "Which one?"

And the answer she received was *"Both."*

They ate the mushrooms first, cooked with the butter kept cool in the river. Then the vegetables were soft in the broth, and they ate that with the remains of the bread. Klara couldn't think much beyond that, and the children were exhausted, too.

The next morning, however, she woke to another delicious smell, and was astonished to learn Georg had coaxed eggs from the chicken.

Earth, she realized, now that she had a clearer head and a belly that didn't ache. Which meant Frieda was Water, if the undines and naiads had any say. But neither child seemed to know; they'd had no training, had no knowledge, in fact, that Elemental Magic existed.

In many ways, that didn't surprise her. Magicians were still looked down upon, feared, outcast. In a time when Old Lutherans and those of any religion not sanctioned by the state chose to seek refuge in America, mages had to be especially careful. Or perhaps their parents hadn't known, either? Frieda had said their mother was dead and their stepmother was strict.

"*Frau* Klara," Georg said after they'd breakfasted, "does the mill no longer function?"

She closed her eyes for a moment. Could they be the answer to her prayers?

"It could," she said, "but I haven't the strength to adjust the face wheel or the runner stones. And the . . . the river has been low."

Before things had become dire, she had tried to hire some help but hadn't been able to find anyone willing to live this far from town for very long.

Plus, the mill had been as prosperous as it had when Hermann was alive, thanks in part to the Water spirits helping guide the wheel, keeping its rotation even and steady.

"We're so grateful for your hospitality," Frieda added, "and we must pay you back for the bread we stole. Please, let us help."

And so Klara led them from the cottage into the mill, where the scent of water and grain was strong, and the air was cool and fresh. It took the three of them to adjust the various wheels so that, finally, they stood back, exhausted, and watched the mechanisms move properly.

Klara went to the storage bins and hauled out a sack of grain.

There would, she thought with the first sense of hope she'd had in months, be fresh bread for supper tonight. And to sell at the market.

The mill would work adequately even without the Elementals' help, but if Frieda had a connection with them. . . .

Klara shook her head, looking down at the moss-covered rocks lining the bank of the river. She didn't yet dare think too far in the future. Right now, though, a glimmer of hope was enough.

The first time they traveled into town for the market, the three of them went together, Klara showing them how to get there and where to set the cart to sell the bread and sacks of fine ground flour. The next time, the two children went together, Frieda scratching between the goat's horns as it pulled the cart, while Klara stayed behind, happier tending to the mill and the garden, staying close to the land.

Cautiously, she let hope trickle back into her life, found it easier to breathe.

The third time, the two children went together again, but only Frieda returned, stumbling next to the cart and the confused goat, weeping to near hysteria.

She could barely speak the words, but Klara figured out, her heart heavy, what Frieda said.

The German Army had conscripted Georg.

Klara couldn't do much more than hold Frieda while the girl wept. She had told the children briefly about Otto, and she hoped Frieda wouldn't think of that, wouldn't assume the same fate would befall Georg.

"Georg is strong and smart and resourceful," she whispered in Frieda's ear. "He led you through the woods; he can take care of himself. When his service is through, he'll find his way back to you."

But she lay awake for many nights, worrying.

Without Georg, the mill's production slowed. Frieda took up much of the slack, and between them they could move the heavier stones, haul the sacks of grain and flour.

Before Georg had left, Klara had tried to broach the subject of Elementals, but any time she did, both children either changed the subject or acted as if they had no idea what she spoke of. She believed Frieda should be trained, however. She just wasn't sure where or how to start.

Her own training had come from family, as natural a part of things as learning to walk and read and bake.

As she baked, she watched Frieda. The girl transferred the shaped loaves to her. Using the wide, flat wooden paddle, Klara slid the loaves into the oven one at a time. Klara could see Frieda furtively watching, her brown eyes darting back and forth as she bit her lip.

Once all the loaves were safely in the oven, Klara left the iron door slightly ajar, then sat Frieda down at the scarred wooden table. She asked one of the salamanders to join her, and it twined about her arm like a weasel, sinuous and playful.

"Frieda," Klara said, "you can see the salamander, can't you?"

The girl's faced paled, and she shook her head so hard Klara thought she might snap her own neck. "No, *Frau* Klara, I don't see anything. Nothing at all."

"Frieda," Klara said. She eased toward the girl, slowly, her voice soothing, as if she were calming a skittish pony. "It's all right. It won't hurt you. I—"

But before she could continue, Frieda burst into tears. The salamander, startled, leaped back into the oven.

"No, no, no!" Frieda repeated, curling into herself and squeezing her eyes shut. "I don't see anything! It's not my fault!"

"Frieda," Klara said again, putting her hands on the girl's arms. "Nothing's your fault, *Liebling*. Why ever would you say such a thing?"

And that was when Frieda finally broke down, her defenses crumbling. They had been cast out of their home, she said, weeping, because their stepmother thought Frieda was a *Hexe*, a witch, because Frieda could see the creatures frolicking in the water.

"Georg . . . Georg can see things, too," she said, and hiccuped. "In the forest. Little gnome-men—*Erdgeists*—he told me. But he doesn't say that anymore. When *she* came, he swore he couldn't see them, and swore I was telling tales, and she beat me to teach me to not to lie."

Klara knew that by *she*, Frieda meant their stepmother.

Klara gathered the girl into her arms and rocked her back and forth. "You're not a witch—not in the way that witches are bad and evil," she said. "But you do have magic in you, a very special gift. You're a magician—a Water Magician, if I'm not mistaken, just as my Hermann was. And it sounds as though Georg is an Earth Magician."

Frieda had stopped weeping, but she was still tense, still frightened, so Klara explained, in simple terms, how Elemental Magic worked.

Eventually Frieda's sobs and hiccups subsided. She rose and went to the marble basin of water on the beechwood washstand that stood between the two bedroom doors, a wedding gift from Hermann a lifetime ago. But instead of splashing her face, she stared into the bowl.

As Klara watched, Frieda bit her lip, reached out hesitantly with one hand.

The water in the bowl shimmered, rippled. Frieda sucked in an audible breath, but she didn't move, didn't pull back.

In contrast, Klara held her breath.

A swirl of water, a tempest in the proverbial teacup, and then a tiny naiad rose halfway out of the water. It cocked its head at Frieda, then held out one little watery hand.

Slowly, Frieda stretched to gently touch that hand with one finger.

The naiad giggled, the sound like a tinkling gargle of delight. It did a backflip, splashed into the water, and disappeared.

Frieda turned to Klara, her brown eyes enormous. She took in another deep breath, squaring her shoulders. Clearly she had come to a crossroads and made her choice.

"Will you—will you teach me?" she asked.

Klara taught Frieda as best she could, for all that Fire Magic opposed Water Magic. It helped that Frieda was determined and talented—and it seemed that the Water spirits remembered Hermann's kindness and didn't hold it against Klara that her own magic was anathema to them.

Klara watched Frieda grow stronger every day in many ways. Not that she hadn't always been strong—not everyone could have survived those days deep in the forest—but previously she'd had Georg to lean on, to share burdens with (and, Klara knew, Georg had shared with Frieda).

The girl blossomed as her relationship with the naiads and undines grew. She never shirked the work that needed to be done to keep the mill running, but when she had a spare moment, Klara always knew to find her down by the river, crouched on the mossy rocks, trailing her fingers in the chill water.

The only darkness was the loss of Georg, of not knowing his fate. Many nights Klara heard Frieda's sobs, no matter how hard she tried to muffle them in her pillow. They both asked their respective Elementals for assistance, but Earth Magic was weaker in cities, if that was indeed where Georg was.

Frieda transformed her fear into determination—determination to learn Elemental Magic, determination to make the mill a success, determination to find Georg, determination to face whatever obstacles came in her path.

At first, Klara and Frieda went to the market together; Klara was concerned about Frieda, an unattended and lovely young woman, as she had to admit Frieda was becoming, going alone. But even in that, Frieda eventually insisted she could handle herself. Georg had taught her to fight, she said. *Ach*, she could hold her own.

To Klara, Frieda was the daughter Hermann and she had never had. To Frieda, Klara was far more of a mother than her stepmother had ever been.

With the forest and the river, the mill and the oven, they were content. When Georg returned, as they both trusted he would, they would have a family together.

But when Georg returned, the reunion wasn't what any of them wished for.

Spring was turning into summer once again, the forest shifting from the bright green of new shoots to the mossy green of thriving growth. The river settled from early-season swollen to a steady flow, the undines playing in the mill wheel.

Frieda had just come in from the mill for lunch—fresh-baked rye bread, *Butterkäse* cheese, and sausage from last week's trip to the market—when the sharp rap at the door brought them both to their feet.

No one ventured this far into the forest.

Klara reached for the butcher knife. Frieda reached for the latch, then stepped back as she opened the door.

The figure in the doorway was silhouetted by the bright sunshine, but Frieda seemed to recognize his form, even changed and grown as it was.

"Georg!" She flung herself into his arms.

But Klara saw a stiffness in him. He held Frieda, his eyes closed, but his body was rigid.

He'd filled out. He was a man now, just as Frieda was a woman. Was that what made him tense?

Klara set the knife onto the table, stepped forward to greet him.

But he released Frieda and straightened, and if he'd been stiff before, now he was a board—no, a rock, braced forever against a stream, unyielding.

He took a few steps inside, and now she could see him more clearly. His uniform was blue, with a red collar and many buttons, and he wore it like a shield.

"*Frau* Klara," he said, his voice distant, official. "I am to take you to the authorities for questioning."

It was Frieda who responded. "Georg, what are you talking about?"

His eyes flicked to her, then back to Klara. "You are under suspicion of being a *Hexe*."

Somewhere, deep down, she'd feared this. When Hermann was alive, their success with the mill and the baking hadn't been unusual to the outside eye. But alone, and then with Frieda's help, she'd wondered if their success would be questioned in these lean and terrible times.

"I am not a *Hexe*, Georg," she said, her voice firm but laced with the affection she felt for him. "I am a woman trying to survive in these harsh times."

"Your mill's production is unusually high," Georg said. He lifted his chin. "And I believe I have seen you consort with demons."

The salamanders in the oven flames.

Klara closed her eyes, shook her head. "You accuse me of something you don't understand," she said. "And are you my sole accuser?"

An uncomfortable look crossed his face. "My regiment is in town," he said. "I asked for time to see my sister and, if necessary, ensure her safety. I said I would bring you in myself, and my success could mean advancement in the ranks."

"Georg, stop." Frieda stepped up to him again. "You're not making any sense. Why would you want to do this?"

His spiked leather helmet made him look taller than he was, but when Frieda faced him, Klara could see that they were the same height. She thought with a small smile that Frieda looked just as formidable as he.

"It's my duty," he said. "To protect. Rules must be followed."

"It's your duty as much as it is anyone's to protect your family," Frieda said. "Not just me; *Frau* Klara *saved* us, Georg. She's your family as much as I am. We've tried everything to find you, sent—" She broke off, bit her lip, glanced at Klara. Although Frieda had accepted and even rejoiced in her Elemental abilities, it was clear Georg's arrival had brought back memories of being beaten for even saying she saw creatures in the water.

And Klara didn't know what Georg would do if he learned about Frieda's magic. He'd no doubt locked away his childhood memories of seeing gnomes in the forest and Frieda seeing Water Elementals.

Frieda was right: You protect family above all else. She didn't need to be implicated. With Klara gone, Frieda could still run the mill, sell the flour.

Klara stepped forward. "I am not a *Hexe*," she repeated. "Elemental Magic is not witchcraft."

She opened the stove, welcomed a salamander, held it out, and tried to explain.

Her words fell on deaf ears. "Witchcraft," Georg repeated, and now he stepped forward, shifting the rifle tucked beneath his arm. Not drawing it up, but preparing to.

"Would a witch have taken you in and fed you after you stole her last loaf of bread?" Klara asked. "Or would a witch have fed you to the fire salamanders?"

"Stop it!" Frieda's voice rang clear and firm. "She's no more a *Hexe* than I am. Her communication with Fire Elementals is no different from mine with Water creatures or yours with Elementals from the Earth. You can pretend they're not real, but they are. Look."

She picked up the heavy marble bowl and brought it over to the kitchen table, its scarred wooden surface still covered with flour from the morning's baking. "Look," she said, pointing.

The little naiad rose cautiously, glancing from person to person.

Georg's jaw clenched. "I see nothing."

So Frieda grabbed his sleeve and marched him to the window, just as she'd pulled him around when they were children, Klara remembered, once they'd settled in with her. "Look there, then," Frieda said, pointing at the river.

The naiads and undines, hearing her silent call, leaped from the water, then fell and rolled like playful otters on the current.

"And there," Frieda said. On the mossy bank, an *Erdgeist*—a gnome—crouched, watching them.

"No," Georg said, but his voice had lost its assurance. "It's witchcraft. She's making me see these things . . ."

"But *I'm* showing them to you," Frieda said. "*I'm* calling the Water Elementals."

"She's making you see them, making you believe you have power," Georg said, clearly grasping at straws.

"No, Georg," Frieda said softly. "I saw them well before we came here. You remember . . . I know you do. And you saw the forest creatures—the little *Erdgeists*, the dryad who sang to you."

He shook his head, a sudden, almost desperate movement, and Klara saw the flash of young Georg in his eyes. The Georg who protected his sister however he could, who led her through the forest, who would have protected her from a witch if that was who Klara had turned out to be.

While they were at the window, she'd taken up the knife again, hidden it in her skirts. Her heart pounded; her mouth was dry as stale bread. She didn't want to hurt him. Didn't know if she had it within herself to hurt another human being. But if he decided Frieda was a witch, she'd defend Frieda, for Frieda was family.

She knew, though, that Frieda would never forgive her, because Georg was family, too.

But the erect military posture Georg had maintained up until now finally shifted; the stiff shell fell away.

"They made me believe . . ." he murmured. "I could believe it of Klara, but never of you. They're wrong, though, the soldiers, our stepmother . . ."

"If you'd stayed, Klara would have shown you what your abilities are, just as she did with me," Frieda said. "They're not wicked or evil."

He gathered her into his arms but still shook his head. "But what can we do? They're waiting for me in town. If I don't return soon, they'll come looking for me—for all of us. I can't protect you against an entire regiment."

With a rush of clarity, Klara knew the answer.

It was an answer she'd feared, but now, she knew, she had to release her fears. Frieda and Georg had been so much braver than she, and they'd done it for each other, because they were family.

As much as she felt rooted to the mill, she knew it wasn't the place that mattered, but the family within it.

"We'll go to America," she said. "We can pack our things and leave tonight. You can help us get through the forest and bypass the town, and we'll go to the city and find transportation there. There are so many people emigrating, we'll just be part of the crowd."

Frieda glanced at Georg, biting her lip, but she was the first to nod.

"It won't be easy," he said, "but you're right. I'll help you pack. We haven't got much time."

Klara turned, hands on her hips, and surveyed the mill house, pondering what to take. Nothing more than what they could carry, she knew. Her possessions, though, weren't the most important thing.

She had lost Hermann and Otto, but Frieda and Georg had given her a new family.

A new chance. An opportunity to live again.

They called America the land of opportunity.

Here, their abilities were feared. There, they might find acceptance.

She smiled. Surely some town there needed a baker whose bread tasted like magic, and her two talented children.

Secret Friends
Louisa Swann

San Francisco always made Nettie feel a little topsy-turvy. Nothing was as it should be. Canvas tents stood side by side with raw-looking buildings and grounded ships that had been turned into shops and hotels. Nettie preferred the mining camp outside where she lived with her adoptive Chinese family. In the mining camp, the gold miners had pitched tents. Ever since the gold rush had started a little over a year ago, it seemed that San Francisco couldn't decide whether to be a camp or a city.

Nettie sighed. There were more buildings than tents now, and the streets were busy with horses and wagons and people going about their business. The bay was filled with ships of all sizes—some bringing in new passengers and supplies, some readying for a return voyage, some abandoned at anchor when their crews took off for the gold fields. She was happy to see the roads were better than they had been; the muddiest places had been covered with wood planking. No more sinking up to her ankles in the slimy muck. But more buildings meant more places she had to search.

The midmorning fog was the same as it always had been, thick and damp and smelling of salty fish. Since it wasn't quite summer yet, there was a chance the fog would burn off later in the day, but Nettie wasn't counting on it. Sea lions barked somewhere out in the bay, and gulls squawked far overhead as horse-drawn wagons groaned up the hills.

She turned away from the world of fog and sea lions and stepped through the door of the dimly lit Palace of the White

Tigress. She sang quietly to herself, taking strength from her mother's old lullaby, the song she'd taught her brother Li when she first came to live with her adoptive family. *"In the woods not far away, secret friends come out to play . . ."*

The air inside smelled softly of herbs and incense, overshadowing the damp scent of the bay still clinging to her hair along with droplets of fog. She sighed. The lullaby always worked best when she and Li sang together. But her adoptive brother couldn't sing with her. He was missing, and no one seemed to care. That was why she was out in the streets, searching all the places she'd thought he could be. She'd finished looking in all the places she'd expected to find him yesterday. Now she was going from building to building, looking for someone, anyone, who'd seen her brother.

Nobody else, not even her adoptive mother, thought Li was in danger, although the doctor he was supposed to be visiting had died in a recent fire.

"Li is growing up," Mama Wu had said. "Do not worry yourself about him. He is trying to find his own way. He will return when he is ready."

That had always sounded so mysterious and unattainable— growing up. Nettie was growing up, too. She could feel it as her body rounded out in ways she did not particularly like. She'd been swimming and running every day since the weather warmed up, but the dresses she had made during the winter were already getting too tight. And she had let down her hems twice in the last two months.

Yes, they were both growing up, but that didn't mean her brother didn't need her anymore. Nettie raised her chin and moved farther into the high-ceilinged room, cautiously extending her senses.

She felt the man's dark shadow before she saw him—a huge man with deep, slanted eyes and a queue almost as long as his tunic. He stood behind a wooden counter, polishing small crystal glasses and setting them carefully on a shelf. Ignoring the sudden knot in her stomach, she carefully scanned the rest of the room. Crystal lamps of all sizes hung from the ceiling, smaller lamps around the outside of the room, and a large chandelier in the center. Silk paintings draped all four walls, and enormous painted vases stood in the corners. Round tables with chairs were scattered here and there. Other than the man behind the bar, the room was deserted.

Nettie didn't feel anything bad here, not like she'd felt at the first place she'd looked after leaving behind what Mama Wu called "the respectable part of town." That first place had smelled worse than sick blankets and dirty men and dead rats all mixed together. She'd barely gotten through the door when a hand had reached out of the darkness, clawing at her arm. A glimpse of cracked lips spread wide over blackened teeth and a whiff of putrid breath was all she'd needed to know Li wouldn't be in such a place. She'd stumbled out the door and run across the street into another building, her feet thumping on the wooden planks and her eyes burning so badly tears ran down her cheeks.

It had been the opium, or so the proprietor of the Spider's Den had told her. The man had helped her dry her streaming eyes without asking why a girl of twelve years was wandering the streets of San Francisco alone. Mr. Bell was a kindly old man who loved spiders so much he let them run free in his establishment. Nettie wished she had found her brother with Mr. Bell. It was the only place she'd felt at home in San Francisco. The old man was not only friends with the spiders, he had little furry manlike creatures he called monkeys and a talkative parrot. He even claimed to have a bear, though it was on loan to a group of traveling entertainers.

Nettie took another step into the Palace of the White Tigress. It even looked like a palace from the outside, with tall towers and fancy woodwork. Mr. Bell had told her this was a gentleman's establishment, though Nettie wasn't sure what he meant. He said he ran a gentleman's establishment, too, but his was an honest place.

Implying, perhaps, that the Palace of the White Tigress was not.

Nettie gathered her courage and walked over to the big man, putting her hands up on the counter she could barely see over. "Excuse me. I'm looking for Wu Li."

The big man tilted his head toward a broad stairway at the back of the room and grunted. Nettie dropped her hands from the counter and hurried to the stairs. She climbed the staircase carefully. A pain started deep in her chest, growing more intense with each step. It wasn't physical pain, Nettie knew that. She was worried that she wouldn't find Li waiting upstairs. And terrified that she would.

A long hall greeted her at the top of the stairway. She followed the ornate rug, quietly moving past a row of closed doors, that led to a room in one of the round towers she'd seen from outside. Thick red curtains draped gracefully along the sides of three enormous windows. The center of the room was taken up by a round table, its dark red surface polished to a shine that reflected the teacup-sized white flowers carefully arranged in a round red-and-white vase. Narrow shelves holding a variety of vases and figurines sat against the slender walls separating the windows. The scent of sandalwood incense was stronger up here, and Nettie stifled a sneeze.

A young man wearing an embroidered Chinese robe topped with a heavy leather vest stood in front of the center window facing her, hands tucked behind his back. The man's hair hung loose around his shoulders in a style she had never seen before. A woven band across his forehead held the hair back from his face, except for two thin sections allowed to drape over the band on either side of his forehead. The hair on top of his head had been gathered together, tied in a knot, then left to hang loose down his back with the rest of his hair.

Nettie peered at the man's face and swallowed hard, her throat suddenly dry. The hair and the clothes were different, but the face was definitely her brother's. "Li?"

"There is no one here by that name."

Li's eyes were always full of light and mischief. This man's eyes were as flat as his voice.

She moved closer, step by step, until the only thing standing between them was the polished wooden table. She squinted at the man, studying the way he stood, the way he held his chin. Then she grinned. It *was* her brother, playing another one of his silly tricks. "You idiot. I was so worried. No one knew where you'd gone." She started to walk around the table. "Mama Wu's worried, too, though she says she's not. She even made strawberry pie." Mama Wu always said Li would climb mountains and swim oceans for a piece of her strawberry pie. Nettie waited for her brother to break into an impish smile, but Li didn't move.

"I'm afraid you have me confused with someone else. Now leave before I have you thrown out."

Nettie stopped, her chest tightening as if all the webs in the Spider's Den had dropped down and wrapped themselves around her heart. She drew in a deep breath. Something was wrong—terribly wrong. "Mama Wu said you were studying with Doctor Low."

"Even if I were this 'Li,' I would never seek teaching from someone like Low." Li lifted his chin. "He is only an Earth Mage and not a very good one. The White Tigress"—he nodded at the woman who'd just entered the room—"is a great Fire Master. She can teach me things Doctor Low could only dream of."

"Doctor Low's store burned to the ground two nights ago," Nettie said quietly. "He couldn't get out. They found his body in the morning. The neighbors said you were gone, but I didn't know . . . I thought . . ." The words tied themselves into a knot in her throat.

The woman glided past her, moving around the table until she stood next to Li. "As you can see, my apprentice is just fine." Not much taller than Nettie, the woman had glittering, almond-shaped eyes like Mama Wu's, a beautifully round face, and shiny black hair piled on top of her head in a round bun stuck through with sharp-looking needles. A brilliant red comb with gold chains draped across her brow. Her dark red kimono shimmered in the dim light, and the comb seemed to writhe in her hair. She tapped Li on the arm with a folded red fan. "Aren't you going to introduce me to your little friend?"

"I do not have any friends." Li's face remained expressionless.

Nettie swallowed again. She watched Li watching her and cringed at the lack of warmth—of any emotion—in his eyes. Li had been excited every time he'd visited Doctor Low. Now he didn't seem to care that the doctor was dead. She took a deep breath. This wasn't the boy she'd grown up with, the boy who had held her when she woke crying in the night from unspeakable nightmares. The boy who had wiped blood from her knee when she had tripped over a log, too busy

talking to watch where she was going. The boy who had visited the woodland creatures with her, who sang the lullaby so
the creatures of the air and stream would come out and
play . . .

"If she's not a friend, then why is she here?" The Tigress's
smile didn't reach her eyes.

Fear crept up Nettie's back, all prickly and tingly, as if a
nest of baby mice had suddenly decided to clamber up into
her hair. She shrieked as something furry darted through the
doorway and ran straight at her, lips drawn back from its
teeth in an angry-looking snarl. It took her a moment to recognize the monkey she'd met earlier at the Spider's Den.
Why on earth had it followed her here?

"Get that beast out of here," the woman said, her voice so
cold Nettie shivered.

Nettie looked down in surprise as the monkey grabbed her
leg. The little creature gazed up at her, lips pursed. Then the
lips spread wide, baring sharp teeth, and the monkey grabbed
her hand, trying to pull her toward the door.

"I'm sorry," Nettie said. "He must've followed me." She
pulled back, trying to get her hand free.

The woman flicked long fingers tipped with vivid red
nails, and the flowers on the table in front of Nettie burst into
flame. The monkey screeched, dropped Nettie's hand, and
bolted back out the door.

Nettie froze. Part of her wanted to scream and run like the
monkey; the other part was fascinated. She stared as the
flowers shriveled in the flames and died. A tiny voice whispered in her mind. *Magic*.

Was that why Li was here? Because this woman could
teach him magic?

In the air, a sheet of flame the size of a window crackled
to life, sending Nettie back a step. Li stood beyond the flame,
one hand stretched out in front of him as if pushing her away.
The flame sputtered as he lowered his arm, then blazed to life
when he brought his arm back up. "I told you to go."

Nettie gazed at her brother as he repeated the motion. He
was the one making the flames. But what was he trying to
do—show her he'd finally learned some magic, or scare her
off?

Ever since his trip to San Francisco last fall, Li had wanted to learn magic. He'd come home with an armload of books he'd gotten from Doctor Low and had spent most of his spare time reading. He started putting names to the unusual creatures only Nettie and he could see, calling the air creatures sylphs and the water creatures nymphs. He'd been excited about what he was learning and claimed he could do strange new things, but throughout all that learning and doing, he'd stayed her brother. Whatever had happened to Li here in the Palace of the White Tigress had changed him. He had learned how to use magic. But at what cost?

"Was it you, Li?" she whispered, gesturing at the flames. "Did you set fire to Doctor Low's store?"

A puzzled look crossed Li's face, and the flames vanished from the air. He glanced at the Tigress, his eyes wide and uncertain. Smiling slightly, she patted his arm. The uncertainty disappeared, and the coldness was back. He glared at Nettie.

"Of course not, you little worm. Now begone." Li thrust his hand out, palm up. Nettie gasped as a ball of flame gathered between his fingers. He tossed the ball up and caught it again. With a quick flick of his wrist, he threw the ball at her.

Nettie leaped backward. The ball landed on the table, spilling across the wooden surface like a puddle of flaming water. She stared in horror as the puddle shrank in on itself, tighter and tighter until she found herself staring at what appeared to be a salamander made of fire. The salamander hissed, then slithered up into the air, weaving its way back to Li. The Tigress's dark eyes danced.

Her brother stepped to the edge of the table, his eyes blazing. "There is no one here named Li. Begone!" He thrust out his hand again.

Nettie backed up a step, then another. She couldn't leave him here, but she didn't know what else to do. "You remember our song, don't you?" she asked in desperation.

"*We* don't have a song," Li started, but Nettie didn't let him finish. She couldn't let him keep shutting her out. Somehow she had to get through.

"*In the woods not far away,*" Nettie sang.

Another fireball grew in his hand as Li's eyes narrowed.

Nettie felt sick. Her voice quavered, but she didn't stop singing. *"Secret friends come out to play . . ."*

He stared at her with a puzzled frown, the fireball slowly spinning.

"I remember when you first told me our special friends weren't spirits, they were nymphs and sylphs," Nettie said in a quiet voice, relieved that she'd finally gotten through to him. "When you told me you were going to learn magic . . ."

"I *am* learning magic," Li said, cutting her off. "Fire Magic . . ."

"Time for your little *friend* to leave," the White Tigress said. Her lips tilted in a slight smile. "Chung Lo will take care of her. Come." She took Li's arm and led him toward the door.

"In the woods not far away, secret friends come out to play . . ." Nettie sang again, her voice loud and strong.

The Tigress whipped around and flicked her fingernails. Nettie gasped and dropped to the floor behind the table as fire streamed over her head. One of the curtains behind her burst into flames.

"Stop!" Li spun around, his face pale.

Nettie cautiously stood back up, singing even louder. *"They make you laugh. They bring good cheer . . ."*

Li stared at her, his lips slowly moving in time with hers.

"They wipe away the blood and tears. So don't you worry, don't you cry. Your secret friends are still close by . . ."

Li closed his eyes, mouthing the words. His eyelashes glistened. Hope bloomed thick in Nettie's chest, so thick she could hardly breathe. She started to walk around the table, to go to her brother. She glanced up in time to see the Tigress flick her fingers again.

The table exploded as Nettie dove behind a group of shelves. She curled into a ball, arms over her face. Pieces of burning wood rained down around her. Pain seared across her bare forearm and then her cheek. She didn't move, afraid to look up as she started the next verse, pouring her heart into the words. This time she could hear Li singing along with her:

"Wind will carry you far and wide, warm your bones by
    Fire's side.

*Keep your feet upon the Earth, and dance with Rain in
    merry mirth.
And if you're still afraid, my dear, rest assured I will be
    near.
My love for you is strong and clear, just close your eyes
    and sleep, my dear . . ."*

Flames cackled like a bunch of old women as little fires
blazed throughout the room. Nettie slowly uncurled herself.
Li gazed around, looking like someone who'd just woken
from a strange dream.

"Time to say goodbye, apprentice," the Tigress said from
the doorway. "We sail in less than an hour." The look in the
woman's eyes made Nettie want to run and hide, but there
was no place left to go. The Tigress raised her hands.

"No!" Li's left hand rose, a massive fireball growing between his fingers. The air seemed to swim as he hurled the
fireball at the Tigress, surrounding her in violent flames. Nettie jumped to her feet, staring in amazement as the small
woman stepped through the flames.

"It is time someone taught you some manners, *apprentice.*"

Nettie never saw what sent Li flying across the room. One
minute he was standing still, the next he was sailing through
the air. He struck the far wall with a loud thump and lay un-
moving on his side.

"Li!" Flames raced across the floor, rising up before Nettie in a fiery wall.

"He is mine," the Tigress said above the crackling flames.
"If not in life, then in death. I will have his power either
way."

The curtain beside Li's head burst into flames.

"No!" Nettie cried. Fire licked at the hem of her dress as
she rushed the flames. She backed off, sobbing in frustration.
Her eyes burned with the intense heat. The skin on her face
tightened. Suddenly, the monkey was beside her again, yank-
ing on the skirt of her dress. Before she knew what was happening, he'd torn the skirt off, jumping up and down as he
tossed the burning cloth aside. Then he grabbed her hand and
yanked her toward the door. Another monkey joined the first.

Together they dragged Nettie toward the door. She stopped in the doorway. She had to get to Li . . .

She stumbled as someone shoved her aside. The big man from downstairs shouldered his way through the flames, snatched Li off the floor, and took the woman's hand. Nettie stared at the woman's impassive face, pale white through the wall of angry flames.

Then the Tigress smiled, and they were gone.

Somehow, Nettie found her way downstairs through the smoke. She stumbled outside, fell back against the wall, and drank in huge gulps of the damp air. The monkeys chittered and squawked, then grabbed her dress and pulled her away from the wall. She followed them blindly down the street, too tired and heartsick to fight. The monkeys finally stopped. Nettie stared down at the wooden planks for a moment, then lifted her head and looked around. It felt like she'd been inside all day, but from the way the fog was thinning, it was only about noon. She had to find Li, had to get him away . . .

"I was beginning to wonder if ya'd make it out."

Nettie's heart leaped into her throat. She stared at the post in front of her, a post that was only half wood. The rest was raven. The black bird was as tall as the monkeys and looked twice as mean. The raven shook his head, ruffling his shiny black feathers, then settling them back into place. "Looks like yer having trouble with the Fire Master."

"Where . . . ?" Nettie started. "How . . . ?" This day was getting stranger by the minute.

The raven clacked his beak. "Ya called me," it said. "With yer singin'. Same as ya called them two fiends." He pointed his beak at the monkeys.

But the monkeys can't talk, she thought, struggling to understand. She studied the raven's glistening feathers and finally nodded. She'd talked to Air and Water spirits before, why not a bird? "Can you help me?" Nettie asked. "My brother . . ."

"She's wantin' his magic." The raven turned his head sideways and peered at her closely with a glittering black eye. "Yer brother's in grave danger."

Nettie chewed her lip, trying to decide what to do. At the

far end of the building, a cart pulled onto the wood planks and rumbled down the street. Nettie stared at the huge man pulling the cart. Inside the cart sat a woman and a small man who looked like he was sleeping.

The Tigress.

"Stop!" Nettie ran after the cart, screeching as she tripped on an uneven plank. She fell, pain shooting through her ankle and knees.

The woman turned to look at Nettie. She held her gaze for a long moment. Then she smiled and said something to the man pulling the cart. The man broke into a jog, pulling the cart out of sight around the next corner.

"No!" Nettie stumbled to her feet and broke into a limping run. She raced around the corner and stopped, panting. The cart was nowhere in sight.

"They be heading for the pier." The raven swooped low in front of her, then rose into the air. "I'll keep watch. Get there as fast as ya can."

Nettie's thoughts raced faster than her feet. Why was the Tigress taking her brother to the pier? She ignored the stabbing pain in her ankle, dodging around a pair of horses pulling a wagon loaded with barrels. Her heart sank as she remembered the Tigress's words. A ship! The Tigress had said they had a ship to catch.

Nettie's stomach twisted. She couldn't let them get on that ship. If they did, Nettie would never see her brother again.

She put on a burst of speed, thankful that she had often raced Li through the woods, leaping over rocks and crossing streams on unsteady logs as they fought to see who could get home first and win the biggest slice of strawberry pie. Li could outrace her with strength and speed, but Nettie had accumulated a number of tricks that let her win every once in a while even with a twisted ankle. She used one of those tricks now, cutting down an alley too narrow for the cart and hoping to catch up to them on the other side. She had never run so fast. She dodged between people, under horses, and around barrels, finally feeling her feet hit sand.

She leaned over, trying to catch her breath. Her side hurt, her heart felt like it was going to jump right out of her chest, and pain stabbed through her ankle every time she shifted her

weight. She drew in a deep breath, trying not to choke on the
dead-fish stench permeating the air. The fog had lifted, revealing the long wooden pier stretching out into the azure
bay. Gulls cried overhead, and a pelican splashed into the
water close by.

Midday wasn't as busy as early morning at the wharf, but
there were still people coming and going along the pier, some
laughing, some cursing, some glowering at anyone close by.
Ships drifted lazily up and down on the waves, their masts
creaking as they swayed back and forth as if waving goodbye. Several ships were tied up to the pier while others sat at
anchor farther out in the bay.

The raven landed in front of her. "They've got him trussed
up like a goat. He's in the boat headed out to yon ship." He
pointed with his beak. Nettie squinted, trying to see what the
raven was pointing at. Finally, she spotted a small rowboat
pulling away from the pier.

"Kin ya row a boat?"

Nettie scowled and straightened up. "Of course I can row
a boat. At least, I think I can." The last time she'd actually
been in a rowboat had been when she was eight years old.
Here, in San Francisco.

The raven pointed again with his beak, indicating a second rowboat tied up to the pier. "Get yerself on board. I'll
take care of the rest."

"Why are you helping me?" Nettie suddenly asked. She
held her breath as the raven looked her over again, tilting his
head one way, then the other.

"I told ya. I heard ya callin'," he finally said. "Singin' that
song. Now get yerself gone. Time's a-wastin', and that ship'll
be on its way back ta China on the next tide."

No one paid attention to Nettie as she limped down the
pier and clambered down the splintery ladder to a small rowboat tied to the bottom rung. She clenched her teeth as a
wave rocked the boat, sending pain shooting through her ankle. She struggled with the coarse rope, tugging hard to get
the stubborn knot loose. Just when she thought she'd torn the
skin off her fingers, the knot pulled free. Quickly dropping
the rope into the bottom of the boat, she shoved hard against
the ladder, almost losing her balance as the boat drifted free.

She plopped down on the seat and glared at the oars propped high on the bow. It took both hands and all of her weight to lift each blade into position. By the time she had both oars in the water, the boat had drifted a good distance away from the pier.

Far ahead she could see the Tigress sitting in the bow of the other boat while the big man pulled on the oars. Li was nowhere in sight.

Nettie grabbed the oar handles. At first she could only manage one oar at a time, sending the boat spinning in circles. She concentrated on lowering both oar blades into the water at the same time, pulling both handles together, then shoving the handles down into her lap, raising the blades back out of the water. One stroke, two strokes—then one blade twisted sideways and slapped down, splashing water across her lap while the other blade dug deep into the foamy sea, sending the boat into another dizzying circle.

The White Tigress was already halfway to the ship.

Nettie gritted her teeth and pulled harder on the oars, managing to turn herself in another half circle. She gave a little gasp of despair. She had to catch the Tigress before the woman got Li onto the ship, or she'd never get her brother back.

The boat rocked ever so slightly, then began to turn. The sound of water slapping against the hull turned into a gentle gurgling and then a hiss as the boat moved faster and faster through the water. Nettie let go of the oars and rubbed her sore hands. The pain in her ankle and knees had dulled to a slow throb.

"Thank you," she said to the two nymphs guiding the boat. Her arms ached, and her hands felt like she'd washed a hundred pots of filthy miners' clothes. The boat moved swiftly between the ships and out into open water.

They were moving fast, but would they be fast enough to catch the Tigress?

Nettie scanned the horizon, looking for a sign of the huge raven, and saw nothing except a small black cloud drifting across the water. Panic bubbled deep in her stomach, a cold fear that threatened to turn her into a frozen statue. What if she did catch the Tigress? She was only a twelve-year-old girl. She had no weapons to fight with, no magic to wield against the woman's fire.

Canvas snapped, and shouts carried across the water. Nettie glanced up at the ship, startled to find it less than a pier's length away. Sailors clambered up the masts, rapidly lowering sails and tying off ropes.

No use getting caught unprepared. Nettie pulled off her boots. Then she slipped off her blackened petticoats. If she ended up in the water, at least she'd be able to swim.

Water slapped her face as her rowboat drew up alongside the Tigress's boat. The big man's oars prevented Nettie's vessel from getting too close, but she was near enough to see her brother crumpled at the Tigress's feet. Though the woman's expression stayed calm, her dark eyes burned like coal. Slowly she raised a hand, displaying the red-and-orange salamanders writhing up her arm.

Nettie's stomach churned, suddenly feeling like she'd just eaten a big batch of sour butter. She sang through gritted teeth as she lifted a heavy oar from its mounting and stood, legs spread wide to keep her balance in the rocking boat. She swung the oar back behind her, then whipped it forward. The blade burst into flame just before it slammed into the huge man's head.

Nettie sat down, startled that she'd actually hit something. A sylph materialized close by and pointed over Nettie's shoulder. Seagulls and crows and starlings of all shapes and sizes descended on the Tigress's boat in a thunderous cloud. The Tigress ignored the raking claws and stabbing beaks, hurling ball after ball of blazing fire into the sky. The air filled with the stench of burning feathers as birds fell by the dozens, their flaming bodies dropping into the water like burning cannonballs. Sylphs whipped through the air, trying to divert the fireballs. Nymphs swam through the sea, thrashing the water into huge waves that rocked both boats violently. The huge man rose to his feet, swinging one of his oars like a madman.

The raven dove into the midst of the battle, claws outstretched. His black feathers glittered as he grabbed the big man's collar, pulled him off balance, and let go. The boat shifted beneath the man's feet, and he tumbled into the sea.

The raven dove again, snagged the Tigress's hair, and dragged her toward the side of the boat. Nettie's heart leaped as the Tigress lost her balance and fell into the boat.

The raven's left wing exploded in fire. The huge bird screamed and disappeared, leaving the Tigress sprawled over the edge of her boat. The woman shoved herself to her feet, a snarl on her normally placid face. Face distorted in anger, the Tigress flung her fists into the air over and over. Fireballs lit up the sky, the rest of the birds dropped like rain, and the sylphs disappeared.

Nettie watched the destruction with a sinking heart. There was no one left to help. No one who could save Li from whatever horrible fate the Tigress had planned for him.

Except her.

Nettie dove into the water and swam toward the Tigress. Nymphs gathered close, swimming effortlessly beside her. The water darkened as she entered the boat's shadow.

"Lift me," Nettie cried as she kicked hard, driving her body up out of the water. Strong hands grabbed hold of her legs and waist as a pair of nymphs rose up beside her. Nettie caught sight of the Tigress's startled face, white in a tangle of black hair, and then she grabbed the edge of the boat and pulled.

The nymphs pulled with her.

The boat capsized, spewing its occupants into the sea. Water splashed into Nettie's nose and mouth. She coughed, then gasped for air as someone grabbed her bare ankle and dragged her down. Strong hands pulled her up even as she sank, nymphs struggling to help her back to the surface. But the force dragging her down was relentless.

Nettie forced her mouth to stay closed. She peered through the water at the hand clutching her ankle. A hand tipped with vibrant red nails. Black hair drifted through the water like lazy snakes around the Tigress's pale face. Nettie drew her other foot up and kicked. Over and over and over again, her heel connected with flesh. Finally, the grip on her ankle relented, and she shot for the surface, kicking hard. Her lungs screamed, and her vision started to darken. Nettie kept her jaw locked, refusing to take the watery breath that would surely be her last . . .

Hands grasped Nettie's elbow—friendly hands, helping hands—lifting her faster and faster. Her head broke the surface, and she inhaled a great, shuddering breath, looking wildly around for her brother. Fear rolled in her belly as the waves lifted and fell.

The water was littered with blackened birds, and her boat rocked gently a short swim away. There was no sign of the Tigress or her big man.

And no sign of Li.

A shadow flowed over the water as the raven circled awkwardly, compensating for his burned left wing. The bird dipped down until he almost landed on the water, then lifted heavily back into the air. Nettie swam toward the spot the raven had touched, refusing to think about what she might find. Her hand touched something cold and stringy, and she almost screamed before she realized she'd found her brother. A pair of nymphs held him faceup at the water's surface. The rowboat eased up beside them, and the next few moments blurred as the nymphs lifted the pair into the boat.

Nettie sat up, cradling Li's head in her lap. Tears streamed down her face as his eyes fluttered open. He coughed, then cleared his throat and gave her a crooked smile. She smiled back, feeling like her heart might explode from her chest.

Li coughed again. Then he struggled to sit up, giving her a weak glare. "What'd you do with my strawberry pie?" he asked.

Fire's Daughter
Elisabeth Waters

"Are you afraid of fire?"

"Not at all," Sophia Pearce replied calmly. This might seem to be an odd question for Lady Mary to ask the new governess to her twelve-year-old daughter, but Sophia knew more about Eleanora than her mother did. Despite being the daughter of a Water Magician, wife of a Fire Master, and mother of twins Albert, Water Master, and Eleanora, Fire Master, Lady Mary did not know that magic existed. Sophia, who was a Fire Magician herself, knew that it did. She had also been extensively briefed on Eleanora before being sent to take this post.

"I'm afraid that my daughter is less than enthusiastic about having a governess, and that her education has been sadly deficient. She has a lot to learn, and only five years before her presentation at court." Lady Mary frowned. "She needs a firm hand."

"I will do my very best to teach her everything she needs to know," Sophia said honestly. *But I have no intention of telling you everything I'm teaching her. Her most urgently needed lessons are things you wouldn't believe, let alone understand.*

Eleanora was summoned to the drawing room to meet her new governess. Her hair had escaped so thoroughly that it was impossible to tell what its style had been when she'd been dressed that morning. Her gown looked as if she had been climbing trees in it, or perhaps simply tried to destroy it; it also had grass stains, bloodstains, and a sleeve that was almost completely ripped off.

Lady Mary sighed. "Eleanora, this is Miss Pearce, your new governess. Please show her where the nursery is." She lay back on the fainting couch and closed her eyes, obviously wishing she could ignore both her daughter and the entire situation. Eleanora scowled at her, then turned and left the room. Sophia followed, somehow certain that they would not be heading for the nursery.

She was not surprised to find herself led to a maze in the middle of the garden. "Can anyone see or hear us here?" she asked.

"No," said Eleanora. "I can do whatever I want to here, and nobody can stop me." Her attempt to look menacing was quite good for a child her age.

The most important thing I need to do is gain her trust. I need her to work with me rather than against me. "Well, if you left my charred corpse here, it would provoke remark," Sophia said calmly, "but we will need private places to work. This is probably a good place to give this to you." She held out a letter. "Albert sent it with me; he didn't want your mother to see it."

Eleanora grabbed the letter from her twin brother as if it were a lifeline, broke the seal, and started to read it. After a few seconds, she gasped. "He's what?"

"A Water Master," Sophia said. "While he was spending all his time with your father and you, your powers apparently hid his." *Or, more likely, completely overwhelmed them. Two strong Fire Masters and one untrained Water Master . . .*

"So you know about me." Eleanora folded the letter carefully and slid it up her intact sleeve.

"Yes, El. I know you're a Fire Master. I know that your father, Sir Nicholas, raised you as a boy and taught you magic, and I know that you helped him in his medical practice. Father Pearce at Christ Church is my brother, and he's very concerned that, despite years of training, you lost control and burned four inches of candle all at once when all you were supposed to do was light it." Sophia smiled briefly. "The ladies of the altar guild are still arguing over who put out such obviously mismatched candles, but he doesn't feel it would help matters to tell them what really happened."

"They're a bunch of stupid old biddies," El said crossly.

"They're always nagging us so a boy can't even play a harmless practical joke. And Father Pearce said I could be one of them when I'm old enough!" Her expression was somewhere between disgusted and betrayed.

"He asked me to apologize to you for that," Sophia said. "He says you're the best acolyte he ever had, and he'd be delighted to have you back if he could be sure the Bishop wouldn't find out that you're female."

"But the Bishop doesn't know!" El protested.

"He would find out pretty soon, no matter what else happened. You're supposed to be confirmed next year, aren't you?"

"Yes, all the younger acolytes were studying for it. Does being a girl mean I can't even be *confirmed*?"

"Not at all, and I'll arrange for you to finish your studies here. The problem is that in order to be confirmed, you have to produce your baptismal records, and the Bishop would notice that Eleanora Victoria is not a boy's name if he were asked to confirm you with the rest of the acolytes. Do you know the words the Bishop uses when he confirms you?"

El shook her head.

" 'Defend, O Lord, this thy Child with thy heavenly grace, that he may continue thine for ever. . . .' In the case of a girl, he substitutes 'she' for 'he,' and many bishops insert your name after 'this thy Child'—I remember having to write mine in large print and hold the paper on the altar rail in front of me so the Bishop could read it."

"Does your brother have magic?" El demanded.

"Yes, he's a Water Magician—in fact, he's Albert's teacher. I'm a Fire Magician, which is why the old boys' club in London sent me here to continue your training."

"The White Lodge?" Apparently El had heard that nickname, too. "So you're not here to teach me embroidery?" she asked hopefully.

"I'm going to teach you enough needlework to keep your mother from asking what else I'm teaching you. It's camouflage, like a salamander hiding in the hearth fire. There are things we need to keep secret from your mother, and the easiest way to do that is to playact so that she thinks she's getting what she wants."

"I don't want to be a girl!" El said petulantly. "Why does Mother think it's so great to be a girl, anyway?"

"Because it's all she's ever known."

El frowned in thought. "You're saying that she's spent her entire life in a cage, so she never noticed the bars."

"Exactly."

"I do see the cage."

"I know. That's why I'm here."

When she found El at breakfast in the nursery the next morning, Sophia got a chance to see both what she had looked like when she was first dressed yesterday and what someone, probably her mother, considered suitable clothing for a female child staying at her grandfather's country estate. Granted, the grandfather in question was a duke, but even so . . .

El picked at her breakfast with the scowl that was becoming her habitual expression. "I can't eat in all this clothing. I can barely breathe."

"I believe you. Are you wearing a corset under that dress?"

"Of course she is," Nurse said indignantly, "but it's laced so loosely it could almost fall off. She has to learn to be a proper young lady!"

Sophia suppressed her first reaction, which was to say "Not right now, and maybe not ever." Instead, she smiled at Nurse and asked if she had been nurse to Lady Mary.

"That I was. She's a beautiful lady, but I'm sure we'll be able to make you just as beautiful, poppet," she said to El.

"I don't want to turn out like my mother!" El snarled. "She's pathetic! Did she really have her lower ribs removed?"

"Young ladies do not discuss things like that."

"I'm not a young lady; I'm an apprentice physician," El retorted, "and I know how harmful it is to remove ribs—and it's done for simple *vanity*! There's a reason she spent most of my life in a sanitarium in Switzerland. She doesn't have enough lung capacity to survive even a month in London. That's why Father sent her here."

From the look on Nurse's face, Sophia suspected there was more to it than that, but all that Nurse said was, "Don't worry, dearie. I'm sure she'll be well enough to be there when you make your curtsy to the Queen."

"Aaargh!" El flung her spoon into her porridge and ran from the room. Sophia quickly followed. As she went, she sent a mental message to the salamanders that tended to hang around her, asking them to lurk in the household fires—especially in the rooms where the servants were likely to gossip—and pass on to her what they heard.

She caught up with El by the lake. "*Nurse*," El said bitterly. "*Torturer* would be more like it."

"She means well," Sophia pointed out. "She just doesn't understand. At all." She looked out at the lake. "This is artificial, isn't it?"

"Yes," El said. "Grandfather had it built. It's odd; water should bother me, because it's my opposing Element, but this feels soothing. Maybe it's because it reminds me of Albert."

"Water doesn't bother me much, either," Sophia admitted. "Perhaps the fact that our brothers both have Water Magic either gives us an immunity to the galloping collywobbles most Fire Magicians get, or maybe we have some small amount of Water Magic as well. Do you know how to swim?"

El shook her head. "It's one thing to sit here and look at it, but I have no desire to trust my body to it."

"Fair enough," Sophia said, "but you will need to learn to ride if you're going to be living in the country, which means you'll need more practical clothing."

"Please!" El said with heartfelt sincerity. "Maybe we can get Grandfather on our side. Did you know he's a Water Magician?"

"The Masters in London told me," Sophia replied. "Is he likely to be any help to us?"

"What do you mean?"

"Who *really* runs this household?"

"What do you mean?"

"Who has the power to get things done or changed? Who can modify the official rules or help you slide around them? It's not always the Master or the Mistress; sometimes it's a key servant, like the butler or the housekeeper." *She thinks of herself as a physician.* "If this were a disease, what are your resources for fighting it?"

"I hear that Grandfather likes chess," El said thoughtfully. "Do you know how to play, and can you teach me?"

"Yes, yes, and that sounds like a good place to start. In the meantime, we'll work on mollifying your mother. Young ladies are supposed to know how to dance, play the pianoforte, sketch, do needlework, and speak French and Italian. Did you study languages other than Greek and Latin at school?"

"No. Father taught us German, because there are medical books in that language. We picked up some French and Italian, but . . ."

"You learned it from patients at the charity hospital?"

El nodded.

"We'll do a quick run through the textbooks and work on your accent. Both French and Italian have a lot in common with Latin, so you shouldn't have trouble with them. We might be able to persuade your mother to help with the accent; that way she'll feel she's contributing, and if she's been in Switzerland, she's probably been speaking either French or Italian for years."

"Don't they also speak German in Switzerland?"

"Very good. Yes, they do, but I don't see your mother as a German speaker. She may, however, understand some of it, so don't try to use it as a secret language. If you don't want most of the household to understand you, use Greek."

"Do you speak Greek?"

"Is my brother a priest?"

"Yes . . . Oh. You studied with your brother, too?"

"Not officially; I didn't get to go to school with him. But we studied together when he was home, and Papa was willing to teach me. He was the vicar in a small town north of Weymouth, and he was willing to teach me anything I could tie in with Bible studies: Latin, Greek, Hebrew, history, geography. . . . Mother made certain I learned all the ladylike accomplishments, so that I could either marry well or be a good governess. So far, I have not met a gentleman I wish to marry." Sophia stood up. "Let's go see what we can find in the way of language texts." As El fell into step beside her, Sophia added, "Instead of embroidery, I think I'll start you with needlepoint. It's not fussy, and it can be soothing; I know several men who do it for relaxation."

Over the next few weeks, El got better at pretending to be a young lady when her mother was around. Fortunately, this wasn't often. Lady Mary saw them for an hour at teatime, during which El wore the dresses her mother had picked out and either read French poetry to her or sat quietly and did needlepoint if Lady Mary had other company. Lady Mary was so impressed with the improvement in her daughter's behavior that she authorized Sophia to buy more clothing for Eleanora. Sophia, who favored the opinions of the emerging Rational Dress movement, got dresses that were much simpler and more comfortable and did not require a corset.

From the salamanders and from her own observations, Sophia was getting a better grasp of the household. The most shocking bit of information was that Lady Mary had not come home from Switzerland because she was cured. She had taken a lover there, and her father had promptly ordered her sent home to her husband, who had sent her back to her father. Word was that the Duke was furious with his daughter, but since he kept to his own rooms, Sophia didn't know this firsthand.

El's other lessons were going well, too. She had, after all, been a trained Fire Mage for several years now. What they were working on most was reestablishing the control that the complete disruption of El's life had shattered.

Unfortunately, there was no way to make El unlearn the things she had learned during the tenure of Sophia's predecessors. Neither Sophia nor El mourned the loss of the wooden paddle that had hung in the schoolroom for generations; that was, it hung there until it suddenly burst into flames when someone with a "firm hand" tried to use it on El. That governess had fled the house shrieking in terror, and she hadn't been the only one. Then there was the governess who had tried for a gentle approach, including stories about beautiful princesses rescued from dragons by handsome young knights.

Unlike that misguided lady, Sophia did not expect El to identify with the useless princess. Indeed, she considered it a sign of progress that El had not identified with the knight. But that left the dragon, considered by El to be misunderstood and beleaguered. Sophia consoled herself with the thought that El's newfound ability to breathe actual fire showed excellent control, and wondered if the departed governess would dare to tell anyone about this. She suspected not. Bedlam was an unpleasant place to reside.

On the surface, everything seemed to be going well, but Sophia knew better. She often found herself fingering the glass vial that she had worn around her neck ever since El's father had given it to her. She tried to prepare herself mentally for the crisis that was bound to come. She hoped she wouldn't need the dose in that vial, but if she did, it was going to be right at hand. And El seemed to be getting, well, twitchy. She was restless, her mood was erratic, and she was frequently downright snappish. Sophia knew what was coming but couldn't seem to find a way to discuss it with El. At least the girl knew how a woman's body functioned, and after years of assisting her father in surgery, she wasn't likely to have hysterics at the sight of blood.

Unfortunately, the morning El woke up and found her own blood on the sheets of her bed, she did have hysterics—not because she didn't know what was happening to her, but because she did. Sophia was nudged awake by an uneasy salamander who flashed her a series of images starting with El's awakening and ending with El's bed on fire. With El in it.

Grabbing her least-flammable dressing gown, Sophia belted it firmly over her nightgown as she ran toward El's bedroom. She ran past a group of hysterical housemaids and through the footmen throwing water on the bed in an unsuccessful attempt to extinguish the fire, reached into the flames to pull El out of bed, and poured the dose from the vial down her throat. El went limp. Sophia rolled her on the floor to extinguish the flames on her clothing while she used her own magic to make El's hair stop burning. With El unconscious, the footmen were able to put out the rest of the fire, although Sophia suspected that the bed was going to be a total loss. Certainly all the bedclothes were.

She supervised having El bathed, dressed in a clean nightgown, and put to bed on a cot in Sophia's room. Then she sent a salamander to El's father to tell him that she needed another dose for the vial. And she sent another one with an urgent message to her favorite doctor. She needed Dr. Sarah Clarke's help, for more than one reason.

The good news was that Lady Mary had taken to her bed in hysterics and been dosed with laudanum, and Nurse was looking after her. The possibly not good news was that the Duke "desired Miss Pearce to wait upon him at her earliest convenience." Sophia shed her charred dressing gown, bathed quickly, used magic to dry her hair, and dressed to look as proper as she could.

The butler led her to the Duke's rooms and turned her over to the valet, who conducted her to the Duke. He was seated in a wheeled chair, contemplating a chessboard, but his eyes were sharp when he looked her over. He pointed to a chair across the chessboard. "You, sit," he said. He looked across the room at his valet and added, "You, out." The man bowed and left the room, closing the door behind him.

"What happened?" the Duke barked at Sophia.

"May I speak plainly, Your Grace, or do you prefer lady-like circumlocutions?"

"I get enough of those from my daughter. Just tell me what's going on. How did my granddaughter's bed happen to catch on fire?"

Sophia sighed. "Oh, El did that."

"She deliberately set her own bed on fire while she was in it?"

Sophia nodded.

"In heaven's name, *why*?"

"She had just discovered she had become a woman, and she doesn't want to be one."

"So she tried to kill herself?" the Duke asked incredulously.

Sophia considered that possibility as well as the damage she had sensed inside El's body, then shook her head. "I don't believe she was thinking straight, but she appears to have been trying to give herself a hysterectomy." At his blank look, she added, "A surgical operation that removes a woman's womb."

"What? But that would ruin her chances of making a good marriage!"

"Why on earth would you think that she *wants* to make a good marriage—or any marriage at all? She's a person, and ever since her mother got home, she's been treated like breeding stock!"

"I know her father dressed her as a boy, but surely she knew she was a girl."

"No, she wasn't just *dressed* as a boy; she was *raised* as a boy. Tell me, Your Grace, do you like doing embroidery?"

"Of course not! I don't even know how—boys aren't taught it. It's for girls."

"Precisely. Eleanora doesn't know how to embroider, either, and she has no desire to learn. What your daughter is insisting upon is essentially forcing a twelve-year-old boy to become a girl—no, worse, a young lady. And while she has a girl's body, she has a boy's experiences. Boys are expected to grow up to be somebody, while girls are expected to marry and become an adjunct to their husbands. Your daughter is asking Eleanora to become less than she is *now*, and Eleanora knows it. This would be difficult for anyone, but for a Fire Master, it's a potentially fatal disaster."

"Particularly when she's just coming into her magic," the Duke said grimly.

Sophia looked at him in horror. "Didn't anyone from London contact you about this situation?"

"I'm afraid they've pretty much ignored me since my legs gave out and I retired to the country."

"Merciful heavens," Sophia breathed, almost in prayer. "The White Lodge trained me for this assignment and sent me here precisely because at least a few of them have enough imagination to predict something like this. El is not 'just coming into her magic.' El is a trained Fire Master; her father has been working with her, both magically and in his medical practice, for several years. She's stronger than I am and possibly stronger than you are. The old boys' club is furious with your son-in-law because they were planning to bring her into the lodge in the next few years. Now they can't—unless they decide to admit women. They sent me here to be her governess because they're terrified that she's losing control of her magic due to the major changes in her life."

The Duke's jaw tightened. "They sent an unstable *Fire Master* into my home and didn't do me the courtesy of informing me?"

"Possibly they thought you would notice as soon as you saw her."

"Haven't seen her yet. Raising a girl is her mother's job."

"In general, yes. In this particular case, I think Lady Mary is the worst possible person to have charge of El's life. For a start, she doesn't even know that magic exists. Her idea of raising her daughter is to dress her up like a doll—imagine a twelve-year-old boy forced to wear pink dresses with all the ruffles and frills that can be squeezed onto them, and you'll get some idea of how El feels about this. She is not happy, and an unhappy Fire Master is dangerous."

"So they sent you to teach her to control magic."

"To reestablish her control over it. It was under control until her mother came back to London, and things were going fairly well until this morning."

"Could Eleanora *really* burn out her own womb?"

"She certainly knows anatomy, and she has enough control of her body to breathe fire."

"She can do what?"

The explanation of the governess and the fairy tale produced the first laugh of the morning.

"So what do we do next?" the Duke asked. "Any suggestions?"

"Several," Sophia said. "First, you should know that I've sent for a woman doctor I know. Not only can she treat whatever El has done to herself, she will serve as an example that being female does not mean that you can't be a doctor, which *is* what El was being trained to do. Second, it would help if you could take an interest in her—as a *person*, not as a girl. She's been learning chess because she heard that you like it, and she's reached the point where she beats me every time."

"I believe I could take over her instruction in that field."

"Third, is there any way you could send Lady Mary back to Switzerland, preferably accompanied by her old nurse?

That woman is a tyrant, and they're trying to force El to be something I don't think she'll ever be."

"I am not sending Mary back to Switzerland. There are reasons for that . . ."

"She took a lover." Sophia looked at him steadily. "The servants talk."

"What did you do, put salamanders in all the fires?"

"And I'm sure you never had an undine hide in the water barrel."

The Duke raised a hand to acknowledge the hit. "What about the Dower House?" He shook his head. "No, too close. I'll look at my estates and find something small and isolated, and I'll send Nurse with her. I never liked that woman, but my wife thought she was a jewel."

"If what you want to produce is someone like Lady Mary, perhaps she is."

"I don't want another Mary. When Eleanora is well enough, bring her to me, and I'll teach her to play chess properly. You can go now."

Sophia rose, curtsied properly, and left. *A bit abrupt, but I think there's a good heart under the gruff exterior. It might serve. I pray it will.*

The drug Sir Nicholas had provided was strong enough to knock his daughter out until he could get there from London. Dr. Clarke arrived just before him, and the two doctors examined Eleanora and talked medicalese over her bed until Sir Nicholas declared there was nothing he could do for her and took Sophia's vial to refill it, leaving Sarah and Sophia to care for El.

"If she was trying to destroy her womanhood, she came pretty close to success," Sarah remarked. "It's sad that her family wounded her spirit so greatly."

"If you're lucky, you won't meet her mother," Sophia said grimly, "and His Grace relieved Nurse of her duties after our talk this morning. I think there's hope if he can come to appreciate El as she is, rather than trying to force her into the 'young lady' mold. She'll never fit. She's not going to be an ornament of their society."

"Of course not," Sarah smiled. "She's one of us." She

looked down at the unconscious girl on the bed. "I'll start the repairs and let her body finish them. She's young and strong; she should be fine. On the other hand, it might be the better part of valor to refrain from making any statement that would suggest she retains her ability to bear children. We'll tell her when she's old enough for it to be an issue, but perhaps it is best if her family does not regard her as a candidate for the marriage market."

"Discretion being the better part of valor." Sophia grinned at her friend. "I agree. Can you stay here until she wakes?"

"I'll stay. If she's going to be one of us, it's best that she start by seeing what we are."

"What we are," Sophia agreed, "and what she can become."

Picking Up the Pieces
Cedric Johnson

On an early autumn's evening, two girls held court on the wide back lawn of an old estate nestled deep in the heart of the Colorado Rockies. Their audience had come far and wide from the forest around them. Had there been any strangers around to watch, they would have said there had been no other sight like it.

The darker of the two, with red hair and ruddy, freckled skin, told the collection of rabbits, deer, and rodents grand tales of adventure that had been told to her. Her vibrant, energetic voice filled the clearing with tales of dragons and damsels, knights and wizards, and the woodland creatures hung on her every word.

The other girl, platinum haired with a smooth, milky complexion, cared for the animals while her sister entertained them. They sat perfectly still as she brushed out their fur and hand fed them spare vegetables from the garden. Occasionally she would join her sister in playing a part of the story being told, adding her gentle, melodic voice to the air.

Clara Wohltat strolled along the terrace of the estate's mansion, smiling with quiet pride as she watched her teenage girls at play. They were a true blessing to both her and her family, bringing life back to this ancient place.

It wasn't all that long ago that Clara and the entire estate had both been held prisoner in the earth itself. It was the untapped courage and unique talent of a down-on-his-luck magician that had set her free. There wasn't a day in the last fifteen years when Clara wasn't grateful for everything the magician Thaddeus Wohltat, now her husband, had done for her, her family, and the love they shared. That she had borne him two beautiful daughters was more than she had ever dreamed of giving in return.

Even though the girls were twins and had many of the same mannerisms, they were still very different. Garnet, with a spirit to match her fiery red hair, was headstrong and a bit rough around the edges. Pearl, as smooth and graceful as her namesake, was as calm and collected as her sibling was rambunctious. Garnet was fiercely loyal and protective of her sister, while Pearl was often the voice of reason whenever they wanted to try something new.

The other thing Pearl and Garnet shared was their family's affinity for magic. Almost as soon as they'd reached schooling age, Garnet had displayed a natural talent for spells for finding plants and coaxing them to grow—what Clara had called "kitchen magic," much to Garnet's distaste—while Pearl had an affinity for spells to sense, communicate, and build rapport with animals.

There was even talk from their great-uncles, Silas and Ephram, of giving them formal training through the family's White Lodge, but only if both of their parents approved—and then only once Pearl and Garnet had "left the girls they were behind and came as ladies."

But when you're a teenager of fourteen, becoming an adult seems a long, long way off, not to mention a very silly notion.

As if sensing her mother's eyes upon them, Pearl looked up and around. Spotting Clara, the girl placed a hand on her sister's shoulder as she pointed at their mother, and they both waved energetically at her. Clara's smile widened as she waved back, then beckoned the girls to her.

Reluctantly, the girls stood and bid farewell to their audience. The woodland creatures Pearl had called dispersed back into the woods as Garnet and she walked up to the mansion and their mother.

Garnet watched the lawn until the last of the animals had disappeared, then turned to Clara. "What is it, Mama?" she asked. "We were still having fun with our friends." Pearl nodded in agreement.

"I know you were, dear," Clara replied. "But the sun has almost set, and it's already chillier than you might think. Go and get yourselves cleaned up; supper will be ready soon. Your father will be done with his studies presently, and we shan't keep him waiting."

"Yes, Mama," Pearl and Garnet said together. They were disappointed that their day's fun was at an end, but just as pleased that there would soon be food to fill and warm them for the cold November night ahead.

Pearl gasped and bolted upright in bed. She clutched at her nightgown, the dream she'd woken from still fresh in her mind. Garnet and she had been running through the forest together toward a distant light. They had been running faster than the strongest wind, but the light never got any closer. Then suddenly, they had slammed into an unseen barrier, the shock of which had jarred her awake.

She lay there quietly for a minute, breathing deeply and calming her heartbeat. When all had returned to normal, she turned over onto her side to see if she had disturbed Garnet, only to discover that her sister had just turned over to check on her.

"I had the strangest dream," they both whispered at the same time.

The two girls quietly giggled at their synchronicity. Then Garnet said, "Could you close the curtains, please? I won't be able to get back to sleep otherwise."

Pearl blinked, then took a good look at her sister. She had put no thought into why she could see Garnet so clearly in the middle of the night. Now, she could see that the room was filled with pale white moonlight, brighter than any she'd ever seen.

"That's odd," she whispered. "The full moon isn't for another week."

Garnet nodded sleepily. Pulling back her covers, Pearl swung her feet to the floor. She stood up and turned, then gasped a second time, much louder than the first. Garnet lifted her head from her pillow to see what had startled her sister, then sprang upright with a gasp of her own.

The light filling the room wasn't coming from the moon

in the window. At the foot of their beds stood a young man not much older than Pearl and Garnet. He was barefoot, dressed all in white, and radiated the pale light. He looked at the girls and smiled, his expression sad yet reassuring.

The glowing figure silently walked over to the balcony door, stepped through it like a phantom, and vanished from sight, taking the light with him. Without a moment's hesitation, Garnet leaped from her bed and ran to the balcony door, throwing it open and going out with Pearl right behind her.

There was no sign of the man. Garnet stepped to the railing while Pearl stayed closer to the doorway, both girls shivering in the freezing night air. Their breath hung in clouds around them as Garnet looked everywhere for any evidence of their visitor.

Pearl was ready to suggest they head back to bed and forget the whole thing when Garnet took her arm and pointed at the back lawn. Pearl rubbed the sleep from her eyes and peered down. Near the edge of the lawn where they had entertained their woodland friends earlier that day was a magnificent stag glowing with the same light that had filled their bedroom. He gazed back up at them. A minute passed in silence. Then the stag turned and walked toward the trees. He paused, looked back up at the girls, flicked his ears, and trotted off into the woods.

Garnet raced back inside and was at the door to the hallway by the time Pearl has closed the balcony door. "What do you think you're doing?" Pearl demanded.

"What does it look like I'm doing?" countered Garnet.

Pearl frowned and shook her head. "We'll be punished for this for sure. That could have been anyone—or any*thing*. And you're just going to accept an invitation in the middle of the night?"

Garnet sighed impatiently. "Are you coming or not?"

Pearl simply shook her head again and followed her sister out of the house, stopping only to grab overcoats to throw over their nightgowns. "We need to get shoes," she whispered, gazing out toward the woods.

Garnet squatted down. "No time for that. But I know a spell that will make the ground soft under our feet. It will be like walking over a blanket." She traced a pattern on each of her feet while muttering the words to the spell, then repeated the ritual on Pearl.

As soon as she was done, Garnet took off across the lawn as fast as her legs would take her. Pearl kept up without a problem, and soon they reached the edge of the woods. They stopped to look around, and Pearl spotted their mysterious creature. He had stopped several yards into the woods and, once seen, made the same beckoning gesture and took off running.

The girls gave chase without a second thought. Garnet's spell held true as they ran, and the exertion drove the chill from their bodies. Garnet even found the breath for an occasional giggle as the stag darted around trees with natural grace. It was a struggle to keep up, but they managed. This was the fastest they had ever run, and the longest.

Just as the girls' stamina was waning, the radiant stag put on a sudden burst of speed, then vanished a few moments later. Pearl and Garnet reached the spot where he had sped up, and with a fearful gasp they skidded to an abrupt halt and clung to each other to keep from falling off the sheer cliff at their feet.

The sisters stared out over the cliff and into the small mountain valley below. There was no sign of the strange visitor. No light shone but the moon, no sounds came from the forest below, nor were there even any footprints but their own.

They stood there for a moment, hoping for a sign that they hadn't imagined the whole thing. Then Pearl silently took Garnet's hand and turned around toward the estate. Garnet accompanied her without protest.

"One of the servants said he saw the two of you head out into the forest last night," their mother said over breakfast. "Is this true?"

Garnet fidgeted with her meal, not looking at either of her parents. Pearl, as usual, spoke up and told of their witching hour adventure, hesitant but not leaving out any truths. When she was finished, she looked up. To her shock, Clara and Thaddeus were sitting stock-still, paying very close attention to her every word.

"And you're sure of this?" asked Thaddeus. Pearl and Garnet both nodded.

Already pale from Pearl's recounting, Clara looked to be on the verge of tears as she gripped her husband's hand. Thaddeus squeezed back before rising and kissing his wife's forehead. Turning to his daughters, he said, "Come to my study when you've finished eating."

He gave no explanation as he departed, and the girls asked for none. Pearl and Garnet had learned quite early on that if something was important enough, they would be told everything in the fullness of time. With that in mind, the girls finished their breakfast, hugged their still-shaken mother, and went to present themselves before their father.

Thaddeus removed a small object from an ornate box on his desk and clutched it tightly as he crossed the room and sat down near the side table. He then bade the girls sit on the divan opposite.

"I'll make this as simple as I can," Thaddeus said. "Not because I think you wouldn't understand, but because there is much that even I don't understand. This spirit you saw is very important to this family. He was your mother's brother. The valley that he led you to was the very same one where I rescued your mother. I daresay that without him, you two would not be sitting here. I wouldn't have broken the curse on your mother and this estate had it not been for his guidance . . . and sacrifice."

Garnet politely spoke up. "You've told us the story many times, Papa. But why would this spirit show up to us now, after all this time, and not to you or Mama?"

Thaddeus shook his head. "I don't know, my little gem. But one thing I've learned from your uncle is to never question the magic that comes your way, because it does so for a reason. I can say this with absolute confidence, though: since the spirit came to the two of you, there may soon be a reason for you to have this."

The Master held out his hand and opened his fist, revealing the pendant he'd been clasping. Pearl and Garnet marveled at the delicately carved crystal bull figurine, its polished facets catching and dispersing the faint light coming through the closed curtains.

"What is it, Papa?" asked Pearl.

Thaddeus leaned over and held the pendant between his daughters, who gazed at it in awe. "It is a focus that belonged to a powerful Earth Master," he explained. "Merely decorative by itself, but in the hands of a skilled Magician, it helps magnify their magic many times over. It is not to be treated lightly, but I trust you two to use it wisely—though I hope you'll not have to use it at all."

Both girls were enraptured by the crystal pendant, but it was Pearl who reached out for it and let it fall into her hand. Normally Garnet would have reminded Pearl that she was the older of the two "by a whole minute," and appoint herself caretaker of their newly shared trinket. This time, however, she made no such protest, and in fact seemed content to see the pendant in her sister's hands.

Thaddeus got up and hugged both his daughters, then placed a hand on each of their shoulders. "Guard it with your lives, dear ones," he said, looking each one in the eye. "It may very well be what guides yours in the days to come."

Before the sun had reached high noon, the clouds had swallowed it, and snow began to fall, the first of the season. It fell quickly and deeply, and within an hour all traces of color save the trunks of trees had disappeared. Not wanting to disturb their parents any further, Pearl and Garnet bundled themselves up against the cold and headed outside.

Pearl loved this time while the snow was still falling. She delighted in the feel of the flakes on her face and how it gathered in her hair and on her clothes. Garnet didn't care about such things. She much preferred running around and playing in the snow to the sensation of it spilling down.

Soon the sisters were in the woods. The high winds and autumn rain had cleared much of the foliage, letting the snow descend unhindered to blanket the forest floor. Once well inside the trees, Garnet stopped playing around and began collecting plants and herbs that wouldn't survive long past the first snow. Pearl stayed close by, whistling different bird songs and listening for replies.

Suddenly, there was a loud *snap* nearby. Garnet stood up quickly and took her sister's hand, standing motionless while they both looked toward where the sound had come from, ready to run back home at a moment's notice.

For a minute, there was only the slight rustling of branches overhead and the occasional bird call. Then, as Pearl and Garnet were about to dismiss it as a branch breaking under the weight of the snow, there was another *snap* ahead of them. A large mound of snow shifted to one side, sending an avalanche of flakes tumbling to the ground.

What the girls had dismissed as a large, snow-covered rock was actually a black bear. It lifted its head and looked straight at them, sniffing the air. Garnet went even more rigid, gripping her sister's hand tightly. They'd both heard stories of prospectors being mauled and killed by bears, and knew better than to startle one with any sudden movements.

After what seemed like an eternity passing, during which the girls and the bear just watched each other, the bear slowly got to its feet and shuffled toward them. The snow was thick on its hide and clung fast, so it must have lain there for some time. Pearl blinked and tilted her head to one side, then took a cautious step forward.

"What are you doing?" Garnet whispered through clenched teeth, keeping tight hold of her sister's hand.

Pearl kept her eyes on the bear as she took another step forward. "I think it's sick, Garnet," she whispered. "It would have found shelter from the snow otherwise."

Garnet squeezed Pearl's hand even tighter and said, "You can't know that! Leave it be, and maybe it'll leave us alone."

Pearl shook her head. "It would have attacked us by now," she said confidently. "I have to try."

Garnet started to ask, "Try what?" when Pearl began tracing a pattern in the air and muttering under her breath. Garnet let her go, and Pearl inched her way forward as she cast her spell, never taking her eyes off the bear.

Pearl stopped and released the rapport spell. There was no way of telling if it had worked. She'd never done it on such a large or aggressive animal before. Leaving her hand outstretched and palm open, she very carefully took another step forward.

The bear sniffed Pearl's hand, now mere inches from its nose, and huffed, then looked up at her. Reaching forward just a little bit more, she slowly put her hand on top of the bear's head. The bear huffed again, but made no move to free itself from the girl's touch.

Garnet sighed with relief. "I wasn't sure that was going to work," she said.

"Neither was I," Pearl agreed, rubbing the bear's head like she would a large dog. "But I can feel it now—he likes us."

Garnet's eyes widened in realization. "Maybe it was the focus!"

Pearl looked down and raised her hand to her chest, where the focus hung on a cord around her neck. "I'd forgotten all about it! You might be right."

Garnet put aside the rest of her caution and approached the bear, likewise rubbing its head. "Do you really think he's sick?" she asked.

"I don't know for sure," Pearl answered. "But for any creature to not take shelter in this kind of weather is very strange." She looked at her sister. "What do you think we should do?"

Garnet thought for a moment and brightened with an idea. "We could use the stable master's house. He's gone for the winter, so maybe we could keep the bear inside for the night. Just until the snow stops; then we can help him find some more suitable shelter."

"I don't know . . .," Pearl said. "Mama and Papa would have a fit. Nursing rabbits and birds is one thing. But a bear?"

Garnet smiled at her sister. "They trust in your magic, Pearl, and so do I. And it's not like we're asking to keep him. It'll be overnight at the most."

Pearl nodded, and the girls led the bear back to the estate, clearing off what snow they could from its fur. The sisters laughed and chatted merrily as they arrived home, and that was what kept Clara from panicking at the sight of the bear.

Pearl, calm and rational as usual, explained their plan. Clara hesitated at first, but finally agreed. "Be extra sure you keep the spell from fading," she admonished. "If he so much as growls at you, go fetch your father straightaway to take care of it."

The girls agreed and took the bear to the stable master's house. It was at the far end of the stables, which were now empty of all but horses for the four of them. Pearl was ready with another spell to calm them, which proved unnecessary.

The door was a tight squeeze for the bear, but Pearl coaxed it through. Once inside, Garnet started a fire in the hearth while Pearl strengthened her spell and explained to the bear that this wasn't permanent, and he would need to find his own place for winter once the snow stopped.

Garnet found a pair of brooms, and the girls brushed the rest of the snow from the bear's fur. He took great delight in this, playfully rolling on his sides and batting at the brooms. Pearl and Garnet were soon laughing and playing with their newfound friend, staying with him until called to supper.

The snow was still gently falling when they returned to the stable master's house, and with night upon them, Pearl convinced their parents to let the bear stay in the empty stables overnight. She fed it some hard nuts from the larder and fresh buffalo berries, while Garnet stoked the hearth.

The girls played some more with the bear, and in their growing attachment talked about how they might be able to keep it around, if not as a resident of the stable, then perhaps somewhere close by where they could visit when the bear wasn't hibernating. Pearl spoke of how she could maintain the rapport spell, maybe even give it some permanence.

It was while Pearl was working out how she might go about such a task that the bear got up and headed toward the door, huffing at the door handle and looking back at the girls. Pearl got up and opened the door to let it do its business.

Once through the door, the bear turn around and gently nuzzled Pearl, looking up into her eyes and huffing again. Pearl understood immediately why.

"You don't have to leave," she said. "You can stay the night here."

The bear looked up at Pearl, then out toward the dark trees, and nuzzled her hand again. Pearl fell to her knees and wrapped her arms tightly around its neck. Garnet walked over and joined her sister in the hug.

The girls stood up and watched the bear as he trundled off into the trees. The cloudy night sky made the bear almost impossible to see after only a few yards. Pearl lay a hand over the focus hanging around her neck and gazed off along the bear's path with longing. With no warning, she started to dash toward the woods, only to be stopped by Garnet grabbing her hand.

"Now who's being the foolish one?" Garnet asked. "The sun is long gone, and you'd just get us lost out there."

Pearl tugged against her sister's grip. "Let go, please!" she pleaded. "He clearly wants us to follow him. This is just like Papa's story, I just know it."

"This is nothing like his story," replied Garnet, holding fast to her sister. "He was carried by the stag, not led. And the stag was what Mama's brother was cursed into being. Why would he come to us as both a stag and a bear?"

She put her other hand on Pearl's shoulder. "Besides, there's no light to guide us this time. All I'm saying is that perhaps we shouldn't be so eager to make Papa's prophecy this morning into a reality."

Pearl looked back at her sister with sadness. "But I can't just let him go, Garnet. I . . . felt something. Something different than the spirit last night. Something stronger than just my usual spell of kinship. What if something happens to him? What if . . ." Pearl's lip quivered. "What if we never see him again?"

Garnet lightly rapped Pearl's forehead with her knuckles. "Don't be silly. He'll be fine; he's a *bear*. Besides, he's much too clever to fall prey to any hunter."

Garnet could tell that her words were of little comfort. "Tell you what," she said, "let's sleep upon it. If you still feel the same way tomorrow, we'll go out and see if we can find any sign of our friend."

Pearl smiled wistfully at the word "friend" and looked back out into the woods. After a few moments with no sound but the wind rustling from the trees, she sighed softly and nodded. Garnet smiled back and released her wrist. This time, she led them back.

The next day dawned bright and clear. The first thing Pearl did was run out onto their balcony and search as far as she could see for any sign of the black bear. The tracks leading from the stable master's house to the woods had all but vanished in the late night snowfall, and there were no fresh disturbances anywhere to be seen.

"I still want to go look for him," Pearl said to Garnet when she stepped out onto the balcony.

Garnet nodded and said, "Yes, I feel the same way. Come on, let's get a good hot meal in us. I know what we can tell Mama and Papa."

After they finished breakfast, Garnet explained that Pearl and she wished to go out into the woods to find more herbs and roots to see them through the winter, and also to check on the animals and make sure they had found adequate shelter. It wasn't an outright lie, but it was a stretching of the truth that Pearl wasn't very comfortable with.

Eager to encourage responsible use of their Earth Magic, and satisfied with how the girls had handled themselves the day before, both Thaddeus and Clara gave their blessing. Pearl and Garnet hugged their parents, dressed for the cold, and headed out with a promise to be back before dark.

The bear's tracks were just as obscured in the woods. Soon they disappeared altogether, leaving the girls to ponder their next move. Garnet suggested they head toward where they'd first found the bear. Pearl agreed, and after casting a spell to alert her of any nearby animals, they set off.

Most of the morning had passed when the girls realized they had gone much farther than where they had originally found the bear. There was no signs that any large animal had been this way, nor did Pearl's spell tell her of any nearby. There were no familiar landmarks around them, either. If not for the footprints they had left behind, Pearl and Garnet would have been lost.

"What should we do now?" asked Pearl, looking all around her.

Garnet reached into her coat pocket and pulled out a bundled kerchief. "I say we have some lunch, then keep going in the same direction. We still have a couple hours before we need to head back."

Pearl nodded, and the girls ate the crackers and dried fruit, washing them down with mouthfuls of snow and chatting about what they might do with a bear as a companion.

"I'd want to take him out into the woods with me," Garnet

said, "and together we'd keep the woods safe from poachers and prospectors that would want to tear all the trees down."

"I would be happy just to have him by the fire on cold nights," said Pearl.

With lunch in their bellies, the girls brushed the snow off their coats and continued on. After walking for a good while, the trees thinned out, and they found themselves in a small clearing. Much to their surprise, they discovered they weren't alone.

In the middle of the clearing was a small camp. The snow was freshly trampled around a fire ring and in front of a tiny tent. They could hear someone on the far side of the clearing, lying on the ground and cursing loudly.

Together the girls slowly walked close enough to get a look. It was a scruffy old man with a few wispy hairs on his head and the longest beard they'd ever seen, both as white as the snow around him. His leg was trapped under a fallen tree trunk.

"Are you all right?" Garnet asked when the old man stopped to catch his breath.

The man twisted around, grabbing the rifle that lay next to him and pointing it at them. Pearl and Garnet both shrieked and leaped back, but the old man held his fire. "Do I look all right to you, you silly goose?" he snapped.

Garnet cautiously took a step forward. "What happened?"

The old man groaned in exasperation. "What does it look like happened, girl? I was hunting a bite to eat, and this dead tree decides to fall on me and pin me here. Now I'm stuck, and I ain't got no food. So unless you plan on helping with the former, get lost!"

Despite the man's cross demeanor, Pearl and Garnet took pity on him and came over to see if they could help. The fallen tree trunk looked very heavy, and the girls weren't sure if they could even manage moving it. They both knew spells that might be able to help in the task, but it was out of the question. The first thing that everyone in their family had ingrained into them was to never use or even talk about magic in front of strangers. Neither of the sisters wanted to find out what would happen if they disobeyed that rule.

Putting their backs into it, the girls managed to roll the

trunk over enough for the old man to wriggle free. He got to his feet, grumbling and brushing himself off. The girls held back their amusement at finding that even if he wasn't hunched over, he was still shorter than either of them.

"I got no reward for you," the old man growled. "So you two run off back to wherever you came from and leave me to—"

The old man stopped and glared. Before either sister could ask what was wrong, he raised his rifle straight at Pearl.

"Where did you get that?" he growled at the terrified girl. When all he got in reply was a whimper, he added, "The focus! That belongs to my Master. Where is he? Where is Master Marco?"

Garnet stepped in front of Pearl, shaking slightly. "You leave her alone!"

The old man fired a shot at the ground near their feet, worked the lever of the rifle, and aimed at the girls again, "Doesn't matter," he said. "I'll take it back, and once I have my prize, Master Marco will be doubly pleased."

Garnet snarled at the old man but didn't move for fear of being shot. Quivering with fear, Pearl clutched the crystal focus and muttered quickly under her breath. When the old man grabbed her wrist, she screamed.

"There's no one out here to help you, girl," said the old man. "So quit that racket!"

Pearl did as she was told, but couldn't help whimpering with the rifle in her face. Garnet clung to her sister, as much out of fear as support. "Please, just let us go," she begged. "You can have the amulet."

The old man shook his head. "No, I'm not worthy to hold Master Marco's focus. I can only work in his name. But you two . . ." He gave them a toothy grin that had more than a few gaps in it. "You would make a fine addition to his empire. I've got prey to hunt, and you're coming with me to find it, even if it takes us to California."

The sisters dared a glance at each other. If everything the man said was true, then his master had been dead for fifteen years. He must have been crazy if he thought there was still an "empire" after all this time.

Keeping the rifle trained on the girls, the old man bent

down to pick up his rucksack. While his gaze was averted, Pearl clutched the focus and quickly whispered the words to the calling spell.

The old man snapped his head up. "What was that you just did? Answer me!"

"N-nothing," Pearl stammered, dropping her hands. "Just a prayer."

The old man snarled. "You lie, girl. I'm old, but I'm not stupid. I've served Master Marco for many years, longer than there's been a state of Colorado. I may not know any magic for myself, but I know the ways of it. So I'll tell you one last time, tell me what spell you've made, or I'll break it by ending you right where you stand!"

Garnet spoke up quickly for her sister. "It was for protection! It would make our skin hard as stone if you tried to shoot us."

The old man squinted at Garnet and scowled. "I'm not going to shoot you, girl. Not yet, anyhow. You're much too valuable. But that doesn't mean I won't reappraise that value if I have to. Now help me break this camp. We've got a lot of walking to do before sundown."

The girls did as they were told without another word. When they had packed up the tent and cooking gear, they were a bit relieved that their captor didn't make them carry any of it. The old man simply told them to start heading west and kept behind them with the rifle ready.

By the time the sun hit the horizon, Pearl and Garnet were numb from the cold and exhausted. They hadn't spoken a word the entire time for fear of angering the old man, making do with holding each other's hand for support. The old man hadn't spoken to them, either, just mumbled to himself.

The old man finally stopped and spoke. "We camp here for tonight. Now how about you work a little magic to get us some meat for dinner?"

Pearl paled and shuddered in revulsion. To ask her to do such a thing was cruel. "I don't know any spells like that, sir," she lied. "But my sister can find us some edible plants."

The old man made a face. "Fine. But don't go where I can't see you. You run, I shoot."

The girls were more than happy to get some distance be-

tween them, even for a little bit. Garnet made herself busy
scrounging around for whatever she could find, while Pearl
kept an eye on the old man making camp and peered off into
the gathering darkness.

"No sign of any help?" whispered Garnet.

Pearl shook her head. "Not that I can see," she whispered
back. "My bear can't have gotten that far. I called for him
specifically."

Garnet smiled at "my bear" but kept the amusement to
herself. "Try casting the spell one more time, just to be sure.
Just say it was to help me, if *he* asks."

Pearl nodded and clutched at the focus, pushing everything out of her mind but the bear as she cast the calling spell.
With the spell away, the girls returned to the camp with a
bucketful of roots and leaves. The old man grumbled about
the lack of meat, but quieted down once Garnet got a stew
going.

After their meal, the sisters sat quietly by the fire while
the old man spun grand tales of Master Marco: the vastness
of his empire, its wealth in gems and gold, and the feats of
magic he had performed. Despite their family's modest
wealth and magical ability, Pearl and Garnet had been raised
to be grateful for what they had and were rather unimpressed
with his stories.

"All right, into the tent with you," the old man finally said.
"We've a long day of walking ahead of us."

As the girls stood up, there was a loud crash of breaking
wood off in the darkness. The old man sprang to his feet,
aiming his rifle out toward the sound, while the girls clung to
each other and edged to the far side of the fire.

There was another crash, closer this time, and the old man
shouted, "You stop right there or I'll shoot!"

A furious roar echoed through the trees. A large black
bear came crashing through the trees, bearing down on the
old man. He raised his rifle. Garnet cried out and lunged,
ruining his aim, but not before he could get a shot off. The
bullet grazed the bear's shoulder but didn't slow him down.

With another roar, the bear swiped at the old man and sent
him flying. The old man hit the ground without a sound. The
bear stumbled back a step, looked at Pearl, and slumped to

the ground. Pearl immediately ran over and put her arms
around him.

"You brave, silly thing," said Pearl, a tear rolling down her
cheek. "Please be all right . . ."

A muted glow surrounded the bear, and to the girls' shock,
it began to shrink and take the form of a man, just like in their
father's story. The glow subsided, and the man sat up on his
knees, taking Pearl's hand and smiling. "I am now, thanks to
the both of you."

Before either sister could find her voice, a man on a horse
came through the trees where the bear had crashed through.
He dismounted and walked toward the trio. To the girls' relief, his was a familiar face.

"Uncle Silas!" the girls cried, running to him and hugging
him tightly. "How did you find us?" asked Garnet.

Silas nodded at the young man. "You can thank him for
that. Three nights ago I felt a strong surge of magic around
here, all the way from St. Elmo. I headed out this way to investigate when I came upon your bear here. I sensed the
magic on him, different from the first. He led me this way,
where I found you two. Now, what are *you* doing out here?"

"Rescuing me," the young man answered, extending his
hand to Silas. "Bernhard Furst is my name."

Silas took his hand. "I know your family. From Utah,
yes?"

Bernhard nodded. "We were, until Marco came along. His
lust for power drove him to claim our family's land and be-
spell us. We were cursed to wander as wild animals. I made
my way here in search of your family, hoping you could help.
Turns out I was right in a way."

Bernard turned to Pearl and took her hand. "Radiant Pearl,
you and Garnet have done us all proud. Your compassion and
strength were a balm to me. I owe you much. Pearl, with your
family's blessing and when you are of age, could I have the
honor of your hand in marriage?"

Pearl blushed deeply, struck dumb and only able to smile
and nod. Jealous of her sister for the first time, Garnet made
a face.

Bernhard grinned at Garnet. "I haven't forgotten about
you, brave Garnet. You are indeed the staff to your sister's

shield. Marco was very powerful in this part of the world, and much of his influence still lingers. I would send my brother to you, to help protect these mountains. I think you would be well suited for each other."

Garnet brightened up at this. "I'd like that," she answered, then hugged her sister in joy at their shared luck.

Bernhard grinned and turned to Silas. "What say you, sir?"

Silas tipped his hat back and said, "It would be an honor to join our families, young man. I'm not their parents, but I don't think they will object."

He looked at the girls and smiled. "So, I'd say that these two little gems have found their fittings. With a little polish, they'll outshine us all."

The Price of Family
Jennifer Brozek

The smell of the cooling pasty in the cold morning air was too much to resist. It'd been two days since Josie had last eaten. Stowing away on a train to Carson City hadn't come with any benefits except for getting away from Salt Lake City. From what little she had seen of the place so far, it was worthy of its title as the capital of the Utah Territory. Not surprising—not with all of the gold and silver miners looking for a claim at the Comstock Lode.

Josie had spent last night in a burned-out shell of a farmhouse. It had been better than nothing, but not by much. There'd been no food. Not even wild grain to scrounge. It had been a bad fire. Her walk in search of something—*anything*—to eat took her from the dead farmhouse into Carson City proper. The town was alive with a bustling Main Street, already awake in the dawn light. It was why she had moved away from the crowd to this side street. And why she now had eyes on the best-looking thing she'd smelled in days. If she were lucky, the pasty would have both savory and sweet in it. It didn't matter either way. What she needed was something to stop the cramps in her tummy.

So intent on her prize in the open window, Josie didn't even know the man was there until she had snatched the pasty and felt bony fingers dig into her shoulder.

"Gotcha, you little mudsill!"

"Lemme go!" Josie twisted and turned, but the man held her tight as he pushed her around the corner of the building. She fought to get free while still trying to keep her prize, but

136

she was small for her age, and he was a grown man. Even as scared as she was, her tummy cried out for the hot food. With a final hard shove from her captor, she tumbled to the ground, the pasty flying out of her hands to land in the dirt.

"Whatcha got there, Bosh?"

"Little thief. He stole one of the pasties I made. Didn't want you to think I shorted you."

The second voice was much deeper than the first, but Josie wasn't listening. She scrabbled forward, grabbing the pasty and hugging it to her chest. She was caught—might as well get as much of it in her as possible before the beatings came. Only when her mouth was full of flaky crust and peas mixed with potatoes and dirt did Josie look up and back at the man who had caught her.

He was a lean man. Clean-shaven, his skeletal face was all angles—as was the rest of his body. Clad in brown homespun trousers and shirt, he wore the half-apron of a baker. He had enough flour covering him to prove her assumption. Josie turned back to the man with the deeper voice.

Standing above her was a tall old man with a full white beard sucking on a pipe and holding a mallet. His shirt was the no-color of dirty white from countless washings, and his patched gray trousers were frayed at the bottoms. Only his thick leather apron looked to be in good shape. Behind him was a forge. He was a blacksmith. His lined face was ruddy from the heat of the fire, and he looked tired, though his eyes smiled at her.

"Looks like your 'he' is a 'she,' and a hungry one at that."

That stopped Josie in mid-bite. She touched her hair with a grimy hand and winced. Her braid had come untucked from her shirt in her fall. She knew she should've cut her hair off. Now it was too late. Things were always worse for girls on the road.

The baker shook his head. "A thief's a thief."

"Bosh, it's a hungry child. Go on, man. I got her."

"I didn't short you."

"I know. Just bring a couple more pasties at lunch and add it to my tab."

Bosh gave Josie a withering look as she stuffed another bite of pasty in her mouth. Then, he turned away and disappeared around the corner of the house.

"Hungry, eh?" The blacksmith nodded to her and then to his left. "The dog's hungry, too. Give him the rest. You can have one that doesn't have dirt on it."

Josie looked around and saw a mutt of a dog eyeing her with keen attention, his tail thumping up puffs of dirt. She didn't want to give up her meal, but the blacksmith was watching, so she stood and offered it to the dog.

"Sit, Dog." The blacksmith's quiet voice was so full of command, Josie almost obeyed him. "He won't bite."

The dog sat, his eyes never leaving the half-eaten pasty in her hand. She walked to him and held it out.

"Go on." The blacksmith's voice was kind. "Gentle."

Dog reached out and mildly took the pasty from her. As soon as she stepped back, he wolfed the food down in a couple of hasty bites. Josie nodded, understanding that kind of hunger.

"C'mon, little one. You can wash up here. We'll have a meal inside and find out your story."

Freshly scrubbed, Josie sat on the edge of a rough wooden chair at the only table in the room, looking around the black-smith's small house while he got breakfast together. It was two rooms as far as she could see. A main room with a kitchen area, rocking chair, and hearth, and then a back bed-room. Based on the fact that his plates looked like the special ones they brought out for important visitors at the orphanage, Josie could see he was doing well in this rough-and-tumble town. She'd expected plain tin plates. These were stone and had a glaze on them.

"Name's Huff. Edward Huffington. But Huff'll do. That's what everyone calls me." He pulled a cast iron pan from the fire and checked the cooking eggs and bacon before scraping the food onto two warmed plates.

"Josie, sir."

"Not 'sir.' Huff." He put both plates on the table, giving her a good, long look as he sat across from her. "What's your story?"

The smell of breakfast made Josie's tummy rumble again, but she made no move to eat. Instead, she watched Huff as she figured out what to tell him. The silence grew. Finally, she shrugged. "Ran away from an orphanage."

"Why?" Huff picked up his fork and shoveled food into his mouth. There was no recitation of prayer, no pretense of etiquette or manners that she'd been forced to learn.

"Girls disappeared from it all the time. They'd show up in bad places, and I wasn't going to be a painted lady." Josie watched the food disappear into his mouth, bits of egg falling into his beard.

He nodded, then waved his fork at her plate. "Eat, child. I ain't gonna bite."

Josie didn't hesitate, and she didn't bother trying to be ladylike, either. Food needed to be eaten as quickly as possible—never mind the taste or the heat.

"What now?" he asked.

She looked up at him, still chewing, and shrugged. She'd gotten this far, but it was as far as she'd planned.

"How old are you?"

Again she debated, then opted for the truth. "Nine."

Huff nodded. "Looking for work?"

"Yeah." She paused long enough to point her fork at him. "But not as anyone's jilly."

He nodded again. "I got that. I'm an old man. No salt left in me anymore. But. . . ." He looked around. "I could use some help around here. Cleaning, cooking, mending, fetching. That sort of thing."

Josie looked around. "Where would I stay?" She couldn't keep the suspicion out of her voice.

Huff threw back his head and laughed. It was halfway between a coughing fit and a crow's cawing. "Trig. The bedroom's mine. I can make you a bed by the fire. For now. We'll see how we cotton to each other." He shrugged. "After that, we'll figure something out. Get another room built or something."

Josie looked around again. The place was a mess, but no worse than Saint Beatrice's Home for Lost Children. Fewer people to clean up after, too. "What's my pay?"

"Room and board." Huff gave her a shrewd look. "A penny a day. More if you help in the forge. But that's hard work, girl."

She nodded. With her plate cleared and her tummy full of warm food, the prospect of a roof, regular meals, and actual money was appealing. She stuck out her hand. "It's a deal, Huff."

"Good." He smiled at her with yellowing teeth and a twinkle in his eyes. "You can start now. I got to get back to work. The new city hall building's keeping me busy."

Josie had slept in worse places. The nest of blankets and Dog made for a comfortable bed. Huff had given her one of his old shirts to sleep in. It came down to her knees and smelled pleasantly of the old man's pipe. Still, something kept her awake. It sounded like someone crying. She put her ear to Dog's side and listened. It wasn't him whining in his sleep.

Sitting up, she listened hard. It wasn't Huff. He was snoring away in his bedroom. The noise sounded like it was coming from the hearth. She leaned toward the fire, the coals giving off a pleasant heat. The crying was louder there. Josie shook her head. That wasn't possible.

She decided she'd ask Huff about it in the morning.

Of course, she didn't. By morning, Josie wasn't certain she hadn't dreamed up the crying. And she didn't want Huff rethinking the deal so soon. It was nice to know where she was staying for a while. Even if Bosh glared at her when he arrived with the day's pasties for both Huff and her. Josie just smiled, politely greeted him, and continued sweeping out a house that had not been swept in months, maybe years.

By lunchtime, the place had a clean look that it must not have seen in ages, and the small window in Huff's bedroom had been pried open to let the stale air out. The biggest mystery was the weird-looking symbols Josie had found scratched into the walls all around the house. Symbols she'd never seen before. She decided she'd ask about them later. After she'd gotten a good gauge of the man.

Huff came in and nodded at the state of the house. He grabbed two of the three pasties, eating half of one in a single bite. He washed it down with water. "Going into town with an order. I'll be back by dinner. Figure something out, eh?"

Josie nodded, knowing the cold box was scant on supplies, but the larder had enough staples to get by. She'd talk about that with him tonight, too.

"And don't forget to play with Dog. He needs his exercise."

She grinned as he winked at her and was gone. Josie took the other pasty and went out to the forge yard. She felt good. Food, sleep, a place to stay, and a dog to play with. There wasn't much more she could ask for.

There was singing. It had been going on for hours. A wordless song in the back of her mind.

At first, Josie didn't realize she was humming along to the tune. It was a sad song, full of loss and longing. It made her think of the parents she'd never had. She finished her pasty, giving the last of the flaky crust to Dog, when she realized that the music she was hearing wasn't just in her head. Like the crying from last night, it was faint, but it was definitely there. Almost like music from the next room, except she heard it in her head and her ears.

Walking around the yard, she traced it to the back of the covered forge area. Josie swore the singing came from the forge itself. Creeping forward, she peeked in at the glowing coals and realized two things at once: the coals and wood were actually stones, and there was something—a creature—cavorting within the flames.

She gasped and jumped back. When nothing followed her, and that wordless singing continued, Josie took two hesitant steps forward and looked into the forge again. This time, when the creature appeared, Josie stood her ground, her heart pounding hard, and watched it.

It was about a foot long, and looked like a cross between a lizard and a fish. Its body was red and orange with flashes of white along its tummy. It was long and sinewy, with a series of small fluttery fins running down its back. It cavorted through the flames on four stubby legs, its claws finding purchase on the impossibly burning rocks. A snouted face toward her, its eyes like white-hot, glowing coals.

"So pretty . . ." she murmured.

The singing stopped, and the creature came to the edge of the stone forge. "You can see me?"

Josie looked around, then nodded, her eyes wide with surprised pleasure. It was something she'd never seen before. Not even heard about. And yet, there it was, fins fluttering in the flames. "You can talk and sing!" She looked around again to make sure no one was watching her talk into the forge, then at Dog to see if he could see what she could see. From his low tail and head, she thought he could and was afraid. Turning back to the undulating creature, she wondered if she should be afraid.

"Yes. I sing." The creature's voice was like the crackling of fire.

Curiosity won over caution as Josie leaned into the heat as far as she dared. "But why is the song sad?"

"I sing for my lost child."

"Lost?"

The creature tilted her head. "My lost child, who feels no flame."

"I'm sorry." Josie stared at the creature. "What's your name? I'm Josie."

"Seneca."

They looked at each other for a long moment. Finally, Josie asked, "Where did you lose your child? I could help you look for him."

"Ask the Master what happened to my Scintil. Ask him."

Josie shook her head. "I don't understand. The Master?"

But Seneca said no more. She disappeared back into the forge and blended in with the flames until she disappeared. Try as she might, Josie couldn't coax the fire creature back out into the open.

Two days passed before Josie could bring herself to ask the questions she knew might change the good thing she had going. A warm bed, a roof, regular meals, and a guardian who didn't yell at her were all powerful incentives to do nothing about what she knew. It was almost like having a real home. But every night she heard the crying by the fire, and it killed her to know that it might be from Seneca's lost child.

"I met Seneca." The words were out of Josie's mouth before she realized they'd bubbled to the top of her mind. She continued wiping the last of the dishes, half-hoping Huff hadn't heard.

Huff kept rocking in his chair near the fire, puffing on his pipe. "Seneca?"

"She lives in the forge." Josie watched his bushy white eyebrows bounce in surprise.

"You can see her?"

She nodded.

"Seneca's her name?" He rocked slowly back and forth, the creaking wood making its own rhythm to fill the room. "Never occurred to me that she'd have a name we could understand."

Josie wanted to know why not. Instead she asked, "What is she?"

"Fire spirit." He gave her a keen look. "You haven't had your menarche yet, have you?" At her blank look, he waved his pipe at her. "Woman's blood."

Flushing, Josie shook her head. "No."

"And yet you can see her. Talk to her." He nodded before she answered, still contemplating her.

"What are fire spirits?"

"Elemental spirits. Earth, Air, Water, Fire. I'm surprised you can see her, talk to her. You've got the talent, Josie. It's rare."

"You've got the talent, too?" She didn't want to ask more. But she knew she needed to figure out if he was the Master Seneca had talked about.

He puffed his pipe and nodded. "Been a Master for decades. It's rare to find them out here in the west. I don't know why. I think the Chinese brought these with 'em. They look like Chinese art."

"You're a Master. What does that mean?"

Huff shrugged. "I can control them. Get them to do things for me. They need that. Fire spirits are wild. Dangerous if not controlled. Burn the whole city down. The one in the forge . . . she *is* the forge. She's the main reason I can make my living without the backbreaking work of getting wood. I'm too old for that now. Just change out the rocks now and then." He looked at her again, a keen interest in his eyes. "I never thought I'd meet another with talent. I could teach you . . ."

Josie put the last dish away and wiped her hands, thinking about that. "Teach me. Is it magic?"

The old man chuckled. "Yes, Josie. It's magic, and it's real."

Josie lay by the hearth, snuggled deep into her makeshift bed of blankets and Dog. She couldn't sleep. There was too much going on in her head. Huff had talked for hours about magic, talent, training, and about the different types of Elemental spirits. He knew about all of them, but his specialty was the fierce and wild fire spirits. The untamed ones. The ones who could kill you where you stand if you didn't have protection.

And yet . . . there was the crying. *In the hearth, up the chimney,* Josie thought, *a baby fire spirit cries while outside in the forge, a mother fire spirit sings for her lost child.* It didn't match with what Huff said about the wild, dangerous, free fire spirits. He'd never even thought to ask Seneca her name.

After one particularly mournful wail, Josie couldn't stand it anymore. She threw off the blankets and crawled across the barely warmed brick of the hearth. Braving the still-glowing coals, she looked up into the chimney and thought she saw metal glinting there.

"Scintil?" Her voice was a whisper, but still sounded loud to her. "Scintil? Is that you?"

The crying stopped.

"Scintil?"

There was a tapping on metal.

"Is it you, Scintil? One for no, two for yes."

There were two taps on the metal.

"Are you stuck?"

One tap.

"Trapped?"

Two taps.

"Do you miss your mama?"

Two taps. Then two more taps. Then a third double tap.

Josie sat back on her haunches. She had a choice to make, and she knew it. On one hand, Huff was offering her a home, a safe haven, *and* magic training. On the other hand, if she accepted, it would cost Seneca and Scintil their family for who knew how long. And now that she knew, she'd be a part of keeping mother and son apart. She could forget this now. Or she could go tell Seneca where Scintil was.

She bowed her head, aching at the choice, and then got up, pulled on her trousers, and padded to the door with Dog following.

It was cold in the darkness of early morning, and the forge glowed the dull orange of banked coals. Picking her way through the yard to the forge, Josie looked into the heat for Seneca. After a moment, the fire spirit came into view. She looked up at the little girl, her eyes dull.

"I found him. I found Scintil."

Seneca flared in a sudden light of flame. "Where? Where is my son?" She flowed out of the forge in a sinewy slither of rasping curves onto the worktable, moving among the tools.

Dog took off, running from the house and spirit. Josie stepped back, too, surprised. "I'll take you to him, but you have to tell me something. If you could leave the forge, why stay? Why not look for Scintil on your own?"

"The Master hid him from me. I had no eyes to see."

Josie tilted her head, looking at the fire spirit that looked more and more like the dragons the Chinese who worked the trains talked about and drew.

Seneca tilted her own head. "And it's a pleasure to burn . . ." Her voice almost sounded guilty. "I didn't want to leave him. I had things to burn."

"So you agreed to work the forge?"

"He had my son. I couldn't leave."

"Why did he trap your son?"

The creature shook her head. "Take me to him. Please. It's been so long."

Josie couldn't resist the longing in that voice. She understood it all too well. The want—the need—for family. She nodded and led Seneca to the blacksmith's house.

Once there, both Josie and Seneca were surprised that the fire spirit was unable to enter. The barrier flared as Josie passed through it, but the fire spirit was stopped at the lintel. "My baby. The Master is keeping me from my baby." Seneca flared brighter in her agitation.

Josie held out a calming hand. "I'll try to get him. If not,

I'll get Huff to free him." She turned and hurried to the hearth on quiet feet. Almost climbing into the still-warm fireplace, careful to avoid the barely glowing coals, Josie reached up into the chimney and felt around. Her hand encountered a small, warm metal thing on a chain. It moved as she touched it.

"Shhh. I got you. You'll see your mama again." Josie pressed herself against the sooty stone as she reached up to find where the chain was hung. It was a hook. A little fiddling, and she was able to free the chain.

"Hurry! Hurry! Before the Master comes!"

As Josie pulled herself out of the hearth along with what looked to be a small incense burner—like they used in church—Huff's bedroom door opened. "Josie?"

She froze, hugging the small metal pot to her, while Seneca gave a wordless cry of rage and began to beat herself against the ward.

Huff took this all in, his eyes widening. He reached for her. "Don't! You don't understand!"

"You've kept them apart. That's not right." Josie's heart broke as she betrayed the man who had been so kind to her.

"He was wild! Burned down two farms. She wouldn't rein him in." Huff nodded at the enraged fire spirit trying to force its way through the wards. "He killed two families! You have to understand."

Josie remembered the burned-out farm she'd slept in as a feeling of horror grew in her stomach. The metal in her hand suddenly flared so hot that it burned her even before she could drop the small, enclosed pot. Josie gasped, looking at her swelling, reddening hand. The burner's heated metal was already making her blankets smolder. Hurrying from the hearth, Josie grabbed the nearest thing she could find to protect her hand—the dishtowel. She wrapped her good hand in it, then returned to grab the burner's chain, pulling the burner from the blankets before they could catch flame.

When she looked up again, Huff was returning from his room, wearing a thick gold ring with a ruby on one hand and holding an ornamental knife in the other. He was focused on Seneca at the door. Josie could see that fire spirit had cracked the ward and was breaking through. Huff was repairing it.

He stepped into the living room, still looking at the ward as he spoke to her. "If you free the fire spirit, we die. Who knows how many more will die?"

"But it's her baby. Her family."

Huff didn't say anything. Josie knew he'd turned his attention back to Seneca and the ward. She could actually *see* the magic flowing from him, feel it like you could feel the air after a thunderstorm. Seneca was nothing more than the embodiment of flame and rage now. Huff pushed her back, capturing her in his magic, forcing her into the yard. Scintil cried out in his prison, a wordless wail of longing and despair.

Josie took one last look at Huff, then closed her eyes and made her choice. It was the hardest decision of her life.

"I'm sorry," she whispered to Scintil's prison. "I'm sorry. If you've killed . . . If you can't be tamed . . ." The wailing grew louder as Josie returned to the hearth and hung the burner in its place in the chimney again. Tears spilled down her face; she knew exactly what she was doing: sacrificing one family for another, the new family and home she had gained.

"I'll find a better way to free you. I promise." Josie spoke to the hearth but wasn't sure Scintil could understand. She turned away and silently repeated the promise. Then she ran to find out what happened with Seneca and Huff.

In the yard, Josie watched as Huff forced Seneca back into the forge. The fire spirit lashed out at him and everything around him, scorching the ground as she went. Once secure, Josie watched him scratch those strange symbols into the forge's stone and metal sides. Seneca raged inside, glowing white hot in her anger.

Huff stepped back and bowed his head. "That was closer than I ever want to admit." He looked over his shoulder at her. "You did the right thing. That fire spirit . . . it would've rampaged. Could have lost the whole town."

Josie was still looking at the white-glowing forge. "Is she a prisoner now?"

Huff nodded. "She has to be. She knows where he is. She won't stop trying to reach him."

Josie stared at the ground, not seeing it as more tears welled and spilled down her dirty face. She knew what she had done. Feeling a warm, kind hand on her shoulder, she looked up.

"I'm proud of you, Josie. You did good."

Sobbing, she threw herself into his arms. The feeling that welled up at his praise battled with the guilt of her betrayal of the fire spirits. She had her family now. She had Huff. Someday, she would free Scintil and Seneca. But not today. Today, Josie had a new father, and that was what mattered.

It was a price she was willing to pay.

Arms of the Sea
Tanya Huff

"Marie! It's time to come in."

She was tempted to pretend she hadn't heard, but that had never worked in the past, and she had no reason to believe it'd work today. "Just a little longer, Mrs. Barton. The doctor said at least an hour a day."

"It's been almost an hour and a half."

Marie carefully sculled around until she faced the shore and the ship-in-full-sail figure of her nurse standing back beyond the reach of spray. "Ten more minutes."

"Only ten!"

"Only ten," Marie murmured as the nearest undine playfully swung her around to face out to sea again. "Only because I can't get the buckles undone."

The straps over her chemise buckled in the back, and she'd never been able to make the undines understand what she wanted. Or perhaps they understood, and they weren't strong enough to manipulate the wet leather. Green-gold hair wrapping around her body like strands of kelp, they'd bat at the buckle with long green fingers, but never managed to get it undone. The undines of the deep would be able to, Marie was sure of that. They were larger and stronger, but she hadn't seen them since the accident, and if she couldn't get free, she never would again.

The line tethering her to the shore was the only reason she was allowed in the water at all. Her doctor had ordered immersion in salt water as therapy, but Mrs. Barton had refused to allow it until she'd made certain her charge would not be swept out to sea. "I don't care how well Miss Hudson used to swim." Arms folded, she'd stared the doctor down. "That was then."

So Marie swam in water that would have once been barely up to her waist, the undines who lived in the shallows and the nymphs of the tidal pools keeping her company, and she dreamed of freedom and enough salt water to save her.

"That's ten minutes, Marie!"

She relaxed into the pull, easily keeping her head above the surface. Her uncle had sent men to clear the loose stones and rough edges from the shelf of rock on the bottom of the small bay so it was like being tugged across a watery dance floor. Not that Marie would ever cross a dance floor again.

"Good heavens, child, you're freezing!"

"I'm fine."

" 'Fine,' she says." With the buckle open, Mrs. Barton tucked large, strong hands under Marie's arms and heaved her up onto a blanket. Marie gritted her teeth and refused to shiver.

The north Atlantic was never warm, not even in late July when Marie wore a thin sheen of moisture under her clothes, her back damp against the woven rattan of her chair. The north Atlantic was never particularly welcoming, either, more often gray than blue, and storms slammed against the outer arm of the small, sheltered bay nearly as often in the summer as they did in the winter. But every day the weather allowed, Mrs. Barton pushed Marie down the ramp her uncle's men had built along the shallows to the shore, lifted her out of her chair, strapped her to the rope, and set her safely down in the water.

Except that the north Atlantic was never safe. Three years ago in the fall, returning from visiting her mother's relatives on Saint-Pierre with her father, a sudden squall had twisted the ship underfoot, slammed it down as she stumbled, and thrown her through the railing. The Atlantic had taken her father's ship, the fifteen men of her father's crew, and her father, but it deposited her alive on L'Ile-aux-Marins.

The fishermen who found her said it was a miracle she'd lived.

When she came home after eight months in the hospital in Halifax, she screamed accusations at the sea. Eventually, she'd had to believe her father was dead before he reached the water and the undines could only guide his body to rest among the bleached bones of other sailors.

"Arms around my neck."

Marie slid her arms from the warmth of the blanket and hung on as Mrs. Barton lifted her, blanket and all, into her chair.

She gripped the arms as Mrs. Barton backed them up to the shore, her fingers white by the time they reached the level path that led to the huge frame house her father had built for his French bride. Owner of half of one of the most successful commercial shipping companies in Nova Scotia, he'd spared no expense. During the long maritime summers, wide, multi-paned windows made in Boston had opened the house to every point of the compass so any passing breeze could freely enter. Now all the windows on the second floor were shuttered tight. Her mother's spirit was as broken as Marie's back, and swathed in widow's weeds, she haunted the upper story of her own house, locked away from her daughter and the winds that had betrayed her.

"Nice, warm bath, and we'll wash the salt from your hair. You'll feel better, you'll see."

Marie knew she was lucky to have Mrs. Barton. Her nurse was practical and pragmatic. While of necessity she ran Marie's life, she never took advantage, and allowed her charge as much freedom as she could. She offered sympathy, but never pity.

Marie also knew she was lucky her family had more than enough money to pay Mrs. Barton's comfortable wages and for the half-dozen servants who kept the house running and food on the table.

She was lucky the break had been low enough to affect only her legs and that she could control the rest of her body.

She didn't feel lucky.

She used to love to dance.

"Marie."

"Uncle Edward." She turned her cheek up for his kiss, then waited, hands folded on her lap until he sat down behind her father's desk.

"And how is your mother?"

Still hiding up a flight of stairs I can't climb. "Mrs. Conway says she's eating a bit more."

"Well, that's something, isn't it. Hard to turn down Mrs. Conway's baking." Her uncle was large and hearty, sweating heavily in the heat. His own wife long gone, his grief muted by time and temperament, he had no idea of how to deal with his sister-in-law's reaction, and tried not to appear grateful he didn't have to.

Her father's shares in the company were Marie's now. Her mother had money of her own, and Marie suspected her father's will had been written in the belief they'd die together. Her uncle's monthly visits always began with company reports and ended with wider-ranging news of the waters around Nova Scotia.

"Four boats lost this month, all just east of Sable Island." Fingers turning a gooseberry tart on its plate, he watched her closely, and when she nodded, her own fingers twisting in the folds of her green muslin skirt, he continued. "Three fishing boats, and then . . ." The tart crumbled. ". . . a Baltimore clipper. One of the older ships of the Black Ball Line. No survivors. Fourteen bloody hours out of Halifax, pardon my French."

His sons, her cousins, captained ships in the company fleet. Brian, the elder, the first of the line's steamships. Bradley, a Water Master like her father and his grandfather before him, stayed under sail in one of the company's big Aberdeen clippers. When Uncle Edward said, *"No survivors,"* Marie knew he saw his sons' bones joining his brother's on the ocean floor.

"You know I'd stay," he'd said, "but I leave tomorrow for the Sydney shipyard."

Marie had smiled and nodded. He wouldn't have lied about leaving for Sydney, but if the weather allowed, he never stayed. Her mother's grieving made him too uncomfortable.

She waited on the wide front porch until Uncle Edward's brougham reached the end of the long drive, then wheeled back into the house and called for Mrs. Barton.

"You want go into the water now?" Mrs. Barton's eyes narrowed. "I don't think so. Look at that sky; it's going to storm."

"But it isn't storming yet." Marie rolled into her room, the old summer parlor remade for her use when the second floor was denied her, and began unbuttoning her shirtwaist. "If we hurry, we'll be done and dry and dressed in time for tea."

"Will we now?" But Marie could hear the smile in the older woman's voice, and when she raised herself up off the cushion, teeth gritted against the pain, Mrs. Barton tugged skirt and petticoat down off her hips and over her legs, waiting until Marie was seated again before lifting each foot and sliding the fabric free.

"I can't believe you received your uncle with bare feet. Like a heathen."

"It's too hot for shoes and stockings, and he couldn't see my feet under my skirt. Not that he ever looks."

"Of course he doesn't. Men don't see what they don't want to see."

"Men don't see me, they see the late captain's poor, crippled daughter."

Mrs. Barton snorted as she draped the blanket over Marie for the ride down to the shore. "That's because men are fools."

The late captain's poor, crippled daughter could bend society's rules, but Marie had never asked about Mr. Barton. It seemed safer.

The undines and tidal pool nymphs usually waited for her by the ramp, as if their enthusiastic welcome—though unseen by any eyes other than Marie's—would encourage Mrs. Barton to faster movement. Today, the bay seemed empty. Although the sky had lowered itself to touch the sea, gray on gray, Marie knew the coming storm wouldn't have driven her usual companions away. She'd watched them from her window, shrieking with laughter as storm-frothed waves tumbled them about, the smaller nymphs skipping from raindrop to raindrop.

She found them at last gathered at the edge of deep water, where the bay became the sea. A wave crested beyond the breakwater, and Marie thought she saw the graceful dance of a deep-water undine in the curl—the lighter curve of a shoulder, an arm, the long, elegant line of tail.

"Are you ready, then? With the air so warm and heavy, it'll be colder today."

"Not possible," Marie murmured absently, her attention on the water.

As soon as her body slipped below the surface, they sped toward her, the nymphs tangling in her curls, the undines winding around her legs and throwing themselves into her arms.

"Is it the ships?" she asked softly, cuddling and soothing where she could. "Did the deep one come to tell you about the ships? Is that what's upset you so?"

She was afraid her hour would end before she could understand what they were saying.

They weren't upset about the ships. Or the loss of life.

It was the serpent . . .

With her uncle in Sydney, Marie had one other option. Three days after she'd learned about the serpent, Conway, the coachman—Mrs. Conway's eldest—lifted her into the family's glossy black clarence as the rising sun painted orange streaks on the sea.

They stopped for tea in Hubbards and again at Upper Tantallon.

"Is it the pain?" Mrs. Barton nodded at Marie's fingers dancing patterns around her saucer.

Marie blinked, confused. Unless she was in the water, pain of one sort or another was a constant companion. Less as time passed, but . . . Then she remembered the reason for their trip to the city. "No, it just takes so long. To get into the city," she added when Mrs. Barton frowned.

"Ah." The frown eased. "Well, I can't deny it would have been much more convenient had the new train route run along the shore. I hear the tracks go all the way to Truro now."

It was just short of noon when they finally pulled up in front of the Victorian General Hospital in Halifax. Conway lifted her chair down and then her into it.

"Wait at the livery, Conway. We'll send a message when we need you. And you"—Marie lifted her hands off the wheels as the chair jerked back—"you may roll yourself about the house all you like, but not here. Here you will behave like the young lady you are."

Mrs. Barton's dignity allowed her to push the chair up the broad flagstone ramp, but once in the cool central hall of the new building, she flagged down an orderly.

Marie locked her fingers together in her lap and fought the urge to wrest control away. By the time they reached Dr. Evans' office, she was about to shake herself out of the chair.

"When you need me, Marie, I'll be right outside."

Marie had no idea how Dr. Evans had first convinced Mrs. Barton that he needed to see her alone; she was just thankful he had. Once in his office, having been deposited in front of his desk as though the chair was the patient, not the person in it, she rolled back and forth, unable to stay still.

The inner door opened. She released a breath she couldn't remember holding and froze, the edge of her wheels biting into her palms. "You're not Dr. Evans."

"Dr. Evans isn't available today, Miss Hudson." Eyes locked on her file, the unfamiliar man crossed to the desk. "I'm Dr. Harris."

He was tall and thin where Dr. Evans was stout, with a neat, dark beard rather than the fringe of Dr. Evans' ginger muttonchops, and his accent was evidence of a much more recent crossing from Scotland. But Marie could feel his connection to the earth, stretching down through the stones of the hospital as secure and unyielding as the roots of a tree, and that was all that really mattered right now.

"There's a sea serpent in the waters east of Sable Island."

"There's a what?" He looked up then and actually saw her. "Oh. Of course . . ." Another glance at the file. "Dr. Evans mentioned your mother is an Air Master . . . to me, personally," he added, setting the file down. "But he neglected to mention you're a Water Master in your own right."

"Why would he?" She slapped the arms of her chair. "This is what he sees. But that's not important now," she added before Dr. Harris could defend his colleague. "Four ships have already been taken with no survivors—three fishing boats and a clipper. It has to stop."

"And you know there's a serpent because . . . ?"

"A deep-water undine brought the news to the spirits of the shallows. When I went in to swim, they told me."

Dark brows rose. "You swim?"

She would. If not for that rope. "You need to send a message to Captain Conner in Greenwood."

"Captain Conner, Water Master, recently retired from Her Majesty's navy?"

What a day for Dr. Evans to be gone. She missed being able to stamp her foot even though she was years too old for such an undignified response. "Yes, *that* Captain Conner. The serpent must be dealt with, without delay."

Dr. Harris spread his hands. "Why would the undines not have told the Captain themselves?"

Marie took a deep breath and counted to five. There wasn't time for ten. "This isn't a stream or pond or a bucket of water, this is the sea. The deep undines saved me when my father's ship went down. They know me."

"I see." He glanced her at her file again as though it would have more answers than she did. "Unfortunately, Captain Conner is laid up with gout. He's not able to leave his chair. But I'll send word to England . . ."

"Fifteen days for a reply, best case scenario," Marie snapped. Captain Conner could leave *his* chair with a cane and a litany of complaints. "There isn't a steamer heading across until the twenty-third, so that's by sail with an Air and Water Master on board. But if we had a functional Water Master, we wouldn't need to send a message to England. I own half of Hudson Shipping, Dr. Harris. I know how long it takes to cross the ocean."

"Of course." Startled, he sounded less patronizing. "There's no ship with a Water Master in port?"

She twitched at the folds of her skirt. "We'd need to check each ship. My uncle spoke of setting up a volunteer registry, having the Water Masters check in at the office when they come to shore, but some work for other companies, and some speak neither French nor English."

"And all of them were suspicious of his motives?" When she nodded, he stroked his knuckles over his beard and sighed. "It might be faster to send the message than to check each ship."

"It might," she acknowledged reluctantly. "Though Boston is closer."

"Boston? In America? Is there a Water Master in Boston?"

"I don't know. My uncle would, but he's in at the dockyards in Sydney." Three days to Sydney even if she could convince Mrs. Barton of the necessity. Three days in the clarence, and the pain wouldn't be a lie. "If I could find a ship to take me, I could . . ."

"No. Not in your condition."

"In my condition?" Marie bit each word off. "I wasn't planning to *walk*, Dr. Harris."

"I don't doubt your will is strong, Miss Hudson, but your body is not." The Earth Master was gone, the doctor in his place. "An injury such as yours will never be entirely healed. The *therapy* Dr. Evans has allowed would be dangerous in the extreme, were you not what you are."

"Were I not what I am, I wouldn't be here." And she didn't have time to linger. "My apologies for taking up your time."

"Miss Hudson . . ."

"I'm sure you have actual patients to see to." Rolling one wheel forward and one back, she began to turn. "Good day, Dr. Harris, I . . ." Interrupted by a brisk knock on the inner door, she paused.

Dr. Harris sighed. "Come in, Ealasaid."

Ealasaid looked a little younger than Marie's twenty years, with bright red hair twisted into a knot it seemed determined to escape, and a heart-shaped face dusted with golden freckles. Not a Master, but something about her lifted the hair off the back of Marie's neck. She wore a dove-gray skirt over modest hoops, a white lawn shirtwaist with a tatted collar, and a starched white pinafore similar to the nursing sisters', although she wore no cap. "I'm sorry to interrupt, Father, but Dr. Kent needs your help."

"Miss Hudson, my daughter, Ealasaid. Ealasaid, Marie Hudson. We're short staffed today, Miss Hudson. My apologies. Ealasaid . . ."

"I'll see Miss Hudson out, Father." And with a gentle shove toward the door, he was gone.

Any other time, Marie would have wanted to make a friend of Ealasaid Harris, now smiling at her with a gleam in her gray eyes, but today, since Dr. Harris had failed her, she had to find a way to deal with that serpent. If she could convince Mrs. Barton to go to the docks, perhaps the undines would know of another Master.

"Miss Hudson, I couldn't help but overhear . . . Actually, I could have, but I didn't. Is there really a sea serpent? Don't worry," Ealasaid added quickly when Marie's eyes widened, "I know what my father does besides medicine. And I have skills of my own." She leaned closer and said quietly, "I help the dead."

"The dead?"

"Move on."

"We're in a hospital."

"Sometimes . . ." The rustle of starched cotton bracketed her words. ". . . sometimes they don't want to leave."

Marie rolled back, noticed that Ealasaid watched her, not the chair, and made a decision. "Yes, there's really a serpent. Men have already died. I have family out on the sea, and I've lost enough family. I have to stop it."

"Of course you do. And I can help. I know a Fire Master at the Citadel."

Of course she did. She looked like the sort of girl young men would want to walk home. Dance with. "How will that help?"

Dimples flashed. "He has a friend with a boat."

"Marie will be perfectly safe with me, Mrs. Barton." Ealasaid spoke with such confidence Marie could actually see Mrs. Barton be convinced. "I'm a doctor's daughter, and I help at the hospital when I'm needed. We'll walk over to the gardens—it's not far—and I can introduce Marie to some of my friends."

Mrs. Barton's brows dipped. "Male friends?"

"One friend is male, yes. An officer in the Citadel regiment and a gentleman, I assure you. They do a luncheon in the garden, and Marie and I will chaperone each other."

"I'm sure you will." After a long moment, Mrs. Barton nodded. "I wouldn't mind a few hours to myself." Turning to Marie, she added, "Keep an eye on the Citadel clock and be back here by four. You have your medicine in your bag?

Good. And wear your hat." She tied the green plaid ribbon under Marie's chin and laid a hand gently against her cheek. "Enjoy yourself, but be careful."

"Thank you. I will." If they spoke of two different things, Mrs. Barton wasn't to know.

A braided belt of turquoise cord and a turquoise half jacket much like Marie's own turned Ellie's near uniform into a stylish walking outfit. Marie shifted her shoulders and tried not to resent Ellie's quick footsteps behind her. Ellie. Not Ealasaid because that was a mouthful, and not Miss Harris because they were going to be friends.

For the last three years, all of Marie's friends had been of the sea.

She wasn't sure she remembered how to be a friend on land.

Captain Alistair Williams was not happy about Ellie's plan. "Begging your pardon, Miss Hudson, but you're . . ."

"Crippled?" Marie tilted her head back far enough to look him in the eye and wondered if he could even see her brows go up under the brim of her hat. "I'm also the only Water Master in Halifax right now, and every moment we delay increases the chance of another attack, of more men dying. I can stop that. But I need your help."

"Ellie . . ."

Ellie glanced down at her, then back up at the captain and grinned. "We won't be walking to the island, Alistair."

When Marie laughed in response, it surprised her almost as much as it surprised Captain Williams.

Getting them to the friend's boat took all the ingenuity of the captain and the cabbie combined. Although Captain Williams had easily lifted Marie inside, without the extra strapping Conway had installed on the family carriage, her chair was causing problems.

"Honestly, they carry sea chests all the time." Ellie handed her a cheese sandwich on a tissue paper napkin.

"I think it's frightening the horse."

"They'll work it out. If you don't mind my saying, you're less fragile than I expected."

"I swim. Dr. Evans prescribed salt water immersion," she added when Ellie looked startled.

"Ah. Because you're a Water Master."

"Because I can't use my legs." Marie crumbled a bit of the bread. "I don't really swim. I just scull about in the shallows at the end of a safety line holding me close to shore. I wish . . ." She stopped and wondered what she was doing. She never talked about this. Of course, if she told Mrs. Barton, she'd never be allowed back in the water, and if she told her mother . . . When did she have the chance to tell her mother? "I wish sometimes I could just swim away and never come back."

Ellie seemed more curious than shocked, but then, she spoke to the dead. "Isn't your mother still alive?"

Marie sighed. "Not entirely."

Then Captain Williams climbed in, triumphant over her chair, and they lost the chance to continue the conversation.

"You don't realize what you're asking. Sable isn't an hour's pleasant sail, you know; it's maybe sixteen hours if the wind is going right and going out . . ." Erik Ahlquist spread large, scarred hands. ". . . it's never right."

"I wouldn't ask if it wasn't important."

"It's always important with you, Williams. Always. My answer's no."

Before Captain Williams could continue the argument, Marie rolled past him. "I'll pay you a hundred dollars. Fifty now." She dug her felted bag out from where it was tucked under her skirt. "Fifty when we're back safely."

Ahlquist looked at the new Dominion of Canada ten-dollar notes. "And if you don't come back safely?"

"Then you'll be out fifty dollars."

Chapped lips twitched into a smile in the depths of his white-blond beard. "Why do—"

"And another fifty to not ask questions."

"Then in the morning . . ."

"We need to go now."

He stared at her for a long moment, his bright blue eyes shifting from the money to her face. Finally, he sighed and turned to the captain. "We should take Miss Hudson and her chair aboard separately."

"Do we even need to take the chair?" Captain Williams wondered. "There's not a lot of room . . ."

Marie could feel Ellie watching her as the two men discussed the best way to secure her. "Did I not mention I was rich?"

"No."

"My uncle gives me pin money every quarter. I don't have anything to spend it on." They used to come to Halifax once a month and stay at Uncle Edward's house. Her cousins' wives would throw parties. She owned half a dozen pairs of dancing shoes.

"How did you know he'd take the money?"

She came back to the dock. "His shirt's been mended with sailmaker stitches, so he probably did it himself, and his left boot is cracked just above the sole. Every cent he has goes into his boat."

"You sound like you approve?"

"It's a beautiful boat." The *Vand Hjerte* was close to a hundred feet long, her cabin rising almost a full three feet above the foredeck, and she gleamed. Not a bit of peeling paint, not a frayed line; no doubt the sails would be mended and tight. She could probably hold a crew of seven or eight, but with the mizzen aft of the rudder post, she could also be sailed by a single man. A single strong man, Marie amended, watching muscles ripple under shirt and vest.

"Does your nurse know you've got so much money with you?" A pause. "Marie?"

"Sorry." She shook her head. "I was admiring the boat. No, she doesn't know."

"What will she do when we're not there at four?"

"She'll go to your father, and he'll explain. He'll know where we've gone." Marie untied her hat and pushed it back, letting the sea breeze dry her curls. "He'd stop this himself, if it were on land."

They were out of the harbor when Ahlquist shouted something that didn't sound polite and Captain Williams shuffled along the tiny walkway linking stern to bow until he could crouch beside her. She'd refused to be stowed in the cabin like baggage. "It's not going to take sixteen hours, is it?"

Marie laughed as a spray of water rose against the wind and drenched him. "No, it's not."

Ahlquist steered by the stars after dark, standing at the rudder with his shirtsleeves rolled up while Captain Williams napped. Once they were in the lee of Sable Island and the sea anchors were out, they traded places. Wrapped in a rough blanket, Ellie curled up on one of the narrow bunks under the foredeck. Marie didn't sleep. She didn't need to sleep, not surrounded by the sea.

Captain Williams came to her at dawn, dark hair and whiskers spiky with salt. "The sea's mercurial enough that Erik's accepted the speed of the journey out, but if he sees the serpent . . ."

Marie pulled a small brown bottle from her bag. "It's calm enough to light the stove; make him a strong coffee and put in half a teaspoon of this. If it doesn't put him out, he'll be sleepy enough to be convinced he's dreaming."

The captain's eyes were a surprisingly pale hazel, with flecks of gold in among the brown and green. "Why do you have laudanum?"

"I have a broken back."

"You're in pain?"

His voice held no pity, so she told him the truth. "Sometimes it's like dancing on knives." But not in the sea. Never in the sea.

The sea rocked the boat slowly up and down, a mother's hand at the cradle.

As the sun rose, Marie slipped out of her jacket and shirtwaist, unfastened her skirt and petticoat and inched her way back out of them, thankful that she was free of most of the complications of women's clothing. Laced into a corset at the hospital, she'd screamed until they removed it. Shoes off, stockings rolled down, she could hear Captain Williams explaining Ahlquist's sudden return to sleep. As she hand-walked to the rope lines, legs trailing behind her, she heard Ellie complain he'd made the coffee bitter enough to hide a pint of laudanum.

Marie slid under the lower rope and pushed herself forward into the water.

Three of the deep undines rose to meet her. Beautiful. Translucent. Bodies twice her size, their tails twice that again. There was no demarcation where their trailing hair and flukes met the sea, flowing one into the other.

When she surfaced, Ellie looked shocked, but Captain Williams merely said, "If there's a serpent in the water, you're going to need a shield."

Ellie turned to glare at him.

Marie laughed. "I know."

"You're going to tell me the ocean is your workroom, aren't you?"

"I am."

The *Vand Hjerte* had fifty feet of rope on her life-ring, so Marie had the undines move her almost fifty feet away. Arms sculling in slow circles, she built her shields layer by layer, currents of blue and green and turquoise wrapped around her.

"Marie! To your right!"

"Starboard," she sighed as she turned. The angle of the light on the water hinted at a long, sinuous curve just below the surface. She felt the currents moving her legs change, then felt the serpent's confusion as it dove beneath her.

The boat rocked violently as it returned. Ellie screamed, the captain swore, and Marie sent the undines. The last thing she needed was a Fire Master in the water.

Then loops of serpent filled the sea between the *Vand Hjerte* and her. It slammed against her shields as it passed—in curiosity, not aggression, but if it could get through her shields, its curiosity would kill her.

She'd be another set of bones on the ocean floor.

When the serpent approached again, she took a deep breath and dove.

Her legs were still useless but so nearly weightless, it barely mattered.

Enormous dark eyes met hers. It was scaled pewter and beautiful the way deadly things were beautiful, perfectly designed to hunt and kill. Driven in from the Grand Banks by the summer storms, far from the deep currents that could have led it home, it was confused by the amount of light, by the relative warmth of the water, and the lack of familiar prey.

Mouth open, teeth shadowed crescents, it lunged.

Shifting the shape of her shields, Marie slapped its nose with power. She'd have laughed at its affronted expression had there been air to laugh with. It was a simple matter after that to instruct the undines to lead it home, although harder to convince the serpent that these were the currents it was meant to follow.

She could see the last sinuous curl of its tail heading northeast as she surfaced, the original trio of undines still with her. Borrowing their strength, Marie licked salt from her lips and remembered how to breathe.

"You didn't destroy it?" Ellie called.

"I never meant to." Marie tipped her weight back and watched the water lift her legs. "It was where it shouldn't have been, so I sent it home. The banks have been fished for centuries; it's probably passed harmlessly under thousands of vessels."

"You were under the water for a very long time."

"She's a Water Master," Captain Williams answered as she stroked her fingers through the fluid length of an undine's hair. "Marie, it's time to come in."

They'd help her if she stayed, help her until they took her down to join her father. She dove under again, just because she could, feeling strong and graceful. Nothing hurt.

"Marie!" Ellie's voice had picked up an edge. Impatience? Desperation? Marie wasn't sure. "We *need* another Water Master. Captain Conner can't get out of his chair."

Marie laughed, got caught by a wave, coughed, caught another wave, couldn't find the line between air and water . . .

Then she was lifted high and laid, nose running, lungs burning, in a puddle on the deck. As her teeth began to chatter and Ellie wrapped her in a blanket, she heard Captain Williams say, "Don't worry, El. If she'd really wanted to stay, they wouldn't have given her back."

Dr. Harris and Uncle Edward were waiting on the dock.

"I had to tell a number of lies to your nurse, Miss Hudson," Dr. Harris said as the captain carried her to her chair.

"And then I had to tell more." Uncle Edward shuddered. "Terrifying woman."

"How did you . . . ?"

"I sent a telegram to Sydney." Dr. Harris glanced at Ahlquist securing the bow some fifty feet away, then lowered his voice. "Is it taken care of?"

"Yes." Marie tilted her head back and met his gaze. "I sent it home."

"Good. However . . ." He turned a distinctly unhappy expression on her companions. "You and I will talk of this later, Ealasaid, but you, Captain Williams, should not have gone along with such a dangerous scheme."

"I'm not going to argue with a Water Master about a sea serpent, sir."

To Marie's surprise, her uncle laughed. After a moment, Dr. Harris shook his head. "Fair enough."

With her uncle instructing the cabbie on how to load her chair, Ahlquist stepped forward and lifted her inside.

"If I don't take the extra fifty," he said quietly, "may I ask questions?"

"Not and get anything like an answer, Mr. Ahlquist."

"Erik."

"Erik." He smelled of salt and hemp and tar. He smelled of the sea. "But I might have need of a fast ship again."

"Then you know where to find me."

"Thank you, Conway." Marie removed her arms from around the coachman's neck as he set her carefully down in her chair at the top of the stairs. If she could get to Sable Island, she could get to the second floor.

Mrs. Barton waited by her mother's door. Opened it. And said as she closed it again, "I'll be out here if you need me." She'd been remarkably understanding about the edited version of the adventure, if a little too interested in Erik Ahlquist.

Rugs tugged at Marie's wheels as she rolled across her mother's room to the windows, but she flexed arms made strong by the sea and refused to yield. Ignoring the protests from the shadowed figure on the chaise, she pulled back the curtains and used the rain to fling open the shutters. "It's time to start living again, Mama. Papa would not want you to shut yourself off like this."

Wrapped in black, her mother raised her hands against the light and whispered, "You can't know what he wants; he's dead."

Marie thought of dead men's bones at the bottom of the sea. "I know he's gone, Mama. And the winds no more betrayed you than the sea betrayed him." As her mother reached to pull the curtains closed again, Marie grabbed her wrist and turned her to face the window. "You got lost. Blown off course by a storm. But the wind has changed . . ."

"No." Thin, pale fingers touched the glass.

Marie released her, leaned forward, and threw open the sash.

There was water enough on the wind she thought she could make it behave, but she didn't have to.

It wrapped around her mother like a lost child.

Her mother was crying now.

Marie gathered her mother onto her lap, wondering when she'd gotten so small, and pressed her lips to her hair while the winds danced round them both and her shirtwaist grew damp.

Salt water.

Salt water to save her.

London Falling

Ben Ohlander

I stepped down from the darkened doorway that looked across to the rooming house that my brother had given as his London address. His lodging proved a decrepit thing, all over crumbling brick, fly-specked curtains, and piled garbage. It squatted in the thick gray fog, flanked by an aging warehouse and a pawnbroker whose cracked shop window displayed nautical pieces of unknown provenance overlaid by a thick coat of dust.

The rooming house fell far below my brother's accustomed standards, a clear sign that he was down on his luck. His preferred prey, the widow of means, had become a wary beast in New England. His presence in London suggested he was attempting more fertile ground, where his quarry might be less bounded by attorneys and male relations who read newspapers.

The noisome stink of the thoroughfare hung in my nostrils and blotted out the view around me, restricting my sight to narrow tunnels, dimly pierced by the Whitechapel gaslights. A single flame danced a moment some yards away before failing, startling me. I absentmindedly reached out, my mind easily coiling around the gas, containing it, and feeling the tiny particles within rub and chafe as I constrained them. I added some small energy until the lamp glowed brightly, and flame returned. The casualness of the act, one I had performed a thousand times before, settled me and calmed my nerves. The dank, fog-enshrouded streets reminded me too greatly of the tunnels beneath Dr. Holmes' hotel, where I had too rashly ventured and only barely escaped.

The memories of the terror as I had been trapped and tormented washed over me. I closed my eyes, and my gorge rose in my throat. I desired nothing else but to flee back to Massachusetts and my beloved woods. The *Campania* was still in port, and I might yet escape the stinks and closeness of the streets.

Steeling myself against my anxieties, I touched the rough paper of my brother's telegram. *I need you. Come at once.* Six words graven into my mind. My brother, so prideful, to be brought so low as to make a naked appeal spoke more to his distress than the terse message. He had been the stronger of us, both physically and in his Mastery of our Art. I had been perhaps the quicker to learn and more deft in application, but the weaker in pure force. I, like others less endowed, served as an object of his derision. My rush to join him served both to protect one whose blood I shared, and also the thought that I might yet prove myself worthy in his eyes. How could I not rise in his esteem if I were the instrument of his salvation?

The thought of gaining estimation in his eyes lent me a courage badly shaken by my time in Chicago, though I confess I drew also reassurance from my father's pistol. The weapon, a heavy horse pistol, proved an object of special contempt in my brother's eyes. He had never understood why Father, a Fire Master and our teacher, kept the thing. Its heavy weight bespoke a totem of a religion I did not worship—technology—but the drag on my coat from its substance lent me courage.

I drew back into the doorway as a gaslight flared to life in what I estimated to be my brother's lodgings. Had he returned while I mused? Had I missed his entrance? I wished I had some sense of his movements and habits, but I had only docked this afternoon, and come straightaway to where he bade me. I stared at the gas-lit windows, seeking a glimpse of my sibling, hoping to confirm that I had found his scent.

First one shape, portly to stout, and then a second, as long and as thin as a beanpole, passed the shabby curtains. Neither man had my brother's broad shoulders. They both moved back and forth in front of the lit shrouds a time or two, their movements more of searchers than lodgers. After some time, they seemed to pace, as though waiting. A long, damp hour passed before the gaslights snuffed out and the room went dark again.

I retreated deeper into my dank abode, uncertain as to how to proceed.

Two men, clearly the same as had been in the chambers above, left the rooming house a few minutes later. They stepped into the gaslights, and I had a clear glimpse of their dress. They both wore hat and coat, natty and out of countenance with the state of their rough surroundings.

Their dress and manner told me they were not from this district, and supported my conclusion that these men might be familiar with my brother's troubles. I suspected that England also had its share of toffs seeking widowed money, and like Boston, possessed a ready supply of consulting detectives to send the rakes on their way. I considered also that they might be relations of a woman my brother had courted or seduced. I'd settled into a comfortable hypothesis regarding my brother's difficulties, and reasoned this was in the same lines as his quick departure from Philadelphia.

I'd no sooner settled into this familiar pattern of familial trouble when I was just as quickly forced back out of it. The taller made a gesture as they stepped into the yellow puddle of gaslight, and the lamp overhead snuffed out. The act bespoke Mastery, either of Fire or Air, and took my brother's situation out of the realm of merely draining bank accounts.

The tall man's casting gesture seemed odd and unnatural, and as he moved in the foggy gloom, I gained a clearer view. Enough light remained from the rooming house's windows to illuminate him as he walked. His steps had a marionette's seeming, a jerkiness of manner suggesting I looked at a puppet manipulated from the outside. I would not have noticed his cohort's oddity had it not been for his own. The shorter, rounder fellow moved with a smoothness as strange as his companion's lack of it. He didn't seem to walk so much as glide, and the movements of his legs did not match his gait. Whatever I saw, it was not two gentlemen of means.

They moved away from me, heading toward the warehouses I had passed as I came up from the dockside where the *Campania* had disembarked. I heard their voices indistinctly, a bass note mingled with a tremulous treble, as they continued up the street toward the end of the block. In a moment, they would pass too deeply into fog for me to see.

The stouter turned into a narrow alley between two buildings across the fetid street. He emerged a moment later, carrying two sacks, each large enough for a single man or a dozen cats. Shouldering one bag that appeared heavy, though he hoisted it with ease, he passed the second sack to his fellow. The bottom half of the sack appeared black in the dim, indirect light. The taller man took it, holding it awkwardly at arm's length as if to avoid staining his clothes.

A trick of the street allowed me to hear their voices clearly. "I'm sorry you broke yours, Mr. Blue," said the deeper voice. I could not see who spoke, so assigned the deeper voice to the stouter. "You shall have nothing for later, I should fear." The voice, now that I heard it clearly, broke into parts. The words arrived in my ears as if spoken by two persons reading the same part, but a fraction of a second apart.

"I will find another, Mr. Grey," the other said. The voice, high and reedy, frightened me less, for it least it came whole and at all at once. Its sound seemed off, though, as though air escaped from a valve as it built pressure before giving voice, the way a steam whistle might. It gave his voice—for I presumed *he*—a sibilant quality, full of esses and long pauses.

"The Master will not be best pleased, Mr. Blue, that you did not share." The stouter one shifted his bag, and I heard a moan. "We should go now, I should think. It rouses."

The taller, his upper body swinging loosely, turned to regard his bag. "I think mine shall be along presently. There shall be plenty for all." He looked up then, and my heart skipped a beat as his marionette head swiveled all the way around his thin neck to look directly at me. I had the sensation of staring at a skull, for all that his face was shrouded by fog, darkness, and hat-brim.

The shorter glanced back as well. He tipped his bowler to his taller friend, then settled it back and tilted it slightly to one side in a jaunty manner. "I see. You play at hazards, Mr. Grey. I commend you. The Master will either reward or punish as he laughs or angers."

He glided into the thickening fog, jouncing his bag a bit for a final moan. The taller shambled after, and for a second I had the sense of the number 1o, fading in the night.

I paused a moment, uncertain what to do. I did not know whether these two had been within my brother's lodgings, for all their suspicious natures. I was torn between lurking here and following after, perhaps missing him if he should return. I dithered a few more moments before deciding to follow. The building would not move, and I might have another chance to encounter him there. The two "men" did move, and would soon become a lost opportunity if I did not seize it now.

I stepped down and hurried after them, then stopped cold as a realization dawned. They had known exactly where I was, that I been watching, and they did not care that I had seen them. A lump formed in my throat, and I grasped my father's pistol tightly. It crystallized my determination to follow, though with abundant caution.

My resolve to keep my distance and remain careful failed almost immediately. I have a quiet way about me, and can move with near silence if I must. Yet as I pressed on after them, I heard not a sound, neither footfall nor voice. I crossed carefully in front of the alley, taken by a sudden fear of something reaching out from the dark and grasping at me, pulling me down, and pressing a wet, acrid cloth over my nose . . .

I stood paralyzed a moment, unaware whether this was memory from Chicago, or a newly conjured fear. There was so much I did not remember, and so much I wished to forget.

Shaking myself free, I hurried to follow the two men, now worrying I had delayed too long and lost them. Walking rapidly forward at intervals for several blocks, I paused often to stop and listen. My racing heart sounded loud in my ears each time I paused, and each time I grew convinced I paused too long. I began to consider dropping back and returning to my lonely vigil outside the rooming house.

The deeper-voiced one spoke ahead of me, frighteningly close now, no more than a dozen steps ahead.

"Are we to be late, then, Mr. Grey?"

I was certain they could hear my heart beating as it thumped in my chest.

"A little, perhaps, Mr. Blue, but it is of no moment. The others will demonstrate the preliminaries." I could see neither of them ahead, for all I was in easy conversing distance.

"Are we just there then, up ahead on the right, Mr. Grey?"

"Indeed, so, Mr. Blue. Look for the small door just below street level."

"Excellent, Mr. Grey. Shall we proceed?"

"Certainly, Mr. Blue. Please, you first. I will come after. I fear I am dripping, and laundresses are put off by blood on the lapels."

I held my breath for two dozen heartbeats, then the same again, until my pulse slowed enough for me to follow.

I took one step forward and felt a brushing against my coat, and then another. A faint but growing sense of resistance pressed back against me, as though the fog itself tried to prevent me from going to the building. Another step, another firming as what felt like faint hands tried to restrain me. What felt like fingers brushed my cheek, and I jumped back, stifling a yell.

Another dead gaslight loomed ahead in the closed-in darkness of the street. I lit it, calling in my Will to heat the cold gas. This task proved more difficult than the earlier act, when the gas had been hot and the metal grill required a only couple of degrees.

Ghostly hands and faces emerged from the fog, each a wisp as it seemed to form and dissipate. The faces of children and women grew in strength, emerging in greater numbers from the fog as I resumed my stride. Their faces grew more distinct as I approached the building, showing expressions of fear and horror. Some, their faces more fully formed, shook their heads in denial. The fog itself began to band around me, and I worried it might begin to act as a physical thing, strong enough to strangle. Fog is the weakest manifestation of Water, the earliest conjuring of an apprentice, and the easiest broken by its opposite, Fire.

I took one final step, felt the resistance tighten again, and called in my Will. I pulled a strand of thread from my coat to use as fuel, for that reduces the amount of the Fire Master's own essence that must be spent. I drew up the flame on my palm, using its heat to drive back the foggy apparitions. They made one final effort to push me back, and failed as I released the flame to fly about me, fending off the ghostly hands. The effect faded, broken by my Fire. I kept the flame going, dancing above my left shoulder to light my way.

I took a tentative step forward, then another, without resistance. I do not know why, but I paused to look back. There in the light of my flame stood a little boy, about ten. He looked at me with an expression of profound sadness, then dissipated, his face and body breaking into millions of pieces as he faded into the fog.

I know little of Air, other than it often serves illusion and false seeming. I assessed this as Elemental conjuring, a spell to keep the unwanted away from the warehouse, too weak in force to draw suspicion while clever enough frighten the credulous and the weak. I was neither.

My confidence returned. So much for Air.

I walked quickly to the small, recessed door in the side of the building. The door opened a foot or two below street level, reached by an ancient step, suggesting that the building had long predated the street, enough for all of London to have risen around it. I glanced at the walls, my impression of great age reinforced by the old, cobbled walls. Brushing one with my fingertips, I felt an old power, a whisper of a foreign tongue I registered as Earth. The large building might today serve as a humble warehouse, but its roots were ancient, and its lineage out of place with its role.

I paused a moment on the step, momentarily overtaken. I had forsworn dark places after Chicago, yet now prepared to enter another. I gathered myself, touched the pistol as talisman, and entered.

A narrow hall stretched before me. I saw doors scattered along the hall, but no sign of either man, and no clue as to which portal they had passed through. I stepped carefully down the narrow passage, wary for a sight or sound that might mean my discovery.

I glanced down and saw dark spatters on the floor a few dozen feet into the hall. I knelt where I could see them more closely, and then removed my glove to touch my fingers to one drop. It proved to be blood, as I surmised. I gathered that it must have fallen from the bag held by the thin man. I wiped my finger clean on my handkerchief and returned it to my pocket.

I followed the blood trail, passing in front of several doors, until it abruptly ended alongside a piece of blank wall. I looked up and back, then passed my flaming ball from my shoulder to my hand and examined the wood on both sides of the hallway. I moved the flame closer still and peered closely at what appeared to be a narrow crevice to my left. The flame's tip danced as though brushed by the slightest movement of air. I focused just there, and saw the tiniest of cracks where a section of wall did not perfectly match the others.

I felt around the wood, my naked hand sensitive to the slightest of rises that marked the door's edge. It proved well concealed, so much so that I might have patrolled the hall a hundred years and never found it. That thought froze my blood a moment.

The feeling grew in my breast that the two men had lured me here, a revelation that gave me both pause and hope. Pause in that while I might now escape the trap, this was still the surest route I had to finding him. Hope in that my epiphany would possibly give me an advantage and allow me to turn the tables. I was slightly built, this was true, but I could yet surprise. Had not Dr. Holmes learned that to his chagrin?

Bending, I found a nail head protruding slightly from the wood. I depressed it, and it gave a satisfying *click*. The hidden door opened a trice, enough for me to insert my fingernail and prize it far enough for me to slip through.

Behind lay a stonewalled staircase, leading steeply down to a lower basement. Smelling the damp and wet, I reasoned that this cellar lay not yet far enough from the Thames to be immune from its effects. I moved down, stepping carefully to avoid a fall that might bring injury, or worse luck, noise.

The stairs gave way into a large, dark room, large enough to swallow the flame from my solitary light. The far end of the room, perhaps sixty paces away, revealed a thin sliver of yellow light, perhaps a door cracked with a lantern beyond?

My nostrils filled with the smells of dank earth and mildew as I stepped onto the dirt floor. I lifted my small flame upward, seeing a wooden floor overhead supported by pillars and rafters. The pillars appeared to be a uniform, square-trunked forest, with trunks spaced every ten feet or so. The room appeared bare except for open barrels scattered around in what appeared to be a random fashion. I glanced quickly in one and saw oil-sheened water, old smelling and unsavory.

I snuffed my light and listened carefully. Was I pursued? Had I been detected? I heard no evidence of either. I waited a few moments more to steel myself, then crossed the open room to the nearest pillar. Somewhere I had lost my glove, so my uncovered hand brushed rough splintery wood, dry as dust. I moved thus, with short staccato steps from pillar to pillar, pausing to listen as I went.

I judged I crossed midway through the room when lamps attached to every pillar burst into flame at once, an exercise requiring more strength than I possessed. The gesture spoke volumes to both a sense of power and a flair for the dramatic. Blinking in the sudden glare, I beheld a figure dressed entirely from head to toe in dark robes marked with suns, comets, and stars. It appeared a richer variant of the fashion worn by side-show conjurers and comic-opera villains. He lacked only a conical hat with *Wizzard* picked out in silver thread to complete the costume.

My eyes adjusted, and I knew I had found my brother. He looked to be in no great distress, standing easily in a conjuring circle some thirty paces away. His hands appeared unshackled, at least as far as I could see from below the hems of the voluminous sleeves. His face seemed as beautiful as ever, and he appeared sleek, well fed, and untroubled.

The frights and discomforts I had suffered in traveling to his side only to find him so well kept made me testy. I made as if to pick a piece of lint from my coat, using my play at nonchalance to mask my distress and fear.

"You said you needed me," I said, not bothering to conceal my irritation. "I came."

"Obviously." His voice, deeper and richer than I remembered, stretched out each syllable, employing them to make me feel small and stupid for stating the obvious.

Stung by his response, yet endeavoring not to show it, I retorted, "I saw your lodgings. You've fallen a long way, then, or has your last conquest cast you aside?"

He flashed his perfect teeth at me and shrugged. I knew him well enough to see he both acknowledged my sally and demonstrated his indifference to its effect.

"Those are not my lodgings," he replied in his quiet voice. "I needed to send you someplace close by where you would be easily found. The rooming house served its purpose."

The fear that I had banked under my irritation flared back to life. I gestured at his comic-opera costume, "Your appearance suggests prosperity, if not common fashion. You said you required my help. Why am I here?"

"You misread the telegram," he answered in the same calm and reasonable tone that drove me mad as a child. "I don't need help. I need you."

"Me? Why?" I replied, startled.

"When you escaped the Chicago Chapterhouse with the ritual incomplete, certain of my fellows wondered if I had aided you." He shrugged. "My commitment to the Cause has been questioned. My order required me to offer a gesture of redress. So I agreed to bring you here in order to restore myself in their eyes."

My mind reeled under the hammer blows of his four short sentences. The memory of being bound naked to a board and screaming while pincers tore my skin burst forth from the locked place where I kept it. I struggled to keep other terrors, as bad and worse, confined in their dark places, lest I be overborne. My brother had known of the torments I suffered in Dr. Holmes' dungeon—had acceded to them, and had brought me here to continue them.

The completeness of the betrayal nearly broke me. I grappled enough with the fact of his treason, but could not fathom the reason for it. "Why?"

He spread his arms, palms toward me, showing me the robe's symbols. "In the ancient days, we were not confined to the one natal Element but could establish Mastery over others, beyond those of birth and sire. That is what this is, these robes adorned with those Elements under command . . . Star for Fire, Moon for Water, Comet for Air, and Diamond for Earth. Those ancient forms, debased by sideshow magicians and fools, now restored to their proper role."

I felt a glimmer of comprehension. "And you've found a way."

"Yes," he replied. "The essence is drawn out of the Master and stored in a vessel. This may then be drawn off by another, if the spells are known."

He reached into his robes and drew forth a cluster of amulets, all on slim chains around his neck. He extended his other hand toward the ground, his beautiful face furrowed in concentration. "And so . . . Earth."

I saw an amulet glow in his hand, shining through his flesh as it brightened. The ground slowly shifted and grew, a small mound that resolved itself into a golem's shape, perhaps knee high, that turned to regard me with an eyeless face.

"Air." A swirling vortex formed around me, entirely free of dust from the dirt below. It battered me, whipping my hair, and driving me to my knees. I tried to stand, and it struck me again, forcing me down. When the buffeting settled, I tried to move and failed. Air, as strong as bonds of iron, held me in place.

"Water. The sign in opposition." His eyes closed in concentration as water from the nearest barrels formed into an arching spout that moved from one barrel to another. The effect proved clearly the hardest and least impressive. Sweat poured from his face, as the last portion of the arc collapsed and fell, a few feet short of the receiving barrel. Had I felt a weakening in his bonds of Air as he struggled with Water, or did this serve only my desperate imagination?

He freed me then, allowing me to my feet, as he mopped his face with his free hand. His other hand grasped the amulets around his neck. His hand, glowing with the energy within, faded.

He both impressed and frightened me by his use of the other Elements, but less than he might have. Fire had come so easily to him that watching him struggle here had been a revelation. He had limits. I had never seen my brother work at anything before, neither in his Mastery, nor in his ability to live on others' fortunes. It diminished him in my eyes. My brother and his ilk had found a way, certainly, but it proved foreign and difficult.

One piece didn't fit. "So, the sending outside was yours, then. A spell of phantasms to ward the building."

He looked askance at me, perplexed. "No. I know naught of that."

Curiouser and curiouser . . .

"Then what need of me?" I asked, striving for a calm I did not feel. I knew the answer before he spoke.

"Masters are the grist for our mill," he replied, in a voice as indifferent as if he were ordering fish for dinner. "The rituals draw the eternal essence, the spark of the divine, or soul, if you prefer the base term. We bind the Elemental energies thus released in order that we may draw from them later. The resonances deplete quickly, so we require steady replenishment."

It confirmed both what I previously suspected and my current suspicion that I had well and truly trapped myself. He was stronger, but I was faster. Could I make it serve me to escape?

I gathered my Will, drawing flame and fuel from the nearest lamps, then sent it hurtling toward him, hoping to catch him off stride. He made no effort to move or evade. Instead, my lancing flame arced away from him, toward one wall where it simply vanished. A sigil there glowed red, then leaped from symbol to symbol around the room, racing at intervals as it picked up my energies and gave them around. In a second the walls glowed, red and hot as embers.

He smiled then, a splitting of his mouth that did not extend to his eyes. "The ritual is begun, and you are still connected to it. The more you cast from yourself, the faster this will proceed." I hurled another ball of flame at him, and watched it arc away and be drunk. The sigils glowed redder still. I saw then that they had not been etched on the wall, but written on some kind of plate or shield that hung there.

"Our investigations have shown that we carry all of the Elements within us, weaker perhaps, but which can still be extracted," he said, speaking as if behind a lectern and I had not just attacked him. He gestured, and I gasped as the air was leached from my lungs. My head reeled, and I collapsed to my knees again, unable to draw breath. Over his shoulder, I saw other sigils light, dimmer blues and greens and whites, less defined, but still glowing. My heart raced, and blood pounded in my veins. My sight darkened as I looked up and saw him make a small plucking gesture with his hands.

The feeling of being pulled through a sieve gave way at once. I fell forward onto my face, hot tears washing away the dust on my cheeks from the dirt floor.

"Pathetic." he stated, his disdain piercing his calm demeanor. "You still represent my family. At least attempt to comport yourself with a modicum of dignity." An amulet glowed, and he raised me to my feet.

I reached my hand into my coat without thinking, and my fingers touched the butt of my father's pistol. I slid my hand around its heavy weight. It gave me a small hope.

"Is this how it ends?" I tried to sound contemptuous, but I suspect my voice merely betrayed my terror.

"No," he answered, again calmly, as though discussing the weather. "I have been given the task of preparing the engine. My trust is not yet restored, so others must complete the ritual."

My voice shook as memories swelled, rushing up from their dark places again. I could neither help the tremor, nor what I said. "Please," I begged. "Please, not that."

His eyes stayed me from further remonstrations. They held no pity. Not a glimmer of concern, or regret, or even embarrassment at what he proposed. His free hand gestured behind me, and I turned to see. Two men, the one tall and the other stout, came into my view and approached me, gliding or on marionette strings, each according to his nature.

I pulled the pistol from my coat, using my turned body to hide the gesture. I then faced him, holding the pistol in both hands as I had practiced on the *Campania*. Using both thumbs, I drew back the heavy hammer.

"Let me go," I said.

My brother's expression remained unconcerned. An amulet glowed in his hand. "I would not, even if I could," he replied.

We stood a few dozen feet apart armed with pistol and amulet. The men's voices cut across us both.

"Do we intervene, Mr. Blue?"

"No, Mr. Grey. These minor dramas will add spice, more

piquant for being a sibling squabble. The fear will keep the engine powered for now. This tableau will resolve itself shortly, and then we may proceed."

A key turned a lock in my head, and the germ of an idea formed. Mine would be a desperate act, drawn from two statements of unknown provenance.

I pulled the trigger. The horse pistol jumped in my hand, shocking me with both its recoil and the loud report in the confined space. Acrid smoke flooded my nostrils and obscured my vision. My ears rang as the gray cloud slowly cleared.

The bullet hung in the air just short of my brother, locked in a wall of Air at the edge of his conjuring circle. It dropped to the ground, the soft lead nose crushed in. He stood poised, ready to defend himself again.

But the first shot had only been a ploy to distract him. Pivoting a quarter-turn, I discharged the remaining shells at the closest of the fiery sigils. One struck, shattering its backing like a dropped clay pot, and destroying the glowing symbol in a burst of flame and energy.

I knew the two men had thrown themselves toward me the moment my intent became clear. They were far too late to prevent my assault upon the symbols. I hoped only to disrupt their rituals and sow enough chaos that I might escape.

Instead, a river, a sea, an ocean of power flowed into me as the sigil ruptured, borne by my connection to the infernal engine. It drew from me, but with its form now disrupted, the energies freed now traveled back along the bindings to me. I had not understood the full import of what my brother had said until that moment. And it nearly destroyed me.

The life essence of five, ten, fifty, a hundred Fire Masters poured into me, far more than I could contain. I threw my head back, my arms out straight and stiff at my sides, as torrents of pure flame poured out of me. The lanterns burst in the heat of my Fire, their fuel blazing it as it flowed down the dry wooden pillars, scorching and catching them one by one. The other Fire sigils detonated in turn, as the power released by the one I had broken lashed back into the others, detonating each in turn. Their torrents joined what already surged into me.

Mad with power, drunk with the energies that infused me, I understood for just a moment what my brother had sought. Then, beneath that, I felt the first energies I had taken fade, felt the first soul fade into ash. A woman, my own age, taken in torment. I felt all her happiness and joys morph into the pain, fear, and despair that marked her final days. My sufferings had marked only the first tastings of the first course.

The life essence of hundreds born to Fire washed over me, powering me, and I became as mighty as any god. And my name was Vengeance.

The two men were nearly upon me when I turned. I clapped my hands together, and a sheer concussive wall of Flame burst away from me, a solid sheet of red, yellow, and blue that shattered the closest pillars, causing the floor above to sag, and sweeping the two men away in a tide of pure, lambent Fire. The heat and force of my rage should have been sufficient to have rendered their bones to ash when I smashed them against the far walls, but it wasn't.

The force did strip their seemings away, however. Mr. Grey stood, a shambling thing of clay and iron and Earth, still moving on his invisible puppet strings, while Mr. Blue roused himself, a swirling ball of Water, oozing and gray as any slug. Mouths and eyes, some against its flesh, others on stalks, emerged and disappeared, tiny tides rippling against its obscene hide.

In any other time, I would have quailed at the sight of them. I had heard of golems of Earth, but as mindless things, incapable of speech or reason. I could not even begin to fathom the creation of a golem of Water. Golems that spoke and thought represented something completely beyond my experience.

My enemies gave me little time to contemplate their natures. The creature of Earth struck first. I walled the Water thing away behind a curtain of flame, and turned to deal with the attack. It made a gesture with its hands, cupping them together and lifting up. Lesser golems began emerging from the dirt, scores pulling themselves upright from the damp ground. I replied with Fire, drawing the flames around me in a maelstrom of heat and energy. When I stopped, the golems stood frozen, baked into hard clay.

Mr. Grey opened and closed his fists again, and the ground opened beneath my feet, pulling me down. The crack widened like a maw, and I scrambled to escape before I could fall, only to have it heave open again as I sought purchase along its edge. I slipped down and inside, clinging with my fingers to the crumbling lip.

I heard another great heave of Earth and saw the other side of the gap closing toward me, seeking my entombment. I desperately directed my borrowed energies against the sagging floor above, bursting it from below. Debris fell around me. One large timber, already on fire, lodged where I could stand, and I leaped out of the crevasse before it slammed closed.

With my coat smoking from the flames and my skin burned where it had been seared by falling embers, I rolled onto my side and saw Mr. Grey closing in on me, his hands now claws opened to rend and tear. He passed between two barrels that remained upright. I saw the heat haze rise from him from his earlier immolation, and I knew his weakness.

I augmented the natural fires, heating them into furnaces, and directing their blasts into Mr. Grey. He was Earth, and therefore immune to Fire. Heat shimmered and rose from his bony frame, and portions glowed red where the heat had been most intense. I waited until he passed near another barrel, but it proved unnecessary. His own heat immolated the cask, bursting it.

Water struck Mr. Grey in a hundred places, cracking his superheated form. His legs burst first, clay shattering as cool water washed over them. Then his arms and chest exploded in shards. He fell heavily to the ground and rolled onto his back. More golems began to form in the mud.

I struck two more barrels with balls of Fire. One proved to contain dirt. It simply failed, leaking dry soil onto the bubbling, steaming floor. The second, filled with water, exploded with a satisfying thunder and hiss, and poured a stream directly onto Mr. Grey's face as he lay there. His head simply burst, throwing sharp-edged pieces of clay about the room, and finishing him.

One piece struck me above the eye. I pressed my hand to it, and it came away bloody. I held my gloved palm to my head to staunch the bleeding.

I turned back toward my brother. I did not need to wonder why he had not attacked me from behind. The amulets around his neck had burst, fusing themselves into a lump that still smoldered. His hand and chest had both been destroyed, cut by molten metal when the amulet burst. I suspect that his death had been instant, from the moment I destroyed the sigil.

I walked toward him, seeing his face beautiful and unmarked. I felt sorrow and regret, not so much for how he ended, but for what he had become. For an instant, I flashed back to our time as children, when he had protected me from an older boy who was tormenting me. He had done it for his reasons, and not mine, but I still had been grateful. I tried to hold onto that memory, but could not. He had taken even that from me.

The energies within me waned more quickly now. I felt each soul winking out as its life essence dissipated. More still flowed in from the shattered sigils, but fewer and fewer, as a flood slows to a trickle. I used a portion of my waning energies to burst the other sigils, freeing those trapped in Air, Earth, and Water. Though I could not feel them as I did Fire, I had no desire to leave them behind for those who made and used this place.

The wall of Fire behind me failed with a hiss and a mighty steam. The gray, sluglike thing, mouths roaring in a hundred gibbering voices, glided toward me, faster than I could run. I saw the doorway I had entered, measured the distance with my eye, and fled.

The thing struck out against me with a dozen small tentacles that flew across the gap separating us. I dodged most, but one wrapped around my bare hand. I screamed as a thousand tiny needles pierced my flesh, each a tiny, jagged tooth determined to saw into my bone. The tentacle pulled my arm backward, spinning me away from the exit. I fell heavily, landing with my brother in sight. He began to slowly burn, his chest now agape and flesh rapidly sloughing into the unholy flames he had wrought.

The thing, its glutinous form erupting in tiny, toothed mouths surrounding a greater maw, pulled me toward it, a gray rope tugging me in great heaves. The agony in my hand flared again, and the sensation grew of ripping skin and tearing muscle.

I panicked, lashing out in brute force. I flailed at it with a pillar of Fire, hurling tree trunks of pure flame, and flogging it with my waning strength, now reduced to a scourge of smokes and sparks. Somewhere in this my control failed, and I smelled my own hair burn away as Fire took it. I was still sufficiently imbued with the power drawn from the shattered sigils, and flush enough with stolen energy and terror, that the separate balls of burst flame merged into a single lambent stream, focused on the horror.

The dry beams and pillars over the creature, awash in the naked heat of my fear, began to smolder and burn, joining those lit when I destroyed the monstrosity of Earth. I sustained just enough of presence of mind to turn the scorching heat away from my own skin as I drove it back and away from me.

The abyssal thing struck back, binding me with the thinning tentacle, and launching a storm of eyes and gibbering mouths. I destroyed the swarm, and the one that followed, and the one that followed that, hurling Fire and Fire and still more Fire, with each mouth and eye detonating in a tiny flare of steam and ichor, as a Creature of Water met a Master of Fire and was thrown down.

In an eternity we strove, though hardly more than a few seconds, before its strength waned, and it could no longer defend the thread that bound us. I broke it with one final heave, forming my left hand into a blazing brand that cut through the greasy tendril holding my right. The strand lost its grayish cast and fell to the smoking ground as a thin stream of common water.

I glanced quickly at my hand. The flesh appeared intact, and not stripped (for all of the sensation), but dotted with a thousand tiny pricks of blood. Something about that chilled me more than seeing bone and torn flesh. The skin heaved as something moved underneath, and I felt faint.

The thing lashed at me again in my distraction. I blocked the dozen tentacles that exploded from around its fanged mouth and drove them back, burning several into steam that immediately regrew. I redoubled my attack, drawing from the fading wellspring of power released into the chamber, hurling pillar after pillar and lash after lash and bolt after bolt, driving Water back with Fire, until I pierced its seeming and my charge struck home.

The thing shrieked. A thousand mouths opened as one, emitting a piercing, keening wail in a hundred voices that pierced my soul and tore at my ears. Gouts of steam burst forth as my Fire struck home. It quailed before my assault, seeking to draw back and flee.

I pursued it, tearing at its flesh with a molten hammer of naked power, fury, and fear. It visibly diminished as I tore its essence, ripping pieces away that fell as simple water. Its flesh rippled and heaved as mouths and then faces pressed outward, as though trapped inside a bladder. One emerged from its side, first the face, and then the torso of a girl, naked and beautiful, her mouth open in a silent scream and her eyes fixed on mine in terrified and mute appeal. She stretched one arm toward me, tiny fingers reaching for me in desperation, before the thing's flesh heaved and she was drawn back into it, like a child drawn beneath the waves to drown. The expression of naked terror as her face disappeared back into its side shook me to my core.

I beheld my own fate in that girl, that night I first escaped from Dr. Holmes' hotel, and what had been planned for me here. I comprehended then, for the first time, just how much danger I had blindly, stupidly courted.

Rage replaced fear, snuffing it like a candle. I had been a foolish child, secure in my arrogance and power, and unmindful of the plentiful warnings placed in my way. I grasped in that moment a truer, deeper understanding of the depths of evil, and the cup of it from which I had nearly sipped. In that moment, a chrysalis opened in my mind, and an adult emerged. A tiny portion of me mourned the loss, but the rest came in glory and anger.

I had squandered the bulk of the energies placed into my hands, wasting the remnants of the captured souls on flailing flashy attacks. In an instant, I drew those that remained into me, marshaling the diminishing streams of power that still flowed through the room. I shaped them into a tiny dart of purest Fire, shaped by Mind, and cast it into the heart of my enemy. The thing simply vanished. In my memory, its seeming vanished the instant *before* I struck it. Perhaps it was a trick of the eye, or of the mind. Either way, it was gone.

I glanced around, searching for more enemies. I saw none. Fires burned throughout the room, clinging to the walls and roof beams where they had sat in the fuel. My brother's chest and belly still smoldered and burned his skull. A line of Fire moved slowly, consuming his perfect face and creeping across his scalp like a grassfire, flaring and burning individual strands of hair. The bone thing against the far wall looked to be hardly more than a pile of ash and dust. I heard a soft sound through the increasing crackle and roar as part of the overlarge arm fell and rolled. I thought I saw a hand twitch, or it was a trick of the dancing firelight?

The last dregs of power dribbled away, leaving me drained and exhausted.

I fell to my knees as the agony in my hand rose. Raising it to my face, I saw the back had swollen into a hard nodule of pustule-covered flesh, where minutes ago there had been just skin and vein and tendon. My shirt, already torn and scorched, gave up a strip easily. I moved to bind the wound. The moment the cloth touched the swollen lump, a ripping agony tore through me. The flesh split open, and stinking green pus laced with tiny worms burst onto the dressing and my fingers, searing them.

I vomited, heaving bile at the pain and the sight of parasites within my flesh. I closed my eyes against a wave of dizziness, then opened them and cleaned the wound as best I could. A flash of movement raised what remained of the hair on my neck.

A single, baleful Eye centered in the back of my hand, nesting in my torn and bleeding flesh. It regarded me with a pure, malevolent evil. I cried out in horror and drew back, stretching my arm away from me. The thing blinked heavily, twice, gobbets of pus and skin clinging to its large pale ball. The eye shifted its glance to my fingers, and they twitched of their own volition.

Abject terror lanced through me, both at the Eye and its claim on the control of my hand. On impulse, I grasped a shard that had fallen near, a scorched splinter riven from the beams overhead in my assault on the mouthed creature. Clutching the blackened wood, without thinking, I drove it deep into the Eye.

Agony as sharp and intense as if I had plunged the splinter into my own eye lanced through me. I screamed again and again, and fell forward, fainting in the warehouse's basement.

I do not know how long I lay prostrate, but I awoke to blazing heat in my nostrils, and the sensation of heat searing my cheek. My hand throbbed as if seared in molten iron, and as I opened my eyes I saw the Eye, hale and whole, staring at me from the back of my hand. The crackle of flame and the searing heat grew as the entire underside of the warehouse floor above burned, close to roasting me. Tongues of flame lapped eagerly at the dry wood, devouring those few portions that did not already burn.

The floor would soon come down, and I had to flee. I lacked the strength to snuff a candle, much less the inferno around me. Gathering my father's pistol from where it had fallen and what remained of my coat, I escaped the burning dungeon. That first breath of cool air as I emerged from the warehouse, so laced with the noxious odors of London, tasted sweeter than the finest ambrosia.

Clutching my maimed hand tight to my chest, I fled into the night.

She unwound the dressing that covered the hand. Ichor dripped from the lesions, staining the desktop. The Eye regarded her, its stare hateful and malevolent. Her hand's own flesh, stinking and enflamed, writhed as the Eye fought to escape the weakening spells that bound it.

Her gaze traveled down from the desk in the second floor room to the small chicken yard below. The hatchet remained buried in the stump. The cautery rested beside it, heating in the small fire.

She picked up a pen and dipped the nib in the inkpot, ready to close her journal's entry.

"One way or another, I shall make an end to this."

The King of the River Rats
Michele Lang

The East River Waterfront, New York City
Spring, 1886

When Fire Master Jane Emerson opened her eyes, inky darkness surrounded her. Deep as the blackness engulfing her thoughts of pirates, of treachery, of death.

She tried to move and found her hands securely bound behind her. Heart pounding, she wriggled on the splintery floor, trying to get free, but it was no use. Somehow, despite her power, Jane had become a prisoner.

With great difficulty, she forced herself to stay still and to think about what to do. She breathed as deeply as she could, smelled the musk of the wooden floor beneath her, pocked with a faint whiff of mold. She heard water slapping against the wood below her cheek. The floor beneath her rolled, and far away she heard the mournful cry of a foghorn.

She was on a boat. And now she remembered how she had gotten there.

"I'm taking you off the white slavery story," Daniel Tappen had said only two days earlier. "In fact, you must come off the Five Points beat altogether. From now on, you'll cover the society balls uptown."

He sat behind his enormous mahogany desk in his publisher's office of the *Daily Clarion*, in the heart of her beat, the Tenth Ward, the tenement district. His protégée, reporter Jane Emerson, took the news of her demotion like a bullet.

His voice sounded apologetic, his face was masked with embarrassment. But nothing could remove the import of his words.

The numbness began to yield to a sharp pain, mortification coupled with grief, but she refused to crumple under the force of his pronouncement.

Ever since the New Year, girls from respectable homes had begun to vanish. One or two a week, snatched from their uptown homes . . . or tempted away somehow. Jane suspected the white slavery trade, which raged in the Tenth Ward, almost completely out in the open. But so far, despite her investigations into the depraved pimps' markets in places like the old Bull's Head Tavern and the Silver Dollar Saloon, Jane had found no trace of the girls.

Jane could not allow herself to accede to her employer's words and abandon her hunt. She paced back and forth on Tappan's gorgeous Persian silk carpet, her arms crossed in front of her so she could hide the trembling of her fingers. Sparks of rage shot out in a nimbus around her head, a corona of heat, and because Tappen was an Air Master, she knew he could see it. She didn't care. Perhaps it would help her in her cause if Daniel could only realize how deeply his pronouncement had affected her.

For he was not only her employer, but her mentor in magic. Daniel Tappen, scion of Old New York, had taught her all that she knew of the arcane arts of the Elemental Masters. A Mage of Air, he had taught the hot-tempered Jane to blend her Fire affinities with the cool azure of Air Magic, and her mastery had benefited from the marriage of such unlike Magics.

She had come from Boston all but untrained, chafing at her ignorance, and Daniel had not only schooled her in magic, but opened the world of Gotham, indeed all the burgeoning Gilded Age, to Jane's reach.

Because of all this, the demotion meant far more than the loss of a job, her livelihood, or her station in the world. Despite the fact that Jane knew she had done nothing wrong, the terrible thought besieged her that somehow she had disappointed Daniel in some fundamental way.

As usual, her temper fought to claim her, and as usual she fought to tame it. So she paced, silk skirts sweeping her ankles as she turned, the hems twitching like a lioness's tail on the hunt. The brass-and-cherrywood grandfather clock leaning against the back wall *tick-tock*ed in tandem with her steps.

Finally, she steadied herself sufficiently to speak. "What is the reason for my dismissal?" To Jane's dismay, she could not keep the trembling out of her voice.

"We both know the reason." Tappen leaned back in his chair and sighed. "Do you really need me to spell it out for you?"

An omnibus clattered by below, rattling the windowpanes behind Tappen's desk. Jane looked at the window and saw a black bird swoop by in the brilliant blue sky, and she thought of her beloved Rose. Her little bird of fire.

The thought of Rose, Elemental phoenix and her dearest friend, put steel into Jane's spine. The trembling stopped.

"Yes," she replied. "I think it would benefit both of us if you explain your reasoning here. I know that I am not an incompetent, and that my stories have enhanced the reputation of the *Daily Clarion*."

Jane knew she had done more than merely enhance the newspaper's reputation. Her exposé of the tenement arsonist, the lady robber baron Imogen Stewart, had not just caused a sensation in New York society at large, but it had cemented her reputation as a rising young star of the mages of the great city. No place as powerful as New York could avoid attracting the cruel and wrong aspects of magic, and it was up to the mages of the world to police their own and to make sure that magic did not spill over into the lives of ordinary folk.

Tappen clasped his hands on the surface of his desk blotter and cleared his throat. "Your work is nothing short of extraordinary. But I have no choice but to remove you from the Tenth Ward, Miss Emerson. Not to dim your brilliance, but to ensure your own safety."

Safety. Jane smelled fire, and the back of her throat burned. She stopped pacing in front of her editor's desk and looked him directly in the eyes.

He didn't flinch or look away. Instead, those all-knowing sky-blue eyes took in the sight of her, her righteous fury, and absorbed all of her teeming emotion without a blink. Ah,

Daniel and his blasted serenity! Sometimes his even-temperedness and calm rationality drove Jane halfway to madness.

"Ah, for my own good," Jane finally said. Daniel arched an eyebrow but said nothing. "You are my teacher, and my mentor, and my guardian as well. I suppose hiding me away will make your thankless job of watching over me a bit easier, at least."

The grandfather clock counted time in the silence.

"Not at all," Daniel finally replied, his voice still easy and calm, at odds with his tense features. "But you don't realize the peril in which you have put yourself. There are powers that do not want you to discover the fate of those missing girls. And I have received word from a lofty source indeed, warning me that if you don't stop your investigation into this latest story, your very life is in danger."

Daniel meant Tammany Hall, the corrupt political machine that controlled New York politics. A fearful enemy, indeed.

"Ah," Jane said. "But what about the safety of the missing girls? What will become of them?"

Daniel's eyes darkened to midnight, and for the first time Jane realized how frightened he himself had become. The power within her balled into an almost painful core of energy, begging for release.

Daniel leaned forward as if that would drive home his intent more effectively. "In your official capacity as the tenements reporter for the *Daily Clarion*, yes, you must stop. You are drawing a tremendous amount of attention to yourself."

He stared deeply into her eyes, piercing her, and she understood in a blinding flash what he really was saying to her. As her employer, the publisher of a daily newspaper subject to political and economic forces, Tappen had no choice but to pull her off the story.

Magic was not the only power rising in New York. The politics here were rotten to the core. For whatever reason, the Tammany machine cared to obscure the fates of these unfortunate girls. But Jane could not bear to forget them.

She drew a step closer and leaned over the massive old

mahogany desk. "Imogen Stewart is dead," she reminded him—herself—for courage. "She will never burn a child again."

The robber baroness had met her end at the hands of Jane's sleuthing and her magic, the cold winter before this new, fresh spring of 1886 in the mighty city of New York, the epicenter of a new world age. But such a new age of power did not come without attendant danger, either corporeal or magical.

Both of them knew that these young girls, most of them from respectable homes, were disappearing from all over the city, and they could sense the strange, malevolent magic at work beneath the surface. Jane, emboldened by her victory against the malignant robber baroness who had succumbed to the power of a dragon Elemental, thought that the light of truth could act to kill the magic that now stalked the innocent of New York.

The cold blue of Daniel's eyes put the lie to her rather naïve supposition.

"And you are afraid for me," Jane whispered.

"Yes, I am afraid for you. There is political danger, yes. But it is worse than that. The thing snatching the girls away is of a magic much more ominous than Imogen Stewart's. And Jane . . ."

He rarely called her Jane, and her name on his lips betrayed his fear for her. Daniel broke their gaze and turned to look out the window behind his desk. His narrow shoulders tensed, and he muttered under his breath, clearly miserable, though he would rather die than admit it to her.

She took a half-step forward. "Surely you know best, but . . . do you think I can simply stay in my gilded cage while these poor girls disappear? My heart is not so hard as that, Daniel. Perhaps I am a silly girl, and too innocent to comprehend the danger. But surely it would be an evil to refuse to use the powers I've been granted?"

Daniel swiveled back to face her. Tears shone in her mentor's eyes. She had never seen him visibly shaken so, not ever. Jane's mouth went dry as cotton.

"My dear Jane, I, too, possess powers. I, too, have taken it upon myself to protect ordinary folk from magic gone awry. But this . . . this magic is most foul. It comes from somewhere the mages of New York have been unable to trace. You are newly come into your powers; you think merely telling the story is enough to change the ending."

"But surely you haven't given up?"

For the first time since Jane had entered the lair of Daniel Tappen's office, he smiled. A small and dangerous smile. "No. You know better than that. Together, in good time, we must find this sickness hidden in the roots of the city, and we will bring it out. But we must do it with discretion. There is no way to report this story without making it worse. Please trust me."

Something hiding in his voice made her heart beat harder, almost painfully. She knew that Daniel meant to protect her from a danger that even he could not yet fight. But if she acquiesced to his protection, the girls who had disappeared would never come to light again. And she could not bear the thought.

She sighed. "Because it is you who ask me, Daniel, I will refrain from investigating the white slavery case in my capacity as a reporter for the *Daily Clarion*. I will write no stories. I will contact no sources."

They both knew she was lying.

The boat creaked in the darkness, and the rolling waves under Jane's head became stronger. She bit her lips to keep back a groan.

After speaking with Daniel, she knew the gambling houses and saloons had too close a relationship to Tammany to risk further investigation there. So Jane followed her hunch and began to ask questions along the East River waterfront, where all manner of wickedness unfolded by night.

The worst of the thugs operated on the water, not on shore. The River Rats and their leader, Tommy Rooster, were renowned as the most notorious of the river pirates operating along both sides of the waterfront, in New York City and across the river in Brooklyn.

They looted the foreign fruit trade in the neighborhood of the Wall Street ferry, and robbed the captains of the canal boats carrying freight from the great California clippers to shore. The canal boatmen and the stevedores on the docks had no love lost for the pirates, and Jane hoped her contacts among the policemen and the sailors near Water Street could give her more information than her Tenth Ward sources had done.

She did not go alone into these dangerous precincts. Walking next to her, in the guise of a penniless tenement girl, was her dearest friend and familiar Rose. This magnificent Elemental, an elusive and rare phoenix, had been drawn to Jane's Fire Magic, and Jane had saved her from a brutal death by ice the winter before.

Jane had provided for the phoenix in her mortal manifestation, and Rose repaid her with a profound and unsettling magic. Each believed they had gotten the better of the bargain, and Jane often reflected that her faith in this cruel, cold world was strengthened simply by the knowledge that a creature like Rose existed in it.

Now they walked hand in hand along Water Street, the power flowing out of Rose's fingers and augmenting Jane's energies. With Rose by her side, Jane felt like she could fight a dozen dragons and triumph.

The full moon glowered down on them like a lone, accusing eye. As they walked along the wharf, Jane heard more than saw the enormous river rats running along the splintery docks and the enormous ropes that tethered the ships to the shore.

A thick black cloud covered the moon and shrouded them in darkness. And the spring night suddenly was plunged into an icy cold.

Rose's fingers tightened inside Jane's. "Danger," she whispered in her low, husky voice.

Jane could hardly speak through the cold, thick magic. "I sense it, too."

A group of men emerged from the boat tethered to the end of the dock, shaking the rotten gray planks with their thick leather boots.

Jane gathered her energy and prepared to do magical battle with these men, who walked within a terrible darkness, a clot of emptiness, a hole in the ordinary night.

She wove her Fire Magic into a braid of energy, planning to bind the men so that they could not harm her—

"Fly away, Rose," Jane whispered with a sudden urgency. She knew to the roots of her hair that she was going to lose this battle to these unknown assailants, and furthermore that they were not the ones generating the superior magic, but merely the minions of that alien power.

If nothing else, Rose could escape, must be safe. All at once, Jane understood how Daniel had felt, helpless to protect her. Rose's safety meant more than her own.

Rose said nothing, only rose into the inky gloom with a shrill cry that split the night. Her brilliant plumage stood out against the darkness like a brilliant jewel set against velvet. The men hesitated as Rose shot through the sky like an arrow and away.

Thank goodness, away.

Godspeed, Rose, Jane thought. And then they were upon her . . .

There was a great outcry . . .

And now, alone, bound and tossed into the hull of the boat, Jane suspected she would soon discover the fates of the missing girls she had tried so hard to find.

The day after her meeting with Daniel, Jane determined to seek information from her new beat uptown, since she was officially barred from the old. Instead of the tenements and workshops of the Five Points, she alighted from a cab to the front door of a fashionable brownstone on Madison Avenue, where Mrs. Fitzsimmons had agreed to meet with her.

Mrs. Fitzsimmons' daughter Molly had disappeared back in February, and the police and the other reporters had already come and gone. Now, in April, Jane hoped Mrs. Fitzsimmons could shed some light on what had happened.

Jane presented her card to a liveried butler, who disappeared down a long hallway, his footsteps echoing away into nothingness. She was surprised when the butler returned with the lady of the house herself, sweeping to the front door to meet Jane.

Every inch the French fashion plate, Mrs. Fitzsimmons was a vision in a green walking dress, with a perfect little white hat and matching gloves. Jane felt quite dowdy in her own best muslin dress.

"Pleasure, I'm sure," the Madame of the house drawled as she held out a silk-soft hand for Jane to shake. "Your reputation precedes you, Miss Emerson. I expected a dirty-faced hellion of the streets."

She looked as far from the image of a grieving mother as could be imagined. *A whited sepulcher*, a voice whispered in Jane's mind, and then she swallowed the bitter thought away.

After a moment of complete shock, Jane managed to laugh. "I clean up quite nicely, don't I? Thank you ever so much for meeting me. You must be terribly busy, all dressed up in your finery."

"Oh, this is my working dress . . . we are to have a ball tonight, and I am all in a tizzy over it."

A restless breeze disturbed the lace curtains at the window next to the front door. "Oh, dear, looks like rain, doesn't it?" the lady said, a little too quickly.

"A ball! How lovely," Jane said, her voice affecting Mrs. Fitzsimmons's careless cheer, her mind churning furiously underneath. "I hope it doesn't rain tonight and spoil it. May I ask the occasion?"

For the first time, the lady looked a bit discomfited. "It is the engagement party for my son, Herbert. He is marrying one of the daughters of the Old Knickerbockers, Emily Van Heusen. We are thrilled to pieces, and as the saying goes, rain will not wash you away . . . they are a grand old family."

Mrs. Fitzsimmons seemed to sense the question hidden in Jane's silence. "Oh. You're thinking of Molly, aren't you?"

Jane nodded. "I am here, as you know, because of her, to see if you have learned anything more of her fate."

Mrs. Fitzsimmons glanced down the hall, her cheeks blushing demurely. Her butler took a step forward, as if expecting to toss Jane out on her ear for her impertinence.

But no. Evidently the lady had decided to speak her peace before bidding Jane farewell. "I know that's why you have come. You want to see me in mourning, secluded, my family destroyed. That is what you expected, what you hoped to put in the newspaper, I'm sure. Read the stories from February, and that is what you will find."

Jane struggled to put her subject at ease, but she saw that she had already lost Mrs. Fitzsimmons, indeed that she had lost her before she had ever knocked upon her front door. "I'm sorry," she finally said. "That is a beautiful dress. Such a green."

"It is a French *piqué*. My seamstress is a miracle worker, isn't she?" Mrs. Fitzsimmons's voice burned with acid. "I know that poor Molly doesn't want me to mourn her, wherever she has gone off to. She would be so happy for Herbert. Perhaps she has access to the society pages and has read of their engagement. As the saying goes, Miss Emerson, life marches on."

"No matter what the tragedy, it is true," Jane replied.

The lady's eyes hardened. "We all make our bargain with the devil, one way or another. And one must do one's best. Poor awkward, jealous Molly. Perhaps it is for the best that she isn't here for the engagement ball. She is all elbows, a skinny, gangly little thing. Happy for Herbert, I'm sure she is, and happy to miss the ball as well."

Jane swallowed hard and bit her tongue to stay quiet.

"Did you know Police Commissioner Alistair himself will be attending this evening?" Mrs. Fitzsimmons continued. "How thrilling for Herbert."

How thrilling for Mrs. Fitzsimmons, the mother of the impending groom. Commissioner Alistair was a tool of the Tammany machine, a corrupt, venal man whom Jane had met in the course of her work.

Jane made some vague murmur of congratulation, and before the butler could show her the door, Jane had already moved to open it herself.

She saw that Mrs. Fitzsimmons had nothing to give her. As the saying went, out of sight, out of mind.

The thud of heavy leather boots against storm-beaten wood shook the little boat in which Jane had been hidden. She smelled rather than saw the knot of rough men enter the hold, and half a dozen hard, cruel hands grabbed at her arms and hauled her to her feet.

"Come on, ye Friday-faced moll," one said close to Jane's ear. His breath, fetid and swampy, filled her nostrils. "Once the Rooster's done with ye, I'll have a turn with what's left."

The other men laughed, an ugly, disquieting sound. Jane took the fear and rage balled in her stomach and sent it out in a sharp spike of Fire off her skin.

The men leaped back in surprise, and the leader cried out

in pain. He punched Jane in the shoulder, so hard that she staggered and almost fell.

"Don't mark her, you hackum Sam," another man said in the darkness. "Rooster will eat yer liver for it."

The man with the swampy breath growled and grabbed her again. "If you try any more parlor tricks like that, you little cow, I'll throw you in the East River, be damned what the Rooster wants."

The Rooster. Jane had heard much of this man's exploits along the East River, for he was the man who led the River Rats, the most terrifying band of river pirates in New York. But more than likely he had heard of her also, or at least knew that she was a reporter for the *Daily Clarion*. Why would the Rooster take the extraordinary step of taking her captive?

She was a defenseless woman in his eyes, true, but surely he knew there would be consequences to what he had done to her. Jane summoned her power and kept it within her as the men hauled her up the narrow, swaying stepladder leading to the deck.

The moon was gone now, obscured behind a thick veil of gray clouds. The docks glowed purple in the shifting shadows of deep night. Jane sent her awareness high into the brooding, unsettled clouds, and found Fire there, energy also held in reserve and waiting for release.

"Storm's coming, a real Nickey," one of her captors noted. She could see them dimly, now, and they looked like a pack of wolves guarding their prize. They pulled her, more gently, onto the wharf and past the other boats tied there.

An enormous warehouse loomed between them and the shore, and when Jane probed it with her inner sight, she reeled back, overwhelmed by the malevolent evil dwelling within. Physically sickened, she swayed on her feet, and the thug who had punched her grabbed her by the arm again.

"Don't go swoonin' on me, you bleak mort! Rooster'll chew me gigg off."

He shook her like a rag doll, and his roughness brought Jane's consciousness back into her body once again. She knew, now, where the girls had ended up. Though given what lurked within the structure, she sadly doubted that they still lived.

She squinted at the hulking monstrosity of the thing. "You do all of this only for money?"

Somehow her question shocked this rough pack of men into silence. "Well, let the Rooster tell," the first man with the rotten teeth finally said. But he sounded sick and hesitant now, as if Jane had punched him back in the gut.

He led her another few yards toward the warehouse, the horrible miasma of evil getting thicker with every step. But to Jane's surprise, instead of completing their journey to the bolted door, her captor led her to a narrow stairway leading off the wharf by the shore.

Instead of stepping foot on Water Street, the pack of men and Jane descended the stairway all the way down, past the street level, to a dark, yawning cave under the wharf itself. Underneath, it smelled like garbage, wood rot, and algae. The broken stones shifted underneath Jane's feet, and bound as she was, she feared falling here even more than she had on the narrow stairs.

This place was no haven against the evil contained in the warehouse. Indeed, the very ground oozed with a malevolent magic. Jane gathered her own reserves around her, muttered under her breath the first protective ward her guardian Polly March had taught her long ago, when her magic had first begun to manifest.

The man sat on a throne, radiating a luminescent glow. Jane was so surprised to see him sitting there, she forgot her fear.

She whispered to the black lodestone hidden in her skirts, where she had tucked it as a precaution. The stone was magnetized by a lightning strike eons ago, and it still retained the traces of the fire that had touched it. Jane used it to focus her own latent Fire.

She squinted to make out the man more clearly. He sat cross-legged on what looked like a settee made of bones, a silk top hat tilted rakishly on his head. His face looked painted on, and his fingers clutched the ends of the armrests as if he was restraining himself from leaping.

"It's her," he said, his voice barely containing a trill of excitement.

A terrible unease settled in like an ache at the base of Jane's stomach. This man had been waiting for her.

"You seem to know me," she said, her voice quiet, still, steady. "But I don't believe that we have met."

"Pity. But now the moment is here. I'm Tommy Rooster, Janie girl, and I been waiting for you."

Jane frowned at his over-familiarity, but she refused to give him any more clues to her mind than that. "It must be kismet, then, sir. I have been searching for you—and the girls you have taken."

He glowed brighter, a terrible greenish cast shadowing his face, and she squinted against the sickly light he emanated. "I am going to tell you some things, and you are going to listen," he said.

"And then you are going to die."

His voice echoed inside her mind louder than his spoken words. That violation, the invasion of her innermost sanctum, made Jane so sick she thought she was going to vomit. She knew that voice. It had whispered to her in the witching hour in the years after her mother died, when despair and loneliness gathered close.

She refused to answer him, either in her mind or out loud before his minions. This creature was Tommy Rooster, or what the world knew as Tommy Rooster. But crawling within him like maggots was a deeper, more ancient power.

"I'm a right friendly gent," he said aloud, his voice booming and pleasant, and his men, gathered around behind Jane, affirmed his words with a gale of fearful-sounding guffaws. "I likes the girls, the girls like me."

"They are all dead."

Alas, she did not need the chthonic voice to confirm what she already knew in her bones. She said nothing, remained absolutely silent. And with the force of her concentration, the hidden lodestone began to grow hot.

A low rumble of thunder far in the distance, beyond Brooklyn, echoed after Rooster's words. He hesitated for a moment, then continued.

"Those girls, lost girls all. They came to me with broken hearts. You came, too."

Jane could not restrain a shudder.

"They came willingly!"

The men behind her murmured under their breath, and

she caught a whispered "not hardly," but nothing more than that.

A low rumble of thunder, again, and the sharp smell of a storm. The sudden patter of rain on the wooden wharf above their heads. Jane strained against the rope at her wrists, but it was hopeless. "You preyed upon those girls," she whispered, her voice hoarse.

"To the contrary. They were unwanted, and their fathers wanted them gone. Don't believe me? Look at their names, ask for gossip if you like. Look at the truth hidden behind the pretty society lies. They were girls instead of boys. They were ugly. They were too racy and naughty, and made their papas angry."

Jane was too horrified to respond. A vision in green, a French *piqué* and a darling little white hat, flashed before her. Mrs. Fitzsimmons' words echoed in Jane's mind . . . *"We all make our bargain with the devil . . ."*

"I do an important job," Rooster went on. "I call those pretty little things to me, a Pied Piper of broken hearts, and they come to me because they know nobody else really wants them. I take 'em in. I'd take you in."

"You sell them," Jane blurted out. As horrible as the white slavery trade in New York was, Jane took refuge in the idea now. Because the alternative . . .

"I sell them, sure. To people who know what to do with them. To people who want what I can get out of them."

"They want power. And power requires sacrifice. These girls weren't worth keeping. I keep their secrets I give them what they want. I am hungry I am hungry I am hungry."

Jane could stomach no more. A flash of lightning clawed out of the sky, and Jane called its power into her. The lodestone grounded the electricity before it could destroy her, and she took hold of the energy for her own purposes.

The human wolves behind her staggered backward, yelling with shock. *"DANIEL!"* Jane called through the chaos, desperately, in her mind. *"ROSE! ROSE! HELP ME!"*

The thing that had been Rooster, now animated by some deep, malignant Elemental of the Earth, rose from its throne of bones. Rat bones, she guessed, creatures that had served their Master before it fed upon them.

Such a Moloch required a constant influx of sacrifice. And the men and ladies of society who consented to the trade received at least a fleeting increase in their own power. This was the underside of the Gilded Age, this evil lurking under the desires of men had led to Daniel's fears for her and for himself.

She could not vanquish such a thing . . . it had lived in New York before any human inhabitant, it propagated itself in the mud and stone of the land itself. The magic that had bubbled out of the ground and devoured Tommy Rooster was utterly alien to Jane and her own Mastery.

Like attracts like in the world of magic. Such opposites as Jane and the Rooster, designed to repel each other. This immutable law of the physics of magic was the only opportunity Jane could find in her desperate situation, and she made the most of it.

She didn't bother with weaving a spell of protection, or binding, or heaven forfend, healing. None of that would save her from this demon of mud. Instead Jane gathered up every ounce of the clean Fire she had gathered from the sky and blasted the Rooster from his throne. Her Mastery called down the lightning, and Fire rained down upon the creature of Earth and blood.

The first strike blasted through the wooden wharf, kindling the rotten wood above their heads. Wet from rain, huge billows of brownish-gray smoke unfolded from the burning wood into the night sky.

The looped ropes binding her wrists incinerated in the blast, and the lodestone burned against her thigh. But it wasn't enough.

The Rooster rose, his skin peeling off in ribbons. The mortal man was surely dead, yet his frame remained animated by something ancient and unkillable. The fire burned away the human, and the Earth element so alien to hers remained.

Another blue-white claw of lightning cracked down, missing Jane by inches. And her Rose, her beloved, true Rose, struck out of the storm. Like called to like, and her phoenix came to her cry.

Swooping out of the sky, brilliant blue, orange, crimson, in her Elemental form Rose rode the storm. And behind her,

Jane sensed not only Daniel's power, but the circle of the great mages of New York. The Western White Lodge, gathered to battle the tremendous evil in their midst.

They could not kill this thing. But with their collective magic, they drove it back underground, into the stone under the city. With a final despairing shriek, the Earth Elemental sank deep into the ground, pressed there by the power of the mages' circle.

Jane whirled to face her human captors, but they had fled. She forced herself forward to see what had become of her tormentor, the river pirate Tommy Rooster.

She sank to her knees by the pirate's side, utterly exhausted. Nothing was left but shreds of fabric, and a scorched and waterlogged silk top hat.

Even as the world turned to gray, Rose gathered Jane into her talons. Nestled safely within the phoenix's claws, Jane rested her head against Rose's flank as she leaped into the air and away from the cursed place.

"Take me to Daniel," she managed to say.

In what seemed to Jane like a blink, Rose and she alighted into the circle of mages, who had gathered to work their magic in the heart of Central Park. Inside the circle, Rose became a human girl again, gasping for air and trembling after the effort of her flight from the pirate lair.

Daniel stepped forward and gathered them both into the protective circle of his arms, and Jane felt the warmth of his breath through her hair. For an eternal moment they wrapped together, and despite the danger Jane felt more loved than since her mother had died.

"I thought I had lost you," Daniel finally said.

Until this moment, Jane had secretly counted herself among the legions of lost girls, in danger of following a Pied Piper into oblivion. The malevolence lurking in the city remained, a dark velvet against which the Gilded Age shone.

But now, safe in Daniel's arms, she realized that despite the evils that could never be vanquished, she possessed all the magic she would ever need, beating right there inside her vulnerable human heart.

Air of Deception
Jody Lynn Nye

The life of an apprentice parfumeuse *is a delight,* Mlle. Aurelia Degard thought, *though one of solid work and hard thought.* The unforeseen revelation that she was an untrained Elemental Magician added further responsibilities and dangers which Aurelia accepted in good part.

One does, after all, complement the other most auspiciously, she thought. She gestured to Hyr, the Air Elemental who lived in La Parfumerie Rupier's workroom, to tip into her mixing bowl a drop of a precious oil so small it would scarcely wet the point of a pin. The scent bloomed in the globelike bowl, enriching the airs already there.

The workroom was a garden of delights to one such as Aurelia. Where better to be able to indulge herself in beautiful fragrances while making a good living doing what one dearly loved? Her parents were proud of her new career and demanded to know every detail. Yet, she reflected, as she peered up at the boy-shaped blue cloud that was the spirit of Air, there were things that she would never be able to tell them. It was possible that if she had known the truth about this shop, she might not have taken the position. But then, she would never have learned the truth about herself, either.

The recent return of her employer, M. Rupier, from his months-long journey to the Levant for rare oils, resins, and other fragrant—and not so fragrant—ingredients for his famed scents, precipitated a very refined and restrained but thorough scolding from Aurelia for not informing her of the dual nature of his shop, nor of her own skills that he had detected. How could he not tell her he was a Master *Magician*? Or she? What was she? It was a matter she could not trust to letters or other correspondence, and so had to wait several months in peril of her soul to find out. She was a good Catholic and did not wish to be burned as a witch.

M. Rupier had immediately apologized to her. He truly had not meant to deceive Aurelia. Time had simply run out for him to have acquainted her with her hidden skills and begun her education in their use before he had had to depart on a long-awaited and necessary journey, let alone to describe his own abilities and responsibilities. How could he know that she had the native talent to discover his hidden workroom and the magical being that lived therein?

But she had done well, very well, in handling the situation, and prevented harm. She had done the House of Rupier proud, and he was glad. A financial reward, a gift of ten francs, had done much to ease the discomfort, but the information she craved was more valuable yet. M. Rupier had promised to answer any and all questions Aurelia had at any time that they were alone, except for the presence of the Air sprite and the door warden, Alfonse, who was a young Earth Magician himself. M. Rupier had also reassured her that her soul was in no danger.

Their first session of questions and answers began the very evening of his return, and went on so long that dawn was creeping over the threshold before Aurelia's voice had gone raspy.

"Is there anything that you have left unsaid?" Aurelia had asked, with the last vestiges of sound she could muster, as the sound of the street sweepers passed by the front door of the elegant shop.

"I am sure there is," her master had said with a twinkle in his catlike eyes, not looking at all tired in spite of their sleepless night. "But this time I promise you, it is neither intentional, nor will remain unsaid, should I realize I had forgotten."

And he had kept his word. Wherever a lesson would fit into her busy day, he offered it. Aurelia absorbed every word, wondering how it was she had gone unaware of magic for her first sixteen years of life.

There was so much to know! A lifetime would not suffice for her education. She ought to have been detected years earlier, M. Rupier had informed her. Her talents could not have gone unnoticed if there had been even one other Master in her district. But how could she know? All she could do was work her hardest at both her crafts, one not only public but famous, and the other secret, never to be revealed to any but a fellow magician. But she was ambitious and hard working. M. Rupier had told Alfonse that she should become the *parfumeuse* after he retired. For that, she would work her fingers to the bone.

For her lessons in magic, she learned how to harness the unseen energies that abounded across the world. Her natural predilection was for the element of Air. M. Rupier was a Water Master, so he did not control the wisps and breaths of her milieu, and could only persuade them to comply with his wishes. She learned from him what she would before have called charms and spells, and all worked in glorious harmony with the skills needed for the making of perfumes.

The labor itself was not physically demanding, but it required infinite care. Formulating perfumes, lotions, powders, bath oils, and other scented products made use of talents she already possessed: a natural flair for combining delicious fragrances in many layers, called notes; a facility for reading formulae from both classic sources and her master's own formulary; and that most precious and irreplaceable gift, a nose. That tip-tilted and unloved feature on her narrow oval of a face had proved the key to her fortune and her future.

She inhaled from the top of the work bowl and checked the notebook beside her. All the ingredients were present, but something was missing. She closed her eyes and imagined what would fill in the deficit.

The Sylph Hyr, a spirit of Air and therefore her willing servant, flew around her as if he would wrap her in a veil of blue.

"Shoo!" Aurelia said crossly.

"But what are you doing, mistress?" Hyr asked. He stopped to hover above her head and took a deep breath from her work bowl. "What a tasty mix! Shall I bring you frankincense?"

"No, you wretched thing, that will make it far too heavy!" Aurelia said. "Bring me calendula."

"You have but to command." Hyr flicked to the high shelves, filled top to bottom with jars, phials, bottles, bags, boxes, and tins. His hand seemed too insubstantial to lift the weighty cream stone jar, but it floated toward Aurelia like a top-heavy white cloud. She lifted the lid and breathed the refreshing scent.

The soft, fugitive fragrance would underpin the heavier oils and temper them. Normally used as a top note, it would be treated here as a middle note. Ten drops, that was all! She counted them as they fell from the pipette into the shimmering golden liquid in the work bowl. Below, the low notes contained frangipani, myrrh, copal, lavender, and a tiny drop of clove oil. It was heady and luxurious, but so was the marvelous customer who had ordered it. Aurelia swirled the bowl to make certain it was right. It was.

"That is perfect, mistress!" Hyr said, gleefully. "Oh, I shall eat all of it!"

"Don't you dare!" Aurelia warned him. Truthfully, he only consumed the scent, not the liquid, but he was such a nuisance sometimes!

M. Rupier, seated at his rosewood desk in the chestnut leather chair in the inner room behind the showroom, chuckled.

Aurelia jumped down from her stool to go attend him.

"Is there something I am doing wrong, master?" she asked, her hands folded nervously against the apron that shielded her dress of black bombazine from splashes.

He smiled at her. His eyes and mustache looked even more catlike because of the expression, but a cat full of cream before the fire, not one on the hunt.

"Not at all," he said. "Your passion reminds me of myself as a youth. Is the preparation complete?"

"I believe so, M. Rupier."

He closed the heavy leather-covered ledger and rose. "Then let me sample it."

Aurelia hovered nervously as he whisked air toward his nose over the globe-shaped bowl. Many *parfumeurs* and scent makers used tall, conical glasses for their mixing, but her master preferred one that would contain all the scents as if in a bubble.

"It is delightful, master!" Hyr cried, whisking overhead. "As spicy as the lady herself!"

"Hush, you bold thing," M. Rupier said, but his smile was indulgent. Hyr laughed and turned somersaults. Aurelia could have stuffed the Air spirit into a bottle. Sometimes he was *so* annoying. "Yes, indeed, it is ready. Decant it. We have new cut-crystal atomizer bottles from Les Cristalleries Baccarat that will be perfect. You know where they are."

"I will fetch one, monsieur," Aurelia said. She hustled into the storeroom. The heavy wooden case in question stood by the rear door. These were the largest bottles that they used, meant to hold ten ounces of scent. Only the wealthy could afford the contents, so the container must be duly impressive. M. Rupier had these made to order for his most select clients. Aurelia chose a bottle made from plum-colored glass overlaid with a sheen of gold flecks. Holding it in both hands so as not to drop it, she returned to the workroom. Suddenly, she heard Alfonse cry out.

"A visitor!" She peered around the door to see. The stocky redheaded boy ran to the door, even though the bell had not yet rung. He knew every inch of the shop and the street beyond, as though he were its special protector. "She is here!"

Three tiny silver bells hanging from a bronze Arts Décoratifs fairy above the door tinkled musically. Alfonse pulled open the portal and bowed deeply. "Welcome, Madame Goltier!"

The woman who entered was like a fabulous beast, wild and untamed, wrapped in exotic furs, one of them a spotted pelt like nothing that Aurelia had ever seen. Her black hair was dressed high on her head, but thick curls tickled her ears as if telling her secrets. The dress she wore was of the most expensive silks and caressed her lush curves. Under a priceless, filmy lace fichu, the décolletage was daringly low, presenting a tantalizing arc of the full upper curve of her bosom without dipping all the way into indecency. Her wrists jangled with bracelets, and rings crusted her fingers, but her eyes, wide, long-lashed and the most astonishing shade of green, needed no paint to make those who beheld them forget all the rest.

Mme. Goltier was famous throughout Paris and, therefore, the world. She sang with the voice of an angel, though she was notorious in other ways. The ladies of the stage had an air of respectable disrespectability that added a *frisson* to those who met them. Rumor had it that she was the *chère amie* of a highly placed Russian nobleman who frequently visited Paris. It was undoubted that she lived in an *appartement meublé* in the very best neighborhood. She had all the confidence in the world but was at the same time was most womanly. Aurelia felt quite shy peering at her from behind the workroom door.

M. Rupier and Mme. Goltier exchanged compliments and fell into companionable chat. Aurelia was not surprised that her employer knew such a famous person—indeed, nobility from many nations wore the scents of the House of Rupier!—but she was not accustomed to conversing with them like old friends.

". . . not at all, it was my new apprentice, Mlle. Degard. Aurelia!" M. Rupier called.

Mme. Goltier's face broke into an enchanted smile as Aurelia tiptoed cautiously into the room.

"A female apprentice!" she exclaimed. Even her speaking voice was musical.

"Not my first, but my best and last," M. Rupier said.

"You embarrass me, monsieur," Aurelia said, keeping her eyes low.

Mme. Goltier reached across the counter and chucked Aurelia's chin high with a cocked finger. The vivid green eyes stared into Aurelia's hazel ones.

"I am all too glad to have you formulate my scent, my child. You shall add a touch of feminine mystery and wiles to my bottle. We understand subtlety better than these rough men."

"She has already added a new flavor to your perfume, one that I would not have thought of myself," M. Rupier said. "I believe it is better. You shall test it and judge."

Aurelia realized that the perfume was still waiting to be decanted. She fled from the showroom and back to the table where the bowl reposed. It was filled with a haze of blue.

"Get out of there!" she hissed at Hyr.

"I was keeping it safe for you, mistress!" the Air sprite said, entirely unrepentant, flowing upward to hover beside her. But he saw to it that not a drop went astray. Aurelia inserted a funnel into the clean atomizer and tipped the globe-shaped bowl above it. All the precious amber fluid flowed neatly into the jar.

She screwed on the top with its gold mesh bulb and carried the jar in both hands out to the waiting client. "Here you are, madame."

Mme. Goltier aimed the nozzle at her wrist and squeezed the bulb. A fine mist of droplets spread across her golden skin. All three of them inhaled deeply. Aurelia frowned, analyzing the aroma before and after it touched flesh. She waited until it warmed slightly, then sniffed again. Yes, it performed as she intended. The heady scents created a mental state of the exotic realm of the jungle, yet draped with an impression of thick, patterned silks that caressed the senses. She relaxed.

"It is indeed better than before," Mme. Goltier said, delighted. "Your little apprentice is already a master!"

M. Rupier bowed to her. "She will surpass me one day, wait and see."

"I do not doubt it," the lady said. Aurelia felt her cheeks turn red. Mme. Goltier touched one of the glowing apples of her face. "Never be ashamed to honor what God gave you, my little bird."

M. Rupier gave one of his catlike smiles. "It is what I have been telling her, madame."

Mme. Goltier peered over her shoulder toward the door, where Alfonse stood guard. "And that other matter that we discussed?"

M. Rupier reached into his waistcoat pocket and brought therefrom a tiny vial half the length of Aurelia's smallest finger. "Be cautious, madame, and be sparing of its use."

An expression that Aurelia never thought to see on the face of the grand diva appeared there: fear. "I will, my friend. And thank you."

She tucked the small bottle in the wrist of her glove. "You will send my perfume to my flat?"

"Of course," M. Rupier said. "It will be delivered within the hour."

With many bows and compliments, he saw her out.

At her departure, Aurelia felt as though the room had enlarged once again. She exhaled. Her master turned his smile on her.

"Mme. Goltier is an intense experience, whether in concert or conversation," he said. "I suspect you are in need of some fresh air. I have a few errands for you to run. First, of course, take the lady's parcel to her apartments. Then, I wish you to inquire as to the progress of our next order of bottles from the Cristalleries. It will be good for you to get to know the staff of the glassworks, so in future years you will know which master or journeyman to ask for when you have a special request."

"Yes, monsieur," Aurelia said, enormously relieved. With more haste than was probably necessary, she fled to the cloakroom to retrieve her summer hat.

If the Parisian summer was hot out-of-doors, Aurelia was stunned at the heat generated within the confines of the Cristalleries Baccarat. Though the kilns and ovens were in the rear of the building, their fire could be felt everywhere. While she sat in the showroom, waiting for one of the staff to serve her, tendrils of hair escaped from her severe coiffure and curled on her cheeks and forehead. She dabbed her face with a handkerchief.

A young man seated in another of the high-backed seats against the white-painted walls leaned over and sniffed.

Offended, Aurelia drew her back more erect than ever. "How dare you, monsieur!" she exclaimed.

"I could not help it, mademoiselle," the youth said. He was very tall and thin, with a shock of black hair that resisted brilliantine as well as the comb. "I could not help but detect an exotic aroma. That is Mme. Goltier's scent, is it not? I apologize. I work for the House of Bourjois, and we are all trained to notice perfumes of distinction."

Aurelia realized that the sample Mme. Goltier had sprayed had touched all of them, and she must smell of musk and calendula. Since the lady was so very famous, Aurelia couldn't help but preen. She put a hand to her modest bosom.

"Yes, indeed. She is a client of the House of Rupier. I am

M. Rupier's apprentice. Mme. Goltier was in this very morning."

The young man's sea-blue eyes widened with admiration.

When she returned with good news of their order, she also told her master of the encounter with the apprentice from the rival house. "He was very impressed," Aurelia said proudly.

Instead of being pleased, M. Rupier's eyes flashed like green fire.

"Are you a common flower seller? *Never* talk about our customers with anyone else!"

Aurelia was deeply taken aback. She bent her narrow body into the very shape of atonement. "But it helps to shine the star of your repute, sir. Others know that you have retained these very famous clients and they cannot steal them."

M. Rupier threw up his hands. "Oh, they can. And they do."

Aurelia lowered her face so she looked up at him through her eyelashes. "How could they compete with your wares? Do any of them do magic?"

M. Rupier smiled his cat smile, his temper assuaged. "No. But let our wares and the words of our devotees speak for themselves. Be above such petty things as gossip and publicity."

With advertisements in every newspaper, and journalists from the social papers stopping by all the time to see who was where, that was a self-defeating policy in Aurelia's eyes. But she was willing to admit that she had been wrong. She kept her head bowed. "I apologize, monsieur. I am yet very young and inexperienced."

He patted her on the wrist. "You will learn, my child. You will learn."

The local church bells tolled five of the clock. Alfonse turned the sign on the shop door from "*Ouverte*" to "*Fermée*." Mindful of the scolding she had received, Aurelia had removed herself from M. Rupier's presence for the remainder of the day, and concentrated on tidying the shop and putting away all the ingredients that had been used. For his part, M. Rupier had secreted himself in the workroom that was hidden to all eyes but those who were touched by the Elemental

Magic. But she needed his permission to depart. Summoning all her courage, she peered in the door.

"All is in order, monsieur," she said. "May I go home now?"

He glanced up from a large marble mortar in which he was grinding herbs. He smiled at her. "Of course, my child. I will see you on the morrow. You did good work today."

"You see?" Alfonse said, as he unlocked the door to let her out. "All is forgiven. Nothing has been done that cannot be undone."

Aurelia heard the door shut behind her, then felt the protections necessary to conceal what was within slide closed like a pair of heavy curtains. She had plenty of time to walk to the Cathedral de Sainte-Chapelle for evensong.

It was her habit to compose her mind from the pressures of the day as she went to church. She rolled over in her mind the blessings she had received, thanks to the Good Mother Marie, and counted the small transgressions for which she would ask forgiveness.

The Rue du Faubourg Sainte-Honoré, the small and very chic shopping precinct on which the House of Rupier stood, was filled with people leaving their places of business. Many women, some with children in tow, departed from the elegant stores, leaving behind bowing shop assistants, the men in old-fashioned tailcoats and the women in modest but good dresses like hers. The August sun was still high in the sky. Aurelia was delighted that she would have hours of sunlight after the service.

She walked southeast along the Rue des Halles, enjoying the mild weather. As she turned onto the Pont au Change that led to the bridge over the north branch of the River Seine, a whirlwind of fabulous fabrics and scents bore down upon her and grabbed her by the arm. It was Madame Goltier.

"For the love of God, my child, hide me! He is sniffing for me! He knows what I did!"

"Madame!" Aurelia exclaimed. Her surprise vanished in a moment, replaced by sympathy for a fellow being in trouble. "There is only one haven none will violate. Come with me!" She seized the lady's hand and pulled her the rest of the way over the bridge. They all but ran, their heels tapping impatiently on the paving stones. Looking this way and that for what may have been the hounds of hell, she opened the cathedral door and pushed Madame Goltier into the companionable darkness therein.

The boom of the great doors shut the wider world away from them. In the embrace of the church, Aurelia felt a confidence she did not have in the shop. The blessed saints would not allow anything to befall her or anyone who sought sanctuary within those walls.

"What is wrong, madame?" she whispered as she guided the distraught Mme. Goltier up the stairs to the chapel. Instead of entering the holy chambers, they remained beside the door, out of the way of other worshipers entering for evensong. "Who is pursuing you?"

The lady gave her a curious look. "Did your master not explain my mission?"

"Mission?" asked Aurelia, her heart beating faster than a bird's wing. "No."

Mme. Goltier produced the small bottle Aurelia had seen her put in her glove. She uncorked it. The air filled with a strong aroma. Aurelia instantly identified rosemary, myrrh, and a dozen other scents, the likes of which she had never known to be combined.

"What is it?" she asked.

"Aide de mémoire," Mme. Goltier said, with a meaningful look at her. "It is a charm for strong memories. Your master formulated it for me."

"A charm?" Aurelia asked, aware that she was blinking stupidly. She was outraged at the notion that bubbled up within her. "You *know?*"

"I do. And you must be a magician, too, or he would not trust you so deeply."

"Why?" Aurelia demanded, feeling as though she had been stripped naked. "Why would he tell you? It puts him and me in terrible danger!"

"We serve the same causes, Mlle. Degard, those of truth and our beloved France," Mme. Goltier said, folding her hands around Aurelia's. "And I swear to you, mademoiselle, I am in as grave a danger."

"From whom?"

A subtle noise near the bottom of the stairs interrupted them. Someone was sniffing the air. Surprised at her own boldness, Aurelia took the older woman by the hand and dragged her into the dimly lit sanctuary. They hurried along the side illuminated by Sainte-Chapelle's famous stained-glass windows and all but fell into a pew that was occupied only by an elderly woman in a black lace veil. Over her shoulder, Aurelia saw a man enter. He wore a dark suit and had a shock of untidy hair. The way he moved his head told her he was Mme. Goltier's enemy. He must have been following her by her very distinctive perfume.

Her hand flew to her bag. Within it, she had vials of rare oils that M. Rupier wanted her to study. Not only were they important ingredients in perfumes, but they had magical properties.

The strongest-smelling was sandalwood, but she needed more than that to hide Mme. Goltier's signature scent. Among the other bottles were lemongrass and sweet bay. Quickly, she dabbed drops of the heady attars onto her small, plain handkerchief and anointed the other woman's wrists and throat with it, all the while praying fervently.

"Mother Marie, preserve your daughters. Give us the protection your beloved son wanted for all the world."

She wished fervently at that moment that she had Alfonse's talent for Earth Magic, that she could form a wall of power around them to keep harm away. Instead, she used her Air talent to draw the fragrances from the oils and mix them between her gloved hands. The fresh perfumes took on a life of their own, forming a cocoon around Mme. Goltier. In a moment, there was no trace of the musky aroma that was her signature scent. Aurelia tucked the bottles away, then pressed her hands together in grateful prayer. She had never done magic within the confines of a church before. So it was true, what M. Rupier said, that God condoned the use of her talents for good. The relief she felt was truncated by the appearance of the dark-coated man in the nearby aisle. He hid his large nose behind a handkerchief. Aurelia remarked that he looked like a foreigner, with dark brows oversized on his square face.

He stopped beside the two women. Mme. Goltier kept her face buried in her hands. He sniffed at the air, his large brows making him look severe. In her mind, Aurelia willed him to go, to go away! It seemed an eternity until he did. She whispered her gratitude to Heaven.

It was not Aurelia's day for confession, so she would not have to tell the priest that she might be sheltering a criminal. She wanted to know more, but an extended conversation in the pews would cause an acolyte to come over and chastise them. Mme. Goltier did not move until the service was at an end. Both women crossed themselves and rose.

"Come with me," Mme. Goltier said. "I need to write all I know as soon as is humanly possible."

Aurelia tried to withdraw, but the other woman put her arm around her and pushed her in the direction that she wanted to go.

They crossed from the Ile to the south bank of the Seine, passing through the fourth *arrondissement*, into alleyways where Aurelia did not normally tread. Discreet bronze plaques announced government offices that she had never heard of.

"We are not walking toward your apartment," Aurelia said. She had been there only that morning with the bottle of perfume. "Where are we going?"

The face that Mme. Goltier turned toward her bore no trace of the celebrity singer, only a frightened woman like herself. "Please, do not ask me in public. Only wait!"

They turned up a narrow passage and were admitted through a creaking black-painted iron gate by a man in a severe suit. Mme. Goltier did not speak to him, only urging Aurelia up flight after flight of stairs.

"Well?" inquired a nondescript man also in nondescript clothing, who occupied the office they finally entered at the top of the building.

"Well. Give me paper and pen!"

"Who is this?" he demanded, looking at Aurelia.

"A friend. A true friend."

Aurelia was quite forgotten as Mme. Goltier threw herself into the chair before a battered desk illuminated by one of the newest of electric lights. The anonymous man supplied a ream of paper and a box of writing implements. The lady seized a pen and wrote out page after page after page of small, close writing. Aurelia could not believe that anyone could possibly have that much to say. No author could compose at such speed and make any sense. She sidled close to try and read over Mme. Goltier's shoulder, but the man gently urged her back. He gestured her to a straight-backed chair against the wall. Aurelia sat, fearful even to move from the spot.

Hours passed before Mme. Goltier put down the pen and massaged her hand. She smiled at Aurelia.

"Is that all of it?" the man asked, gathering up the papers.

"Every word," the lady said. She looked exhausted but certain.

"France thanks you, madame," he said, with a bow, the first human gesture Aurelia had seen him make. "If only we could protect you."

Mme. Goltier rose and straightened her back. She took a handkerchief from her bag and wiped away a trace of sheen from beneath her nose. "Then this is likely to be the last time we meet, my friend. I have no choice but to go tonight, perhaps to my death."

The man dipped his head. "Your service is deeply appreciated, madame. Go with God."

With head high, the lady walked toward the stairs. Aurelia scrambled to her feet, and raced after her.

"What did he mean, madame?" she asked, her whisper hissing in the stone stairwell. "Where are you going?"

Mme. Goltier stopped and put her finger under Aurelia's chin. The strong fingers trembled slightly. "Where I must, child."

"How can I help you?"

"You have already done as much as anyone could. More."

"But what have I done?"

"You gave me safe haven when it was needed." Mme. Goltier smiled. "Come back with me to my rooms. I would like to have my story known, even if only to you and your good master."

Night was wrapping Paris in its dark blue cloak bespangled with gems of the new electric lights and stripes of the old gas lamps. Mme. Goltier did not hail a cab.

"Within the confines of a carriage or a car, who knows what could happen? We are safer on foot."

Aurelia felt as if she would burst with curiosity. "Please, madame, safer from what? What were you writing?"

"What do you know of my life?" the lady countered, with a sideways glance at Aurelia.

The question caused her to stutter, holding back the scurrilous gossip that Alfonse and she had pored over in the society papers. "Well, madame, I know you are very famous. I have never heard you sing . . ."

Mme. Goltier waved a hand. "I know what you are not saying. It is true that I have found affection in the arms of a man not my husband. Many men, if I am frank. But what do you know of the dance of nations?"

"Nothing," Aurelia said firmly. "We border with a few. Some are our enemies, and some are our friends . . ." Her voice trailed off.

"But none are always one or the other. They do not trust one another. Every subterfuge is employed to make a friendship, but we know it will not last. That is the normal human condition. We deceive to gain our ends."

Aurelia was taken aback at such a negative view of the world. "I am sure that is not true."

"Oh, but it is," Mme. Goltier said. "Your Master creates airs that deceive all the time. You are part of that deception. You cause men to believe that women are more appealing than they truly are."

"Madame!"

The lady smiled but kept her gaze moving around the crowded street. "Oh, it is all for a good cause. The sexes must mix, or our race is doomed. But I was asked to make myself appealing—and available—to a certain man. The Count Boris Ouspeskiy. He is a very well-placed individual in the foreign service of the Tsar, the confidential assistant of Count Vladimir Lamsdorf, Foreign Secretary to His Highness."

Such things were beyond Aurelia's experience, but she could not help but ask. "Why are you not Count Vladimir's friend?"

The lady shook her head, smiling. "He is not interested in

me, or any woman, but his secret is kept for the sake of foreign relations. Count Boris loves a charming lady who resists only a little. I am only his woman here in Paris."

"And Count Vladimir negotiates with France?"

"No. France is like the belle who attends the ball, but no one dances with her. While we woo Great Britain, so does Russia. If we are not to be shut out entirely from the party, we must know what is going on between them."

"What did you write out?"

"A great treaty is being negotiated between Britain and Russia. Count Vladimir came here in secret, to confer with his opposite number from the Court of St. James in my apartment, since it was bought for me by Count Boris. But the draft treaty was kept locked in a private office maintained by the government of Russia. I gained access under pretext of waiting in its anteroom for my dear friend, then entering as soon as the clerk left for a short while. Thanks to the oil provided for me by your master, I was able to read it and memorize it, though the effect lasts only a short time. I brought that information, as you saw, to those they call my handlers, in the French foreign office. Fool that I am, I realized only too late that I should not have worn my personal scent on my quest. It is too distinctive! The clerk who pursued me is a servant of the Tsar. He did not see me, that I swear, but he scented me. That was enough. If I was detected in that office, where I had no business being, I would next be mentioned in the society papers as a corpse found floating in the Seine, my purse and valuables missing. So sad! The notorious singer a victim of yet another robbery by *apaches* or other cutpurses in the dangerous, mad city of Paris."

Aurelia shivered. This was a world beyond the small village where she had been raised. They crossed the Boulevard Opera, heading toward the lady's apartments.

"But he did not catch you. Soon he must go back to Russia with the Tsar. Can you not stay out of his way until then?"

"Alas, no. Tonight there will be a ball given by Count Boris. I will be his hostess. If I do not come, suspicion will fall on me. If I do," she said, her head drooping on her lovely neck, "I probably will not survive."

"But you will, madame," Aurelia said, with determination. "Since you serve our nation, I will help you if I can. Where is this ball to be held?"

In her most exotic dreams, Aurelia never thought she would attend a grand gala. Men in black suits with stiff white collars and ties or a host of pristine military uniforms danced with ladies dressed like a cloud of butterflies, in all the colors of silk that the designers at Hermès had ever devised. All of them wore different perfumes, the scents of which clashed and bumped elbows like so many coster boys at a market.

Many women in modest black dresses like hers huddled in the retiring room, waiting attendance upon their employers, dabbing a brow, anointing a cheek with fresh rouge, buttoning gloves up to past their ladies' elbows and reapplying more perfume as their ladies wished. Privacy was to be had only in the small dressing rooms along the rear wall. With her master's name as bulwark and shield, Aurelia claimed one of these as her particular province and waited.

Mme. Goltier swept into the retiring room. Her dress was of her favorite deep green, the same color as absinthe. The neckline was so low as to be almost indecent, yet it was scarcely lower than those of the other ladies present. She wore fabulous jewels at her throat and wrists, twinkling like a whole galaxy of stars. A jeweled fan hung by a silken cord from one wrist. And she bore with her the scent that was familiar to thousands, the aroma that was forever Mme. Goltier, the brilliant singer and woman of questionable morals. Only a few knew for certain that her heart as true as a saint's.

As they were her guests here, all the ladies in the retiring room greeted her from their chairs or couches. She returned the gestures grandly. Aurelia could only imagine how majestic she must be on the stage.

Spotting Aurelia, Mme. Goltier swept toward her, in no seeming hurry, but bustled into the tiny chamber that Aurelia indicated. Once the white-painted door was closed behind them, she lowered her rouged lips to the apprentice's ear.

"My patron has arrived," she whispered, "along with his employer and that man. What can you do? I do not wish these to be the last moments of my life."

Aurelia felt shy, but now was not the time to be hesitant.

"I thought deeply about what you told me," she said. "Your scent is so distinctive that no one who breathes it will ever forget it. That is M. Rupier's magic. Therefore," she continued, taking from her handbag a small bottle, "I made one similar, but it is meant to make one forget."

"How? How can it work?" Mme. Goltier asked. "I bathe in the scent. I wear it to bed. It is in my skin, as is every sin I have ever committed."

For answer, Aurelia brought forth another bottle and uncorked it. Hyr flowed out of it in a stream of blue mist, then assumed his usual boyish form.

"What, a genie?" Mme. Goltier exclaimed, her green eyes wide with wonder.

"He is a sylph, a spirit of Air, and my servant. Do what you can," she instructed him.

"Oh, it will be easy!" Hyr trilled. "She always smells so good, I would adore to consume her scents."

"Hush!" Aurelia commanded, glancing toward the door. She hoped the other ladies thought they were merely gossiping. But eager to please, Hyr flowed around the lady, surrounding her like a veil. When he withdrew, Aurelia leaned close, and sniffed.

"It is a miracle!" Mme. Goltier said, lifting her hand to her nose. "I smell of nothing, not even my own body."

"That will allow this—this *spell*," Aurelia stammered, hesitant to say the word outside the safety of M. Rupier's workroom, "to function without impediment."

She offered the small bottle and waited while Mme. Goltier anointed herself.

"It is very like my own scent. Did M. Rupier instruct you so?"

"He was not in the shop," Aurelia admitted. "There was no time. I prepared this myself."

Mme. Goltier smiled at her with an expression Aurelia believed to be admiration. "You have initiative and courage," she said. "*You* could be a spy."

"Heaven forbid!"

Mme. Goltier laughed. "What must I do now?"

"Touch the man's skin," Aurelia insisted. "And anyone else you feel is a danger to you. Then return to me."

"What will it do?"

Aurelia smiled. "It will deceive. All who touch you while you wear it will forget everything they know about you."

Mme. Goltier laughed again, a trifle ruefully. "A fresh slate. Perhaps I should shake hands with all of Paris." She shook her head. "Ah, but no, I am too fond of my fame." She extended her hand to touch Aurelia's cheek, who withdrew in haste. "Yes, you must not forget me. Watch over me, my guardian angels."

Aurelia opened the door for her and trailed her into the ballroom. Mme. Goltier sallied forth, her head high, and made straight for the handsome man in uniform who held out his hand in her direction. The lady was careful to avoid contact with him. *She follows instructions well,* Aurelia thought. *It must be how she avoids catastrophe in her secret life.*

The handsome man, who must have been Count Boris, introduced her to the Tsar's foreign secretary, Count Vladimir, a slight man in faultless evening dress. Mme. Goltier gathered her poison-green skirts in her hands and curtsied to him.

At the secretary's side was the dangerous man with the thick black eyebrows. The dignitary made her known to the man, who bowed, then straightened in haste, his large nose working. He had recognized the lady's scent. Aurelia's heart pounded in her chest. The man tugged Count Vladimir's sleeve.

But Mme. Goltier was quick. She reached out and shook the man's hand, surprising him. Aurelia just caught her words in between the sawing of the violins and the polite chatter of the guests. "Sir, I am pleased to make your acquaintance."

In a twinkling, the man's face changed from anger and suspicion to the beguiled expression men normally wore when first beholding Mme. Goltier. He was, from that moment, her devoted servant, Aurelia could tell. He looked her up and down and was charmed by what he saw.

"And there goes his memory!" Hyr cackled in her ear.

"Hush!" Aurelia said, hoping no one else heard. The man began to bow over her hand, clicking his heels and talking rapidly. Aurelia could not hear him, but Mme. Goltier fluttered her fan as if embarrassed yet gratified by his outpourings.

The elegant party went on around the small group like eddies dividing around rocks in their path. After a time, Mme. Goltier curtsied deeply and begged to be excused, deftly escaping a move by Count Boris to touch her. Aurelia could read the pantomime. Mme. Goltier regretted her departure, but she would return in but the smallest of moments. She hurried back to the retiring room.

"Oh, I thought I would die of fright!" she burst out as soon as Aurelia closed the door behind them. "He said nothing! I am saved. Well done, child, well done! Now strip me of this potion, or Boris shall forget me, too. Someday I may use the scent to escape him, but not yet. I am too fond of my apartments."

Hyr obliged, whisking up and down her lush body. When he swirled back into his bottle again, Mme. Goltier drenched herself with her signature scent. The lady leaned forward and embraced Aurelia, surrounding her in a heady, sweet cloud. "Ah! I feel myself again. Mlle. Aurelia, I am forever in your debt."

"It is for France," Aurelia said modestly. "The House of Rupier would never let her down."

"In her name, then," Mme. Goltier said, highly amused, "I gratefully accept your service."

"Will the danger to Mme. Goltier pass?" Aurelia asked after she had informed her master of the evening's events in the safety of his hidden workroom the next day.

"Perhaps, perhaps not," M. Rupier said, toying with a jar of priceless musk. "That is the risk she takes. You should be proud of her, as I am of you."

"I am . . . though she intimidates me. We have so little in common."

M. Rupier laughed. "She intimidates me, too! But I am grateful to have one such as her to protect the rest of us. It does not matter what the shape of the bottle, my cherished apprentice, but what good God pours into it."

Aurelia agreed. "In that, there is no deception."

Fly or Fall
Stephanie Shaver

Zephyrs once enticed Aurelia with secrets; now they left her alone. She briefly wished that she could summon them into her kitchen to cool it down, then immediately cast the thought aside and cursed herself for thinking it. No more. Never again.

Chicago shouldn't be this hot, not this late in autumn, but the weather didn't care what should or shouldn't be. She'd flung open the back door and done everything she could to minimize her time at the cookstove, but even so, the kitchen was hotter than the seventh circle of Dante's Hell. When this was over, she vowed to take a bath. And if she had to go jump in Lake Michigan to do so, well, she'd take that chance.

"How are you feeling, Miss Foster?" Aurelia called as she pulled the charlotte russe from the icebox and prepared to unmold the pudding by setting a plate over it.

"I feel fine, Miss Weiss," Alice Foster responded. And she did sound fine—better than Aurelia, in fact, and in no way affected by the sweltering heat of the kitchen.

Aurelia glanced over to where Alice played with her doll by the pantry door. Mrs. Foster had assured Aurelia that she'd find a nursemaid for her only child soon, but "soon" had yet to happen. Instead, Mrs. Foster saw to her daughter's lessons and upbringing, and on nights like this—when entertaining dinner guests—Alice was sent to the kitchen. It wasn't a burden on Aurelia; Alice usually took her dinners in the kitchen regardless, and she was a good child. Mostly.

"Just a little while more." Aurelia said a little prayer and gave the pudding mold a ringing *thump*. It slid out with no trouble, and she allowed herself an undignified grunt of satisfaction. "I'll get you your dinner shortly."

"That's okay," Alice said, stroking her doll's hair. The cloth poppet had been decorated to look like her—golden yarn for hair, blue glass buttons for the eyes. "I'm playing with my friend."

The pudding was the capstone on what had been a challenging meal. The Fosters were entertaining visitors doing work for the World's Columbian Exposition coming next year, and at least one had informed Mrs. Foster only a day before the dinner that he would "rather avoid meat." The season was late, but Aurelia had thrilled to the challenge. She'd broiled mushrooms and glazed them with wine, prepared a cold potato omelet *española*, and cracked a can of French peas, which she'd seasoned heavily with butter and chervil. Other delights wove their way through the courses: crisp lettuce drizzled with Roquefort dressing, split artichokes with drawn butter, and a plate of fresh cheeses. The relish platter was a foregone conclusion, piled with her five favorite homemade pickles. She'd even given up some of her precious half-sours, as the guests were all from New York City, so she thought they might like a taste of their hometown.

And there'd been meat, of course. She'd sent out platters heaped with raw oysters on ice, garnished with lemons from Florida. On another platter she'd put boiled calf's tongue over a bed of spinach. A side of dark mustard and pickled onions had gone with that course, along with thin slices of rye bread. At the meal's heart was a larded tenderloin of beef carved tableside by Oscar, the house butler.

She finished the charlotte russe with dollops of sweetened whipped cream, and blew the pudding a kiss as it was carried out to the dining room's boisterous crowd.

Victory. That's what this felt like. The rush and panic of food service was enough to drive all the worries out of her mind. For a few moments she stood there, wiping her hands on her apron, feeling confident and sure. Like she'd finally run far enough to escape her curse.

"Very well. Alice," she said, turning around, "it's time for your—"

The girl lay on the floor, thrashing.

Alarm welled up inside Aurelia. She bolted over to find Alice's eyes rolled up in her head and her hands clammy. Aurelia heard the door from the servant's hallway scrape and turned to see Julius, the butler's son, standing there.

"Find Mrs. Foster. Quickly," Aurelia told him, and he dashed off.

Moments later, Grace Foster arrived, moving as quickly as her petticoats would allow her. She knelt by her daughter, a glass bottle in her hand. The many jeweled rings on her fingers flashed as Mrs. Foster swiftly uncorked the bottle. Aurelia caught a brief whiff, like incense and alcohol. Mrs. Foster measured out a teaspoon of syrup and extended it to Alice.

"No—" the girl moaned, but the moment her mouth opened, her mother stuck in the spoon and held it there, waiting until Alice swallowed.

"She'll be all right," Grace said calmly, tucking aside a stray strand of golden hair that had dared to escape her tightly coiled bun. "Julius, would you be a dear and carry Miss Alice to her room?"

The young man nodded and picked up the semiconscious girl, her limbs flopping limply at her sides.

"She hasn't had her dinner yet, Mrs. Foster," Aurelia said as Julius carried her down the servant's passage, toward the flight of stairs that led to her room on the third floor. "Should I make her up the usual? Milk toast and broth?" After an episode, Mrs. Foster always wanted her daughter fed invalid food.

But Grace shook her head. She looked weary and drawn, nearly as pale as her sickly daughter. "She'll be dull after taking the Soothing Syrup. Best let her sleep, Miss Weiss. If you could have something prepared for the morning, though, that would be ever so kind of you."

"Very well, Mrs. Foster."

With her evening unexpectedly cut short, Aurelia grabbed a bottle from the pantry, then sat down on the back doorstep and unlaced her shoes. Toes wiggling in the open air, she opened the bottle of ginger beer and took a long sip. She was too hot and weary to care who saw her.

The sun had long since set, leaving only the ambient glow of gaslight from the Foster mansion's windows. The gardens were an enigma of smudged outlines, darkness upon darkness.

The kitchen door banged, causing her to start. She twisted mid-sip to see Oscar entering with a stack of finger bowls.

"Ah, Miss Weiss," he said, setting the silver bowls in the copper sink. "Our guests send their regards. One asked if you had ever lived in New York?"

She swallowed her ginger beer, aware that her cheeks were burning slightly. "I did once," she said. "Why?"

"Something on the pickle tray," Oscar said. "He said he had only seen the like there."

So the half-sours *had* been appreciated. She felt a certain pride in that—and relief that the question entailed nothing more.

When he'd gone, she gazed out over the darkened garden. Tonight's work may have been done, but tomorrow's required her to set out a few things. She needed to soak salt cod and beans and start the day's bread rising. Finishing her drink, she climbed to her feet and turned to go back inside.

The dishes began to rattle.

Aurelia froze in the doorway, heart hammering, mouth dry. The hum and vibration of glass, china, and metal surrounded her. The old fear filled her as she waited, ears straining, terrified of not hearing it—

In the distance, a train whistle blew. Her shoulders drooped with relief. One day she wouldn't have this involuntary reaction every time a door banged or the railroad that ran too close to Prairie Avenue sent a locomotive barreling down the line. One day, the feeling of freedom wouldn't be so fleeting, or so easily demolished. One day she could start having a life.

Maybe in a year.

Maybe in ten.

Probably never.

Straightening her spine, she headed to the pantry to start scooping out flour for the bread.

In her dreams . . .

. . . she entered the opium joint with the sylphs and the

zephyrs swirling around her. The cheap wall hangings fluttered. The proprietors backed away, fearful.

In her dreams . . .

. . . she pointed, and the gleeful children of Air set forth, knocking over pipes and snuffing open flames, sending the poisonous smoke swirling both up the stairwell and out the basement windows.

In her dreams . . .

. . . there was no question of her Mastery. The zephyrs obeyed. The sylphs whispered in her ears. And Millicent knelt at her feet, sobbing, begging to be let back in. To be forgiven.

That was, ultimately, how she knew it to be only a dream. Millie had never begged.

Aurelia drifted awake, allowing the dream to float away. She opened her eyes on her spartan bedroom in the Foster mansion. A bed, a dresser, a chest, a nightstand, and a washstand. Nothing as sumptuous as what she'd grown up with, but she found she didn't really miss all the frills and ruffles. She'd rather have a kitchen packed full of tools than a bedroom trimmed in eyelet lace.

She washed up, then put on her shirtwaist and skirt and wandered into the kitchen, her hair untidily tucked into a bun. Oscar sat at the long table in the middle of the kitchen, polishing silver in the predawn light.

"Good morning, Miss Weiss," he said, setting down the tureen he'd been working on.

"And to you, Mr. Pannier," she replied, walking over to wash her hands in the sink. "Would you like me to start some coffee?"

"I would rather tea, if you do not mind." His English was faintly stilted. Despite a decidedly French last name, Oscar Pannier had emigrated from Germany to escape discrimination for being a Jew. Aurelia rarely heard him speak German—usually only when he was frustrated or angry. Two things that Oscar rarely exhibited.

"Of course not," she said, shaking droplets off her hands. "I'll have it going in a moment."

Oscar snapped his fingers, recalling something important that had slipped his memory. "Mrs. Foster asked that you stop by the chemist and procure a fresh supply of Soothing Syrup for Alice. They are on the dregs of the last bottle."

Aurelia remembered that one pungent whiff of the medicine that Mrs. Foster had given Alice last night, and a shiver ran down her back.

There was a reason she'd been dreaming about Millicent.

The only people in the kitchen were Oscar and her; indeed, they were probably the only ones awake in the house at this hour. Even so, she lowered her voice for what she had to say next.

"I don't like that . . . that *nostrum*, Mr. Pannier," she said. "Isn't she long past teething? Don't you think it's odd that we have to keep giving her more and more?"

When next he spoke, Oscar's voice had lost its warm familiarity. "Is Alice your child, Aurelia?"

"No, sir."

"Then do as your employer requests, my girl."

"Yes, sir."

But as she set about getting the morning meal ready, Aurelia could feel an idea forming in her head. And by the time the house had awakened to plow through plates of her biscuits, codfish cakes, eggs, and bacon, she knew what else she'd need to buy when she was out and about.

Aurelia sniffed the mostly empty bottle, then touched one small drop to her tongue. Bitterness flooded her mouth. Yes. No doubt. The aroma alone gave it away—Mrs. Winslow's Soothing Syrup was little more than adulterated laudanum.

It was said that the poison was in the dose. If so, Aurelia could think of no dose of opium that was not poison. Her sister's downfall had only confirmed this notion. That such a substance should be marketed to children was despicable.

She also knew herself to be alone in this thinking. Women like Mrs. Foster didn't deliberately poison their children. Aurelia suspected Grace even thought she was doing Alice good.

Aurelia sat on her heels in the pantry, eyes closed, the flavor rolling in her mouth. There was nothing quite like the earthy-incense bouquet of opium, so reproducing it would not be easy—if possible at all. Then again, an *exact* duplicate might not be necessary; her nose, she knew, was far more discriminate than most, and Mrs. Foster and Alice probably wouldn't detect a minor difference.

Sugar was added to the nostrum to offset both the opium's burnt bitterness and the sting of the alcohol in which it had been dissolved. The bitterness could be likened to a tincture of blessed thistle, a common enough decoction for nursing mothers, and of no harm to a child. But what she really needed was something to ease the transition as Alice's body was weaned off the drug.

She had found such an herb once, in her old life. She knew it by scent rather than name: burnt and green. And finding it hadn't been easy, despite her knowing where to go. She'd been to nearly every shop in Chicago's thriving Chinatown before she'd found it. She'd watched as the herbalist poured a mix of charred leaves and sticks into a waxed bit of paper, thumping the jar to get the last of it out. Now she shook the contents of that packet into a blue glass jar half-filled with strong spirits. She capped the jar and shook it violently. The herbs would need a week to extract, and then she could strain and set about using the resulting tincture.

She heard movement in the kitchen and poked her head out to find Alice opening the door to the cookstove and peering inside. Aurelia cleared her throat, and Alice spun about, a guilty look on her face.

"Checking my cookstove for small cakes?" Aurelia asked.

Alice grinned. "No," she said. "I was looking for my—" She began to cough, great, wracking spasms that tore at her lungs and turned her even whiter than she already was.

Mrs. Foster suddenly appeared, looking annoyed.

"Alice!" she said sharply. "What are you doing in here?" She looked to Aurelia. "I'm sorry, Miss Weiss. My daughter needs to learn to not be underfoot. Come here, young lady."

Alice recovered from her spell and closed the cookstove door, then reluctantly walked over to her mother. Grace gave Aurelia a short nod before herding her daughter out, one hand on the back of the child's neck.

When they were gone Aurelia walked over to the cookstove, opened the oven door, and peered inside.

Empty.

Well, what did you expect to find? she thought as she shut it. *Salamanders?*

Still, Alice was a very peculiar—but sweet—child. Aurelia had to wonder what it was she'd been looking for.

Aurelia went back to the pantry for some jam jars and pickles. She thought of her sister, who had never been so good at making preserves, but had composed the most beautiful cakes and pastries—partly because she'd employed Air spirits to whip her egg whites rather than spending the time and effort to do it herself. Despite being very well off, Aurelia's grandmother had used her kitchen for teaching magic. The discipline of following recipes combined with the intuition to adjust them translated neatly to magic, as did the grueling hours spent in too-hot kitchens. Aurelia had loved it. Millie had hated it. It was probably why she'd been the first to test her magic—the sooner she got out of that kitchen, the happier she'd be.

But she failed, Aurelia thought as she separated eggs, putting the whites in a shallow pie plate. *And I didn't fail, but I didn't succeed. I just . . . didn't finish.*

Fly or fall, her grandmother had always said. But Aurelia had picked neither.

The crash of glass and a scream broke her reverie.

Aurelia hurried down the servant's hallway, poking her head out the foyer door. Two people—Mr. Foster and Oscar—stood in the foyer. Shards of crystal glinted on the floor.

"Good heavens, a hair more and it would have hit me!" Mr. Foster was saying.

"You are sure you are all right, Mr. Foster?" Oscar asked.

"Quite! But I can't say the same for our bank account once we fix this. We'll need to replace that gasolier, and preferably before next week's soiree. Mr. Pannier, could you—"

Aurelia retreated back to the kitchen.

There was a rational explanation for this, she told herself. Sometimes, things fell. It didn't mean—

It couldn't mean—

She looked toward the pantry, where the blue glass jar was.

It didn't mean anything. It was just a coincidence. She *needed* it to be a coincidence.

Just for a few weeks more.

*   *   *

Unfortunately, the "coincidences" refused to cooperate.

After inspection, Julius had proclaimed that the gasolier's ceiling hook had come free of the joist it had been bolted to.

"Must've been too heavy," he told Aurelia one day as she whisked fresh cream into lofty peaks. She'd nodded and then went back to ignoring him, keeping her mind as far from the mysterious accident as she could take it.

Once the herbs had extracted into the spirits, Aurelia faced a new challenge: getting to Mrs. Foster's bottle. Which would require her to somehow access Mrs. Foster's purse. She wished she was better friends with Agnès, Mrs. Foster's personal maid, but Aurelia's overtures had failed to build any friendship between them. Like Oscar, Agnès was originally from Europe—France, in her case—but unlike Oscar, her grasp of English was not terribly strong. She kept to herself.

And so days went by, and in the meantime, things kept getting stranger. And less coincidental.

They were still waiting for the gasolier to arrive when nearly every portrait in the drawing room was discovered hanging upside down.

"Funny thing is, that room's locked tight," Julius told Aurelia the day it was discovered. "Not sure how it could have happened, unless my dad or one of the Fosters did it."

"Oh? Very interesting," Aurelia replied, and had immediately gone into the pantry to reorganize all the jams and pickles she'd prepared for winter.

And then. . . .

Weeks passed without any more incidences, but there were also no opportunities for Aurelia to act with her mock-nostrum, or "mockstrum," as she'd begun to think of it. Thanksgiving came with a flurry of dishes and activity, and then Christmas and New Year. January closed its grip on the city, the wind whipping off Lake Michigan, and every night the stoves were lit and fires built in the hearths.

Aurelia was icing a coconut layer cake, Alice playing under the kitchen table with her doll, when an awful groan filled the house.

Alice popped out from under the table. "What was that?"

The groan happened again, coming from the front parlor. The walls shuddered.

Aurelia gave Alice a look that said "stay put," and hurried down the servant hallway to investigate.

Mr. and Mrs. Foster weren't home, but Julius and Oscar were. Oscar had opened the parlor; they both stood in the doorway, dumbfounded.

The piano had moved from one end of the room to the other. Rips marred the rug where it had been dragged.

The three exchanged looks.

"That's not possible," Julius said at last.

Oscar frowned at his son. "Of course it is possible. You see it, do you not?"

Between the three of them and Wing Lee, the Chinese laundryman, they managed to move the piano back in place before the Fosters got back. Mr. Lee muttered a few curt syllables in his native tongue when they'd finished, then retreated back to his domain in the basement. It fell to Oscar to explain the rugs and the piano to Mr. and Mrs. Foster.

That night, Aurelia retired to her room and curled up on her bed. It wouldn't be long now. Someone would start saying *it*. They would start believing in *it*. And *it* would only get worse because of that. Escalation wasn't just inevitable—it had already begun.

Her greatest fear, though, was that someday someone would chance to talk to her previous employer. The subject of queer goings-on might come up. Things that had started while she'd been there . . . and stopped when she'd left.

She'd been lucky so far. But luck never lasted.

Julius said the dreaded word the next day.

"What's next? A floating cookstove?" he asked as the house staff sat about drinking coffee and waiting for Aurelia to finish making their breakfast.

Please don't give it ideas, she thought as she poured beaten eggs and cream into the bacon drippings and gave them a stir.

"What are you babbling about?" asked Mary Campbell, one of the housemaids.

"Mrs. Foster is talking about bringing in a medium," Julius said, "on account of the house being haunted."

And suddenly there it was. *It.* Haunted.

Aurelia froze, her ears straining.

"Silly gossip," Oscar said.

"That piano didn't move itself."

"Trains," his father muttered.

"Trains didn't move the piano, Father!"

Aurelia scraped the eggs onto a platter and turned around, forcing a too-bright smile. "Breakfast!"

But Julius refused to be distracted. As they all piled biscuits, eggs, and bacon on their plates, he kept talking.

"Mr. Grant from New York claims to be a Spiritualist," he said. "He told her he can suss it out."

I very much doubt that, Aurelia thought as she slathered jam on her biscuit.

"There is nothing to 'suss,'" Oscar said, his normally kind countenance rendered gruff with annoyance. "There is no ghost!"

"But have you considered that Mrs. Foster has had five miscarriages—"

"Enough!" He slammed his fist on the table, causing them all to freeze and stare at him. "I will not have my own son talking that way at his employer's table. No more talk of ghosts!"

"Papa—"

Oscar rattled off a rapid stream of German at his son. Julius sat back, his lips pressed tight together.

The rest of the meal concluded in uncomfortable silence.

That night Aurelia curled up on her bed, a book in her lap. The tension between father and son had become palpable. Yet one more thing that she was to blame for, though they didn't know it—and hopefully never would.

Things would only get worse. She needed to run, though she now wondered where she could go that she wouldn't be found by her curse. San Francisco? Los Angeles? Perhaps there was an Elemental Master in New Orleans or Saint Louis who could help her? Probably not, though. In the beginning she had tried to find someone. A simple dismissal command would have freed her. But every Master she'd found had been a man telling her a woman "wasn't worthy" of his precious time.

It had made her realize how unique her grandmother was as one of the few female Elemental Masters in America. And it made her wonder what happened to all those women with talent who didn't have her grandmother to teach them.

Not that it had done Millie any good.

Aurelia remembered the last time she'd seen her sister: curled up in an opium joint on Mott Street, a pipe to her lips. She'd changed shockingly. Her hair had once been like Aurelia's—so dark brown it was nearly black—but it had turned pure white and brittle in mere months. Scabs dotted her arms and legs. For all that she'd been glad to see her sister—up to the point when Aurelia told her she was going to summon her first sylph and face the same test that Millie had failed: resisting the temptations of Air.

Millie had laughed. "You'll fail."

Aurelia frowned. "No, I won't."

"Fly or fall. Isn't that what the old bat always says? I fell. I haven't stopped falling." Millie's eyes had grown distant. "They still talk to me, you know. Whispering in my head. Whisper whisper whisper . . ." She rubbed her cheeks. "The smoke is the only thing that drives their incessant chatter out of my mind. Secrets. Endless secrets. The city is lousy with them."

Aurelia drew away in horror. Her sister had been disinherited months back, and it had taken considerable effort just to find and visit her. Her grandmother hadn't told her what had happened, and had even bargained with the Elements to keep the truth from Aurelia.

She'd ultimately gotten around this by finding an Earth Master and paying him a great deal to send his gnomes to suss out Millie's location. Her grandmother couldn't control gnomes. Earth was a slow Element—at times maddeningly so—but eventually they'd found her sister.

Aurelia wondered if she'd have preferred if they hadn't.

Millie had smiled and stroked her sister's face. "Of course, you'll still try. And you'll fall. And when you do"—she patted the empty seat next to her, and then drew on the long opium pipe, her eyes drifting shut with exquisite bliss—"I'll be here, saving a place for you, dear sister."

Back in her bedroom in Chicago, Aurelia leaned over and turned down her lamp until it was only a faint glow.

I didn't fall, Millie, she thought. *I just didn't finish what I started. And that failure of courage has come back to "haunt" me again and again.*

She lay back, wondering where her sister was now. Wondering if she had, in the end, stopped her fall.

Aurelia wasn't sure she had the courage to know the answer.

The next morning at the Foster Mansion, opportunity finally chose to smile on Aurelia.

"Mrs. Foster wanted to know if you could get her more of the syrup from the chemist?" Oscar asked.

Aurelia's head snapped up from where she'd been setting water to boil for the coffee. "Yes. Absolutely!"

Oscar gave her a curious look but said, "It is appreciated. Thank you."

Aurelia had to quash a giddy giggle as she returned later that day, a fresh bottle of Mrs. Winslow's Soothing Syrup clutched in her hand. She'd probably need to stay a few weeks more, titrating down the amount of syrup Alice received, but if this worked, she'd have at least done *some* good before she ran away from Chicago. That *had* to be worth whatever calamity would result from her staying longer.

She replaced half of the bottle's contents with her own decoction, then delivered the adulterated Soothing Syrup to Mrs. Foster. Aurelia walked on eggshells from that point, waiting at once for both the next supernatural event and one of Alice's episodes.

Alice usually took dinner with Aurelia, who was expected to teach the girl formal dining manners. It was one of many things a governess would have done if she'd had one, but Aurelia knew a thing or two about table manners, and in the absence of a nanny she'd absorbed this responsibility as well.

Tonight was different—Grace Foster had joined them, as Mr. Foster was out of town, and on this rare occasion, Grace had nowhere to be and no one to entertain. She sat at the table, observing and correcting her daughter's manners, when Alice suddenly toppled out of her seat, hitting the floor in a crumpled pile.

Aurelia quickly pushed away from the table, running to pick up Alice, as Mrs. Foster produced a familiar bottle and spoon from her purse. "Step aside, Miss Weiss," she said.

The china began to rattle.

And then the bottle flew out Mrs. Foster's hand and smashed on the tiled floor—inches from Alice's head. Shards of glass sprayed, but hit no one. The room filled with the sweet stink of the nostrum.

Aurelia cradled Alice in stunned silence. Grace trembled visibly. "M-Miss Weiss," she whispered. "D-did you see that?"

Aurelia nodded, and realized that she probably wasn't showing the correct reaction. Afraid. She should be afraid.

Not *livid*.

It wasn't just that weeks of planning and preparation and waiting had suddenly shattered on the floor. She could have endured a little longer if it would help Alice. It was that she wasn't being *allowed* to help. That if she tried again, she'd be sabotaged again. And worse—that the sabotage had involved Alice and her mother. Had directly threatened their lives.

"Stay here, Mrs. Foster," she said. "I may have something in the pantry that will help Alice."

Grace nodded, though Aurelia suspected she was too shaken to do anything else.

Aurelia gently set Alice down and ran into the pantry, pulling the door mostly shut behind her. "I know you can hear me," she said, her voice a low growl. "Leave them *alone*. This quarrel is between you and me."

Something laughed in the darkness, a malevolent trill. She felt a draft where there should have been none, and smelled elderflower and ozone.

In the little light from the mostly shut doorway, she found the half of the syrup she'd set aside, and slowly poured a small measure of it into a Winslow's bottle she'd rescued from the rubbish pile.

She held up the bottle. "Does this make you happy?" she asked as the wind grew, making the jars rattle and her clothes flap. "Is this what you want?"

The wind died the moment she touched the door handle,

and she returned to Mrs. Foster, who sat silently beside her daughter, stroking her hair and whispering softly to her.

"There was a little left over from a previous order," she explained, kneeling down beside Alice.

Grace Foster reached for the bottle, and in that moment, a silent war burst into life in Aurelia's head. *I don't have to support this,* she realized. *I don't have to give her this bottle.*

She would lose her job, but she'd already lost it. She had nothing left to lose.

Aurelia drew the bottle back, leaving Grace grasping at empty air. "What are you doing, Miss Weiss?" she asked.

"You know it's not good for her, don't you?" Aurelia said quietly. "It's laudanum. It's poison."

Grace's jaw tightened. "Give me the bottle."

"Her 'cure' is the source of her malady—"

"*Enough*, Miss Weiss! I will not tolerate this kind of talk from a—a *cook*!"

Aurelia's face twitched with barely contained rage. *Would you tolerate this from Aurelia Weiss, New York socialite?* she wondered. *Or Aurelia Weiss, Elemental Master?*

"All the doctors prescribe th-this for the common maladies that plague children," Grace said. "It is a well understood remedy!"

On the floor, Alice moaned. Aurelia leaned forward, holding Grace's gaze. "Do you believe that, Mrs. Foster? Truly?"

Grace's eyes unexpectedly filled with tears. "It's the only thing that keeps her safe."

Behind her, the cookstove's oven door creaked open. A small, scaly creature hopped out and flicked a forked tongue in Aurelia's direction.

A salamander? she thought as it flowed like a line of fire across the floor, stopping just short of them. Grace Foster stiffened.

Aurelia gave her a sharp look.

"You can see it," she said. "You can see the Elemental."

Grace widened her eyes and stared. "You can, too?"

The salamander blinked slitted eyes at them, then slithered closer to Alice. Grace shrieked and swatted at it, and the salamander skittered back, flicking its tongue in vexation at her.

"Get away from her!" she yelled. "Get away!"

Aurelia blinked, dumbfounded. She stretched a hand out and whistled to the salamander, which cast a speculative look at Mrs. Foster, and then—skittering in a wide arc around her—came over to Aurelia, poking its nose at her hand.

"Are you . . . *petting* that creature?" Grace sounded horrified.

"It's a salamander," Alice replied. "And yes. As much as it will let me. Fire isn't my Element, though it is my ally." She looked at Grace. "Is it yours?"

Grace trembled. "I don't know what you're talking about."

Aurelia sat back on her heels. "Mrs. Foster, do you know anything about the Elemental Masters?" Something most scandalous suddenly occurred to Aurelia. "Is Mr. Foster Alice's real father?"

Grace turned white as a sheet, then regained some of her regal composure. "How *dare* you—"

"So many miscarriages," Aurelia said. "It's not always the woman's fault, you know. Sometimes the father—"

Grace slapped her.

The salamander hissed and snapped. A wind suddenly sprang up in the kitchen, whipping around Aurelia and shoving Grace across the floor and into a wall. Aurelia turned to see an elfin figure floating in the air behind her.

"The ghost!" Grace gasped.

"No," Aurelia said angrily. "Not a ghost. Never a ghost. An Elemental that refuses to leave me be." To the sylph she said, "*Stop it!*"

The sylph laughed. "I don't need to listen to *you*," it said.

The wind blew harder, feeding the flames that licked the salamander's scales. The kitten-sized creature began to grow, its Fire fed by the sylph's Air. It advanced on Mrs. Foster, who stared, dazed.

"Stop!" Aurelia commanded again, but the Elementals ignored her, the sylph swooping around and hovering above the salamander, laughing like a bedlamite.

Tears spilled down Grace's cheeks as she crawled across the floor and back to Alice. She pulled her daughter into her arms, shielding the girl with her body. Aurelia could hear her whispering Psalm Twenty-Three into her daughter's hair.

Aurelia stood and took a deep breath. It had been years since she'd invoked her magic. The last time she'd tried had been in the attic her grandmother had converted into a kind of magical atelier, and the subject of her arcane attentions had been the very sylph that floated before her.

Aurelia was certain her grandmother had deliberately chosen not to dismiss it. The sylph had spent the last three years chasing her, "haunting" every household she'd worked in, and Aurelia had played the good victim every time.

She drew the threads of magic around her—Air from her own breath, Fire from the oven, Water from the broth bubbling on the cookstove. Magic swirled around her as she cried, "I invoke our Pact!"

The salamander froze. The sylph turned and glided over until they were nose-to-nose. "There is no *Pact*, you silly goose," the sylph said. "We are not bound. You never finished."

"So let us finish now," Aurelia said, holding and keeping the sylph's gaze. The intense blue eyes of the creature brought the memories of her grandmother's atelier into sharp focus: the smell of cedar, the motes of chalk powder floating in the air, and her grandmother standing to one side, watching like a hawk.

"Why would I answer to a creature such as *you*?" The sylph tittered indelicately. "You're no Master. You're just a *cook*. You allow this woman to treat you like *nothing*. And poor Alice. What has she been doing to her?" It leaned close to whisper in Aurelia's ear. "You're right about the child's father."

Aurelia looked down at Grace, who still had her face buried in Alice's hair.

"Grace was quite the naughty girl," the sylph continued, its words a private seduction of knowledge. "She acts proper now, but oh, the men *she* entertained when she was young! Would you like to know about them? Would you like to know about the Fire Master she met on summer vacation in St. Louis? The things I know would destroy her. She'd pay handsomely to keep them secrets."

The sylph's implication was all too clear to Aurelia. Grace Foster would do anything to keep her husband from knowing about her past indiscretions—would *pay* anything. Aurelia would probably never have to work another day in her life.

"Would you like to know the secrets of the city's great men, the names and addresses of their mistresses?" the sylph whispered. "They would pay you, too. Oh, and they'd *deserve* it, every single one. Things will be like they used to be. You'll be rich without having to go back begging for your inheritance."

Try as she might, Aurelia couldn't look away from the Elemental. How had she even managed to run away the first time? She couldn't remember. Her mind swam, and she could feel it slipping.

"I can show you corrupt politicians and businessmen," the sylph said. "They'd be all too happy to pay you to keep their secrets."

"Secrets. Endless secrets. The city is lousy with them," Millie had said.

Words formed on Aurelia's lips. "If you know so much," she said, "then tell me where my sister is."

The sylph looked pleased. Its voice wound through Aurelia's ears, echoing in her skull. "Your sister sleeps under the dirt in a potter's field on Hart Island. She's not alone, though. The grave is full of bodies, and she was six months quick with child when she drank her last drop of laudanum."

Tears formed in Aurelia's eyes. She clung to the pain in her chest, and used it to form a single word. *"Stop."*

The sylph swirled in blessed silence around her. Across the room, Alice shifted in her mother's arms, moaning through her unconsciousness.

Aurelia took a deep breath. "Stop," she said again, in a much calmer voice. "Do you swear the Pact with me?"

In an instant, the sylph's malevolence evaporated, and it retreated to fold its arms across its chest like a sullen child. "Your sister was more fun."

"Do you swear it?" Aurelia asked again.

The sylph threw its head back and laughed—not the malevolent trill from before, but happy, clear laughter. It rushed forward and, surprisingly, kissed Aurelia's forehead. The kiss felt like the caress of a fogbank. "What a merry chase you have given me! Yes, we will swear the Pact with you, and I shall haunt you no more. Farewell, Aurelia Weiss—until you summon me again."

It turned and swooped away, flying into the hearth and up the chimney, stirring the coals to briefly blaze into life—then fade back down again.

Aurelia was folding a dress when she heard a knock at the door.

"Come in," she said.

Grace Foster opened the door, took two steps in, and paused. "Packing?" she asked.

"Yes, ma'am," Aurelia replied. She smoothed the dress and laid it down in her chest.

"You already have another position elsewhere?"

"No, but I don't imagine you want me staying." *Not with what I know.*

Grace twisted the ring on her finger. "Miss Weiss, you are the first person since . . . him . . . that I have been able to talk to about this."

Aurelia sat on her bed. Normally she would have remained standing, but she was too weary to bother with formality at the moment.

"Robert and I were supposed to be married," Grace went on. "When he died, and my parents learned I was early with child, they acted quickly and had me married to Ellis Foster." She stood silently a moment, gazing into the distance. "And Ellis, bless him, never asked too many questions. My mother coached me, told him the baby was early, even though she weighed a full eight pounds and popped out fat as a Christmas goose."

"It's my experience that men don't want to know about how the babies come about," Aurelia said. "They just like the part at the beginning."

Grace laughed. "Too true," she said, pulling up the only chair in the room and plunking down in it. "She has her father's eyes. We told Ellis she inherited them from my long-passed grandfather." She smiled and shook her head. "I didn't think she'd also have Robert's . . . talents."

"Mrs. Foster, you should know that I don't care," Aurelia blurted. Grace raised a brow at her, and Aurelia quickly said,

"I mean, I don't care in the sense that I won't use it against you. All I care about is that Alice is healthy and . . . aware of her talents."

"But not her heritage," Grace said. "Not yet, at least. Ellis is a good man. I have grown to love him, even if I will never be *in* love with him like I was with Robert. But I don't know how he would cope with finding out his darling daughter is not his, and his wife came to him as sullied merchandise."

Aurelia nodded. "Did Robert ask the Elementals to reveal themselves to you?"

Grace made a soft noise. "Is that what he did? All I know is that after he learned I was with child, I began to see them. I never understood why. Honestly, I was happier when I was—er—blind. I certainly can't control them like you."

I couldn't, either, until a few hours ago, Aurelia thought, and then wondered if Robert had had a premonition of his fate. And *how* he'd done what he'd done. She'd only heard one story of a nonmagical person seeing the Elementals, and that had involved one of the old British Isles spirits.

Grace twisted her rings. "I know dosing Alice with that horrible stuff isn't the best way to make those—things—go away."

"If you let the salamanders come to her," Aurelia said, "they can heal her." Grace's eyes widened. "She wouldn't be as sickly. She could easily quit that dreadful syrup with their help."

"Would they hurt her?"

Aurelia shook her head. "No."

"I don't know these things, Miss Weiss. I see a fiery lizard, and all I can think is that my daughter needs to be protected from it. Not invite it into her bedroom!"

Aurelia chuckled. "Well, I can tell you now that you can't run away from them. I've been trying for years. What your daughter needs is a teacher."

Grace regarded her. "She needs a governess, too."

Then she smiled, and Aurelia found herself smiling back. "Well," she said. "I guess I should unpack."

"Miss Weiss!" Alice said excitedly, pointing to the enormous contraption. "We *must* ride it!"

The Columbian Exposition had opened with much fanfare, but for all the amazing architecture and exotic goings-on, the thing that had most captured Aurelia's attention had been a giant steel monstrosity towering over two hundred feet in the sky.

She wasn't the only one. Alice wanted to climb into one of the great cars: at least a dozen sylphs and zephyrs danced excitedly around the Wheel, unseen by the throng of Exposition attendees.

In fact, now that she allowed herself to summon them, Aurelia realized that between the skyscrapers and the wind coming off Lake Michigan, Chicago had much for the Elementals of Air to love. The wide use of electricity at the Exhibition also seemed to entertain them. The Ferris Wheel made them positively giddy.

She paid fifty cents each for Alice and herself, and they climbed into the car, taking seats on the far end. The sylphs swarmed as they lifted up, the car shuddering and swaying, the metal groaning. Aurelia smiled, and Alice, being a child, got to wave and giggle back at the Elementals without anyone looking at her sidelong.

Someday, she'll need to go through her own test, Aurelia thought. *And I'll be here, Providence willing, to get her through it.*

And maybe someday she'd leave and find another young girl who needed the instruction of an Elemental Master.

Maybe in ten years.

Maybe fifteen.

The choice was hers when to stay or go.

The car shuddered and rose to its apex. It wasn't quite flight, but it would do. Aurelia closed her eyes and leaned into the wind.

Bone Dance

Rosemary Edghill
and Rebecca Fox

It was pouring rain when Captain Frederick Wentworth left the club. He'd planned to stay at least another hour, and he might have done, if the evening's only annoyance had been George Cliburn holding forth yet again on the great triumphs of modern science.

Cliburn was a minor Water Magician and a moderately talented alchemist, but he fancied himself a Naturalist, and was prone to holding forth at considerable length—and long past the point when his audience had lost interest—on the writings of Huxley and Darwin and their colleagues, though of late he'd become rather obsessed with Robert Louis Stevenson's lurid tale of Jekyll and Hyde.

But tonight Cliburn had left early, pleading personal business, and discussion had turned to the story buried in the back pages of the *Police Gazette*, a publication not normally welcome within the walls of the club—*though somehow, Frederick thought, the copies I bring with me do not lack for readers.*

"Come now, Frederick, you can't possibly believe that penny dreadful rot is true," Sir Henry said, taking a sip of his brandy. "If I believed everything I read, I'd be afraid to leave my house."

"True or not, don't you think it's worth investigating something so . . . unusual?" Frederick asked.

Major-General the Earl of Chawleigh snorted. "If the

Council stepped in every time a rabid dog bit some drunkard in Whitechapel, we'd have no time for dealing with real threats. I'll bet you half a crown this 'Wolf of Whitechapel' business is nothing but gin and idleness. You know how those people are."

There were nods of agreement around the room.

"Superstitious, the lot of them," Sir Henry agreed. "Irish— and worse."

"It killed a woman," Frederick protested, more sharply than was really politic. "According to the report it gutted her and left . . . what was left . . . lying in the middle of the street."

"People ought not let their boarhounds run loose," Lord Chawleigh said firmly. "I'm sure it will find its way back to its kennel presently."

"And what if it's a real problem?" Frederick asked. "*Our* sort of problem?"

"Oh!" Lord Chawleigh said, as if something had suddenly occurred to him. He gazed around the room. "Captain Wentworth is afraid this Wolf of London is going to bite his Goose Girl!"

Frederick stormed out of the club with the sound of laughter at his back.

After a few blocks, his temper cooled enough for him to realize he'd left his umbrella behind. He was weighing the prospect of a sodden journey home against another encounter with Chawleigh's cronies when the gnome dashed out of the alleyway just ahead. The Earth Elementals didn't care for London—too many cobblestones and too few growing things—so the sight of one here brought him up short.

Squat and fat, with hair the color of moss, the gnome's voice was the hiss of gravel sliding down a slope. "*Come, Earth Master,*" it said. "*Something's happened.*"

Creatures with names didn't belong in cages.

Bounce knew that the way he knew that barges brought rats. The way he knew the sun came up over the river every morning. The way he knew how to shake his prey by the neck until it died.

Bounce had a name. A real name. A name given by Smell-Gives-Bite when Bounce was just a pup.

The other creatures here had names, too.

"Percy," *said the Raven,* "from the Ravenmaster."

"Bright Eyes," *said the cat,* "from Tinker Tom."

"Jingo," *said the monkey.* "I picked it myself." *Monkeys were impatient creatures. That was no surprise. They were the closest cousins to Man.*

They were all here in the dark and the damp together: Bounce and Percy and Bright Eyes and Jingo.

And the bear.

Bounce was sure the bear had a name, too, but no one had asked. His very smell turned Bounce's bowels to water and left him whimpering. If he'd been free, he'd have run from the bear as fast as he could. But none of them was free, so Bounce tried to ignore the bear as best he could. It was really the only thing he could do.

Bounce wasn't sure how long he'd been here when Bad-stink Man brought the Girl. She was sleeping. Bounce didn't think she was dead because she didn't smell dead, and because Badstink Man threw her into another cage and locked the door before he clomped back up the stairs to wherever he went when he wasn't here.

Frederick wasn't really surprised when the gnome led him to Whitechapel, but he really wished the little Earth Elemental had waited until daybreak. After weaving a small glamour about himself, he offered up a silent prayer to remain unmolested. At least it was raining; even villains liked to stay out of the wet.

Frederick knew this area rather better than he liked. He'd been coming here for going on four years now, hunting what Sir Henry and Lord Chawleigh and the rest of that lot insisted was nothing but a phantom, a figment of his overheated imagination.

"You heard from a cart horse there's another Animal Speaker in Whitechapel!" Henry had laughed, slapping his knee. "Next thing we know you'll be getting the news from the pigeons instead of reading the *Times*!"

The men at the Club might poke fun, but Frederick knew *someone* had been Speaking with the animal denizens of Whitechapel for the last few years, and it certainly wasn't him. He'd wondered from the beginning if it might not be Claire Prentiss' daughter. A little girl, the animals said, who shared her food even if her own belly went empty.

"Here," the gnome said, pointing down the alley.

There was a faint taste of Water Magic, like the last streamers of dawn fog, and a smell of sulfur. Over that, the feeling of something utterly *Wrong.* Twisted. Frederick shivered involuntarily. If he'd been a dog, his hackles would have gone up instantly.

"The Wolf?" he asked the gnome.

"Worse," the gnome said in his loose-gravel voice. *"The Poison Master took Her."*

Frederick didn't know who the Poison Master was, but he didn't have to ask whom the gnome meant. There was only one *Her* in Whitechapel the Earth allies would care about enough to bring word of to him. His Goose Girl.

"I am sorry, Earth Master," the gnome said. *"She did not want to be found before. But now she must be found."*

"Then take me to her!" Frederick whispered. His neck prickled with the sense of dark forces of the human sort— cutpurses and bully boys and hugger-mugger—lurking in the shadows, and his skin crawled with the Wrongness in the alley.

"I cannot," the little Earth Elemental said apologetically. *"The Poison Master hides behind his magics. But there is one here who might be able to find where he dens."* The gnome motioned to something lurking in a doorway, and Frederick tensed.

But what emerged from the shadows was a puppy of indeterminate color, all soaked, matted fur and heaving ribs. He limped along on three legs. One ear was chewed away, and the other lay flat against its skull in fear. It looked as if it might be a little terrier.

"Don't hurt. Don't hurt . . ." The mind-whisper was faint and desperate.

"I won't hurt you," Frederick said in a low voice, squatting down and holding very still. *"Friend,"* he Spoke in his mind.

Warily, the little dog slunk closer. Frederick carefully held out his hand. "I won't hurt you," he said again.

The puppy sniffed his fingers and whined. *"Danger,"* the puppy whispered. *"Wrongthing. Took her away. Took her away."*

"Do you know where?" Frederick asked. His thighs were starting to ache from squatting, but he held himself still.

"Smell gone," the puppy said, tucking his tail tightly between his legs. *"Too much rain. Smell gone. The Girl gone."*

"Maybe you'll be able to find the smell again when it's not so wet," Frederick said. "Will you let me help?"

Tentatively, the trembling puppy leaned against Frederick's leg. *"I Bucket,"* he whispered. *"Girl Named me,"* he added proudly.

I have to find her, Frederick thought desperately.

Bounce did not expect the Girl to talk. As a general rule, Men didn't. They made plenty of noises with their mouths, but they didn't have names, and they didn't talk. So when the Girl asked Bounce where she was, he was shocked clear down to the tip of his stumpy little tail.

He wished he could tell her, but he didn't remember how he'd come to be here in a cage in the dark. All he remembered was Badstink Man, and the others who had been here before Bounce came disappearing one by one. First all the mice, and then Long Toes the pigeon and her mate White Feather, and then the three-legged cat named Sharpteeth, and finally Black Joe, who had been a guard dog before he woke up in his little cage. Now Bounce and Percy and Bright Eyes and Jingo and the bear were the only ones left, and Badstink Man had stopped feeding them when he had taken Black Joe away.

He had no answers for the Girl, but he could ask her the one question that mattered: "What's your name?"

"People call me Cinder," *the Girl said.* "But it isn't a real name."

That was too bad, Bounce thought. People should have names.

Bertrand was at Frederick's side with a large towel and a look of tolerant amusement not thirty seconds after the night footman ushered him through the front door of the Wentworth townhouse. Despite the opinions of certain visitors, Bertrand owed his uncanny ability to appear just when he was needed not to any Gift, but to whatever instinct it was with which God blessed superlative valets.

"Best I take care of that coat of yours at once," Bertrand said, proffering the towel. "If you will forgive me for mentioning, it has a certain . . . air . . . about it, sir."

"Wet dog," Lady Mina pronounced, coming into the white-tiled foyer on the heels of the night footman, her maid behind her. "With a hint of open sewer." She wrinkled her nose in distaste. She was wrapped in a green silk dressing gown; clearly she had been preparing for bed when curiosity got the better of propriety.

Frederick's pocket chose that inopportune moment to yip sharply.

"Good heavens, Frederick, what have you brought home *this* time?" Mina demanded.

"This is Bucket," he said, plucking the sodden, shivering scrap of brown and white from his pocket and holding the puppy close in the crook of his arm. Bucket blinked at the light and whined.

"Oh!" Mina said, folding her arms. "First it was those filthy sparrows, then that awful one-eyed cat, and now it's some mangy little mongrel. Get that thing out of the house, Frederick. It almost certainly has fleas."

Frederick shook his head. "No," he said. "I need Bucket's help."

"What possible help could it possibly be?" Mina scoffed. She wrapped her dressing gown more tightly around herself and glared. Behind her, Mrs. Lange sniffed disapprovingly in sympathy.

"Bucket's seen her, Mina," Frederick said urgently, toweling his hair dry one-handed. "My Earth Magician. She's been kidnapped—"

Mina blinked at him, her dark eyes narrow. "You've been in Whitechapel at this hour? Have you a death wish?"

"I didn't mean to," Frederick protested. "I—"

"Took the word of a *dog* that Claire Prentiss' imaginary daughter has been kidnapped to Whitechapel," Mina said, tossing her head in annoyance. "It's been *four years*, Frederick. When are you going to give this nonsense up? If the girl ever existed, she's long dead."

"If Claire Prentiss had married Lord Marbury instead of eloping with that Russian lion tamer," Frederick snapped, "you'd want to know whether her daughter was dead or alive." *And so,* he thought grimly, *would the Council.*

"If that . . . *thing* is still here in the morning," Mina said as she turned to stalk back upstairs. "I'm going to Bath. Mother told me marrying an Earth Master would be trouble."

"Well," Frederick said, gazing down at the puppy after she was gone, "that went well, don't you think?"

Bounce was almost sleeping when Badstink Man came back, even though he was hungry and thirsty and the air was full of bear smell.

The Girl had tried to talk to the bear earlier, but he had merely grunted and whuffed and growled threateningly.

"I think he is a circus bear," *the Girl told Bounce.* "I think people"—*by which she meant Men*—"have been very cruel to him."

Bounce might have answered her, but the Badstink Man opened the door that led to Above and came down the stairs, whistling cheerfully. He left the door open, but it did none of them any good, trapped as they were in their hard iron cages. Badstink Man stopped to pet Bright Eyes, who hissed at him and showed her teeth, before turning and strolling over to the Girl's cage.

Bounce couldn't help but growl uselessly as Badstink Man crooked a finger under the Girl's chin and crooned to her.

"You are my precious treasure," *he said to her in the babble of Men.* "You will be my triumph. The men at the club laughed at me, but you, my child, will help me prove Stevenson's elixir is real. His novel points the way to the next stage of human evolution."

"I don't know what you're talking about," *the Girl said in the same language.*

"Watch and see," *Badstink Man said, taking something long and sharp and gleaming out of his pocket. Bounce couldn't see exactly what it was, but it smelled Wrong. Badstink Man walked over to the bear's cage and reached inside*

*where the bear couldn't get at him. He did something, and
the bear roared in pain.*

And then the bear Changed. *He grew until he pressed
against the cage on every side. His teeth grew, and his claws
grew, and the smell of Wrongness came from the bear now,
and that was the most terrifying thing of all.*

*Badstink Man backed away to the other side of the room,
but his voice held no fear as he said, "Be free, precious one."*

*The bear tore the cage open, and when he stood, his head
nearly touched the ceiling. For a moment Bounce hoped the
bear would kill Badstink Man, but then his muzzle wrinkled
as he sniffed the air of freedom. He opened his jaws and
roared, then flung himself up the steps that led to Above.*

*"He is free," Badstink Man said. "Not merely of his cage,
but of every restraint of Nature. It is a pity you cannot understand the wonder of what you have seen."*

"Water," the Girl said. "They will die without water."

*"What is that to me? I no longer need them." After a few
moments, Badstink Man followed the bear.*

The rain didn't let up until half past two the following afternoon, but Frederick had slept until noon. Bucket had to be
bathed and fed and bandaged, and he hadn't wanted to disturb Mina by then, so he'd slept in his dressing room, with
the puppy curled up under his chin.

When he awoke, Bertram brought him *The Illustrated
London News* and a summons from the Council in its usual
tidy vellum envelope, complete with sealing wax and ribbons. The *News* was more interesting. On the front page,
complete with a lurid sketch, was the story of an attack on the
sexton of St. Matthew's on Church Row. He'd been dismem-
bered by what witnesses swore was an enormous *bear*—the
only witnessed attack, but a dozen people had died in the
same manner last night.

Frederick regarded the unopened summons balefully. He
already knew what it contained. A dozen murders, whatever
their cause, would spark a panic. And so Captain Wentworth,
as the sole Animal Speaker on the Council, would be dispatched to deal with the matter—after suitable lecturing
about how this wasn't their problem in the first place.

He got to his feet and began to pace. Bucket, who had been lying at Frederick's feet, stood as well.

"*Go now?*" Bucket asked. "*Find the Girl?*"

"You know," Frederick said, ringing for Bertrand, "I think we might as well."

It would spare him a conversation with Alderscroft, since the Poison Master was probably the one responsible for this plague of werewolves. And stopping him was undoubtedly what the Council wanted Frederick to do in the first place.

Even if it wasn't, it was always better to ask forgiveness than permission.

It was a long time before the smell of Wrongness faded, and even longer until the Girl stopped weeping. But when she finally spoke, there was iron in her voice. "We have to get out of here before he comes back."

"*How?*" *Jingo demanded, hooting and leaping.* "*We are all trapped in little boxes.*"

"Not all of us," *the Girl said firmly.* "The rats in the walls are free."

"*They won't come here,*" *Bright Eyes said, and Bounce knew she was right. Rats were clever, and the cellar was filled with smells that promised death.*

"*I think I can persuade them,*" *the Girl said as she produced something from her pocket. The smell of food—even if it was nothing but a piece of stale bread—made Bounce's mouth water. It had been so long since he'd eaten.* "But you have to promise to be still," *she said firmly to Bounce and Bright Eyes.* "If you frighten them, they will not help us."

Bounce lay down and rested his head on his paws. "*All right,*" *he said.*

"All right," *Bright Eyes agreed.*

And the Girl called the rats.

If he hadn't been able to draw a glamour around himself, Frederick wouldn't have ventured into this part of London for a hundred guineas, even dressed as he was in his oldest and most disreputable clothes. He began in the alley where he'd found Bucket, hoping the puppy could pick up the scent. Day turned to evening and then to night as they walked the streets, circling and backtracking as Bucket found the scent and lost it again. At last Bucket struck a strong trace, at almost the exact instant Frederick caught a hint of Water Magic. It was like something glimpsed out of the corner of his eye—there and gone and there again. It made him a bit dizzy.

"*Man,*" Bucket whispered. "*Man who took the Girl.*" He leaned against Frederick's leg and trembled.

Frederick squatted down and stroked his head. "Do you know where?" he asked gently.

"*This way,*" Bucket said, putting his nose to the ground and taking a reluctant pace forward. Frederick followed. The Water Magic lay that way, too. He was pretty sure he didn't like this any more than Bucket did.

Finally, an enormous gray rat reluctantly emerged from the wall. Bounce knew there had to be others. Where there was one rat, there were many. The smell was nearly enough to drive him mad. He imagined the rat between his strong jaws. He imagined the swift shake that broke a neck. He whined softly with longing.

"I promise Bounce and Bright Eyes will not hurt you," *the Girl said to the rat.* "They have given me their word." *Unafraid, she held out the bread.* "And I will give you this for your help."

Frederick began to understand why the gnome had been unable to track the man who kidnapped the Goose Girl. The Water Magic wasn't the work of a Master, but it was cleverly woven. All around him, the world seemed to ripple and shift, dissolving here and there into bright sparks of light. It dazzled the inner eye and drew the attention first here, then there, and then to still another place on the horizon. If not for Bucket, he would have gotten hopelessly lost, and even forgotten why he was here in the first place. Fortunately, the Poison Master hadn't thought to ward his domain against the puppy's sensitive nose. He kept on walking, nose to the ground and hackles up, and Frederick followed.

Stumptail clambered up onto the crate where Percy's cage rested and stood on his hind legs in front of the door. The cage was made of wire, but a rat's teeth were strong. Suddenly the cage door sprang open, and the raven hopped out, flicking his wings to settle the feathers. Stumptail leaped from the crate to the ground and darted back to the hole in the wall from whence he'd come.

"Now you must free Bright Eyes," *the Girl said to Percy.* "I know you're clever enough to figure out the latch."

"Of course I am," *Percy said, and flap-hopped across the floor to where the cat's cage sat, his talons clicking against the stone. Percy hopped around the cage a couple of times with his head cocked, studying it, before he nudged up the hook and the door swung open. Bright Eyes leaped free and whirled to face the raven.*

"I am not supper, you stupid feline," *Percy said, spreading his wings in unmistakable threat.* "Try it and I'll peck your eyes out. Free Jingo. You promised."

Bright Eyes lashed her tail and fixed Percy with a stare that would have made a lesser bird take wing, but finally— reluctantly—she sprang up to the crate over which Jingo's cage hung. Percy and she both inspected it carefully, but the latch had been designed to defeat a captive with hands.

"If it falls, it will smash," *Bright Eyes finally said. Without waiting for any reply, she sprang upward, clinging to the cage as it rocked. Jingo whimpered.*

Then it fell, and Bounce yipped despite himself. For a moment nothing happened, but the fall had sprung the bars enough for Jingo to reach through them. In a moment he was free. He bounded over and drew the pin from the latch on Bounce's cage.

"Here you go, old chap," *the monkey announced, swinging the door wide. Bounce crept out of the cage, savoring his freedom. Jingo turned to the Girl's prison.*

"A lock," *he said.* "I cannot open a lock."

"Is there a key?" *the Girl asked hopefully.*

Just then the door to Above slammed open, and the scent of Badstink Man filled the air.

"Go!" *the Girl cried.* "Save yourselves!"

"The window!" *Jingo said. It was the work of a moment for him to unfasten the latches. He paused on the sill, then leaped through the opening. Percy and Bright Eyes followed.*

Bounce hesitated. The Girl would be here alone. He could stay. He could protect her.

"Hurry!" *the Girl said. There were footsteps on the stairs.* "Go! You must go now!"

Bounce sprang onto the table beneath the window and looked up at the window. He was not a cat or a raven or a monkey. He did not fly or leap. He dug. He pounced. He ran fast.

But the Girl had asked this, and so he crouched down and jumped up as high as he could. His forepaws hooked over the sill, and his hind legs scrabbled against the wall. For a moment, he thought he would fall back.

Then he was through.

Frederick nearly shouted in surprise when a cat, a terrier, a monkey, and an enormous raven burst abruptly from an alley not three yards from where he nursed the headache that damned Water working had given him.

"Here!" Bucket cried. "Here! Girl! Here!"

"Earth Master!" *t*he raven said in surprise.

"Help the Girl!" the monkey shouted, his lips going wide in a fear grimace as he sprang from the ground to a box and then to Frederick's shoulder. "Help the Girl!"

"This way!" said the terrier, and Bucket followed. Frederick ran after them, the monkey on his shoulder, followed by the cat and the raven.

Kits, cats, sacks, and wives, he thought giddily, as he followed the dogs down the alley from which they'd just come. There was an open cellar window through which his new friends had clearly made their exit, and next to it, a door.

It would have had to have been a much stronger door than Whitechapel usually boasted to resist Frederick's efforts to enter. The Water Magic wrapped around him like a stifling blanket, and he stumbled across the kitchen, barely catching himself against a wall before he fell down the stairs to the cellar. But now even the Water Magic wasn't enough to keep him from sensing the presence of another Earth Magician.

The Goose Girl. Claire Prentiss' daughter. It had to be.

He headed for the stairs. He could hear voices.

"What did you do?" a man snarled, and the voice was startlingly familiar.

Frederick flung himself down the last ten stairs.

In the cellar stood George Cliburn, holding a soot-streaked, rag-clad street urchin by the upper arm. The girl was struggling, but while Frederick could sense the latent Earth power coiling around her, it was clear she had no idea it was there, let alone how to use it.

Cliburn turned at the sound of Frederick's footsteps on the cellar floor. His eyebrows lifted. "Well, if it isn't Captain Wentworth, here to rescue another one of his strays."

"Let her go, Cliburn," Frederick said through gritted teeth. "I'm here to bring you before the Council."

"The Council is finished. I've done it, don't you see? My lovely hound and my beautiful bear are only just the beginning. I've mastered Stevenson's elixir. Magic is dead, and Science is king. Men shall become as gods."

"You're mad," Frederick said flatly, reaching into the ground beneath him for the tiny trickle of available Earth power. He wished now that he'd thought to bring a pistol. *Come on, Wentworth, you're a Master, not an untutored child,* he told himself.

Cliburn *tsk*ed mildly. "Oh, come now, Frederick, you're a forward-thinking man. Surely you can see I'm the future. Imagine an army of soldiers augmented by my elixir. What force could stand against the Empire then?"

"You can tell Alderscroft all about it," Frederick said. He drew a deep breath and began haltingly to weave a net of compulsion around Cliburn. The bright flickers of Water power darted around him, dizzying him, disrupting his focus.

"Now, now, my good Captain, I'm not ready to publish yet. But I have been working on something else that might interest you." Cliburn reached into his pocket and flung the contents of a little vial into Frederick's face.

Blackness swamped his senses as the ground rushed up to meet him.

The Earth Master crashed to the ground, and the Girl cried out. Badstink Man laughed delightedly.

Jingo leaped to the windowsill, and Bounce cringed back into a corner, but Badstink Man didn't seem to notice them now.

"I'm sorry," *Bounce whispered, gazing up at the Girl.*

"You tried," *she whispered back. Her Voice was full of pride, even though her eyes were full of terror. And then she went utterly still, as if listening to something.* "Wait," *she said.* "Do you hear that?"

Bounce didn't hear it, but he could smell *it. The bear. Close. He must have come back to the only familiar place he knew. The Girl had called him a Circus Bear and said Men had treated him badly. Perhaps the Circus Bear thought cruelty meant Home.*

Bounce didn't think Badstink Man heard the Circus Bear or smelled him, for Badstink Man merely adjusted his grip on the Girl's arm and dragged her toward the staircase that led Above. "Where were we before we were so rudely interrupted? Ah, yes. You shall be my first human subject, my darling. Aren't you pleased? A few minutes in my laboratory, and you'll be a completely different woman," *he promised.*

The puppy whimpered in terror, smelling the Circus Bear, smelling the Wrongness that surrounded Badstink Man.

"Hush," *Bounce said. He had an idea.*

It was a foolhardy idea, the sort of idea that led Hunters of Rats to glorious deaths. Bounce threw back his head and sang to the Circus Bear. Softly at first, and then louder.

"Here," *Bounce called to the Circus Bear.* "Badstink Man is here. He waits for you. Come and close your jaws around his throat."

Badstink Man kicked at him, and Bounce dodged. He scuttled out of reach and Sang again. "Badstink Man is here. He waits for you."

For long moments Bounce wasn't sure the Circus Bear had heard, or whether he cared to listen to a Hunter of Rats at all.

Badstink Man set his foot on the first step, pulling the Girl with him.

And then a dark Shape shouldered its way through the door to Above.

Frederick wasn't sure if it was the scream or the *smell* that roused him, but he opened his eyes just in time to see an enormous bear take George Cliburn by the throat and shake him the way a terrier might shake a rat as it dragged him up the stairs.

Exeunt, he thought hysterically, *pursued by a bear.*

And then the darkness reached up and claimed him again.

Bounce did not know where the Circus Bear and Badstink Man went, but as long as they did not come back here, he didn't care. The Girl found food for all of them in the rooms above, and water, too, and they stayed. Percy could fly home again, and Bright Eyes did not care, but Bounce did not know how to find Smell-Gives-Bite again, and Jingo did not know where he belonged. For now, here was as good as anywhere.

The Earth Master slept for a long time. The puppy Bucket never left his side. Finally, when the window near the ceiling brightened with day, the Earth Master stirred and sat up, putting his hands to his head in the way Men did when they didn't feel at all well. He sat for a moment, apparently unperturbed by the assortment of creatures peering at him closely.

Then he turned to the Girl and said the one thing that mattered. "I'm Frederick. And I know your name."

The Flying Contraption
Ron Collins

On an evening late in August—a hot month in Dayton, Ohio—
ten-year-old Daisy Mae Fuller dried her sweaty palms on her
dress as she peered out the bicycle shop's dirty window.

She plucked a feather from the duster, like Mr. Cash had
suggested. And just to make sure the feather knew what it
was there to do, she brushed it over some dirt that had gathered in the window's corner. Then she hummed a little tune
and opened her thoughts to the Elemental, just like Mr. Cash
had taught her.

The feather jumped from her hand and danced down the
window, dusting all the way.

With a gleeful yip, she clapped her hands with such vigor
that her palms turned red.

She discovered that the harder she hummed, the faster the
feather twirled. So Daisy hummed, and she whistled, and she
even sang, starting with "Daisy Bell" (a song her daddy sang
to her every day on account of that being her name) and moving into "Ta-ra-ra Boom de-ay" (a song she just liked to
sing). The feather danced with her songs, it floated on her
melody, and it dusted. Oh, yes, how it dusted.

It was the most exciting thing she had ever seen! Better
than her wildest dreams—and let me tell you that being ten
years old and full of thoughts like beating Timmy, her
freckle-faced older brother, in a race across town, or pulling
a never-ending string of fish out of the creek that ran behind
Franklin's Curio Shop, Daisy Mae could dream of many wild
things.

In fact, she dreamed all the time. The century had just turned, after all, and everyone was talking about what might come next. She imagined having her own horseless carriage, setting its choke and getting out of the cab to turn its crank until it roared to life with a plume of oily smoke and a rumble that sounded like a big old grizzly bear. If she did have her own automobile someday, she might go to Boston, where she heard there was a train that ran completely underground, or maybe she would drive to Alaska, where Uncle Carl said they'd found mountains of gold. Daisy could barely imagine what that might look like. She dreamed about places from the stories that Mama read her, too. Places like the Sahara desert and the Amazon rain forest.

Ever since she had started coming to the Wright brothers' shop, she found herself thinking of Kitty Hawk, too. Kitty Hawk, where the Wrights were going to fly their contraption. Kitty Hawk. She liked how saying it made her lips stretch over her teeth. She liked how it sounded so exciting.

She dreamed of flying, too, you see, though she had never told anyone at all about it because she knew how they would laugh and say that no ten-year-old named Daisy Mae Fuller, a girl no less, could ever be allowed to touch a flying contraption, better yet captain one. But dream about it she did, and in her dreams she imagined it would be like swinging out over the lake on that big rope Timmy had strung up, only better. Daisy had to admit that when she saw the contraption's parts spread over the bicycle shop's floor—the wiring, the canvas, and the box framework—she had felt that same thrill. And when she had seen the drawings pinned up all over the shop walls, she dreamed of flying even more.

Her only defense was that when you're ten years old, everything is interesting. At least that's what her granddaddy said. He said she had the curiosity in her, and he said that was a good thing.

Auntie Ida didn't agree with Granddaddy. She said a girl needs to sit on the porch and find her a young man, and that even ten years old isn't too early to practice being attractive. Luckily, Mama agreed with Granddaddy, and shushed Ida every chance she got. Daisy didn't really like Auntie Ida. Not just because of her ideas, but also because she smelled like powder, and because Daisy had no patience for sitting on the porch and fanning herself all day like a lace doily waiting for the wind to come along and take her wherever it wanted her to go.

Mama would just smile at Ida when she started talking about her grandniece.

"I don't think Daisy Mae's cut out for courting just yet," Mama said to Ida earlier this spring. "I think she's got places to go first."

Ida blanched pale as a sheet and rolled her eyes up to the sky as she sipped her tea.

Mama glanced at Daisy out the corner of her eye. With a grin on her lips as cool as a cat's, she said, "Who knows, Ida. Daisy Mae might even be the first woman to cast a vote."

Auntie Ida choked on her tea then.

And Daisy laughed and ran off to play in the creek. She remembered that day especially because it was springtime, and she had chased tadpoles all over the shallow flats.

She was worried, though.

Even at ten years old, Daisy knew there were more people in this world who thought like Ida than there were who thought like Mama. She knew most everyone thought it queer that she still played in creeks rather than got her hair done up, and she knew everyone expected her to be learning how to cook and sew rather than be dreaming of underground trains or mountains of gold.

All this made Daisy Mae feel strange. Since the day of that conversation, she had grown more wary. She tucked her thinking into the back of her head more often than not, and she kept her dreams to herself. She still had those dreams, of course. But now they made her wonder if she was broken. Was she so different? Was she supposed to think like this? Wouldn't it be better if she just learned to darn socks or to serve tea?

Usually she didn't worry so much, though. Usually she let her dreams run free inside her head, even if she didn't talk about them as much as she had when she was seven or eight or even nine.

The problem with dreams that are left to run free, though, is that they can sometimes get a person into trouble. And as

Daisy watched the feather dance over the window, she should have known that trouble was just around the corner.

You see, everything started one day about a month before when Mr. Cash stopped her while she was walking home from the park.

"I'll purchase you a soda if you would take a moment to speak with me," he said as they stood on the street corner, he primly in his suit jacket, cane, and bowler, and she in her dress stained with grass at the elbow and hip (she and the rest of the girls had been playing red rover, and she had broken through with such a run that she'd gone tumbling over the grass).

No one liked Mr. Cash much. He was one of those adults who always seemed to be around, but considered himself above the dignity of participation. The kids around town told stories about him. Jessie Martin said Mr. Cash was crazy as a loon, and Jimsie Pitoski told everyone that one day he saw Mr. Cash out in the woods all alone, making the wind do all sorts of tricks. It wasn't long after that common tattle talk at school was that he was a wizard, or a warlock, or some other witchy kind of thing.

That made Daisy curious, of course. She couldn't help herself.

Daisy was curious about magic. She admitted that fully and without any sense of shame. Magic didn't scare her. Not much, anyway. She figured that if it was real, it had to be about like everything else—something you could learn if you were interested enough. So when Mr. Cash offered her a soda that day, she was excited enough about the chance to learn a bit of trickery that she accepted.

She ordered a cherry float.

They took seats at a tall, round table in the drugstore window.

"The Wright brothers are looking for someone to clean their shop," Mr. Cash said once they were settled. He played nervously with his cane.

"That's interesting," Daisy said, more because she felt like he expected her to say something than because she actually found it interesting. The ice cream was very delicious.

"I would like you to consider pursuing the job."

"I don't understand."

"I'm very interested in the Wrights, you see. If you were to take that job, I would be willing to pay you a nickel a day if you would tell me stories about what they are working on."

"I see," Daisy said, though she didn't really. "You want me to spy on the Wright brothers?"

"Oh, no," Mr. Cash said, dismissing that notion with a sharp wave of his spindly hand. "Nothing untoward like that, of course. I'm, uh, thinking that perhaps I'll write a book or something about them, and so I could use some inside perspectives."

"So why don't you just talk to the Wrights yourself?"

"I would," Mr. Cash said. "But well, let's put it this way. Have you ever noticed that people do things differently when they know someone's watching?"

"Sure."

"Or do you ever notice they don't always tell you the full truth when you ask about something directly?"

"All the time."

Mr. Cash's lips pulled back in a smile. "That's why I would rather not speak with the Wrights myself. I want to know what they're really up to. So, I need someone else to keep an eye on them, someone they wouldn't think of as watching them all the time."

"All right," Daisy said. "That makes sense, then."

He waited while she drank more of her float.

"You'll give me a nickel a day?"

"That's right. A nickel a day on top of whatever the Wrights pay you for the actual cleaning you would do."

"And all I have to do is tell you stories about what happens while I'm there?"

"Correct again."

Daisy considered the offer. A nickel a day! *On top of what the Wrights might give her!* She would be rich. And the best part was, she could spend time in the Wrights' shop with all those tools and machines and other shiny gizmos the adults talked so much about, and Timmy would turn all shades of green.

*   *   *

She met Mr. Wright that afternoon.

"You can call me Wilbur," he said as he shook her hand. Can you imagine that, an adult actually shook her hand and said to call him by his first name? Wilbur was the kind of thin that made him look taller than he was, and the fact that he was bald over the top of his head made him seem taller still.

Wilbur didn't smile a lot because, as Daisy would learn later, he didn't have his teeth in, but he was big, and he moved with confidence like her daddy did. She liked him right away. And he seemed to like her, too. He said she had gumption, which she also took to be a good thing even if it did sound like a disease. He introduced Daisy to his brother, Orville, a quiet, serious man, who looked a lot like Wilbur, but with a bushy mustache and considerably more hair. And finally, he introduced her to several other men hovering over a big sheet of paper, scribbling notes and arguing about angles and pressures.

"Are they working on the contraption?" she asked.

"Contraption?"

"You know," Daisy said, "the flying contraption that everyone talks about."

Wilbur chuckled and patted her on the shoulder. "Yes, they're working on the contraption, all right—though we prefer to call it our little flying problem—which right now is focused on the fact that our wind tunnel is not working as well as we might like."

"Wind tunnel? It sounds like a hole in the sky."

"A hole in the sky," Wilbur said with a pleasant drawl. "I like that, Daisy. But no, a wind tunnel isn't a hole in the sky. It's that big, long thing over there."

He pointed to a wooden box that stood on a set of sturdy legs made of crossed lumber. It was the size of a casket and had a built-in fan at the front. A square glass window let you look inside, and a small engine sat on the ground beside it. "We want to use it to push air over things to see how they work."

"So what's the problem?" she said.

"Well," Wilbur sighed, "the air going in is too messy."

Daisy wasn't certain what he meant, but she studied the wind tunnel as they returned to the front of the shop. "Flying would be so dreamy," she said.

Wilbur gave her a look of keen assessment. "Yes," he replied. "I believe it would."

They stopped at the counter.

"I think you'll do just fine, Daisy," Wilbur said. "How would you like to start right now?"

She nearly jumped for joy but managed to restrain herself. "I'm ready."

Wilbur showed her where to clean and what to stay away from (which was basically the back part of the shop, where they kept all the paperwork about the contraption), then left her to her own devices. She dusted around corners and ran wet rags over bicycle racks full of Ramblers and Spaldings and Waverlys. She loved the advertisements for the Waverly. *America's Favorite!* it read, and it had a picture of a lady of refinement riding down a lane.

There was even a bicycle from a company in Middletown, Ohio. Imagine that. A place that made bicycles right there in Ohio. Daisy smiled. She felt like she might actually be able to go to Middletown someday.

Pleased with her work, Wilbur gave her a nickel. She twirled it between her fingers as she walked home. A whole nickel! And another in the morning when she spoke with Mr. Cash! She was going to be so rich.

It wasn't until later that night that Daisy realized she hadn't asked Mr. Cash about his magic.

Everything was just peachy for a couple weeks.

She cleaned, she kept her eyes open, and she reported to Mr. Cash every morning. She told him about Elmer, a cat that was adopting the shop as its mousing territory, and about a stranger who came into the shop to get his spokes fixed—tensioned, Mr. Taylor called it. Mr. Taylor—Charlie—was a nice man who worked in the bicycle shop. Orville and Wilbur were always out back, so Charlie seemed to keep the bicycle business all by himself. She told Mr. Cash about that. And she told him about the kites Wilbur had showed her one day. Mr. Cash was more interested in those kites than anything else.

"How are they shaped?" he asked. "What are they made of?"

When Daisy answered, he nodded, scowled, scratched his chin, or mumbled things to himself that she couldn't catch.

Something didn't feel right about the way Mr. Cash's eyes grew slitted and calculating when she talked about things in the Wrights' flying shop. That's why she didn't tell Mr. Cash about the drawings she had seen, or about the test plans the Wrights were changing for the next time they went to Kitty Hawk. That's why she only told him about a few of the models they were building.

Instead, she gave Mr. Cash simple stories and walked home with two shiny nickels in her dress pocket every evening. Mama was happy because Daisy gave her one of the nickels. Mr. Cash said it was important that no one know she was working for him, so she put the nickels he gave her into a shoebox and stashed them under her bed. By the time three weeks had passed, Daisy felt rich as Rockefeller.

But as time passed, shadows crossed Mr. Cash's face, and he grew impatient. Daisy knew this was not going to last forever.

Indeed, things changed the very next morning.

"When are you going to bring me something useful?" Mr. Cash demanded. He sat on the park bench like he always did, his bowler primly beside him, his mustache so perfect across his upper lip that Daisy thought it might be drawn on. The park smelled of dry yellow grass.

"What more do you want?" Daisy asked, thinking this might be the moment she had been looking for.

He dabbed at his forehead with his handkerchief. It was warm, even for the morning, and the sun was coming out.

"I want to know what parts the Wrights are ordering, what designs they're contemplating. I want to know *what* they're planning on testing, and *when* they're planning to test it."

Daisy looked at Mr. Cash and thought, yes, this was definitely the moment. She stood in front of the bench and twisted on one heel. "I'm too busy cleaning," she said. "There's no time left to sleuth. I could probably learn more if you would teach me a trick that made the cleaning go faster."

"Now, now, little girl. You don't need to be fooling around with any *tricks*."

"I understand, Mr. Cash," she said, pouting just a bit. "But all my friends are jealous of me because they think you're a *powerful* mage. I just figured if that was true you could teach me something to make things go faster—something little, of course. Just enough to give me time to look around. I'm a kid, after all. I can't handle much. But it's okay if you can't teach me. I understand. I'll just use what time I've got, and it'll take longer."

Mr. Cash sighed and stared out over the grassy park.

Daisy looked away then, too, careful to avoid showing just how anxious she was to know if the rumors were true.

"All right," he replied. "You show every sign of having ability, and I don't see that learning a little dusting cantrip can do you much harm." He put his bowler on his head and patted the bench with his palm. "Sit up here, and I'll give you one *small* lesson."

Daisy squealed with delight.

"Hush, child," Mr. Cash said, pulling his handkerchief from his pocket once again to dab his forehead. "You have to promise not to tell anyone."

"Oh, I promise, Mr. Cash. I promise not to tell a soul."

And there, in open daylight, Mr. Cash taught Daisy how to clear her mind, and how to think about a leaf, and then how to ask a tiny favor from an Air Elemental.

The touch of magic felt light to her. It was like cool fire—she could feel it, but not touch it. After the power built a bit, Mr. Cash had her focus on a leaf on the ground, and then had her hum just bit to get a rhythm going.

And then she did it.

Can you imagine?

She, Daisy Mae Fuller, made that leaf *move* with her little gust of wind.

And that's how she managed to be in the corner of the Wright brothers' shop, serenading a feather and making it do the dusting dance. This was fun, but one feather did not a dusting machine make. She needed more. She looked at the duster, realizing she had several more feathers at her disposal.

So she plucked another and she added to her song, asking the Elemental to take that feather from her hand and dust with it, too. Which it did.

She sang and sang, and was having such a grand time that

it was several minutes before she noticed all the other feathers in the duster had loosened and were dancing and dusting, too. What a miraculous sight it was! The windows were sparkling, and Mr. Taylor's workbench was soon going to be free of ash from his pipe and from those big cigars he smoked. He would be so pleased!

She danced and pranced and clapped with such joy as she might never have felt before. She did a two-step, and she waved her arms about like she was a conductor in a grand hall, leading a parade of feathers as they dusted their way around the shop. She raised her hands and wiggled her fingers in celebration, and the feathers joined her, shaking themselves out and becoming ready to do it all over again.

She kept her voice up, of course, humming and singing a symphony so that the dusting would continue as she wandered around the shop. She picked up a rubber mallet and felt its weight as she pounded a beat on the bench. She spun a gear wheel, listening to its chain rattle and rasp. Everything she touched made its own sound and moved to its own rhythm, and everything she did added to the music. The feathers kept on dusting while she rolled bearings and twirled sprockets and fiddled with that odd sort of thing Charlie had called a self-oiler.

She wasn't sure what it was that finally caught her attention, but when she looked up, Daisy saw a plumey cloud of dust had gathered in the center of the room and was starting to swirl like a tiny tornado. The air smelled like a touch of lightning, and Daisy heard a rumbling chuckle that might have been the Elemental itself. The cloud looked almost exactly like she imagined a sandstorm from the *Arabian Nights* might look, except it was black and brown rather than orange and yellow.

"Stop!" she yelled.

But the cloud still billowed, the air still swirled, and she could still hear gears and chains grinding.

"I'm not singing anymore!" she yelled again, feeling ice-cold fingers of panic across her back.

The feathers were still dusting, but now they moved out of the bicycle shop and into the Wrights' flying lab. Sheets of butcher paper filled with penciled drawings rose up like laundry on the line. One of the kites tumbled to the floor. Every tool or piece of machinery in the shop was lifting up now, or screeching and rattling.

"Stop it!" she screamed again as she ran through the shop and grabbed papers out of midair to clutch them to her chest. "I said stop it!"

Windows. Maybe opening a window would help. But it was as if too much air was inside the shop pressing on them, and she couldn't get one to budge.

The cloud grew more forceful.

Small nails flew in its grasp now, nails and grommets and bits of other things that came from workbenches. She saw Mr. Taylor's pipe and Orville's favorite pen. *That's it,* she thought. They were going to kill her.

Her eyes lit on the wind tunnel.

If she could get the engine going, maybe it would suck up all the air, and then she could gather up all the papers.

Daisy ran to crank the engine.

It didn't start, so she cranked it again.

Nothing.

She looked around. What could she do? Nothing. Nothing. She was doomed. She had been silly to think she could do this. She was only ten. And worse, she was a girl, a girl mucking around in an adult world where she clearly didn't belong.

And look what she had done!

Tears welled in her eyes. She didn't want to cry. Yet despite her resolve, a tear ran down her cheek. She gritted her teeth and grabbed the starter one more time. She hit the choke and pulled as hard she could pull.

The engine coughed once, then caught. The belt loop turned, and the big wooden blades of the fan slowly twirled up to speed. She had never been so happy to hear a machine run at any time in her entire life.

With a huge whoop, she pushed the box to get the fan pointed at the cloud, which was now heavy and black and whirling with such force that she could see loops of wire and old saw blades flying around the room. All that wood and metal all bolted together was heavy as a rock, but if she strained and pushed and hit the wind tunnel hard with her shoulder, she could nudge it here and there. The front end slowly came around to suck air away from the cyclone. Daisy put her back into the effort, pushing so hard, she thought her eyes might pop. Then she got to the back of the box and pushed some more, shoving the entrance deeper into the cloud.

And it seemed to work.

An advertisement wrapped itself around the fan blade for a moment, then disappeared into the tunnel.

Stuff flew into the box, bigger things clunking against its walls. She looked at the far end of the tunnel and saw a paper flutter out onto the floor for her to pick up.

Yes! It *was* working!

Then the wind tunnel sucked in a kite wing that got tangled with the fan blade, and wedged it against the box. The engine choked and died, and the whole thing came to a shuddering halt.

"No!"

Daisy clawed at the kite to get it unstuck. She cracked a fingernail, but couldn't dislodge the fan blade. Air pressure grew once again as she scraped and pulled.

But the wind tunnel was broken.

Daisy was done.

She heard the Elemental chuckle again as the whistling rose around the room. Force grew so great around her that she worried the roof might blow off.

Then the door burst open.

It was Mr. Cash, wearing his suit pants and a jacket, but not his customary bowler. His cheeks were red as cherries against his white face, and his hair stuck out at wild angles. He stepped into the room and sang his own song.

The cloud stopped swirling. Debris clattered to the floor, and the shop instruments stopped grinding.

"What in the blazes are you doing?" Mr. Cash yelled, striding across the shop with angry little steps. His hand clamped over Daisy's shoulder with strength enough that it hurt. His dark eyes glanced around the shop with a nervous twitch. He spoke from deep in his throat. "I told you to *be careful.*"

The door opened from the other side of the shop.

This time it was Wilbur—with Orville trailing right behind.

Wilbur stepped to Daisy's side and forced Mr. Cash to release his hold. Blood flowed through her shoulder.

"That's a very good question, Artemis," Wilbur said. "What *is* happening here? Do we need to call the sheriff?"

"That won't be necessary," Cash said, brushing dust off his jacket and straightening his vest. "I ran over to help this young lady."

Wilbur took in the disaster around the room. Tools were scattered everywhere, and half the shop was covered in loose-leaf paper.

"I see," he said. "And just *how* did you know she was in such dire need of your help?"

Mr. Cash looked like a dog that had been caught digging in Mama's tomato garden.

"We told you to stay out of here," Wilbur said.

"I can't let you fly," Mr. Cash said between gritted teeth.

"You can't stop us, Artemis. We've been through this before. Not you, and not these suppliers who seem hell-bent on ruining half our plans. No one. Only God himself can keep us away from solving this little flying problem. And if it's not us, it'll be somebody else. You need to relax, stop using little ones like Daisy here to do your dirty business, and realize there's enough sky for all of us."

Mr. Cash pressed his lips together.

Wilbur shook his head.

"I think it would be best that you leave, Artemis. Or else I believe we *will* need to call the sheriff."

Mr. Cash drew a breath through his nose, then walked tersely out the door.

"And you, young lady." Wilbur looked down at Daisy. "What are we going to do with you?"

"I'm sorry, Mr. Wright," Daisy said. And then she spewed a long string of words that rushed out like water through a hose, and that told the entire story of her snooping and spying and how she learned enough magic to call the Air, but how the feathers got to dancing and the papers flying and the tools and . . . by the time she got to the end, she was crying a river of remorse.

"I feel so awful, Mr. Wright. Just awful. I wouldn't blame you at all if you fired me and told me to never come back!"

"Will?" Orville said. He was leaning over the window that looked into the wind tunnel. "You want to take a look at this?"

Wilbur joined his brother at the window. Then they both peered into the entry of the wind tunnel, where spoke wire, paper, and a hacksaw blade had gotten all wrapped up together and stuck.

"Did I break it?" Daisy said. "I'll pay for it if I did. I've got a lot of nickels, and I can work harder."

Wilbur bent down in front of her. "No, Daisy Mae. You didn't break it. In fact, that saw blade got stuck in just such a way that it made the air smooth out as it went through the tunnel. Come on and see."

He walked her to the window. "See how all the dirt you sucked up left patterns on the wall?"

"Yes," she said.

"See how they're straight lines here?"

"Yes."

"Those are air-flow paths," Orville said from the other side of the tunnel. He had a dopey smile on his face. It was the first time she had ever seen that kind of expression on Orville.

"The lines," Daisy said, looking up at Wilbur with wide eyes. "They aren't messy. You said before that the air was too messy. But these lines are straight."

"That's right," Wilbur said. "We were having a problem with turbulent air."

Turbulent. The air was turbulent. Daisy liked that word. It sounded right for what it was, and it made her mouth move just like it did when she said Kitty Hawk.

"That blade," Orville said, "seems to have straightened some of the air flow right out."

"If this is right," Wilbur said as Orville finished, "we'll be able to test all the models we've been wanting to test. So you see, Daisy, your work tonight might have helped us solve this little flying problem once and for all."

"You're not mad?"

"Oh, we're mad all right," Orville said with an edge to his voice. "Look at this mess." He reached down and picked up his pen.

Wilbur nodded. "Daisy Mae, you're going to have to do two things if you want to keep your job." He stopped and looked at her. "Well, make that three."

"Yes?"

"First, you're going to have to work as long as it takes tonight to get this place picked up. Charlie will be mad as a hornet if he comes in to a messy shop tomorrow morning."

"I already planned to do that, Mr. Wright."

He smiled. "Second, from here out you have to promise not to tell Artemis Cash about our work."

"I already planned that, too."

"That's good."

"What's the third thing?"

"The third thing is the most important."

Daisy swallowed hard.

"The third thing is that you have to promise me that no matter what happens, you'll never stop making mistakes."

"What?"

"You made a big mistake tonight, Daisy Mae. No doubt about it. But you've got the dreaming disease. I see it in you every day. You're young, and you need some learning. But the world needs folks like you, people with interesting questions and ideas who are willing to make mistakes, so long as they're also willing to clean up after them."

"Thank you, Mr. Wright."

Wilbur rose up and ran his hand over the wind tunnel, then looked at Daisy with a sideways glance.

"But you're so much trouble, I'm thinking we'd best keep our eyes on you throughout the day. So whenever you're not in school, I'm thinking we'll need you to come and help us out while we test these models. Don't you think that's wise, Orville?"

Orville raised his eyes to the heavens, as if asking powers that be for forbearance.

"You mean it, Mr. Wright?" Daisy asked, stunned. "You mean I can come help you with the flying contraption?"

Wilbur laughed. "On one more condition."

"What's that?" she asked, crestfallen.

"You have to remember to call me Wilbur."

"Deal!" she said, squealing with delight.

*   *   *

Over the next two months, Daisy learned there is as much magic to staying true to a dream as there is in spells or staffs or pixie dust. She heard people snickering about the Wrights, and about her work. But she didn't care.

Every day she got up early and went to the shop. When school started, she left, then came back and stayed late to clean. By October, Orville had the tunnel working, and they took to testing. There were wings that got twisted, and wings with droopy backsides. There were blocky models, and models with two wings and with three. There were models made of wood, and of canvas stretched over frames, and models made of metal that Mr. Taylor would pound into various shapes. Daisy helped set up the tunnel, and she cranked the engine. And sometimes she wrote down information in the logs.

By the time the leaves turned red, the Wrights were ready to test their glider once again.

"Wilbur?" Daisy asked one day.

"Hmm?"

"Do you think I could go to Kitty Hawk with you and Orville?"

He smiled. "I think you've earned that, Daisy Mae. But I'll have to ask your daddy and your mama first."

She knew then she was going to Kitty Hawk.

The rest of the day she found herself imagining the contraption flying over flat sand. That night she dreamed of smooth, looping pictures of air streams, and in that dream, if she squinted just right, she could see those streams flowing across wings as she piloted the contraption on a flight over mountains of gold and forests of pure green.

A Peony Amongst Roses

Gail Sanders and Michael Z. Williamson

Mei-Hua Walsingham sighed wistfully. She enjoyed her position at the Royal Botanical Gardens at Kew, working with the rainbow of flowers and riot of decorative shrubs. But sometimes she missed the Harton School. Sometimes she missed it more than she missed her parents, which was distressing.

She took that uncomfortable discovery to her parents' shrine in the corner of her boarding room. Lighting some incense, she sat in front of the little Chinese table that she had so carefully arranged. It held a white peony and the official portraits Mrs. Harton had located for her once her memory had returned.

"Mother, Father, it's not that I don't miss you, but I know that you're still here watching over me. It's just that you're not a part of my life, and the school became my home after you both were murdered. I miss my friends, and I miss Memsa'b and Sahib Harton. I found a place there, but I'm still not sure that I'll find one here."

It had all come out in a rush, because she had to say it, and had no one else to say it to.

A little breeze caressed her check, but it could have been just from the open window. That it smelled of her father's pipe tobacco and her mother's white peony perfume rather than the London air was also surely a coincidence. Feeling strangely comforted, she rose to her feet and prepared for her day.

She had challenges ahead.

*   *   *

Last May, the King had died.

There was nothing to be done about it. He smoked heavily and had been ill for months. It was not related to the previous Elemental attack on His person, but Mei felt hurt just the same. He had been gracious to her, had offered the financial support and the position she now enjoyed, unheard of for a woman, much less one of mixed blood.

He died clutching one of the peonies she'd had delivered to the Palace to protect him. They were the legacy of her parents and could ward against evil. They couldn't ward against simple ill health and old age.

Now in the present, her peonies were being moved to a new location by the Pagoda. It had been built by an Englishman a century and a half before, and while it appeared to be a pagoda at a distance, up close it was obviously English and not Chinese. It was half native, half foreign, and out of place. Mei realized that description could apply to her, too.

She had to coordinate the move with Mr. Burkill of the Herbarium. He wasn't trained in magic and hadn't been given all the details of the peonies' power, but he knew they were special and essential to the Royals, and he accepted them as his charges. The peonies weren't famous, but they were noted in several high circles. That was enough for the staff.

"Good day, Miss Walsingham," he greeted her. "Are we ready to start the move?"

"We are, sir," she agreed. "One plot every three days for the next three weeks."

"As you say, miss." He was agreeing because he'd been told to. He'd rather move them all at once and had said so. Mei was worried about a drop in the peonies' energy if they were all to be uprooted and distressed at the same time. Mr. Burkill was an expert botanist, and well read, but what she did wasn't in any book.

"I'll manage it," she said with a smile. "It means they'll have plenty of blooms for the Coronation."

"Well, the beds are ready by the Pagoda. I think that's a nice match, don't you?"

"It's all right," she said noncommittally. They all meant

well, she realized. They didn't grasp the intricacies of China, and to be fair, most had never visited it and never would.

"Let's hope the rain holds off," he said, pointing up at the gravid gray clouds overhead.

The bed was nicely dug, the soil black and rich. The gardeners had their wheelbarrows lined up like taxicabs and were carefully digging up each peony, placing it in a pot, and laying it in a barrow.

By eleven, the entire first bed had been relocated and replanted, and she fussed along the rows, using the edging bricks as stepping stones. She made sure to touch each plant, reassuring them that they were as they should be. She told them to hold off on blooming until they were ready and refreshed.

By Midsummer, they should be fully recovered and lush for the Coronation of King George V.

The transfer of the first bed complete, she moved on to her regular duties.

From the second bed she chose a full, healthy specimen, dug it up most carefully, and transferred it to a large pot. That was placed in a wagon and rolled off to be taken to the Palace. The new King didn't know why peonies were always in bloom at his residences. He'd be told when the time was right.

A light rain rolled in from the steely sky, and Mei sought shelter in the Temperate House.

Burkill had tea served and invited the laborers to join them. He was a middle-class, Cambridge-educated botanist, but he politely ignored some of the class rules and kept in regular conversation with the workers. He did sit at his own table, though, and chose who would join him. Mei was the only subordinate who gained that privilege.

"Your flowers are very strange, Miss Walsingham," he said. "I've taken to analyzing them. They're stronger than other peonies I've seen, but still very tender and delicate. I can't explain it."

"My mother bred them," she said. "I don't know exactly what she did."

"I see," he said. "Have you seen the Chinese delegation for the Coronation, miss? They've been through the garden twice this week."

"Only from a distance," she admitted. "They wouldn't know me, so I have no reason to visit with them." That, and she was a half-breed. Some English accepted her as a "colonial," others as the daughter of a diplomat. A goodly number treated her as a foreigner of lower station. The Chinese nobles and Imperial servants would think no better of her. Her mother's exile and marriage to a foreigner would mark her just as outcast to the Chinese, if not more so.

Ironically, the diplomatic delegation all wore English-style suits in their visits and business. Mei wasn't sure if she was glad or annoyed that they weren't in Chinese dress.

"They might not be overly friendly, given your father's station," he agreed.

"I'm all English now," she said. If for no other reason than the forces she'd fought previously would be delighted to have her on their ground. She was here to stay, where Elemental Mages, her Talent, and her peonies kept her safe.

And she did love the Gardens.

Her boarding room was in a house three miles from the Gardens' main entrance. She was glad of her bicycle, which made the trip much easier, though many of the new automobiles were a problem in traffic.

She arrived home at ten after seven. Mrs. Seton, her landlady, had baked fish on the table. The other residents were girls who worked as housekeepers or seamstresses and weren't home yet.

"That smells lovely," Mei said. "But I have work to do. I hope you won't think it rude if I take it upstairs."

Mrs. Seton smiled. "Of course, dear. But don't work too hard. You need rest and fresh air."

"I get fresh air all day, madam," Mei said with a smile.

"Yes, but what about the rest?"

"I will, thank you." She placed a slab of lemon-seasoned haddock on a plate with some fried potatoes and took it upstairs.

Once in her room, she set the plate down and removed her shoes. She did intend to rest. She also had to review the schedule for the protective peonies. Several plants were dispatched to the Royal quarters biweekly. Out of season, they were forced to bloom in a greenhouse. As they wilted, they were brought back to be nursed into renewed vigor, and others took their place. The entire replanting matter was interrupting that schedule. Then she was tasked with the water lilies in the same area. Those would be moved next, to a new pond. She was less tense over those, though she still wanted their move to be gentle. It showed her priorities, she realized, as the lilies would require more care in the move than regular peonies would.

A beautiful, formal garden was spread out beneath her. Mei could see two people in this garden. It was a hot and sunny day near the height of the sun, and there was a quality to the air that told Mei that this was not in England, or even in Reality.

The man said, "Well, hulloo there! Gads, what a lot of beautiful flowers. Are these all your doing?"

The woman started, not expecting to hear voices in the gardens at this hour of the day. Usually the workers did the rough tasks just after daylight broke, and the nobility, diplomats, and bureaucrats preferred early evening.

She pulled her mouth into a neutral smile, gracefully rose from her kneeling position, and bowed. She hoped that he would mistake her for one of the lowly workers and thus escape his presence and his memory. She had not figured on his English "arrogance" and his willful ignorance of Imperial "civilized" behavior.

Henry Walsingham hadn't been appointed the King's Representative to the Emperor of China without proving his skills in a different pool of sharks than the Imperial court. The unknown gardener's grace and her expert and unobtrusive application of Earth Magic had actually gotten Walsingham's attention weeks before. However, mindful of the proprieties he was bending, he had waited to approach until he was sure that they would be unobserved. After a quiet word to one of the sylphs hanging around him to keep watch, he had enacted his ambush.

With a much moderated tone and a properly respectful return bow to one who might be an equal, Walsingham inquired in perfectly executed Mandarin, "It is my imperfect understanding that your Mastery is responsible for these humble gardens achieving their present grandeur. Would the Master Gardener consider imparting some of her wisdom to me?"

Visibly realizing that she had strayed from the polite blankness that was proper to astonishment, the young woman schooled her expression. "If the worthy gentleman wishes to receive wisdom, he might try someone more appropriate to his station."

With another bow, she gracefully turned and walked away.

Walsingham was forced to concede the encounter—but not the battle. The glint of amusement in her almond eyes was almost a dare for the war to continue.

Mei woke from the dream with a start. Why was she dreaming of how her parents had met? While she had been told the stories, these dreams were too vivid to be just a mere retelling. Shaking her head, she looked around her small room.

She was still dressed, and her clock said it was close to two a.m. She shivered slightly. She didn't remember how she got to bed, but she was atop the blankets, and England could be quite chilly even in summer. She slipped into her nightgown and under the covers.

Why that dream? It was almost as if she were watching it in person. It bothered her. Was she obsessing over the past? Was it some sort of coping mechanism? What was she missing?

She drifted fitfully back to sleep.

The next morning, Mei took tea and toast with butter and marmalade. It wasn't the same as rice porridge, but she did like the contrasting flavors of the tart orange and the savory bread.

She reflected back on her dreams of last night. Why was she imagining how her parents had met? It was almost as if her parents were trying to tell or teach her something. Well, she would wait to see what developed. Signs from the other world came as they would and couldn't be forced.

She pedaled her way to the Gardens. Today she had to supervise moving another bed of flowers, review the orders for compost and minerals, and then encourage the recently transferred plants. The previous bed was being converted to something else, but Mr. Burkill would see to that. Her specialty was the Asian varieties that were becoming so popular now that England was promoting its Chinese connections, and above all, to keep the white peonies for the Royals.

After rolling through the front gate of Kew Gardens, she parked her bike and secured it with a lock. From there, she went on foot to her station. She reflected on how much she enjoyed her walk in the mornings. It would become unbearable come winter, but for now it gave her a chance to see the other plantings before starting work. She courteously greeted the planters and other gardeners, and for every smile returning her greeting, she received a frown or a hostile look. Mei sighed. She hoped that it wouldn't take long for the others to understand that she was no threat to their position or standing. For an Empire that "the sun never set on," England's people had a very narrow viewpoint.

She walked down the path toward the Pagoda, and took the long sweep toward her beds. Then she gasped.

The peonies were blighted. Not only would they not make a proud display for the coronation, they might not survive at all. Nor was it just the new bed. The old beds were suffering, too.

She didn't understand. Flowers responded to her touch, if not her presence. That was her Talent. She'd had her hands on them only two days before, but now they were wilting into a wrinkled, stained, soggy mess.

"Oh, no!" she cried, and ran forward.

"Miss!" Burkill shouted.

Mei stopped and turned.

"Begging your pardon, miss, but the Director said you should stay back."

"Why is that?"

Reluctantly he answered. "They're saying you did it, miss—the Chinese diplomats. They're saying that you're out to get revenge because of your mother's exile from the Imperial Court."

"Mr. Burkill—Isaac, do you truly believe that I would kill my mother's legacy?" In her desperation, Mei broke both protocol and propriety. "These peonies are the only gift I have from her."

"I know, miss, but I don't know what else to do. I have to obey the Director."

Mei-Hua Walsingham drew herself up with dignity. "Yes, but I know who the Director has to obey."

It was time to make a telephone call.

"I don't know who you contacted, miss, but the Director didn't half act as if he had seen a ghost." There was certainly a hint of both glee and astonishment in Burkill's voice.

"You'll have a chance to meet him. He's meeting us here to have a look at the peonies. I'm afraid that there is more going on than meets the eye, and he sees deeper than most. Even if he spends most of his time in that silly Men's Club of his." That last comment was voiced tartly enough that Isaac raised an eyebrow and yet held his peace.

Mei and Mr. Burkill didn't have long to wait. Shortly, they saw a very dapperly dressed man with a shock of white hair, almost like a lion's mane, walking toward them along the path. He plied his walking cane briskly and was within speaking distance after only a few minutes' wait.

"Miss Walsingham," he said courteously.

"Lord Alderscroft, this is Mr. Burkill. He is in charge of the Herbarium and this section of the Gardens." With a twinkle in her eye, Mei went on to say, "He's a Cambridge-trained botanist, and sure to achieve Director himself someday."

"I don't know about that, miss." Mr. Burkill held out his hand to shake Lord Alderscroft's. "I'm just a simple gardener," he said a little stiffly.

"I'm a Cambridge man myself, you know." And with that mysterious alchemy of attending the same college, even if in a different discipline, the ice was broken; Mr. Burkill beamed. "I recall we met once or twice in school," Alderscroft said, "and your credentials prove you are no simple gardener."

After a few moments' courtesy talk, Alderscroft excused himself and walked slowly among the peony beds, leaning over to examine several. He spent quite a few minutes wandering around, and the frown on his face deepened.

Eventually, his travels brought him back to Mei.

Mei looked questioningly at Alderscroft. They had discussed the possibility of Elemental interference on the phone when she had asked for his help. Alderscroft shook his head; there was nothing he could detect.

"No?" she asked aloud.

"I find no signs of any foul play," he said.

Her heart sank. She couldn't have done anything to harm them. She hadn't. All was as it should be. Except they were dying.

"Please let me look for myself?"

With Lord Alderscroft standing as surety for her conduct, Mei was allowed to approach the wilting beds. She knew that she should feel insulted by the need to have him here for that purpose, but she was too intent on the task before her. The conversation of the two men occasionally penetrated her concentration.

". . . they're making a lot of fuss over having the daughter of an exiled and disgraced Chinese high-caste family in charge of an Imperial treasure, by which they mean the peonies . . ."

Mei felt the ground; it was sufficiently damp, but it clumped oddly.

". . . there's a lot of people who don't have anything better to do than spread around what I put on the beds . . ."

She stroked the leaves and stalks. *Tell me what is wrong,* she asked the peony. It responded slowly, as if through a fog, that it didn't know.

". . . the Director's not the only one listening. I hope she can solve this, or there may be an Incident . . ."

The peony couldn't tell her, but Earth and Air could. There was a vague smell that was neither peony nor rot. Something had been added to the soil around the plants.

It was either poison or some kind of magical equivalent. Certainly the other side was eager to suppress the peonies and their healing agency. But was this attack on them via Elemental intervention, or by simple contamination?

"It is either a poison, or something has been added to the soil," she announced.

"You don't think it is a common blight?"

"There is an easy way to tell," she said. "We plant an unrelated species and see how it responds."

Alderscroft said, "We have less than a month until the Coronation. There isn't time." He emphasized the last word to remind her that they needed live peonies at the Palace within days.

"There is time enough for me. But I must be left in peace. I need a rose."

Alderscroft gestured. At a nod, one of the gardeners, Mr. Higgs, came over to consult, then strode briskly to the greenhouse. For fifteen minutes, Alderscroft and she waited silently. He pretended to observe the garden. She used her hand to dig a small planting hole.

Mr. Higgs returned with a rose cane, its root in a burlap wrap.

"Thank you, Mr. Higgs," Mei said politely, then turned and placed it in the ground.

Shifting her long skirt, she sat on her knees in front of the rose, whispering to and caressing it. It visibly grew as she coaxed it. She moved from sitting to squatting and back, keeping as comfortable as she could on the damp earth. Lord Alderscroft was nearby, she knew, checking on her every few minutes. She paid no attention. The plants needed her. Mr. Burkill kept a more discreet distance.

When the rose was only an hour old, it was already a foot high with a tiny bud blushing through sepals.

However, the bud was dark-tinged and oozing.

Poison. That was what had happened. Nothing magical was involved, which was why no amount of Elemental effort had found anything.

Lord Alderscroft cleared his throat. "Is that grotesque color what you refer to?"

"It is," she said. "Now I need a lot of roses."

He raised an eyebrow. "If that's what you need."

Mr. Burkill came over, worry on his face. What he'd seen wasn't natural, and he clearly knew that.

Alderscroft still wasn't convinced, but he gave her the benefit of the doubt.

"How many is a lot?" Mr. Burkill asked, less skeptically than Lord Alderscroft. He could see the effects of the poison for himself.

"Probably all we have. Have the planters run them in a line along the edges, right against the bricks. Then we'll need to run a hose and pump from the pond."

She expected to be told it was impossible, but Mr. Burkill stood, stiffened, and took off at a smart walk, almost an un-gentlemanly run.

Twenty minutes later, five gardeners Mei didn't recognize trundled over barrows containing a half gross of roses.

"Here, miss?" one of them asked.

"There. All the way along, please. Just a handbreadth in will be fine."

They produced trowels and started digging.

"The water should be pumped slowly, just to keep the barest puddle on top," she said.

Another team of men arrived with a hose and pump on a cart, and unrolled it toward the water.

Mei felt guilty at what she was to do. The poor roses were a sacrifice. As they drew more water, they would draw out the poison, and she'd force them to strain unto death to do so. People told jokes about flowers feeling pain. They weren't jokes to her. But the peonies were wards of the Royals, and the roses were the soldiers she intended to use to protect them in turn.

Alderscroft watched her, convinced at last she was right. And what power she had. Who would have thought a Talent over something as mundane as flowers could be so key? And now, it seemed that Talent could force entire fields of growth. But it was draining her.

He motioned for one of the staff. The man hurried over.

"Sir?" he asked.

"Please ensure Miss Walsingham has sandwiches and water. Some lemonade might be nice, too. If there is a parasol available, bring that as well."

"At once, My Lord."

She sat there all day, encouraging and stroking the roses, roses that visibly crept from mere canes to mature shrubs, then died. Each wilted, tattered rose represented poison drawn from the soil. Was it enough? As each rose wilted and died, it was replaced by yet another immature cane brought by selected staff. Were there enough plants?

Mei grew tired and ragged, her eyes bloodshot. By the time of the long dusk, she slumped alongside a row of dead English roses.

Inside that perimeter, the peonies stood proud, bright and healthy.

Mei awoke to voices in the next room. Her surroundings were unfamiliar; she was not back at the boarding house where she lodged. The room was bright and airy, featuring a floral wallpaper and late afternoon light streaming into the room. The last thing she remembered was the gardens and then darkness.

". . . Look, I don't care how she did it; it *could* be magic for all I care. Those peonies are now right as rain. Those so-called diplomats were wrong about Miss Walsingham, and you know it!"

"The problem, Burkill, is that while I, King Edward, and now you, all knew the value of those peonies, no one else does. Except whoever is trying to kill them off."

"The other problem is that King Edward is dead. King George is too busy getting ready for his coronation to even know what danger he could be in."

"That's my problem, Burkill. We can bring the King into the fold after things settle down a bit. Meanwhile, those peonies are additional protection until we can. They have to stay healthy!"

"I'm just a gardener, my Lord. Miss Walsingham and I can handle the flowers; you just make sure we don't have to deal with any of those deuced foreigners while we do so."

"A Cambridge botanist is not a simple gardener, and Mei is one of those deuced foreigners in some people's eyes."

"Yes, that's the other problem—now they're saying that maybe the peonies might have contributed to King Edward's illness. After all, there was one clutched in his hand when he was found . . ."

The voices faded off as Lord Alderscroft and Mr. Burkill

headed out of her hearing. Mei would have liked to have heard Alderscroft's reply; things would have been much easier if she knew what he thought of such rumors. Well, it didn't matter. She had to get up and see for herself just how the peonies were doing.

She was still very weak, and being light-headed didn't help her progress. They'd removed her shoes before covering her up. Bending over to lace them up almost caused her to faint again. She had really pushed her Talent past her limits. Leaning up against the door, she listened, then slowly opened it.

"Miss?" a female voice said.

"Yes?" she asked, turning.

"Are you feeling better? Mr. Burkill said we was to take care of you." The reflection of the gaslights off the housekeeper's starched white apron almost made Mei's headache worse.

"I'm all right now," she said. "Thank you. Is this his house?"

"Yes, miss."

Taking her time and frequently leaning up against the wall, Mei made her slow and careful way to the front doors. She had to politely shoo the housekeeper away. She'd be fine. She just needed to get back to the Gardens.

She hoped the cabs were still running in this neighborhood.

The brief rest in the cab restored Mei enough for her to walk with some semblance of her normal energy through the entrance to Kew Gardens. While she kept to a decorous pace, inside she could hear her peonies crying out, *"Hurry, hurry, hurry."* She knew something was wrong. Everything in her felt it. There was a gathering of energy ahead, a swirling of air and a spattering of rain where the sky had been largely clear shortly before.

Undeterred by the weather, she approached the peony beds. The area was deserted as the visitors took shelter from the sudden storm. Weather had never bothered Mei. Even though she couldn't see them, her father's Air allies watched over her still. A quick pause to reach down and touch the earth confirmed her feeling of something amiss. Earth, too, was troubled and for the same reason that Air was troubled: magic was stirring ahead—dark magic.

Quickening her pace as much as she could in her long skirts, she reached the peony beds around the Pagoda. Those closest to her appeared to be unharmed, and she sighed with relief. Reaching down, she stroked the leaves and flowers of the shrub nearest her. The peony practically screamed into her mind. Shocked, Mei staggered back, then noticed a furtive figure skulking near the beds closer to the Pagoda.

Near the crouching figure, there was a ripple of color running through the white peonies. They were changing from white to red and then to black. Without pausing to think, Mei approached the unknown person. Straying slightly to the side of the paved path, she grasped a hoe one of the planters had left behind from the planting yesterday. With her steady stride muffled by the rising winds, the figure was too involved in whatever he was doing to notice her.

Hesitating slightly at the vague sense of recognition at the man's clothing and the touch of the magic spilling over, she stood poised above him with her hoe—and then she swung.

"Earth and Air, our daughter. Earth and Air will find you. Earth and Air will aid you. Earth and Air will bind you." Mei-Hua Walsingham heard her parents' voices in the caress of the wind on her cheek. She smelled her father's pipe and her mother's favorite flower carried on that breeze.

Then she was awake.

She looked around. She was in a tower looking out over the gardens. She was in the Pagoda. How did she get here?

A gust of wind slapped at her, and she turned while clutching at the wall. She was on the top balcony, and the man from the garden was standing near her.

"Mei-Hua Wang, you have been most aggravating," he said in Mandarin. But his accent placed him to Shandong, where the Boxers arose. "Your ancestors would not approve of you consorting with *guizi*."

Guizi. *Foreigners*. But she was English, too, caught between worlds.

She wasn't sure if the wind had been Elemental, but he hardly needed it. He could loft her over the balcony in a moment. If he was a Boxer, they were called that in the West because they were skilled in Kung Fu.

He started chanting and staggered, almost as if drunk, but she knew that was a fighting technique, and that it hid spirit possession.

She leaped lightly back and had to steady herself again against the balcony rail. She needed a way back inside the building, and then perhaps she could race down the stairs.

A voice said, "We're with you, miss."

She stole a glance over her shoulder to see Mr. Burkill, with a pruning hook. He sounded nervous, but sure.

The Chinese man was in full fury, now, swaying and waving and whirling. She understood some of his incantation, calling for spirits to possess him.

Then she heard Lord Alderscroft's voice. "It is spirits you want? Then you shall have them, sir. Miss Walsingham, you must focus on the wooden dragon."

Unsure what he meant, she cast her eyes about. There, at a roof joint above them, was a stub. At one time in the past, it had been a carved dragon. Each roof peak had had one. They were rumored to have been gold and sold off, but they'd been lacquered wood that rotted away.

Wood! But it was dead wood. She had no Talent over it. However . . . was that a hint of moss? A few vines?

She did focus on it, coaxing it, urging it to grow.

Trees were a product of Earth and Air, her parents' elements. This was dead wood, but there was plenty of air, and the decay under the moss was earth, and it was growing.

In a moment, the lump flowed and shifted, and she yelped in fear, but it resolved as a dragon's head with a twisting body and furled wings of moss and ivy—an Imperial dragon.

Her attacker staggered and shouted, and the wind rose to a howl.

Then Lord Alderscroft said, "Air, sir, against a winged dragon? But I am a Master of Fire."

The dragon twisted and wove, blocking the space between the Chinese mage and them. Then it snorted a breath of sulfur, and followed that with a burning blast that singed Mei's hair.

The heat rolled over her, with the smell of scorched and

dried wood and fumes, and the wind dropped to a hot breeze, then to nothing, and the dragon evaporated into dust, fragrant with the smell of damp moss.

The mage had disappeared.

Mr. Burkill said, "His goose is cooked."

Before Mei could make sense of the horrible joke, he continued. "So, this is what you do for entertainment, sir and miss, playing with spirits?" He sagged back against the wall and breathed deeply.

"I've partaken of spirits ever since you and I read together at Cambridge," Lord Alderscroft said. "But we should get Miss Walsingham to the ground for some tea."

Yes. She found herself shaking in reaction and fear. But she felt a rush of relief under it.

The peonies weren't precisely "featured" at the Coronation, but as the Royal Carriage rolled past, Mei could see a plant inside. It was one of her peonies, contrasting against all the pageantry with its brilliant white. Here and there, men wore other peonies as boutonnieres, as did some ladies in their corsages. There were enough scattered about to dissuade any interference. The beds at the Gardens were in full bloom, and that much energy should shield the whole city for now.

There wasn't much to see of the parade. Her main reason to be present was to see her flowers, both from pride and duty.

Lord Alderscroft and some other ranking personages had explained the nature of Elemental Magic to the King, and advised him on several defenses, including the peonies. Her work was to continue.

Back at the Gardens, Mr. Burkill was congratulatory in his own calm way.

"The flowers look spectacular, miss," he said. "You have done well, even better than I'd have thought possible."

"Thank you, sir," she said. "I wish there were more I could do. People are starting to grow more peonies in their gardens, and I hope it will be enough."

"I hope so, too," he said. "There has been some more work in that direction, though."

"Oh?" she asked.

Mr. Burkill said, "His Majesty reviewed the events and has asked that I take a post at the Botanical Gardens in Singapore in a year or so. That will give us a broader knowledge of your Oriental flowers and their strange powers."

"In a year or so?" she asked.

"Well, miss, first I have to learn what I can here, if you don't mind sharing your knowledge. And while ladies can't be awarded degrees, a study of natural science at Girton College in Cambridge seems like a fair exchange."

"And perhaps my mother's peony could be brought back to China." It would be fitting, she thought, ending her mother's exile in a way. The next few years looked to be very full.

She had challenges ahead—and looked forward to them.

Into The Woods
Mercedes Lackey

Mutti and *Vati* were talking again. It wasn't quite arguing, and Rosa pretended that she couldn't hear it. Children were not supposed to hear when grown-ups were talking about them.

It wasn't exactly about her, anyway. It was about the fact that they were living in a cottage in the little village of Holzdorf in the Schwarzwald instead of in Wuppertal, as *Mutti* wanted. The reason, of course, was Rosa. Living in the city had nearly killed her; she had felt poisoned all the time and was sick all the time, and it hadn't been until *Onkel* Hans and *Tante* Bertha had come to the house and told them about the magic that *Mutti* and *Vati* had understood that being in a city was just not going to be possible for Rosa until she was much older, at the very least. Maybe not ever.

Mutti and *Vati* had only a little of the magic, so at least they knew it was real, and *Vati* hadn't sent his brother and sister-in-law away with taunts of madness. But Earth Magic had never been in their families before; it had been two unbroken lines of Fire Mages until Rosa was born. A Fire Mage had no problem with living in a city. Some even found it pleasant.

But for an Earth Mage, well . . . no wonder Rosa had always been sick and felt as if she was being poisoned. She *was* being poisoned. All of the industries spewing filth into the air, the soil and the water, all of the smokes and the soot, all of the nastiness caused by too many people living too closely together—all that made the Earth sick, and that made *her* sick. So living in Wuppertal was no longer an option, unless they wanted to send Rosa away alone—and that plan had made *Mutti* even more unhappy than the prospect of leaving the city.

"It's so *lonely* here," *Mutti* said plaintively.

Rosa knew what *Vati* was thinking, that it would be less lonely if *Mutti* just tried a little harder to fit herself into village life. Her city clothing alone set her apart, and it wasn't as if *Tante* Bertha hadn't supplied her with the right costume and more than enough fabric to make more. Rosa thought the black skirt and black laced jacket with the beautifully embroidered blouse and apron and shawl looked wonderful on *Mutti*, but her mother would not part with her stiffly corseted, voluminous, and highly impractical gowns.

And it wasn't as if the women of the village would not have welcomed her! They felt sorry for the *"junge Frau"* who always looked so shy and sad. They were eager to share recipes and needlework patterns and gossip. They were always happy to see Rosa, and if she hadn't by nature had a modest appetite, she would have been as round as a Christmas goose from all the good things they tried to coax her to eat. Everyone here knew *of* magic, even if they didn't have any themselves, and they sympathized with the city folk who had exiled themselves here in order that their daughter might thrive and learn.

"*Liebchen*, you must try harder," said her *Vati* wearily. *He* had fitted himself right into the life of the village almost as soon as they'd arrived. Now, in his black suit, the long coat with red lapels and brass buttons, and his little round black hat, he could not have been told from one of the locals until he opened his mouth. The village had lacked a proper schoolmaster; the local priest, a very old man, had served double duty in that regard for decades, and he was more than happy to give over the position to *Vati*.

And oh, yes . . . religion. That was another thing that made *Mutti* unhappy. The village was Catholic, mostly, and she was staunch Lutheran. Not that such a designation made any difference to the village. How could it, when there were Elemental Masters in their forest? Even the priest, gentle old man that he was, would have happily served Holy Communion to *Mutti* as he did to *Vati*, without so much as a hint that she should convert, even though his bishop would probably have died of a fit if he found out. "We are all Children of the Good God," he would say. "The bad days that Master Luther railed about are over. We should accept one another in God's Peace and make no fuss about names and credos."

Well, Rosa had faith in her father. Eventually he would wear *Mutti* down, as he always did. One day she would put on the pretty black dress and hat bedecked with fat pom-poms and go to visit the neighbors. One day she would meet the gentle priest and discover he was not a baby-eating ogre.

"Rosa!" *Mutti* called from the kitchen. "It's time to visit *Großmutter* Helga!"

That was what Rosa had been waiting—a bit impatiently—for. "*Großmutter*" Helga was not really her grandmother. Both of her *real* grandmothers had lived back in the city. *Großmutter* Helga was a very learned and very powerful Earth Master who was teaching Rosa her magic, because one day Rosa was expected to be just as learned and powerful—although no one knew yet what direction her magic might take.

Rosa was never happier than when she was sitting beside the old woman, listening so hard her face would ache afterward. And sometimes—sometimes she was allowed to do a very little magic herself. Or try. Sometimes it didn't work. She didn't seem to be very good at coaxing things to grow, or at healing. *Großmutter* said that this was all right, that not every Earth Master was adept at nurturing.

And when Rosa was tired, *Großmutter* would make her tea and give her a little meal and tell her stories. Many of the stories were about the *Bruderschaft der Förster*, the Brother-hood of the Foresters, the arcane guardians of the Schwarz-wald, for there were many dark and dangerous things that lived here, and the paths through the shadowy trees could be perilous. Listening to those tales, Rosa was very glad that the Brotherhood was there.

As she entered the warm and fragrant kitchen, *Vati* ruffled her hair and left for the schoolhouse by the kitchen door. The kitchen—indeed, the entire cottage—was the one thing *Mutti* did like about their new life. Living space in the city was cramped, and Rosa remembered *Vati* always complaining about how expensive it was. Here, thanks to *Vati*'s school-master job, the spacious cottage cost them nothing. It had three rooms below, and the loft where Rosa slept above. The kitchen had a red-tiled floor, a spacious hearth with an oven built into it for baking, a sink, cupboards that held all manner of good things, a sturdy wooden table in the center, and real glass windows—it was ever so much nicer than the tiny little kitchen in their city flat. They had a real parlor and a bed-room for *Mutti* and *Vati* as well, whereas in the city flat they'd had to hide their bed behind a curtain, and Rosa had slept in a cupboard-bed.

"I have your basket for *Großmutter*," said *Mutti*, folding the top of the napkin that lined the basket over the contents. "Some lovely apple cakes, a nice pat of butter, and that soft cheese she likes so much." *Mutti* always sent Rosa with a basket to *Großmutter*, as if she needed someone else to do her cooking for her, although Rosa knew very well that *Großmutter* was as good a cook—or better—than *Mutti*. But she was too polite to say anything, and *Großmutter* always accepted the contents of the basket with grave thanks, so Rosa supposed that this was one of the many things children were supposed to be silent about.

Then *Mutti* tied Rosa's pride and joy about her neck—a beautiful, bright red cape with a matching hood. Rosa always felt like a princess in this cape, which was a miniature copy of the riding capes that fine ladies wore to go hunting in. *Mutti* had copied it from an illustrated magazine that *Vati* had had brought from the city for her.

"Now go and take your lessons with *Großmutter*, and don't dawdle on the way," *Mutti* cautioned.

"I won't, *Mutti*," Rosa promised.

"And don't speak to strangers."

"I won't, *Mutti*," she promised again, although she could not imagine what strangers she could possibly meet on the path to *Großmutter*'s cottage. But *Mutti* had said that back in the city every time Rosa went out to play on the doorstep, so she supposed it must be habit from that time.

"And if you are kept too late, you may stay with *Großmut-ter*," *Mutti* concluded, albeit reluctantly. "I don't want you wandering in the forest at sundown. There are wolves. And bears."

Rosa stifled a sigh. Of course there were wolves and bears. Everyone knew that. That was why there was a wolf or a bear on practically every piece of Schwarzwald carving. And stags, but her mother never warned her to beware of stags, even though *Großmutter* had told her that they could be just as dangerous as a bear. "Yes, *Mutti*," she said dutifully.

"Now off you go."

Finally, Rosa was free to scamper out the door, through the vegetable garden that was *Vati*'s pride, and out the gate to the path that led to *Großmutter*'s house.

The first part of her journey was out of the village and through all the village fields. She always ran through this part; the farm fields and small pastures held very little interest for her. The land had been tamed, controlled, and confined. Everything was neat, everything was regimented. She always felt a little stifled when in the village or its farmlands. It was *nothing* like as bad as it had been when she'd lived in a city, but . . . well, it was akin to being forced to wear your Sunday best all the time. You couldn't really be yourself. The land wasn't itself.

She was always glad when she got out of the farmlands and into the water meadow. While the meadow and its pond weren't exactly wild, not like the forest, they were still much freer than the farmed land. Nothing grew in the meadow or in the pond that was deliberately planted. The village ducks and geese grazed here, and the village goats, but that was about the extent of the hand of man. Rosa slowed to a fast walk as soon as the path crossed the boundary of the meadow.

Here was where she finally saw the first of the Elementals—other than brownies—that lived around the village. The village was *full* of brownies, of course, even if no one but Rosa and her parents were aware of them. It was a wholesome, earthy place, and brownies were the Elementals not only of Earth, but of hearth and home. Virtually every household in the village had at least one brownie seeing to it that all was well in the house, and that any accidents were small ones. Rosa's household had three, because of her magic.

But here in the water meadow was where she started to see the wild ones. There was a little faun that she thought lived here. Not like the ones in the woods, who were older, somehow more goatlike, and were always looking at her slyly out of their strange eyes. This was a very little fellow, shy, and often found napping in the sun. There was a tree-girl here as well, though she held herself aloof from the faun. There were entire swarms of the sorts of little creatures that were in picture books, little grotesques with fat bodies and spindly legs, or made with parts of ordinary animals, birds, and insects. She didn't have names for them, and neither did *Großmutter*, who just called them "*alvar*." No matter how odd they looked, they were playful and friendly, and Rosa wished she had lived here when she was younger, because she could have run down here to play with them.

She was not free to do so today, though, so she waved at the ones she saw and plunged into the forest. "Plunged" was the right word; the Schwarzwald was a very old forest, and once you got onto the paths within it, you found yourself in a dark and mysterious place. Tree trunks towered all around, like pillars holding up a green ceiling high, high above. Here and there shafts of sunlight pierced the gloom. The forest floor was thick with old leaves and needles, soft with moss, rippling with roots. And normally, it felt welcoming to Rosa. But today . . .

Well, today the forest felt . . . uneasy. Not so much near the village, but the deeper she got into it, the more it felt as if the forest were holding its breath, and that many of the animals and creatures that dwelled here were hiding from . . . something.

Rosa had had that same feeling in here before, now and again. Nothing had ever come of it, but when she asked *Großmutter* about it, the elder Magician had pulled a long face. "There are dark tales in the forest," she had said. "And most of them are true. Hurry your steps, and do not tarry when the trees hold their breath and the fauns hide in their caves. And never go there after dark until you are older and *much* more powerful." That seemed like good advice to Rosa . . . and she was heeding it now. Instead of sauntering along her way, stopping to look at something interesting or to collect bird feathers and the mushrooms *Großmutter* had taught her were safe, she sped up, gathering her little cloak about her, for suddenly the shadows beneath the trees seemed cold.

She was halfway to *Großmutter*'s cottage when she rounded a twist in the path and was stopped dead in her tracks by the sight of a man she did not know ahead of her.

Now, the forest was very famous. And her village was well known for wood carving. Strangers were known to trek through the forest for pleasure, especially in the summer, although this was the first time that Rosa had encountered a man she didn't recognize inside the forest and not in the village.

But there was something about this man she did not like, and she could not have said why.

Whether or not he had been walking before he saw her, he had stopped now, and was waiting; she could not go farther without passing him, and he watched her every move with eyes that gleamed with an unfathomable expression. Slowly, and with deep reluctance, she approached him.

He was dressed like a hunter—leather trousers tucked into leather boots, green wool jacket, green wool hat, and game bag—but he wasn't carrying a rifle or a bow. But maybe he was one of those foreigners. A foreigner would think that hunting gear was the sort of thing you should wear to walk in the forest.

The hat looked a little odd on his head; he had longish, shaggy hair of mixed brown and gray, although he didn't look all that old. He was clean-shaven, but his features were—well, she'd have called him ugly if she'd dared. But she was only a little girl, and children were supposed to be respectful of their elders. His eyes glittered beneath his hat-brim, a strange yellow-brown. She really didn't know what to make of him, except that if she hadn't been halfway to *Großmutter*'s—and if she hadn't been half-scared he would chase her if she ran—she'd have turned around and pelted all the way back home.

"Hello, little girl," the man said, when she finally stopped on the path, unwilling to get any closer. "What would your name be and where are you from?"

"Rosamund Ackermann, sir," she said politely. "I come from Holzdorf." He must be a foreigner. The only way the path behind her led was to Holzdorf.

He nodded approvingly. "And what is such a little creature like you doing out here in the dark forest all alone?" He didn't move, yet somehow he seemed to loom over her, and the place where he stood got a little darker.

Magic. It must be magic that I feel on him. Maybe he was Air . . . Air and Earth did not get along at all. She gathered her little power about her and inched a bit sideways off the path, trying to move without looking as if she was doing so. "I am going to my grandmother's house, sir," she said, still remaining polite. "Mother says that she is old, and it is hard for her to cook now." It was *very* important that a magician not lie! But this was not a lie. *Mutti did* say that, even though it was not true.

"And what does your grandmother do, all alone in that cottage in the woods?" the stranger asked, his eyes glittering. "Does she make potions? Does she have any strange animals about?"

Oh! Now she knew why she didn't like him! *Großmutter* had warned her about men like this. They were looking for witches, and if they found any, would hurt them! *Großmutter* had even warned her that such men might have magic themselves and not know it, or pretend they didn't, or tell themselves it was some sort of God-given power.

"She knits," Rosa said truthfully. "And sews. She has two little hens for her egg in the morning." She wouldn't tell him about the goat. "And she mends stockings. Mother has her mend all our stockings." Also true. *Mutti* hated mending stockings, and *Großmutter* didn't mind.

The man looked vaguely disappointed, which made her think that her guess was right. He *was* looking for witches. "Why does she live by herself in the forest? Shouldn't she move to the village where it is safer?"

"My mother says there is no room for her in our cottage, sir," she replied, which was not strictly true but also was not a lie. *Mutti* had not *said* so, but every time *Vati* mentioned the idea, she made a face. It wasn't as if *Großmutter* was Rosa's *real* grandmother. after all, and *Mutti* always replied with, "But what if your father or mine needs to move in with us?"

Rosa didn't think that was likely to happen. Both grandfathers were vigorously pursuing pretty young widows. She knew *Mutti* had gotten used to having her own little house with just *Vati* and her in it, and didn't want to share, particularly not with an old lady who might be demanding, interfering, or critical. Rosa might be very young, but there was a great deal she understood quite well.

The man made a stern face. "Your father—" he began, then shook his head in disapproval. Rosa began to inch her way around him. "Women should know their place," he told Rosa sternly. "It is for the man to say what is to happen in his own house."

"Yes, sir," Rosa said automatically. She was almost halfway around him, although she had to go a good five feet off the path to do so.

Fortunately, he was now so engrossed in his own lecture that he didn't seem to have noticed what she was doing. "Women and girls do not have strong enough minds to know what is best for them," he said, looking thunderous. "Women and girls must be obedient to men in all things. They must confine themselves to the tasks that God suited them for. Work in the home, childbearing, and childrearing. They are too given to emotion to make any good decisions—like your mother, child."

By this point she was all the way around him and back on the path, and this seemed to be the opening she needed to get away from him. She ducked her head. "And my father has said I must take these things to Grandmother, and hurry, and not dawdle on the way, sir. So I must be going. Good day to you! Holzdorf is just ahead of you!" And before he could respond to that, she turned and scampered up the path, putting as much distance as she could between herself and the unpleasant stranger.

She was afraid he might call after her, but he did not.

The forest, however, remained strangely dark, and unusually quiet, as if something in it was disturbing everything. She didn't see a single Elemental, which made her unhappy and uneasy. Then again, that stranger had made her very disturbed, and she could easily see him having that effect on the entire forest. He was just nasty—and if he had been going off the path, poking about in the forest a bit, snooping, well . . . if she had been an Elemental, she would have hidden, too.

As soon as she was sure he wasn't going to call after her or, worse, chase after her, she slowed to a fast walk. Normally she took her time going through the forest, because she liked it so much, but today, well, she just wanted to get to *Großmutter*'s house as quickly as she could.

It seemed to take much, much longer than usual, as if the path had somehow doubled in length, although she knew that could not possibly be so.

She almost sobbed with relief when she finally saw the little branching path that led to *Großmutter*'s cottage. She ran again, all the way up the path, through silence that was so thick it felt like fog around her, ran until she reached the door, pulled the latch-string, pulled it open, and shut it tight behind her.

The cottage was very dark, darker than twilight. Something was not right.

"Grandmama?" she called into the dark.

The cottage was a single room, with *Großmutter*'s bed in a little nook at the rear, which was now deeply in shadow. Something stirred back there.

Something was very wrong. She felt it deep inside her, worse than when she had been in the forest. But how could that be? This was *Großmutter*'s cottage, the safest place in the forest!

"Rosa?" said a strange voice. "Is that you, child?" There was a cough. "I am not well. Come closer. Did you bring me something from your mother?"

Rosa took a cautious step toward the bed. It should be *Großmutter* there. She couldn't imagine how it could be anyone except *Großmutter*. "Grandmama? You sound strange."

"I took a chill," said the hoarse voice. "Come closer, child."

Another step. "Grandmama?" She could see *Großmutter*'s nightcap in the shadows around the bed. "Why is it so dark?" She peered anxiously into the shadows, her little heart pounding. A pair of eyes seemed to gleam in the darkness beneath the cap. "Why are your eyes so bright?"

"So that I may see you better, my dear," said the voice.

Rosa shivered at the shadows, clutching her basket. It felt as if an icy drop of water were creeping down her spine. "Grandmama? Something is not right—"

It was a good thing she was poised to flee, because whatever was in *Großmutter*'s bed suddenly heaved up and leaped right over the top of her. It might have pounced on her, too, if she hadn't ducked and scuttled out of the way. It landed between her and the door.

"Enough!" howled the thing as she backed away from it. It lunged for her.

She shrieked in pure terror. And the thing winced back, clapping its paws over its ears, an expression of acute pain twisting its features. That gave her enough time to run for the pantry, wrench the door open, slam it shut behind herself, and lock it from the inside.

She could lock herself in, even though most pantries were made to lock on the *outside,* because *Großmutter* had had it made that way—one safe place that she, or Rosa and she, could hide in if something bad happened.

Something bad, very bad, like the horrid creature with the stranger's eyes, a hoarsened version of the stranger's voice, the body of a man, and the pelt, paws, and claws, and twisted facial features of something that was a half-man and a half-wolf.

The door shuddered as the thing flung itself against the wood. She wanted badly to just drop onto the floor, pull her cape over her head, and hide. But *Großmutter* had taught her better than that. Despite her terror, Rosa twisted her fingers in frantic patterns as she made the wood come alive, knit itself into the door frame, and start to grow at preternatural speed. At least that was what she was trying to do—she couldn't actually *see* what she was doing, but a moment after she made the magic, she put her hand on the door and felt the rough bark of a living tree instead of the hewn wood of the door. The wood still vibrated under her hand but no longer shuddered. She was safe for now.

But she was also trapped.

She felt along the shelves until she put her hand on the wooden box of candles. Beside it was the box of Lucifer matches. Carefully, she struck one and lit the candle.

And screamed. For sharing the pantry with her was the mangled body of *Großmutter*.

She clutched the candle and screamed and screamed and screamed, weeping with terror and loss.

She screamed until she ran out of breath, took another breath, and screamed more. From the other side of the door came the shriek of terrible claws rending the wood.

The bare tip of a claw gleamed in the candlelight, reawakening her to her danger. Frantically, she put her hand against where the door had been and felt the talons tearing it away. Feeling the power drain from her, she made the wood grow again, and from the other side came a terrible howl of rage and frustration and the sound of claws shredding wood with renewed fury.

She didn't know what to do. Somewhere out there, there were people who could help her, but *Großmutter* had not told her how to call them yet!

She didn't know why she did what she did next. She just *did* it, out of pure fear and desperation. She dropped the candle, which rolled and went out, leaned into the living door, put both palms against it, and cried out in terror.

"HELP ME!"

It was as if a shudder went through everything, and a moment after that . . . an enormous *silence*. Even the thing outside the door paused. It really *did* seem as if everything held its breath—

Then the monster howled in triumph, and every hair on her head stood straight up. She had thought she was frightened before. She was so terrified, she couldn't even shriek. She couldn't even breathe.

The creature redoubled its efforts on her door, and she kept trying to renew the wood, her little strength fading more with each try. She began to feel faint each time she made the wood grow. She hardly had the strength to stand upright, and supported herself against the rough bark of the door—

Then the cottage shook with a crash and a drumming of hooves.

The monster barked in surprise and stopped clawing at the door.

There was another crash, and another, and the bellow of

an elk. Rosa knew what it was because she had seen an elk trumpeting one day in the forest. Then another crash, and the entire cottage rocked, the monster shrieked, and chaos erupted on the other side of her wooden barrier.

She fainted.

She could not have been unconscious for too very long, because the fighting was still going on, although it sounded distinctly as if the elk was losing. She curled her fingers into the bark of the tree and tried to will it strength, tears pouring from her eyes.

The elk was going to die. The horrible thing out there was going to kill it. And then it would break through the wood, and it would kill her—

And then, out of *nowhere,* the cottage rocked again; a thunderous roar shook the walls. Rosa screamed. She couldn't imagine what it was—

And then she heard the voices calling her. "Rosa! Rosa!" muffled by the wood.

"Here!" she cried out, pounding her little fists on the bark. "Here!"

Then she fell into a widening gap as the wood parted, dropped into arms that plucked her out of the pantry and pulled her up onto a huge, strong shoulder.

The cottage was no longer full of shadows. The door was *gone.* She got a glimpse of her savior, the elk, with its head hanging but still standing, hide gashed in dozens of places, being tended to by a woman with short-cut hair, dressed as the stranger had been, in well-worn green loden hunting gear. She got another glimpse of the monster, a hole in its chest, head hacked off, and hid her face in her rescuer's shoulder.

And she cried and cried and cried while her rescuer carried her out into the woods, patting her back awkwardly.

"There there," he murmured. "It's all right now, Rosa. You're safe."

Her rescuer carried her over to some horses, somehow mounting without ever putting her down. She looked up for a moment through eyes streaming with tears and saw the elk stumbling out of the ruined door, staggering a little, but looking determined.

"That's one fellow that will never become cutlets with

mushrooms," said one of the other green-clad hunters mounting his own horse.

"Aye. Gilda will bring him back to the Lodge, and he'll live to be a ripe old age, and die having fathered a hundred more like him," her rescuer rumbled. "And well done, he. If it had not been for him answering the child's call, we'd never have got here in time."

Rosa put her head back down on the man's shoulder, sobbing, and clinging to him.

"Hans, Fritz," the man ordered, "go to the girl's parents. Tell them we're taking her. It's clearly not safe for her to be with them anymore. The next time, the beasts might come into the village, and the Good God only knows what would happen then."

"Aye, Hunt Master," said another fellow, and there was the sound of hooves trotting away.

Wait . . . It wasn't safe for her to live with *Mutti* and *Vati*?

"Where are you taking me?" Rosa asked, pulling her head off the man's shoulder, and scrubbing her eyes with the back of her hand. "Who are you?"

Again, the man patted her back. "Don't be afraid, Rosa. I am the Hunt Master of the Schwarzwald Foresters. We have been watching you, and watching over you, ever since you arrived. Your aunt and uncle told us about you. We are going to take you to our Lodge, where you will be safe and learn about your magic all the time."

Rosa blinked, took a deep breath, about to object—and stopped. Because . . . this felt *right.* This was what she . . . wanted.

"But *Vati* and *Mutti*—"

"Will come visit you all the time. Unless they wish to return to the city—and if they do, we know powerful men who will make certain that they are well taken care of." The man put his horse in motion; the rest of the group followed him.

Rosa could see the elk limping along at the end of the group. She put her head down on his shoulder, and thought.

Was it wrong that she loved her *Mutti* and *Vati*, and yet felt . . . as if they never really understood who she was and what she wanted? Because that was, indeed, how she felt. She could not explain it, but she had felt, instantly, more at home with this man whose name she didn't even *know*, than with them.

"You are very quiet, little one," the man murmured. "Are you troubled? Do you not care for what we have planned?"

"I—I am troubled because I *do*," she almost wailed softly, feeling a desperate sort of confusion come over her.

"Ah . . . that is because your magic speaks to mine. We are more alike than if you were my daughter and I were your father." He patted her. "I will gladly be a second father to you, child. If you would care for that."

The *moment* he said that, she knew it was true. This man, this Hunt Master, *was* more like her father than her own *Vati*. He understood the hunger to learn about her magic. And he would be able to protect her as her own *Vati* could not.

She thought about that monster breaking into her own little home, and her blood ran cold. Her parents would have had less chance against that thing than *Großmutter*.

Even if she *hadn't* liked these plans—and she did—she could not endanger them like that.

"I would care for that, Hunt Master," she said with a sigh, laying her head down on his shoulder and closing her eyes. "Please take me home."

About the Authors

Jennifer Brozek is an award-winning editor, game designer, and author. She has been writing role-playing games and professionally publishing fiction since 2004. With the number of edited anthologies, fiction sales, RPG books, and nonfiction books under her belt, Jennifer is often considered a Renaissance woman, but she prefers to be known as a wordslinger and optimist. Read more about her at www.jenniferbrozek .com or follow her on Twitter at @JenniferBrozek.

Ron Collins has appeared in *Analog*, *Asimov's*, *Nature*, and several other magazines and anthologies. His writing has received a Writers of the Future prize, and a CompuServe HO-Mer Award. He holds a degree in Mechanical Engineering, and has worked developing avionics systems, electronics, and information technology. Today, though, he finds himself living in the truly arcane world of a Human Resources department in the heart of Corporate America. How that happened, he'll never know. He lives in Columbus, Indiana, with his wife, Lisa. The obligatory cat's name is Keiko. He reports that he's been looking for an excuse to retell "The Sorcerer's Apprentice" ever since he used the Disney version of it to teach storytelling structure to middle-school kids. So you could say that writing this story was a dream come true.

Samuel Conway holds a doctorate in chemistry from Dartmouth and currently lives and works in the environs of Raleigh, NC. When he is not doing research he serves as the chairman of Anthrocon, the world's largest anthropomorphics convention, which is held annually in Pittsburgh, PA. Somewhere between the two he somehow finds time to write. This foray into the world of the Elemental Masters is his third published work outside of the small-press circuit."

Dayle A. Dermatis' short fantasy has been called "funny (and rather ingenious)," "something new and something fresh," and "really, really good!" Under various pseudonyms (and sometimes with coauthors), she's sold several novels and more than 100 short stories in multiple genres. She lives and works in California within scent of the ocean, and in her spare time follows Styx around the country and travels the world, all of which inspires her writing. To find out where she is today, check out www.cyvarwydd.com.

Rosemary Edghill's first professional sales were to the black & white horror comics, so she can truthfully state on her resume that she once killed vampires for a living. She has worked as an SF editor for Avon Books, as a freelance book designer, as a typesetter, as an illustrator, as an anthologist, and as a professional book reviewer. She has written Regency romances, historical novels, space opera, high fantasy, media tie-ins, and horror, and collaborated with authors such as Marion Zimmer Bradley, SF Grand Master Andre Norton, and Mercedes Lackey—*Mad Maudlin*, her third Bedlam's Bard collaboration, was a 2002 Voices of Youth Advocates (VOYA) selection as one of the best Horror and Fantasy novels of the year. You can find her on Facebook or Dreamwidth when she ought to be writing.

Rebecca Fox always wanted to be John Carter of Mars when she grew up, because of the giant birds. Since that career path didn't look like it was going to pan out anytime soon, she got her Ph.D. in Animal Behavior instead. She makes her home in Lexington, Kentucky, where she shares her life with three parrots, a Jack Russell terrier named Izzy, and the world's most opinionated chestnut mare. When she isn't writing, Rebecca teaches college biology and spends a lot of time outdoors doing research on bird behavior.

Tanya Huff lives in rural Ontario, Canada, with her wife Fiona Patton and, as of last count, eight cats. Her 27 novels and 74 short stories include horror, heroic fantasy, urban fantasy, comedy, and space opera. She's written four essays for BenBella's pop culture collections. Her Blood series was turned into the 22-episode *Blood Ties* television show, and writing episode nine allowed her to finally use her degree in Radio & Television Arts. Her latest novel is *The Silvered*, and her next will be the third Gale girls book—*The Future Falls*. When not writing, she practices her guitar and spends too much time online.

Cedric Johnson was born and raised in Lincoln, Nebraska, where he began writing short stories and poetry at an early age. While attending Lincoln Southeast High School, Cedric was a top-placing contributor, layout editor, and senior year editor-in-chief of its multiple-award-winning annual literary publication *From the Depths*. Cedric currently resides in Commerce City, CO, where he continues to write while working with other form of digital media, including 3D modeling and virtual world communications.

Michele Lang writes supernatural tales: the stories of witches, lawyers, goddesses, bankers, demons, and other magical creatures hidden in plain sight. Author of the *Lady Lazarus* historical fantasy series, Michele's most recent book in the series, *Rebel Angels*, was released in March 2013. Please visit Michele at www.michelelang.com.

Jody Lynn Nye lists her main career activity as "spoiling cats." She lives northwest of Chicago with one of the above and her husband, author and packager Bill Fawcett. She has written over forty books, including *The Ship Who Won* with Anne McCaffrey, eight books with Robert Asprin, and a humorous anthology about mothers, *Don't Forget Your Spacesuit, Dear!*, and over 115 short stories. Her latest books are *View From the Imperium* and *Myth-Quoted*.

Benjamin Ohlander's previous short fiction has appeared in *Sword of Ice and Other Tales of Valdemar* and *Crossroads* *and Other Tales of Valdemar*. He has also written novels with David Drake and in the *Wing Commander* series, both from Baen. He lives with his family in Mason, Ohio.

Fiona Patton was born in Calgary, Alberta, Canada, and grew up in the United States. She now lives in rural Ontario with her wife, Tanya Huff, two glorious dogs, and a pride of very small lions. She has written seven fantasy novels for DAW Books, and is currently working on the first book of a new series, entitled *The King's Eagle*.

Diana L. Paxson first worked with the four elements in the Chronicles of Westria, including *The Earthstone*, *The Sea Star*, *The Wind Crystal*, and *The Jewel of Fire*. She has written two dozen other fantasy novels, mostly with historical settings, such as the Avalon series, which she took over from Marion Zimmer Bradley. She is also the author of several nonfiction books, most recently *The Way of the Oracle*.

Gail Sanders and **Michael Z. Williamson** are married veterans who live near Indianapolis. Gail is a veteran combat photographer and construction equipment operator who works as a unit administrator for the Army Reserve. She graduated Basic Combat Training a week shy of her 36th birthday. Mike is retired from the USAF and US Army. He was a Mechanical Section shop chief in Engineer and Forward Support units. He is a full time SF writer, consultant and researcher who has worked with several TV production companies, private and military clients. Mike also tests and reviews gear for disaster preparedness, and is a bladesmith when he can find the time.

Kristin Schwengel lives near Milwaukee, Wisconsin, with her husband, the obligatory cat (named Gandalf, of course), and the eternal hope that this year she will have a productive garden. Of "Sails of the Armada," she says, "In its original incarnation, this was about the battles between Spanish priest-mages and English Druids for control of the winds. Then the sea serpent who becomes the Loch Ness monster appeared, and things got a lot more interesting."

Stephanie Shaver lives in Southern California, where she works in the games industry as a producer. She has one lovely daughter and a husband who cheerfully edits out as many of her prepositional phrases as he can find (and that she will allow). When she isn't working or writing, she's probably cooking, camping, or cat-herding. You can find her online at www.sdshaver.com.

Louisa Swann was born on an Indian reservation in northern California, and spent the first six months of her life carried around in a papoose carrier. Determined not to remain a basket case forever, she escaped the splintered confines and proceeded to participate in, make a living as, or halfheartedly attempt the following: student, maid, waitress, receptionist, flight attendant, secretary, ski instructor, ski patrol (volunteer), and engineering assistant. She finally settled down on an eighty-acre ranch in northern California with hubby, son, two horses, cat, a varying population of rabbits, deer, coyotes, bobcats, cougars, snakes, frogs, birds, bugs, and no electricity. The human members of the family put up with Louisa's writerly eccentricities with only a few minor squabbles. On the other hand, the horses, dog, cat, and miscellaneous wildlife understand her completely. She often goes to them for grooming when the rest of the world becomes too difficult to handle.

Elizabeth A. Vaughan writes fantasy romance. You can learn more about her books at www.eavwrites.com. Any historical errors are hers and hers alone, but one should never let history accuracy get in the way of a good story. Special thanks to Mary E. Gustafson for answering a myriad of odd raven questions!

Elisabeth Waters sold her first short story in 1980 to Marion Zimmer Bradley for *The Keeper's Price*, the first of the Darkover anthologies. She then went on to sell short stories to a variety of anthologies. Her first novel, a fantasy called *Changing Fate*, was awarded the 1989 Gryphon Award. She is now working on a sequel to it, in addition to her short story writing and anthology editing. She currently edits the *Sword and Sorceress* anthologies. She also worked as a supernumerary with the San Francisco Opera, where she appeared in *La Gioconda, Manon Lescaut, Madama Butterfly, Khovanschina, Das Rheingold, Werther*, and *Idomeneo*.

About the Editor

Mercedes Lackey is a full-time writer and has published numerous novels and works of short fiction, including the bestselling *Heralds of Valdemar* series. She is also a professional lyricist and a licensed wild bird rehabilitator. She lives in Oklahoma with her husband and collaborator, artist Larry Dixon, and their flock of parrots.